CW01642269

Under an Irish Sky

Nicola Kearns

INFINITY

Published by Infinity Books, Malta

ISBN 978-9918622009

Front cover painted by Artist Nicholas Kearns, Dundalk, County Louth, Ireland.

Dedicated to my beautiful granddaughters,

Aria & Céala McShane.

Bíodh an lúcháir a thug tú dom mar chomhluadar agat sa saol amach romhat[1]

[11] *May the joy you have given me, be your companion in life.*

Foreword

There are very few books written regarding the untold story of Ireland's brave young women who decided to join Cumann na mBan in order to fight for their country. The courage of these rural women who felt it their duty to take part in both the Rising and Civil War are knowledgably represented in this novel and I commend author, Nicola Kearns, for taking on this mammoth task.

My Grandmother, Nancy O'Rahilly, attended the foundation of Cumann na mBan held in Wynn's Hotel Dublin, in 1914 and was its Vice President. Her husband, The O'Rahilly, founded the Irish Volunteers a year earlier and was Director of Arms.

I was delighted when approached by Nicola Kearns, a Leitrim based woman and originally hailing from Dundalk, after she noticed the plaque I had erected on Rooskey Bridge, honouring my mother, Bridie Clyne. The plaque is strategically placed and overlooks her family's island on the majestic Shannon and old homestead down river, now planted with trees.

Nicola was so taken with the roles my mother and grandparents played in their fight for Irish freedom she decided to write them into her novel 'Under an Irish Sky'.

Having met Nicola Kearns, uncannily in Wynn's Hotel, I could see her enthusiasm regarding her latest personal project.

I do not doubt this novel, which has a great slant in the story, will be yet another best seller for Nicola and I sincerely thank her for allowing me to be a part of it.

The butterfly has spoken!

Proinsias O'Rathaille.
June 2023.

Acknowledgements

During the writing of this novel, I was fortunate to have the assistance of some wonderful people whose kind support and invaluable historical information made this book possible. In order of my meeting them on my book's journey;

I want to thank firstly, Miss Kathleen Moffat, Dromod, County Leitrim, whose parents Michael and Lily (nee Frayne) Moffat were both Volunteers for the Republic and served time in prison during these years for their beliefs. Kathleen kindly allowed me to use her mother's personal documents for research on this book.

Mr. Tony O'Connell, Fenagh, Leitrim, author of 'Atlantipedia' and 'Joining the Dots' and expert on Atlantis, for his unstinting support and ruthlessness with his red pen.

Majella and John Toolan, Ballinamore, Leitrim, Honorary Secretary of The Kilmainham Board of Visitors, for their knowledge on Irish history and Majella's expertise on Irish police history.

Mr. Prionsias O'Rathaille, Wexford, for sharing stories of his grandfather, The O'Rahilly, and his grandmother Nancy O'Rahilly, who attended the first meeting of Cumann na mBan at Wynns Hotel, Dublin in 1914 and later became Vice-President of Cumann na mBan. Prionsias also shared stories and information on his mother Bridie Clyne (Cumann na mBan member) from Dromod, County Leitrim, which are included in this story.

And for the consistent encouragement, love and patience, I acknowledge my parents Nicholas and Mary Kearns, siblings Jonathan, Christabel, Genevieve, Elizabeth and Bronwen, and their families; my amazing sons, Adam Curley-Kearns, Darragh McShane and his beautiful fiancée Paula Lynch and their daughters, Aria & Céala McShane; my friends of which I am blessed with many, Jeanette Appleby, Tony & Margaret Kelly, Elaine Broderick. Jolanta Gołuki, Mary Martin, David and Anthea Price and many more. Thank you all.

And most importantly, to those mentioned in this novel and those who are not, who fought and died for this country of Ireland; Go raibh mile maith agaibh go léir. [2]

---

[2] *A thousand thanks to you all.*

Table of Contents

The End of the Beginning

In the hot summer of 1921, a Truce was declared in Ireland after the bloody War of Independence and in July of that same year, the despised Black and Tans were finally taken off the country's streets. On 6th December 1921, the Treaty was signed in Downing Street, London, by representatives of the British government including Prime Minister David Lloyd George, head of the British delegates and by Irish representatives, including Michael Collins and Arthur Griffith. Michael Collins later claimed that at the last minute Lloyd George threatened the Irish delegates with a renewal of 'terrible and immediate war' if the Treaty was not signed at once.

Most of the British army leaves Ireland and a new Irish Free State is born. People get married once again and life begins to return to some kind of normality. Sporting events resume as villages and towns once more have a full quota for making up a team now that their young men, what is left of them, have returned from fighting for their country. Markets resume their place on Fair Day and the air is filled with a sense of celebration as a new future for Ireland has been achieved. The Irish Free State, as contemplated by the Treaty, came into existence when its constitution became law on 6 December 1922, by a royal proclamation.

But an even more brutal Civil War is about to begin, which will incite a bitterness and shame that will linger for generations. This war turns brother against brother, neighbour against neighbour - those who are for the Treaty, which Collins brought back to the Irish people, giving Ireland only twenty-six of her thirty-two counties and keeping the Northern six counties under British rule - and those for whom this was unacceptable. To the people who opposed the Treaty, this was seen as traitorous and an insult to the Irish men and women who fought and died in the Irish Rebellion of Easter, 1916.

In 1921, the new Irish State executed twice as many Republicans as the British had done in 1916-1921. Even after it passed the 'Public Safety Bill', there was no legal standing for the Provisional Government's killings of a further eighty-one Republican prisoners. Many of those executed were just eighteen and nineteen years of age.

On 16th April 1922, 200 Anti-Treaty IRA, under Rory O'Connor occupied the Four Courts. The Battle of Dublin was a week of street battles from June 28th to July 5th, 1922, that marked the beginning of the Irish Civil War. Six months after the Anglo-Irish Treaty ended the recent Irish War of Independence, the Civil War was fought between the Forces of the new Provisional Government and the Irish Republican Army (IRA) that opposed the Treaty.

The Civil War was won by the pro-treaty National Army. The guerrilla phase of the Irish Civil War lasted another ten months, before the IRA leadership issued a 'dump arms' order to all units, effectively ending the conflict. The conflict left Irish society divided and embittered for generations. Today, the three largest political parties in the Republic of Ireland, Fine Gael, Fianna Fáil, and Sinn Féin are direct descendants of the opposing sides of the war; Fine Gael from the supporters of the pro-Treaty side, Fianna Fáil party formed from the bulk of the anti-Treaty side by Éamon de Valera, and Sinn Féin, descended from the rump anti-Treaty and irredentist Republican Party left behind by De Valera's supporters.

Introduction

In my research for this novel, I reached out to many sources for information and I was largely faced with a wall of silence. So many of my emails to people and places I hoped would give me assistance went unanswered and for this reason, my novel took a long time to write. Keeping written records of events of this time was discouraged to prevent classified information being disclosed. This lack of the female voice in the historiography of the period circa 1916 - 1923 was strengthened by an insufficiency of archival material and unwillingness on the part of the female revolutionaries to discuss their part in the Republican campaign. The story of female participation in the fight for Irish Freedom was not so much written out of history, as never written at all. Thankfully, some did share with me accounts of their own family member's history of these terrible times and these narratives are included in this book. My novel was completed, eventually, with the knowledge this book is historically accurate, but some of the people and places mentioned are works of fiction and you, the reader, can decide what you choose to be the true accounts – because some of the events you will read in this novel, you may decide are too difficult to believe.

I also found them hard to comprehend, because these occurrences took place at a time when my grandparents were alive, and yet neither she nor the rest of her generation, ever spoke of such events in my time of knowing them.

As a woman living in the 21st Century, I am humbled and proud of what the women just two generations ago endured, and kept silent about. This enabled the peace we now live in to thrive and it was their sacrifice that made this possible. For that, I humbly salute them.

Now, I will tell their story.

Nicola Kearns

June 2023

Prologue

Nothing spectacular happened today, apart from the fact I died. I left the world as I knew it, much swifter and with significantly more silence than I arrived. Neither was by choice. My life began and ended on the inclination of another. Both occurrences a result of consequences and events in which I was a pawn, moved around under the control of others in the game of life.

My life was not meant to end this way.

And I was not meant to be born at all.

Perhaps I had cheated my way into my mother's womb. Indeed, I had caused the death of my brother who shared that cocoon with me. That's what I had been told. This may be the reason why throughout my life I carried guilt inside me, like a heavy stone I could never put down.

I never allowed myself to put down.

For this reason, I did the work of two on our small farm. To make up for the son they never had and the brother I had supposedly killed.

And one day, the day that turned into a heavy thunderstorm and swept my old life away, I was reborn and I remembered.

I remembered I hadn't died at all.

1

Leah
Dundalk, Ireland
2016

The sleet came down hard, heavy flakes splashing angrily against my kitchen window. I reached over, removed the string of the blinds tied around the handles and pushed the window open wide. Cobwebs dislodged themselves from the corners of the sill and I blew their debris away with my coffee-coated breath. Breathe in, count to seven, breathe out, count to seven, and again and again. But it was still there, that feeling of a hard lump that had taken home in my throat. It was made of tears I would not shed and words I could not say.

I sipped from my cup. The strong Italian coffee warmed my tongue and for a second it scalded the lump and gave me a moment, a short moment, of relief. I knew the wine would give me a longer time of relief, but I had to be careful. Wine and grief do not mix, not with me. They make the words and the tears come out, and where would that leave me?

It was dark and I had an overwhelming urge to be outside, even though the weather was bad. It was a cold, January night with frost beginning to form on the windowpanes, but I opened the door to my back garden and stepped outside. Bare feet on icy pebbles made me wince and the door slammed shut behind me. I fumbled for the battery switch hidden under the huge flowerpot. The twinkling Christmas lights Jill had still not taken down sprung into a flickering array of colours.

I sat on the pink, cast iron garden seat under the pergola, put my mug down on the matching pink table and lit a cigarette. I had begun smoking again after years of abstinence and this evening I bought a pack with some groceries while waiting for my taxi at the airport. Just in case I had the urge later, which I did within five minutes of getting home, just because I knew I had them. I removed the blue, fringed throw from over my shoulders and wrapped it around my legs and feet, trying hard not to think about him.

He was an anti-smoker and an anti-drinker and now he was also an anti-me.

I leaned down and picked up a blue flowerpot knocked over by the storm, now picking up an angry pace. At least it hadn't broken. I looked around the small garden in the backyard, picking out what state it was in by the scant amount of light afforded me by the string of fairy lights on the pergola window, and wondered when I had last sat out here. As a teenager, I had persuaded my grandfather (Grandy as I called him) to make a garden for me one summer.

'Make a garden?' he had repeated. 'And how does one make a garden, tell me?' he joked, raising his hands theatrically in the air.

'With grass and a spade and stuff,' I had innocently answered, to which he had roared laughing.

But he did make me a garden with grass and stuff. My little wild garden where bees were welcome and no weed killer was allowed. Marc laughed at that when I told him about it. His garden was landscaped and huge. It had taken my breath away when I first saw it. How did I end up with a man who had a gardener and a fountain and sprinklers that came on from an app installed on his mobile phone? Of course, I later found out it hadn't even been his home at all.

He had all the gadgets. iPhone, Apple this, and Apple that … newest Tesla car, and yet he'd wanted me. I never quite got my head around that. Now I knew why, and it hurt and that was why the tears could not come and the words could not be said.

Leah
Germany
2013

'*Nein,* '[3] he'd shouted brusquely, opening the lid of the huge blue bin in the city park and gesturing at the little plastic bag in my hand containing left-over lunch. I could at least understand that German word, but I looked up at him quizzically.

'*Es geht heir,* '[4] he'd said, taking the bag from my hand and throwing it into another garbage can. Then he walked away, leaving me with a red face and my mouth hanging open.

Then I saw him again, this time in a lift. One of those tiny lifts you get in official buildings in Germany that just about fit two people and make it so awkward. What do you say? Nothing? Or say hello, even? They don't do small talk here like we do in Ireland. But he nodded at me and although the few seconds of our being transferred from ground to middle floor seemed like eternity, I sensed

[3] *No.*
[4] *It goes here.*

friendliness. Have you ever had that experience … of bumping into a stranger several times and feeling that somehow you know them, but you don't? It began like that. Just like that.

He'd be at the bakery, or the cake shop where the Germans like to go on a Sunday afternoon. Tables filled mostly with divorced Dads and their kids, or elderly women surrounded by noisy grandchildren and then me. Women like me. Alone, with a book they pretend to read while their eyes scan the tables around them, wondering when their lives will start. Of course, it had to be my fault we met again. A spilled coffee and his polite acknowledgment that it was okay, even though I could see the black coffee run down his grey, suit jacket. Our hands grazed as I handed him another of those scant see-through napkins that would do nothing to clean up the mess I had made.

My embarrassed offers of payment for dry-cleaning and another coffee were refused and when we next met in the lift of my office block, he looked at me in recognition and we both laughed. We didn't laugh a lot after that. I put it down to his being German and well, it is known they are a bit reserved, right? By the time our relationship had ended I had begun to laugh less, or at least with less gusto than I used to. His look of distaste as I loudly sang along out of tune to the

Mamma Mia show at the Millennium Hotel in Stuttgart made me stop mid-flow during 'Dancing Queen' and although my feet still tapped unrestrainedly for the rest of the evening, my mouth stayed shut. But I sang inside.

Oh, how easy it is to look back on a bad situation later on and to ask yourself, why didn't I do this and why didn't I say that? I had that familiar feeling I would get, thanks to my gift of second sight passed on by grandmother – I will tell that story later – the feeling I was inviting danger into my life, or if not danger, then something that would not be good for me in some way. But I ignored it. Hindsight is always an easy thing, as they say. Because in the beginning, I believed I was in love. Because I was afraid to ask questions that might rock the already shaky boat we were in. Because of a hundred other reasons, like, he made me feel safe and with his gentlemanly ways, he reminded me of my grandfather. He opened me up to the city I lived in, in a way I had never imagined and there were lots more reasons to add to where they came from.

I'd been in Germany for almost three years when I met him. Three years of working round the clock and I was happy doing that. My routine was, well it was routine. The same one I had everywhere I worked, no matter what country or what newspaper I was stationed in. Thankfully my job as a freelance crime journalist meant that generally, I could write anywhere that I wanted, once I got those articles in by whatever deadline my boss, Bernard Schmidt of *Die Mainzer Zeiten Zeitung* (The Mainz Times Newspaper), decided upon. I had been head-hunted for this job by him and it did take some persuasion as I was quite happy where I was in Italy. I had been writing for *Il Mattino*, a well-known newspaper from Naples, on the Mafia in Southern Italy for years and was enjoying life in that noisy, passionate city. But, I did have to admit I had unwillingly put myself very much under the spotlight, not in a good way, and it was now time to go a bit incognito as some were beginning to think I needed to be *messo a tacere* (silenced.)

After receiving a couple of anonymous threatening letters (the Italians are quite fond of the use of these) I thought getting a transfer to a different country, even for a little while, would be a good idea. I had some grasp of the German language, but that was not a problem as my work would simply be translated by somebody else before being published. My assignment was to keep Germany abreast of news in Ireland and the UK, most particularly on any criminal activity from those countries in Germany, of which there was much more than I had anticipated. Drug smuggling/human trafficking/supply of counterfeit goods were just some of the crimes I wrote about, but sometimes there would be missing persons or other such news events which I also covered. One thing for sure is that no matter what country you lived in there would always be crime and always people who wanted to read about it.

I lived the same life, just in a different country. I woke late and before even getting out of bed I could easily spend an hour scanning the headlines in various newspapers, reading emails, and then finally get up. If I was working from home, which was most days, I didn't even bother to get properly dressed; instead, I'd just throw on a pair of leggings and a t-shirt, pile my hair up on my head in a top knot and the only thing I put on my face was moisturiser. Breakfast was coffee, always coffee and it had to be Italian and it had to be made from coffee beans. With that I would have fruit, pancakes, and if I had any, a dollop of freshly whipped cream to top it all off. I did like my food. Living in Italy taught me the importance of the freshness of ingredients, flavour, and quality and it was a lesson that was now a way of life.

If the weather was good, my office would be on my little terrace where I had a table big enough to spread my work and a sun umbrella overhead that meant I could easily read my screen. I also had an office in the newspaper building, and guess where that was - directly across the road from my apartment. I could wave over at my colleagues and hold up a cup asking if they fancied a jaunt across the road to join me in a coffee which they often did, filling me in on all the office gossip without me having to be there in person. I went into my office if I needed to use their equipment such as microfilmers/photocopiers ... you get the picture, also sometimes I just needed some human interaction. But mostly, I worked better alone as I always had done. I was grateful for a job and a boss who allowed that.

My at-home days involved mostly working on an article, either writing it or researching it, and having phone calls with my large network, a mixture of police inspectors, solicitors, people who knew what was going on in the street, other journalists ... and criminals many of whom I had built up a friendship with of sorts. However, I was not a workaholic. I made time in my day for my love of reading, anything from the newest chick-lit to the classics, and as a lover of anything vintage, I also loved watching old movies, in any language.

I enjoyed having colleagues around for dinner sometimes and occasionally went out for meals at their homes or joined them for an after-work drink thing. But usually, I was quite happy to fly solo. Almost all my work friends were either married or living with their other half and had children to look after. And yes, they revelled in trying to set me up, which meant dinner at theirs usually entailed a convenient single male friend, who out of courtesy I would chat nicely with, but so far none of them made me want to continue chatting any further with on a date.

My weekends were also taken up with work, but on these days I strolled around the city, mostly raking through markets that sold vintage clothes/handbags/shoes and buying groceries at the food stalls, which is where I met him once again. Later I realized that we had not been simply 'bumping into each other' as I had thought, with romantic notions of it being fate, but that he had been carefully stalking me for some time.

Holding a blue silk 1940s dress towards the warm June sun to check for stains, I heard a voice behind me.

'You know, I think that would look good on you.'

Spinning around, I was aware my face flushed on seeing bin/elevator/coffee-spill man smiling at me. Gosh, he was so handsome. He had it all. Gleaming white teeth, smiley eyes, plenty of brown hair, good physique, well dressed … need I go on? Today he wore a blue Ralph Lauren shirt and dark jeans. I, on the other hand, was wearing a long plain cream, maxi dress with a floor-length, pink kimono over it and a floppy cream hat.

'Do you think so?' I asked him, checking the label. It was almost unreadable. I could just make out *100% silk*. That would do for me. At the bargain price of just ten euro, I couldn't let that go and already had ideas of teeming it up with my strappy, blue shoes with the block heels.

'Most definitely,' he replied.

As I pulled a ten euro note from my cream shopper bag, he handed a twenty over to the stall-holder.

'Here, let me,' he offered, telling the guy to keep the change. Oh, out to impress me, was he? It was working.

'There was no need,' I told him, putting the money back into my bag and accepting the dress, unceremoniously given to me in a blue plastic bag and scrunched into a ball. Immediately I removed the dress and carefully re-folded it, then returned it once more to the bag.

'It would be nice to see you wear it,' he suggested, raising an eyebrow. 'Perhaps while sharing dinner with me?'

My heart did a little happy flip, but my head told me; Not so quick Leah!

'Perhaps we could have a coffee now and then if that goes without any mishaps, maybe dinner another time?' I replied, hoping I hadn't put him off.

'Agreed. But this time let me drink the coffee please, instead of wearing it.'

We both laughed at that and I must say we got on so well that the coffee we had at a little Kaffeehaus turned into a glass of wine for me and a non-alcoholic beer for him. By the time we departed, I had a date for the following Saturday night. I would have loved to go for dinner that very night, but a woman needs a week to prepare and also to discuss the preparations with her friends beforehand, right? And so it began - the most significant, the longest, and the worst relationship of my life.

2

Maggie
Aghameen, Ireland
1917

There it was again.

Maggie stopped walking and held her breath. The air was crisp with a bite of February frost. Clutching the front of her woolly scarf in her left fist, she took a tentative step. It was no bird that she had heard, nor an animal. Monks Lake to her left was still. The huge white swans that usually dotted the lake had taken refuge in the waterlogged field next to it. Later, when the sun had risen and warmed the water they would return, dipping their graceful heads underneath its depths for their meal.

She didn't mind getting wet. It was different from the soakings she regularly got while running from pig-pen to cow shed with pails of scraps and meal, getting drenched to the skin and her fingers nearly frozen to the handle of the galvanized bucket. Those times it was just a pure nuisance. Or like when she helped her father in the bog, with the rain pouring down on her and every stitch of her clothing heavy with rainwater. But this kind of rain was nice when she had nowhere to be going. Nobody was calling for her or waiting on her to finish up one job before she started another.

What was beyond the mountain, she wondered? Oh, she'd heard many a story of what it was like. Some of them were good and filled her heart with a yearning to experience the tales herself. Other tales were not so good. Of people who were out just to harm another for no other reason but greed, or those who crossed beyond that mountain and were never heard tell of again. The further she'd ever travelled so far was to the nearest large town of Carrick-on - Shannon, or in Irish, *Cora Droma Rúisc*, meaning 'Weir of the marshy ridge'.

As far as Maggie's eyes could see were fields and more fields, and mountains and trees; hundreds of them and cattle in the next field and everything was a washed-out colour of green and grey. Maggie knew in the spring and the summer, it was a different colour. The trees, most of them nothing but bare branches now and the hedges, they would all be full of colour and humming with the birds that nested and mated in them, and the bees that stole nectar from the flowers that grew on them. Mam even had a garden where she grew colourful flowers from seeds Daddy had bought her from Daly's grocery shop. Mam took great pride in her flower garden. It was looked on as wasteful by some, those who wouldn't waste a patch of ground where they could grow something they could eat or sell. But sure, her family had plenty enough land, thank God, to keep them going and the English garden made her mother happy, and that was reason enough for her husband.

Sketches of this garden of her mothers were piled high on every surface in Maggie's bedroom. Most were simply drawn in pencil, but some were in bright water colours when she could get her hands on some. Instead of saving these precious boxes of paint, Maggie used the lot within days of acquiring them, so excited was she to create on paper what her eyes looked at every day. In winter she enjoyed placing her paintings around her bedroom as a reminder of the promise of summer and in the warmer months, she swapped them for drawings of the fields around her, covered in a blanket of snow. She had sketches of her father sitting by the fireside, stuffing his pipe with tobacco and her mother always at one chore or another, sewing, knitting, or kneading dough. Other sketches were of her friends and other family members, her good friend and cousin, Ernie, and his surly brother, her dog, and farm animals. Some paintings and drawings were hung in pride of place in the parlour, in frames that her father had crafted and varnished himself. On the back of all her artwork, Maggie would write in pencil the place where it was painted, the month and the year, and then her initials. Her parents encouraged her pastime and took a quiet delight in her talent.

Tending the flower garden was her mother's favourite activity. Brigid McGuill had great regard for the finer things in life and liked to copy the past-times of the English ladies, much to the amusement of her husband and everyone else. Unconcerned with politics or land or the famine or any of the rest of it like her husband was, it was the class of the English that mother hankered after. Before her marriage, Biddy, or Brigid O'Hare, had worked under Lady Goodville, up at the Big House, or Goodvilles as it was known locally. Brigid O'Hare's mother had also worked there, right up until her death. The kindness of the Goodvilles at her mother's demise always stayed with the young woman. They'd kindly allowed the bereaved family to hold the funeral wake in their private drawing room, even having the coffin carried in a horse-drawn carriage to the parish graveyard. They had also paid for a meal in the local hotel for all the family afterward and the gravestone was paid for by the Goodville family. There were those in the town who raised an eyebrow at this unusual show of loyalty towards a staff member, but nobody would say a derogatory word against the Goodvilles in public. In the young Brigid O'Hare's eyes, the Goodvilles were angels sent from heaven. But for some reason, Maggie's father hated every last one of them and never held back on telling everybody around him why he did.

'Land-grabbers,' he called them – a story he often reminded the family about. It was he who insisted his wife ceased working for the Goodvilles the day she married John-Joe McGuill and it didn't take much coaxing, relieved she was not to be a housemaid any longer, but her head was already full of fanciful ideas and one of them was her flower garden. John-Joe felt it was one thing he could give her that she wanted. God knows he felt he had failed her at everything else.

☘

Bare feet in damp boots made her wince and a blister from yesterday still smarted on her heel. I should have worn socks, Maggie thought. They would be warm too from hanging over the fireplace all night. Placing the heavy galvanized bucket in her left hand down on the ground, she tied a knot in front of her shawl. The pigs had already run towards the metal gate, grunting hungrily as she lifted the latch.

It happened so quickly that later Maggie had trouble recalling the event at all. She felt a strong push on her back and splayed her hands out, palms down in the frosted mud. The pigs brushed past her as they bolted out the little gate and she felt a sudden sharp pain in her knees as they hit the ground.

'And you didn't see anybody at all?' her father asked again later, tapping his pipe on the sooty hearth.

'No,' she repeated, wincing as her mother dabbed gently at her palms with a warm, damp cloth. 'But I thought I heard a noise in the whin bushes just before.'

'What kind of a noise?' her father asked, warily.

'It was like a …,' she hesitated, trying to remember the sound exactly. 'It was …,' then she went quiet. Her cheeks grew hot, remembering now where she had heard that sound before. 'Ah, it was probably just the birds,' she added. 'I'm sure it was nothing.'

But her mother noticed. What was Maggie hiding, she wondered?

'You might fool your father, but you can't fool me,' Brigid McGuill winked, whispering into her daughter's ear, as she hung the wet rag over the fireplace.

Maggie lowered her head, her face camouflaged behind the heavy curtain of blond hair. He was back. Nothing else mattered right now. Her sweetheart, Conall Daly, had been on the run for some time after his involvement in an ambush that caused the deaths of some British Armed Forces. That whistle sounded like one of their childish codes, she was sure it was from him. But where was he hiding?

'Our family has been Irish Republicans for over sixty years. My grandfather had to flee Ireland in 1848 because of the failed rebellion and his Fenian ideology.[5] He and many more from around here went all over Europe trying to make a life for themselves before ending up in America. It wasn't till 1858 that he came back, along with his good friend, that great man, James Stephens.[6] He vowed he'd never be forced to leave his country again, nor any of his own.'

The women were quiet. When John-Joe started on this long biography of his forebears and their part in

---

[5] *The Young Irelander Rebellion was a failed Irish nationalist uprising led by the Young Ireland movement, part of the wider Revolutions of 1848 that affected most of Europe.*

[6] *See Historical Notes*

Ireland's long fight for freedom from Britain, they knew better than to firstly, interrupt and secondly, leave the room. To do so would cause a tirade that could go on for days, with John-Joe recalling to his family every single injustice done to the Irish, including a lengthy narrative on the horrors of the famine[7] and going as far back as Cromwell's[8] attack on Ireland in the 17th Century. No, better to let him have his say, and agree by comments such as 'Up the Republic' and all would be well in the household.

Maggie completely concurred with her father's beliefs and unlike her mother, she relished these times with her father, when he spoke to her as an equal instead of like the flighty young girl he sometimes treated her as. Instead, she indulged him, asking many questions about the Cause he vehemently spoke of and coaxing even more stories from him. These were private times between them which she greatly cherished. Kneeling by his feet in front of the blazing warm fire, she laid her head against his knee, watching as the flames danced with wild abandon and throwing their shapes against the darkening room. Feeling the warmth from his hand which he often laid on her head as he spoke, Maggie felt a sense of security and love from him that she would have given anything to

---

[7] *See Historical Notes*
[8] *See Historical Notes*

preserve. As she listened, Maggie closed her eyes, absorbing every precious word he spoke and oftentimes wishing she was the son he had longed for. Then she too could fight for a free Ireland and win the respect she so desperately yearned for. This particular diatribe was due to the upcoming election in Roscommon in which an acquaintance of John-Joe's was standing for office.

'There'd be no better man than George Plunkett[9] to see this country treated right,' John-Joe proclaimed. 'Sure, Pope Benedict XV himself gave him his blessing just weeks ago in Rome, and it was he who gave him the title of Count. What more could you ask for in a leader? And Plunkett's son was executed for his great bravery.'

'Yes and his other two sons are serving ten years for their part in the Rebellion,' Bridget McGuill added sourly. 'So their bravery came at quite a cost. I pity their poor mother.'

'Pity her?' John-Joe exclaimed, gently rounding on his wife. 'You should be praising her for rearing such courageous and loyal young men. Even the bible says *Greater love hath no man than to lay down his life for his country.*'

---

[9] *See Historical Notes*

Bridget scoffed. 'You've changed the words of the bible to suit yourself. It's *for his friends*, is what it says in the bible. Not country!'

'It's the same thing,' John-Joe replied, defensively. 'Friends, family, faith and a free Ireland. They're all the same thing because they are the only things … the only things that matter.'

'I think it's a disgrace that women can't vote in the election,' Bridget retorted. 'It says in that Proclamation[10] from Easter-time that men and women in Ireland shall have equal rights and equal opportunities. If we are good enough to produce sons that can go out and get themselves killed for Ireland, then we should be able to have a say in the running of this country, the same as any man.'

Then she fell silent and Maggie knew the sudden wince in her mother's face was because she was thinking of her deceased son.

'I agree with you, Mam,' she said, nodding her head and moving towards her mother who had silently taken a seat at the large, wooden dining table. 'But you never know, with the ruckus Emmeline

---

[10] *See Historical Notes*

Pankhurst[11] and her suffragettes are making over in England, it is looking more and more like they will get the vote there and we will as well. Just wait and see. I'm sure of it.'

'I hope you're right, Maggie,' Bridget replied. 'If we get the vote, who knows what else it might get us? Men have had the run of the country for long enough and look at the state it is in!'

Her words surprised Maggie. Her mother never usually gave an opinion on politics, or on very much else. Uncharacteristically, she smoothed a strand of her mother's hair behind her ear. It was still golden in colour with just a fleck of two of silver at the temples and as usual, was clipped into a loose bun on the back of her head. Her mother was still a beauty.

'She could've had any man in the country and she chose me,' John-Joe McGuill was wont to be heard saying many times after a few pints in Daly's public house.

It was a well-known fact that many thought he was punching above his weight when he snared the beautiful Bridget O'Hare and made her his wife. The story was that he had seen her pegging out washing in

---

[11] *Emmeline Pankhurst was a British political activist who organised the UK suffragette movement and helped women win the right to vote.*

the gardens of the Goodville House where she worked as a maid and told his mate 'Do you see that girl there,' he pointed where Bridget stood. 'I'm going to marry her.'

At which his friend had laughed outright and told John-Joe he'd marry her only in his dreams. A statement he recounted as part of his best man's speech just a few months later, to his amazement and that of the rest of the wedding party. For John-Joe McGuill was known more for having his head in a book instead of going courting, so how he had successfully wooed the beautiful Bridget O'Hare was his secret, and hers.

It was precisely because John-Joe always had his head in a book that made the young eighteen-year-old Bridget take a shine to him. She admired anybody that was well-read as they were always more interesting to talk to. Not like most of the people around, especially the men, who were unable to talk about anything except farming and the state of the country. She cared about neither. Besides, the McGuills may have been only farmers, but since his father's death, John-Joe McGuill now owned his land and house, and the McGuill family down the generations had always been well respected in the area with no blemishes against their name for decades. They were particularly acknowledged for their staunch Republican beliefs and John-Joe's father and father before him had played significant roles through the years in the Irish Cause. There was no one around who would have a bad word to say about them. Or who would dare to.

'Who would you vote for in the election, Mam, if you could?' Maggie asked tentatively, hoping to draw her mother's attention away from what was making her face look so pitifully sad.

Bridget sighed heavily.

'Sit with me a minute, love', she answered, pulling the chair next to her out from the table and gesturing for Maggie to sit down. 'You are a young woman now,' she said, taking Maggie's hand in her own. 'When I was about your age I had so many lofty ideas. I was going to travel the world, see things and learn things. Every single penny I got from my work at Goodvilles was saved for getting as far out of here as I could. When the other girls spent their meager wages on frivolities such as ribbons for their hair or going dancing, I squirreled mine away. I'd no interest in landing myself a local lad like they had. I didn't want to be married to some farmer and spend my life making babies and a home and … '

‘… and then you met Daddy and fell in love,’ Maggie interrupted, winking playfully.

Suddenly, her mother pushed Maggie's hand away irritably, and then placed a palm on each of her daughter's cheeks, firmly holding Maggie's face in her hands, she said. 'Don't you go looking for love to make you happy.' Her green eyes looked right into Maggie's, so close that Maggie could see her reflection in them.

'Do something with your life,' she continued. 'Find something important to you. You have a good brain, so don't let it go to waste.'

'Like my painting and my writing?' Maggie asked, eyes wide, knowing that this moment of being brought into her mother's confidence was going to be important.

'Like those suffragettes, you were talking about in England,' her mother replied. 'Yes, keep at your painting and making stories. You are good at it. But painting is not going to change anything in the world or your life. Unless of course you become as famous as Michelangelo and go painting the ceiling in St. Agnes church!'

They both giggled.

‘You never know,’ Maggie laughed. ‘It might be a good place to start.’

Then her mother’s face grew serious once again.

'Be who you want to be, Maggie,' she said, and this time it was she who smoothed her hand over her daughter's hair. 'If what you want to do with your life means going against what others say, losing people is better than losing yourself. Never let anybody or anything stand in the way of what you believe is the right thing for you. Not even me!’

Maggie raised her eyebrows. ‘What do you mean?’

‘I mean love, if what you want to do is leave here and go out foreign, go without worrying about me. I will be all the happier for knowing that you are living your life out there and away from these mountains and lakes, and the small minds of the people that live around them.’

‘But I am happy here, Mam,’ Maggie implored, sincerely. ‘I love the mountains and the lakes and my friends here. I love this country and never want to leave it. I’m never happier than when I am near our trees and streams and meadows. If I had one wish, it would be to live right here forever and also to see a free Ireland like Daddy wants, and for him to know that his friends and relations did not die in vain last

Easter[12]. I wish I was a man and I could make Daddy proud of me and help somehow to get that for him.'

'That's three wishes, Maggie,' Bridget winked. 'Your father *is* proud of you and loves you very much. I don't think he expects you to lead another Rising!'

'No,' Maggie agreed. 'But there are other things I can do.'

---

12 *See Historical Notes*

3

Leah
Germany
2016

When did the alarm bells begin to ring or the red flag begin to wave? Not for a while. As in most relationships, ours started as the quintessential, perfect love affair. He was charming, attentive, generous, funny and romantic. I was on my best behaviour and although sometimes I gritted my teeth at being interrupted by yet another of his many daily texts and calls, I always replied cheerfully. Then, the first almost unnoticeable stain smeared what was up to now our unblemished relationship. It was a very simple, very slight admission he made that caused a worrying seismic shift, for me. He had scraped somebody's car very badly on reversing and instead of leaving a note with his insurance and contact details he simply drove off, which horrified me. On questioning him about it he told me he wasn't currently insured, that his cover had lapsed a day ago and he was in the process of renewing it.

But, of course, that was forgotten about and I put it down to a simple oversight that anybody could be guilty of. Then on another occasion, we were eating at a very swish restaurant on a weekend trip to Paris when one of the customers started shouting at Marc in broken English saying 'You are a thief. You are a fraud. Police! Somebody get the police. He is a thief. He stole almost a million euros from me.'

As we all looked at Marc in horror, he nonchalantly continued to eat and the person shouting was removed. But that incident always stuck in my mind. He brushed it off as a disgruntled customer whom he had reported for non-payment of tax and didn't seem a bit fazed by the allegations. As for me, I was so aware that every fibre of my being was screaming he is NOT the right one. RUN! But to my detriment, I ignored the warning signs of anxiety and nervousness my body gave me now and then.

I enjoyed him picking me up for dates and being told I was beautiful. I enjoyed the wonderful places he took me to. He seemed to know all the best restaurants, got invited to many parties and openings and I loved the wining and dining and inclusion into the whole social world I had never been part of before. My wardrobe now sported stunning evening dresses with matching shoes and I finally got to show off my large array of costume jewellery and sequinned clutch bags. Mornings in bed got longer and my days of wandering around market stalls were replaced with shopping trips to Paris and Milan.

I had money you see. My grandfather left me everything he owned after he died. All his businesses in Ireland and Europe and all his assets now belonged to me. During my time abroad and making a name for myself in the world of crime journalism, I hadn't touched any of it. I wasn't ready to acknowledge his death and to use his money would do that, so I kept putting it off. Grandy's solicitor and friend, Seán Keenan, and his son, also named Seán, dealt with anything business related and to date, everything remained the same as it had been when my grandfather was alive. I earned quite enough for myself to live on and had no plans to begin running a thriving transport business. I was quite happy to keep the same people in the same jobs and let the staff deal with it all. Seán Jnr kept me updated weekly on the business and sent me financial reports and monthly/quarterly and yearly reports but I only glanced over them. Once these trusted friends of Grandy's were happy, I was happy. Whenever I went home I always met up with Seán Jnr and over dinner and a drink, he would fill me in on what was going on with the business and try to coax me into taking a more involved role.

'You never have to work a day again, Leah, if you don't want to,' he'd tell me. 'Sit back and enjoy what Grandy left you. He'd want that for you.'

But I wasn't ready to do that, not yet. Marc had money too, or at least seemed to have. He was a financial consultant – one who swooped like Superman into businesses experiencing problems and he apparently made their problems go away. His work was specialised and he had to be suitably discreet, so apart from his sleek-look website he was not visible anywhere else on social media. He wanted his clients to know he was scrupulously guarded and private and their collaboration with him was treated the same way. It all sounded very glamorous to me with his many long trips to various cities and countries, staying in five-star hotels and receiving some wonderful gifts and even one time, a car.

The longest he had been away was his trip to Dubai for six months helping an oil tycoon discover the reason for a missing large sum of money. I did not join him there because of the secrecy involved in the company. If I did go, I would have to spend my whole time indoors in the compound where he was staying and working in. That did not appeal to me. Even though I could easily stay indoors for a week at a time if working on a project, I would feel claustrophobic if I knew I couldn't go out if I wanted to. He rang me often and I was quite happy to use the time he was away catching up with friends and going on a trip to Italy for another friend's wedding. I never felt the need to be with somebody 24/7 and to be honest I did find sometimes that he was a bit too full-on. There were weekends when I just wanted to lounge about at home instead of dressing up and going out and days when I wanted to write without the phone going off every hour or so. I usually put my phone on silent when working, but he didn't like it if he couldn't get hold of me. He bought me a new phone with a number just for him, and he didn't like me to turn it off or put on silent, even at night. Not that he rang me much at night, but if he was abroad he sometimes did regardless of the time difference.

☘

There were things I should have paid more attention to, but the occasional question mark that flashed into my mind was interspersed between fantastic times and when a random warning light bulb went off in my head intermittently, I chose to ignore it.

Ninety percent of the time he made me feel like the most attractive, sexy and intelligent woman in the world and any female would find that hard to give up. He had traits like my grandfather in that he was old-fashioned in his way of opening doors for me, walking on the outside of the footpath, always had impeccable manners and my favourite … protecting me. I had missed that. As a single woman I had grown used to looking after myself, but it was nice the time I broke my ankle to have somebody physically carry me to the car and then into the hospital. To have somebody harass the nurses and doctors to get me seen immediately, to do my shopping, cook my meals and take me to appointments when I could do none of these things for myself. I especially liked when the landlord ignored my calls regarding a late partying neighbour - one conversation with Marc and the new tenant soon became a previous tenant. I trusted him when it came to business affairs due to his seemingly amazing success with his own. He gave me advice about how to go forward with my grandfather's business and every day he kept at me to get Grandy's assets changed into my name, including his bank account.

And I lied that I did. I didn't intend it to be a lie, but it was. He asked me again during a conversation if I had finally got around to having Grandy's money changed into my name and I said that I had. He kept telling me to have my grandfather's money put into my bank account as he said since Grandy was deceased there were fraudsters out there who would be able to lay their hands on it. He was an expert in this field and so I chatted to Seán (his dad was now deceased and the business handed over to him) and he did what I asked. So, when Marc asked me if I finally did what he advised, I said that yes, I had. He was delighted because he said it took the worry from him about me being ripped off and he even bought champagne to celebrate.

But I hadn’t changed it. It was in the process, but first I needed to go to Ireland to sign papers before it could happen formally. I just kept this information to myself to avoid Marc coming with me to Ireland, because I didn’t want him to come with me. I guess I knew in my gut that he was not going to be in my future and I didn't want Ireland to be tainted with him, if that makes sense? In reality, that should have been a get-out-of-jail-free NOW card for me, but I still hung in there. Another huge deal-breaker for me was he repeatedly told me not only did he not even *like* children, but he never intended to have any; not something I wanted to hear as I approached the age where this would become a priority on my list. He was a like a drug I kept meaning to quit, but not yet. Until he quit me.

☘

Who would have ever thought of it? He did.

But how could I have known that a simple trip to the beauty salon would have changed it all? They didn't take credit cards. When he arrived to pick me up he offered to get cash from the bank machine opposite with my card. As I watched him walk across the road, he looked back as he waited for the green light and when he waved, I blew him a kiss.

Then a few minutes became forty-five minutes. I rang and his phone was dead. Handing my empty coffee cup to the receptionist, I stayed waiting in my seat and blew on my nails, needlessly, they always dried immediately. The wonder of acrylic nails. I rang again. The phone was still dead. Rummaging in my handbag, I found enough cash to pay for the nail treatment but not enough for a tip.

Anrika laughed, 'Don't worry,' she'd said. 'You have given me enough tips over the past years to pay for my annual holiday.'

Still, I felt embarrassed and squeezed Anrika's arm. 'I'll sort you out next time,' I promised.

There never was a next time. It wasn't far to walk back to my apartment. Kicking off my shoes in the small hallway, I peeled off my coat and hung it on the coat rack. His coat was gone, so he was still out. I rang again. His phone rang out again. When I tapped my card on the machine in the coffee shop the next morning and it was refused … and when I checked my online account minutes later, I knew. He was gone and my money was gone. With the small amount of change I had in my coat pocket, I bought a pack of cigarettes, then went home and emptied the fridge of any alcohol in there.

Waking up the next day, I opened my online banking account, tapped in a different code and sighed with relief. At least he hadn't got that, for this was Grandy's account and there was well over a million euro in it. You would imagine that spending the last number of years of my life writing about the criminal world, I would be able to spot one from ten metres away. Not so. For while I was busy researching and interviewing some of the most notorious underworld gangsters in Europe, I was unknowingly being groomed in the most hurtful and deceptive of ways.

How does one become so gullible and trusting? Oh, so easily. Men, like Marc, know exactly who their prey is and exactly how to strike when least expected. He was an expert in his field. His methods were simple. First, discover their weaknesses, second, gain the victim's trust and third, rob them blind. For blind was what I was, blinded by romance, blinded by desire and blinded by him. Marc Lewis, even his name sounds made up, doesn't it? It is too neat. Too much like a brand of some sort. Of course, I Googled him after we met. Isn't that what any sensible crime journalist would do before going on a date with a gorgeous new guy? What I found out before our date – his age first of all, six years older than me, a respectable age gap; never married with no children. That would normally send up the first red flag. Come on, at that age most men have had at least one divorce or one child. But when it comes to the men in my life, when I see red flags, I think it is a party!

He somehow was able to use my bank card to clear out my account, I presume with an accomplice who would pass as me. But oh, how I would have loved to have seen his face when he realized I had not yet transferred my grandfather's money to my account as I had said. I had approximately 50,000 euro in my account, made up of good wages and a lump sum from Grandy for a birthday gift, who suggested I invest it. I never got around to that. It was not the millions Marc had hoped for. Stupid man. Cruel man. But he had been my man.

I did not miss him one little bit. I did not pine for him or even my money. But my self-esteem took a huge bashing. Here was I, a well-known crime journalist finding myself the victim of the oldest and most common crime of all. Robbed blind by somebody they were romantically involved with. Did I love him though? No. He had become that plaster I was slowly trying to remove bit by bit but needed to just peel off quickly and forever. But that didn't take the sting out of being duped. Pardon the pun. I was hurt that he played me like a cat with a mouse and I had no idea I was his prey. I was hurt that all the things he told me and I had naively believed were just lies and I allowed myself to be so easily fooled. I was furious, but more with myself than him.

I could have written about him. I could have reported him and I could easily have paid one of my criminal friends to find him and sort him out, at least get my money back, but I was too proud to let anybody know of my stupidity. So, I told my editor that I was taking a much overdue holiday and told my friends I was nursing a break-up and I booked my flight home.

The journey back to Ireland was a blur. A hastily packed suitcase, full of odd shoes and bits of him, and leaving behind bits of me. I remembered a sweeping of green fields, factories, and a plastic tumbler of wine on the train, a headache and two Solpadine in a plastic bottle of water warmed by the sunny window seat. Two drunken lads on their way home from a stag weekend and their kindness of giving me the aisle seat so I could run to the Ladies when nausea overcame me. They gave me Diorlyte sachets.

'Good for the hydration,' they'd said.

It helped. Of course, there was nobody to pick me up as nobody knew I was coming home. No cash for the bus. A quick run to the bank machine made me miss the only Express Bus leaving that night. I spent €160 on a taxi home. That made the tears start again because home had been with Grandy and that life with him was over. And my life in Germany as I'd known it with Marc was over too and now all I had were a bulging suitcase, a hangover, and a self-confidence now torn to shreds.

4

Maggie

Aghameen, Ireland
1917

Unknown to her parents, Maggie had recently joined Cumann na mBan,[13] translated as the Women's League. Cumann na mBan was originally formed in April 1914 at a meeting held in Wynn's Hotel, Dublin, as an auxiliary formation to complement the Irish Volunteers. Under its constitution, the primary aim of the organisation was to advance the cause of Irish liberty and teach its members first aid, drill, signalling, and rifle practice in order to aid the Volunteer men who were fighting for Ireland.

It was a former school pal, Josie Fox, who first suggested to Maggie she might like to join the organisation, but Josie had been a bit of a bully at school and Maggie was hesitant. Then her best friend Alice brought the subject up, saying she had thought

---

[13] *See Historical Notes*

about joining but only if Maggie did too. The first night, the girls, under instruction from Alice's brother Conall, turned up where the meeting was to take place. It was in the attic of a Republican House and they were advised to make their journey over the fields to avoid running into a roadblock. Alice and Maggie both giggled nervously as they steered their way past cow pats with bicycle lamps lighting the way.

Arriving at the house situated up a long, winding boreen they found many other bicycles and two ponies and traps outside the large two-storied house. The front half-door was open and timidly the girls entered a narrow hallway where coats and hats were piled onto coat hooks nailed into the white-washed walls. There was a long, narrow hallway on the left-hand-side which led to an open door, from where they could hear chattering and somebody badly playing a mouth organ. Cigarette smoke billowed out of this room. Opposite them, there was a green, velvet curtain pulled aside revealing a matching carpeted staircase. Looking at each other and raising their eyebrows, they both shrugged, wondering where to go next when a lady came out from a doorway which they had not previously noticed underneath the staircase.

'Oh, hello ladies,' she exclaimed. 'Are you here for the induction?'

They both nodded yes, although neither was sure what an induction entailed.

'Very good and you are most welcome. Follow me,' they were told and the lady began to climb the stairs, while the girls followed suit.

Apart from three officers, there were fifteen young women in total, including Maggie and Alice and both girls were impressed with how formally the meeting was conducted. They were given small brown membership cards with Cumann na mBan written on the front and a place to write their name. Inside the Constitution was written as follows;

CONSTITUTION

(CORÚGHADH)

Cumann n na mBan is an independent body of Irishwomen pledged to maintain the Irish Republic, and to organise and train the women of Ireland to work unceasingly for its international recognition.

All women of Irish birth or descent are eligible for membership, except that no woman who is a member of an organisation doing any kind of work for the enemy can become a member.

There was a membership fee also of 1d to be paid each week and a part in the card where their fees were recorded. On another part of the card the *POLICY AND AIMS (CUSPÓRA)* were written and they were also given several papers which included a longer list of Cumann na mBan's Constitution with their badge on the top, information on activities such as Educational – to learn Irish and use as much as possible. Military – First Aid, Nursing, Intelligence work, Scouting, Despatch carrying, Drill. Publicity/Social – organise Irish drama clubs, sports and dances. Economic – Only buy Irish, fundraise for prisoners and their families and for the expenses of Republicans. Agendas had been handed out to everybody at the beginning of the meeting and there were several topics brought up, including a lot of discussion about accessing uniforms. The Officer in Command, (O.C.) Sheila Daly, had this to say on the issue.

'Ladies, I appreciate very much you all want to support our organization by being observed wearing the uniform, but I am afraid to say the quality of some of the homemade attire is just not acceptable. We cannot expect to be taken seriously if our uniform looks like it was made with a knife and fork.'[14] This diatribe caused some of the women to look shamefacedly down at their own outfits which indeed had been roughly designed and sewn.

'The various hues of emerald which are being sported here tonight definitely must make up Ireland's forty shades of green,' she continued, with a hint of a smile. 'There is a Co-op in Dublin making these uniforms at present and orders will be taken along with measurements at the end of the meeting. And of course ladies, the uniform is not compulsory. As you must pay for it yourself, it is only optional, and where possible materials should be Irish made.'[15]

'Will you order one?' Alice asked Maggie. 'I will if you will.'

Maggie nodded her head, grimacing a little, as Alice always needed Maggie to do things with her, no matter what it was. It had been that way since they were children, even though Alice was the elder of the two. Another topic on the agenda was the upcoming by-election in Roscommon for which Count Plunkett would be canvassing and women were needed to help

---

14 *Commenting on the poor quality of the women's uniforms, Kathleen O'Doherty commented that they looked "as if they were cut out with a knife and fork".*

with the campaign. Both Maggie and Alice volunteered for this role and on their way home they discussed the different ways in which they could assist.

'We can design some banners and posters,' Alice suggested. 'Do you think we'll have to come up with the materials ourselves or will we be given them?'

Maggie didn't answer. She was lost in thoughts of whether or not to tell her parents she had joined Cumann na mBan.

'Wakey, wakey,' Alice called, swerving her bicycle past a rabbit trap. 'I nearly got my wheel caught just now,' she added. 'Those traps are a danger. You'd barely see them in among the long grass.'

'Where did you see it?' Maggie shouted back, slowing her cycling to a stop.

Alice slowed down too then indicated with her head where it was. Maggie jumped off her bike and laid it down on the ground before walking over to the trap.

'It's not a rabbit trap,' she stated. 'The Crown Forces set those traps for the men on night manoeuvres. If they are being chased over the bog it slows them down. We'll have to let Conall know where it is and if there is one here, then there are bound to be more.'

Conall was grateful when he heard from the girls where the trap was and immediately he and a group of other men went out to the fields with their torches where, along with Maggie and Alice, they carefully searched for more. They found six in all.

'But, does that mean the bog-land needs to be searched daily?' Maggie asked.

'We can't spare men just to watch the area day and night,' Conall replied. 'But we will have to spread the word that any movement by the Armed Forces[16] on it needs to be reported to Volunteers. The soldiers know the bog is a short way through to the mountains and the men hide out there.'

'Well,' Maggie thought. 'If they go into the bog at night to set traps, can't we set traps for them first?'

Conall stared at her, then threw back his head and howled with laughter.

'My, you are a crafty one,' he cried. 'And are you going to be part of this ruse then, Miss McGuill?' he teased.

---

[16] *See Historical Notes*

‘I will,’ Maggie answered. ‘Do you want me to come up with a plan?’ she added.

‘I would most certainly like to hear of any plan you come up with,’ Conall replied, appraising her canniness. ‘I will pitch the idea to the men and call over after dinner this evening to discuss it with your father. Is that alright with you?’

‘It is,’ Maggie replied. ‘And bring Alice with you. We are Cumann na mBan women now, so this can be our first assignment.’

‘God help us all with you two as our aides,’ Conall teased, as he walked over towards the men on their hunkers, carefully removing the traps.

☘

Maggie’s father was surprisingly pleased when she nervously told him about joining Cumann na mBan.

'I am proud of you, Maggie,' he said, hugging her. 'Ireland needs its young women to support our fight for freedom. After all, you are the backbone of society, the ones men listen to when they are at home. The ones who will teach the future generation from a young age how important it is to be brought up in a free Ireland, out from under the foot of Britain.'

Her mother wasn't as supportive.

'I'll be even more worried sick now every time you go out the door,' she lamented. 'You'll get yourself killed or put in prison. They shoot women too you know.'

'I won't be involved in any fighting, Mam,' Maggie replied. 'You know I despise that killings have to be part of securing a free Ireland. I don't believe that anything is worth the life of one person.'

'You are naïve,' her mother said, shaking her head and leaving the rest of them to their talk.

'I have to agree with your mother,' John-Joe said. 'Death and killing are part of war. Talking never won a war, unfortunately. Not one of us likes to have to cause the death of another but sometimes it is necessary. The Crown Forces have brought us to our knees and the only way we can get back up is to fight our way up.'

'Your father is right,' Conall agreed. 'It's an eye for an eye out there right now.'

'I have an idea for the traps,' Maggie answered, trying to steer the subject. Death was not a topic she relished discussing. 'At the moment the field is clear but we know that they will be putting traps out for the men but we don’t know when. Isn’t that right?’

The men nodded and her father tried to keep a serious face, unused from taking direction from his daughter.

‘Those man-traps that are in our outhouse,’ Maggie said. ‘The ones that you said have been illegal since 1820 except as a defense against burglars between sunset and sunrise. We can put something in the field we can say we were afraid of being stolen, like a plough and a sign on the gate saying, Keep Out. After all, Daddy, it is your field.’

‘What are these man-traps like?’ Conall asked, impressed with her idea.

'They are mechanical security devices for catching poachers and trespassers,' John-Joe answered. 'They have different designs. The ones I have are like a large foothold trap. It mainly consists of steel springs armed with teeth that grab the victim's leg. They were used by my grandfather to discourage poachers getting on their land illegally to hunt for game, in the days when there were more poachers about.'

‘How many do you have?’ Conall asked.

‘Come out and we’ll have a look,’ John-Joe replied. ‘I suppose you want to come too, Maggie?’

'No,' she answered. 'I came up with the idea as promised. I will leave the rest of the plan to you two. If Mam sees me in the shed with you both tinkering with man traps she will have a lot to say about it,' she added, with a knowing look.

'You are a source of constant surprises,' Conall teased, taking her hand as they meandered down the tree-lined avenue.

‘So are you,’ Maggie replied, swinging his arm. ‘I couldn’t believe it when you asked me in front of Daddy if I wanted to go for a walk.’

‘Why? He knows we are always together.’

Maggie searched the face that she had known since she was born. He who had at one time been just the older annoying brother of her best friend almost overnight had suddenly become so much more. It had been a warm sunny day in May when he eventually returned from Dublin, not even a full year ago yet, when Maggie had seen him from her front garden, jumping wearily from the back of a cart on the dusty road. At first, she had thought him a stranger and an older stranger at that. Filthy dirty, he looked exhausted with his right trouser leg flapping against a bloodied rag wrapped around his calve. It was only his floppy fringe that made him recognizable to Maggie and she immediately dropped the stick she had been throwing for her golden Labrador, Marley, and ran out the gate towards him.

'Conall,' she called and he turned towards her. He had a look on his face that made her do something completely uncharacteristic and she flung her arms around his neck.

'Thank God you are back,' she cried. 'We have all been worried sick. There have been so many deaths.'

Conall threw his knapsack on the ground and hugged Maggie tightly. 'It was hell, Maggie,' he murmured.

'But you are home now. You are safe. I am so sorry about Eddie.'

'Edward[17] was the same age as me you know. We were born just a day apart. The executions, Maggie, have been horrendous. I almost feel guilty for having escaped.'

---

[17] *Edward Daly was tried by court-martial and executed by firing squad on Thursday, 4 May for his role in the Easter Rising.*

‘Tell me everything.’

Conall looked towards his home, just opposite Maggie's own, and nodded his head.

‘Yes. But first I need to go in. I don’t want them to suffer any longer than they have to waiting for my return.’

‘Come across when you can and we’ll go for a stroll.’

He gave her a quick hug again. 'Thanks, Maggie. I'll be over soon.' Then he walked slowly up the laneway to his home, no longer the same man who had left it just a month ago.

‘When I got to the Post Office that first evening in April I found the windows were barricaded with bags of sand and at each of the tall windows were two or three men armed with Lee Enfield rifles. They were taking it in shifts. What had been the front office had been turned into the headquarters of the leaders, and I saw James Connolly[18] there who was in charge of the GPO garrison made up of Irish Volunteers and the Citizen Army; the two brothers Padraic and Willie

---

[18] *See Historical Notes*

Pearse, Michael O'Rahilly[19] and Joe Plunkett. Tom Clarke and some others I didn't know were sitting at tables writing out orders and receiving messengers. Do you remember Seán Mac Diarmada[20] from Kiltyclogher who stayed at your house that time?'

Maggie nodded her head. 'Oh yes, he and Daddy stayed up the whole night chatting with the rest of the men and Mam was giving out because she never slept a wink with the fiddle playing.'

'I heard that she gave Seán's father Donald[21] a right earful the next morning. I was gone by then but my father told me.'

Maggie laughed. 'Yes, she told him that he and your uncle, John Daly[22], could make the breakfast for the men because they were the eldest and should have sent them to bed.'

'Seán was at the GPO too and he was the one who introduced me to Pearse. It was due to Pearse that I

---

[19] *Michael Joseph O'Rahilly, known as The O'Rahilly, was an Irish Republican and nationalist; he was a founding member of the Irish Volunteers in 1913 and served as Director of Arms. Died in combat, Easter Rising 1916.*

[20] *Seán Mac Diarmada, from Kiltyclogher, Leitrim, was an Irish Republican political activist and revolutionary leader. Executed for his role in the Easter Rising.*

[21] *Donald McDermott was a member of the IRB and a friend of John Daly (Uncle of Edward Daly).*

[22] *John Daly, a prominent Republican who had taken part in the Fenian Rising and Fenian Dynamite Campaign.*

didn't get arrested with the others. Otherwise, I'd be on my way to Frongoch[23] now with the rest of the men.'

'How did he stop you from getting arrested?'

'On Friday the GPO was in flames from an incendiary bomb that landed over the doorway. Pearse sent me with Michael Joseph O'Rahilly who was leading a group of men to a new fortification at the Williams and Wood Factory on Great Britain Street. The O'Rahilly knew the building was a secure one. Thirteen of us were the first to evacuate the GPO, twelve Volunteers and O'Rahilly himself. We were under heavy fire the whole time. He and several others got hit by a British machine gun at the intersection of Great Britain and Moore Street. A civilian man pulled me into a bombed-out pub and I ducked down under the window with my rifle. I saw O'Rahilly get hit in the chest, then slump into a doorway on Moore Street and he seemed to be bleeding badly but then he made a dash across the road towards Sackville Row and I didn't see him after that. I presumed he was safe. Later I heard he was hit after ducking his head out to see if the coast was clear for his men to advance. He was shot several times by machine gun fire and died

---

[23] *Frongoch internment camp in Gwynedd, Wales. It was used to hold Irish Republican prisoners from the 1916 Rising.*

from his wounds after lying there for over a whole day. Maggie, the soldiers wouldn't let anybody come to his aid or even let them move the body after he had died. They wanted people to see him lying there.'

'Oh, Conall, how awful, how could they have done that?' Maggie shuddered. 'But I am so grateful he saved your life by getting you out of the GPO. It must have been horrific.'

'At first, when I arrived it was almost exciting, Maggie,' he said, lying back on the freshly cut grass near the edge of the lake, his hands underneath his head. 'All of us together there for the one cause, to fight for our independence. Ah, Pearse was a great man for the speeches. I could have listened to him talk all day. He stirred the men up. You know, everybody was sort of in good enough spirits at the beginning. We were full of bravado and in a strange kind of way it was some of the best days of my life. Listening to James Connolly talking was a privilege. I can't believe what they did to him.'

Maggie, who was sitting up and watching Conall as he spoke, lay down now beside him and reached out for his hand as it was easier to do so when she could no longer see his face. He took it.

‘We have been getting snippets of information these last few weeks but it is hard to know what is true or if what they are telling us are lies, just to scare us all. Some of the soldiers have been gloating and sneering about the executions to anybody they see. Is it true they shot James Connolly while he was tied to a chair?’

'Worse, Maggie. They shot him while he was still on his stretcher. They tied him to it and then leaned the stretcher against the wall because he was too injured to even sit in the chair.'

Maggie horror-stricken couldn't reply. Biting her lip she looked up at the golden, yellow sky above their heads. It was one of those beautiful Irish evenings when the sun is beginning to set and the sky looks like an artist's palette, with its colourful conglomeration of orange, yellow, and tinges of prismatic pink and red reflecting on the shimmering surface of Monks Lake.

‘To think of never seeing this again,’ Maggie whispered, squeezing Conall’s hand. ‘It is unthinkable. How did you manage to get away? There must have been soldiers everywhere.’

'There was. After a while, I made it to a house on Moore Street via the back of the pub I was in. That's where I was when we got word of Pearse's[24] surrender. We were expecting it but it still came as a hell of a blow to us all. We had given it everything we had, but we were simply outnumbered and under-armed.'

'And then?'

'Then I went with Ernie O'Malley and a few others into hiding in some house on a street called Leinster Road near Harolds Cross. The soldiers were arresting anybody involved in the rebellion and even many of those who were not. But when we heard about the executions[25] it was an awful shock. It was a Cumann na mBan woman whose house we were staying in who told me about my cousin Edward. It was our uncle John Daly who was at your house at that time. They are from Limerick. His older sister Kathleen is married to Tom Clarke and they executed him the day before Edward.'

'Oh, Conall, the poor family, I can't imagine. Don't they have a couple of children?'

---

[24] *29 April 1916 – Patrick Pearse surrendered, ending the Easter Rising, in his words, "to prevent the further slaughter of Dublin citizens."*

[25] *Sixteen of the Rising's leaders were executed starting in May 1916.*

'Yes. Three and Kathleen[26] was expecting their fourth.'

'Was?'

'Yes. Sadly, you know with the shock of Tom's execution and everything, she …'

'Oh, no, that is awful, Conall.'

'It has changed me forever, Maggie.'

Turning on her side to look at that face she knew so well, she could say only one thing. 'I could see that the moment you jumped off the cart.'

'For one thing, the executions have made me even more determined to get these barbarous intruders out of our country, no matter what. The other thing is that after witnessing the deaths of so many men who have now left widows and young fatherless children behind them, I realize I cannot make any sort of commitment to a woman until Ireland is free. It would be only selfish of me to do so. Do you understand what I am saying?'

Maggie felt as though her heart skipped a beat as immediately she felt tears spring to her eyes and was grateful that Conall could not see her face. He turned

---

[26] *See Historical Notes*

towards her when she didn't reply and pulled her closer to him.

'Do you understand, Maggie?' he repeated.

She snuggled her head into the crook of his arm like a chick under its mother's wing and reached her arm across the wide expanse of his chest.

'I understand,' she answered.

'You'll wait?'

'I will.'

'You won't go off with that Matthew Goodville?' he asked, tickling her ribs.

Maggie giggled now. 'Sure, you never know. I might,' she teased, well aware that he always held a jealousy regarding her friendship with Matthew.

With that, Conall jumped up on his good leg but Maggie was quicker, taking off over the field towards her home as though the hounds of hell were after her. But of course, she was no match for his long legs and speed despite his injury and soon he tumbled her to the ground, kissing her as though there was no tomorrow and she let him. Of course, she did. Afterwards together they lay in silence holding hands, both lost in thought of the brutality of the war that was going on around them, as the sun kissed the land they loved farewell, for another day under an Irish sky.

5

Leah
Dundalk, Ireland
2016

The house held that stale smell that all buildings have if unused for a time. I know that Jill, our long-time housekeeper, still kept an eye on it. She picked up any mail and took it to the office, weeded my little garden when required and ensured the heat was on a timer in winter, and still on for a little while in summer. But a house needs to be lived in. Smells of cooking, laundry drying, an open fire and windows open to let the air in, were all needed to keep a house smelling fresh. To me, every single home has its unique smell and I often found if a person moved to another house, within time, that smell would follow them. It's a very personal thing. Nobody uses the same scents, perfume, soap, washing powders, air fresheners, floor cleaners, or choice of flowers as another, so every single person's home has its familiar essence which can instantly make a returned family member feel brought back to the fold. I suppose it is a pre-historic animalistic thing, for each tribe to have its scent and therefore recognisable to their clan.

Pushing open the door I did not get that initial smell of coming home because Grandy was no longer here. Nobody knew I was arriving and if Jill had known she would be here, probably with something cooking in the expectation that I'd be starving. She would have my bed freshly made up that would smell of the washing powder we always bought and no doubt the bed would also have a hot water bottle in it 'to take the chill out of it' she would say.

The fire would be lit even in the height of summer and it would just smell like home. Now it no longer did and that immediately caused sadness on my entering the small hallway. As this had initially been Grandy's home business, instead of a front door there were two high wooden gates with a sort of latch door inserted where we went in and out if the gates were not opened. On entering the yard from the latch door there was a door to the right and entrance into the house. I had insisted on it being painted bright yellow as a teenager because I felt everything inside the brown gates, the yard and outhouses that used to be Grandy's garages, were all very drab colours and I believed the house where we lived should be different and brighter. It needed to be more welcoming, I had said. To the left was a stairway with a large landing in the middle and a long, tall window that looked out onto the yard, with a window ledge big enough to sit in, and I often did right up to adulthood. It was usually where I waited for Grandy to come home and I had it bedecked with comfortable cushions. Sometimes I would be found asleep there if Grandy was home late and he would gently guide me from my reading nook up to bed.

Over the fireplace in the sitting room was a beautiful black and white portrait of my grandmother holding my infant mother on her knees. My grandmother had very long, dark hair which hung down over one shoulder in the photo and beautiful big eyes. In the drawing, she is wearing what I know is a blue frock with wide, cream lapels but in the picture, the dress looks white. My mother's blond curly hair is just beginning to grow and little ringlets decorate her head. She has the cherubic look of a perfect baby, chubby cheeks and rosebud lips, and both dimpled hands are clasped in my mother's. Grandy had a sentimental tradition of blessing himself and touching this drawing every time he left the house and every time he did it my heart ached for our loss.

As a child, I thought this house was massive, but now as is the case for most people; it didn't seem very big at all. Despite being three stories high, the rooms were not that large, in keeping I suppose with the fashion of the time it was built, in 1835. The rooms were smaller then as easier to keep warm and three bedrooms upstairs all had fireplaces. The third floor was initially where servants slept but I had always known it as a playroom and had thought it full of mystery. Running the length of the house, it had creaking floorboards and a sloping ceiling. The walls had flaking white plaster and cobwebs lurked in corners. It was accessible from what looked like an ordinary door on the second landing but when opened it led to a long, narrow and steep staircase. A cord at the top of the staircase lit the room when pulled and for a long time I could only go into it if Grandy or Jill pulled the cord first and the door was left open.

But oh, what wonders were held up there. Till this day it remains largely untouched, even the bed-frames belonging to servants of almost a hundred years ago are still there. There were so many suitcases with treasures inside, old tea chests with clothes from several eras myself and my friends frequently used as our private old-fashioned clothes shop. I guess that is where my love of vintage clothes came from. There were items that I only realized as I got older were quite valuable, little black Chanel bags from the 1950s, fur stoles, and leather gloves which eventually and unfortunately became too small for me as I grew up. There was even lingerie from decades ago, things with clips and bows and basques, most of which I had no idea how to wear. It was a veritable Aladdin's Cave and to my delight I had *carte blanche* to use its treasures in any way.

My bedroom was the largest one upstairs and looked out onto the road. It had once been my grandparents' bedroom but after my grandmother died, Grandy could no longer sleep in it. My bedroom had two large windows overlooking the street. These had the old-fashioned wooden shutters that kept out the sound of traffic including the bells of the nearby St. Patricks Cathedral that rang out every hour. Against the right wall was a long wooden dressing table and a curved back, cane chair with a pink flowery, cushioned seat. In the mirror on top of this was where I watched my face change from a twelve-year-old to a teenager, to a young woman and the person I now am. Here is where I practised putting on my make-up, from the childish painted doll look created with my grandmother's old cosmetics found in the bathroom cabinet, to my teen too-dark foundation that ended at my jaw-line and eventually moving on to almost getting it right with regrets for over-plucked eyebrows and gratitude for inheriting my mother's flawless skin.

From my bedroom window I could see the varying heights of multi-coloured rooftops of businesses and homes and I loved this view for its sameness. In all these years the view had never changed. It was the same one my mother had looked out at as a child and that thought kept me grounded during times when I most needed to be. When I began to show an interest in boys Grandy didn't freak out as I expected. He even allowed me to bring them home until I realized the reason why. They were grilled more than if they were a spy being interrogated by the Gestapo, to no avail because Grandy could probably tell them more about themselves than they knew already. He knew everybody in town, their parents, and even their pets' names. If he didn't know, he would soon find out. Many in the town worked for him and some had even emigrated to various parts of Europe where he had businesses. He was the pulse of the town and if his granddaughter was going to have a boyfriend, he would know about it.

Therefore, it was just as well that Grandy was not around to witness this recent debacle, and as I carried my bags into the little porch, it was the first time I felt relieved he was not at home.

6

Maggie
Leitrim & Roscommon
1917

Maggie stamped her feet up and down in the snow, now mostly turned to filthy slush with the number of people traipsing through it at the train station in Carrick-on-Shannon. The air was scented with the smell of wet coats and cold bodies. Cigarette smoke wafted above the heads of the crowd, mixing with the condensation they exhaled with their raspy coughs and chatter on the dull and cloudy February day. Snow fell quietly, landing on hats and coat shoulders, not even getting a chance to fall to the ground with the thick throng surrounding the station, all eagerly awaiting the train which carried Count Plunkett[27], along with one of his daughters into Leitrim.

Maggie had been instructed along with a fellow Cumann na mBan Volunteer to hold up high a placard

[27] *See Historical Notes*

mounted on each side with a wooden pole, inscribed with the words *Why you should support Plunkett,* at the top in bold, black print and underneath was written a list of reasons, such as *Because he is a man of dignity and a man of learning,* with another six points following that.

On the lapel of her uniform, Maggie wore the election badge *Vote for Count Plunkett - The man for Ireland.* This was also written in black print and inserted inside a badge, the shape of the recognisable shamrock. Some people said the shape was to represent the Holy Trinity - especially as Plunkett had previously received a special blessing in Rome from Pope Benedict XV, just three weeks before his part in the Easter Rising. For this reason, Plunkett was almost seen as a prophet amongst his followers and the populace had huge hopes if he won this election, he would surely bring about a free Ireland.

By now Maggie's arms ached, as did Alice's.

'Let's put this down for a few minutes,' Maggie suggested. 'My arms are hurting.'

'Mine too,' Alice replied, thankfully lowering the placard along with Maggie.

Suddenly the sound of a train approaching could be heard and the young women quickly swung the placard into the air again.

'Aaagh, my head!' somebody roared behind them and they both swung around, realising they had knocked the hat of a distinguished-looking gentleman, whose head-gear was now being trampled on by many feet.

Maggie's eyes opened wide when she realized who it was.

'Bartle!' she exclaimed. 'Why are you dressed in your finery?'

'I am to accompany Count Plunkett and his daughter and a Fr. Conlon to the hotel and then we are making a procession into Roscommon,' he answered, dusting the dirt of the hat he luckily retrieved in one piece.

'When was this arranged? We are also going to be part of the procession,' Alice replied.

'It was a last-minute request from Laurence Nugent. He is a leader of the National Committee for National Volunteers and has been campaigning for Count Plunkett's election. He sent a message last night requesting I meet them from the train and take them to the hotel before the procession so they can freshen up and get a bite to eat.'

'Oh, that is quite an honour,' Maggie said, impressed. 'We might see you later on then, in Roscommon?'

'Probably,' Bartle agreed. 'It will be a bit of an endurance test in this weather. You ladies already look frozen to the bone.'

Both Maggie and Alice nodded to confirm this.

'I won't deny we are cold,' Maggie said, stamping her freezing feet again. 'But it is important to show support for Count Plunkett and the more campaigners there are out to show that, the better for the Cause.'

Bartle tipped his hat at the ladies, and replied 'You are doing great work, the pair of you. It hasn't gone unnoticed.'

The young women couldn't get a look at the Count at all or his daughter when they arrived at the train station, so great was the crowd around them. They could understand why Bartle and the other volunteers were tasked with getting the Dublin visitors to the hotel, as Bartle had borrowed his father's delivery van and that was the humble way they travelled, without being hindered by the several hundred people who had turned out to welcome Count Plunkett.

The torchlight procession to Roscommon from Carrick-on-Shannon was a noisy affair with some people giving speeches along the way and many Republican songs were sung, all passing the time on the long walk in the cold snow blizzard. On reaching Roscommon there was a substantial throng of people considering the bad weather and Fr. O'Flanagan gave a rousing speech before the Count took the platform, where he also gave an impressive oration, electrifying the listeners. Since they carried the banners, both Maggie and Alice this time had the advantage of being in the fortunate position of front row, ably seeing and hearing all that took place on the stage. By now their arms were painfully sore and they gratefully handed their burden over to Volunteers from Roscommon who offered to take their turn.

'I hope we don't have to carry them back again,' Alice pleaded, rolling her shoulders up and down to ease the knots that had formed there.

'Bartle told me he would give us a lift home with them,' Maggie answered.

'Thank goodness. I was dreading the walk back in this weather.'

'There are some women serving tea over there, shall we get some?' Maggie asked, pointing to where a makeshift stall was set up.

‘Oh yes, please,’ replied Alice and they made their way through the swarm of bodies.

'Tea for two please, with milk and one with sugar,' Maggie asked, while fishing in her coat pocket for some coppers.

‘No charge for the Volunteers,’ she was told.

It was easy to spot they were Volunteers with the green Cumann na mBan uniforms the ladies serving tea also wore. Maggie thought of what her O.C. Sheila Daly, had reminded them a few times, that everybody's role in the organization was an equally important one and right now the tea-ladies role was a much-needed one.

'Excuse me, please,' a voice asked, and Maggie turned around to see a well-dressed lady also very warmly clad.

‘Yes, can I help you?’ Maggie asked her.

‘I am afraid I have gotten myself rather embarrassingly lost,’ the lady replied. ‘I am Miss

Plunkett.[28] Is there a possibility you could please help me locate my father? I seem to have been swept along in the crowd and cannot find him.'

'Oh, goodness,' Maggie exclaimed. Taking a long drink of her tea she put the cup back on the stand. 'Here, take my arm,' she said, offering Miss Plunkett her elbow and nodding to Alice to take the other arm. 'We will help you locate your father. Don't worry.'

They walked quickly among the crowd until finally reaching the area where the stage was. It now stood empty but Alice climbed the steps to it and began scanning the area for the Count while Maggie and Miss Plunkett waited below. Although it was dark, the space was well lit up with the many torches people carried and it wasn't long before she spotted Volunteer Bartholomew Daly first and then the priest, Fr. O'Flanagan, who had also escorted Plunkett. They accompanied Miss Plunkett to where she eventually found her father, still surrounded by many well-wishers.

'My dear,' he said. 'I was quite worried. Where did you go?'

---

[28] *The gathering was big for a country town and most enthusiastic. Miss Plunkett got lost in the crowd and some of the local Volunteer women took possession of her and she was certainly well cared for.*

‘I am embarrassed to say I have no idea how or where I ended up, Father,’ she replied. ‘Thankfully this kind lady Volunteer came to my aid and found you on my behalf.’

The Count turned to Maggie and took her gloved hands in his own.

‘Thank you very much for looking after my daughter, Miss …?’

‘Margaret,’ Maggie answered, a bit shyly. ‘Margaret McGuill.’

‘And you are a Volunteer from the Roscommon and Leitrim Brigade I take it?’

‘Yes, I am,’ Maggie answered.

‘I must thank you again for your support. We greatly appreciate the outstanding welcome we have received in both Leitrim and Roscommon. McGuill you say?’ the Count asked. ‘Are you a relation of John-Joe McGuill then?’

‘Yes. He is my father,’ Maggie answered, turning to Bartle who was beginning to load banners and other materials into the back of the van.

Just then Alice had reached the small group and Maggie introduced her also.

‘Well, it is a pleasure to have met you ladies and once again I thank you for coming to the aid of my daughter, and especially in your support for the Cause. I hope I can come to your assistance sometime if needed and I do hope we meet again.’

The Count once more shook the ladies' hands and after they said goodbye to Miss Plunkett, Maggie and Alice joined Bartle in the van for their journey home.

7

Leah
Ireland
2016

I believe there is something exceedingly comforting about wakening in your childhood bedroom. The familiar, out-of-date furniture around you of which you know the story behind every scratch or cigarette burn and even every scuff mark on the wallpaper tells a tale. After spending as long as I could bear last night outside in the cold night air, I eventually went inside to the slightly warmer house and carried just what I needed for the bedtime routine upstairs, including a half glass of red wine and a bar of Cadbury's milk chocolate, with my current read 'Pale Fire' by Vladimir Nabokov tucked under my arm. This book was chosen because despite the controversy created by the novel, the author's words are the most luminous and beautifully composed writing that exists in literature. This works perfectly as a recipe for calming anxiety and heartache. The absence of any romantic plots made it the perfect companion for when I wanted to receive a sense of cleansing the soul through fiction.

Now wide awake and refreshed after a restful night's sleep, I opened the white shutters wide allowing the morning sun to creep into my bedroom. I felt filled with a new sense of optimism and after slipping my arms into my cosy blue, fleece dressing gown and my feet into my comfortable Uggs I padded downstairs into the kitchen and filled the kettle. The airport shop did not stretch to Italian coffee, but Nescáfe was sufficient for now. I also put two slices of bread into the toaster, retrieved butter and milk from the fridge and while waiting on the kettle to boil and bread to toast, I turned the dial on Grandy's ancient radio.

It always seemed more like I had come home when I could hear the local accent across the airwaves and notices being read out about what was going on in town during the week. Picking up my mobile I pressed the number I needed.

'Jill, it's …'

'Aw, Leah,' she interrupted. 'You're home.'

'Yes,' I replied. 'How did you …'

‘Sure, I don’t know how many people told me this morning already that you were back,’ she answered. ‘You forgot how fast word gets around here,’ she added, with a laugh. ‘How are you, pet?’

‘I’m grand, Jill. I’m grand,’ I replied, already falling back into the local dialect.

‘How long are you home for?’

‘I am not sure. How …’ I laughed to myself as Jill interrupted once again. Nobody could ever get a word in with her.

'Well, I'll call this evening for a chat. I'm taking myself to Dublin on the train now in a minute for a bit of shopping in the sales, but I'll pop in on the way home for a catch-up. Okay?'

‘Sure. Yes, of course,’ I replied. ‘Have a good time in Dublin.’

‘Oh, I’ll try,’ Jill laughed girlishly. ‘And call around to Seán won't you? See you soon, pet. God bless now.’

And she was gone. I loved Jill to bits but somehow I always felt exhausted after speaking with her. She talked ninety to the dozen and used to drive poor Grandy demented with her constant prattle when she was going about the house cooking or cleaning, but we were very fond of her. In many ways, she made up for my not having any female role model in my teenage years. After putting away the strange collection of hastily packed clothes I had taken with me, I went upstairs to the attic and began to pull out cardboard boxes where I had stored all my old interviews and research notes. Of course, as what usually happens to people when they begin to go through storage boxes, hours pass until eventually, they get cramped from sitting too long and all around them is a heap of long-forgotten letters, photos, and mementos. Then I saw the blue, flowery plastic box containing all the notes I had taken when interviewing Lise. As part of my journalism course, I had to do a series of interviews and while trying to come up with ideas of who to contact, Grandy had suggested a woman whom he said may be of some interest.

'She is somebody who you may find intriguing,' he had said. 'And who both I and your grandmother knew from a long time ago. She is known as quite an enigma in the town or village as it is now, where your grandmother is from. One or two of the local women bring her food and things. She doesn't go very far from her surroundings. I think it would be good for you to meet her. It is a bit of a journey, but will be worth it to you, I am sure.'

‘Oh, she sounds interesting, Grandy,’ I replied. ‘I’d love to interview her. Will you take me?’

And that was how I had gotten to know Lise. I remembered I grew extremely fond of her and she of me. We became quite close friends despite the huge age difference and I recall finding her lively and young at heart. It was hunger that made me get up from the attic in the end and I carried down the box containing all my interview notes and put it on the kitchen table. I couldn't help but feel bad about the fact I had more or less vanished from Lise's life. I had interviewed her over several months and I felt as though I had known her a much longer time and recalled even the very first day I saw her, she had seemed so familiar to me. She told me later that she had felt the same way, hence the reason why she hugged me so warmly when we met.

Sorting through the several workbooks and folders, I put them into order according to the dates and balancing them along with a tray containing a toasted sandwich and a coffee, I carried them into the front sitting room. Stretching my legs out on the long sofa, I began to read the words I had typed many years ago.

Her name was Lees, or Lise. She didn't know for sure. I suggested it was maybe from the name Elizabeth. She did not know her birth name. She simply told me this was the name she was known as. I couldn't imagine not even knowing what your real name was. It was something that immediately cast her as an anomaly.

She lived in what used to be a huge shed for storing coal and firewood, in the basement underneath the hotel. The door was set in the middle of a long, white wall circling the courtyard where the hotel was situated. It was a white wooden door, almost as though intentionally camouflaged into the wall. It was slightly warped and didn't close properly. There was no key for her to lock herself in and when I pushed the door open that first day I was hit by two things, the warmth and the smell of lavender. Her living place was next door to the boiler house, so she had heat. The floor was stone flagged but covered in a mix-match of rugs. To the right of me, I could see her, sitting in her red, woollen shawl on an old rocking chair. She stood when I entered, held her arms out and I went into them, and she hugged me tightly, smelling of soap and her hair tied up in a bun, smelled clean.

I wondered later who the kind people were who brought her food and any other necessities as she told me she never left the grounds. She pointed to a chair opposite. The seat was soft red velvet. I sat. She stayed standing and moved towards a yellow dresser, left of the room. It was one of those old ones you could pull part of the door into a small table.

'You'll have tea?'

I hesitated, seeing it was obvious electricity was not part of her living conditions. I could tell as there was no light bulb. Her home was dark and although I had called to her in the early afternoon, the only light was from the windows either side of her door. Perhaps she used candles. Indeed, there were those old-fashioned Tilley lamps on the walls.

'I heat the water on the gas cooker and then fill a flask for the day,' she said, holding up a huge thermos flask, she was already screwing open.

I nodded.

'Yes, lovely thanks,' I replied, sitting upright, already feeling the chair wobble on the uneven floor.

As Lise fussed around her small kitchen area, I scanned the room. It felt cosy. What I noticed most of all were the picture frames or canvasses along the white-washed walls where normally a skirting board would be. I longed to pick one up but dared not. I couldn't help but feel compelled to turn them around and see what she was hiding. Lise moved slowly as she silently poured from the flask into the teapot and then poured tea into a white cup. This one she offered to me. The tin cup from the flask she kept for herself.

'I have bars too,' she said, opening an old biscuit tin and offering me a Penguin Bar.

I sat, sipping from the white teacup and tore the wrapper open with my teeth. Lise sat unhurriedly in the chair opposite and leaned towards me, looking intently into my eyes.

'Why did you come here?'

I was surprised at her question and immediately felt embarrassed. I had not been invited to her home. I just called, expecting to be welcomed. I would not just call to anybody else's home uninvited or unexpected. Immediately I realised I was thinking of her as somebody for whom social niceties do not exist. I judged her just as probably everybody else in her life had done … and in doing so thought I could treat her differently and I felt ashamed.

‘I am sorry. I should have asked before if I could call. I thought my grandfather would have had somebody tell you.’

She sat back in her chair, took a sip from her tin cup and after a minute or two of silence, replied;

‘You are here I believe,’ she said. ‘Because you are going to tell my story.’

I did, but it took me many years to do so and for that, I am also ashamed.

‘How did you find out about me?’ she asked. ‘Was it from one of my callers?’

‘Yes, in a round-about way,’ I answered. ‘My grandmother came from around here, but I had never heard anything about you. It was my grandfather who mentioned you. I live with him.’

‘What was your grandmother’s name?

‘Charlotte. Charlotte McKeown,’ I told her, looking for some kind of recognition in her face, but there was none.

Lise sat quietly for a few seconds then lifted her head and smiled.

'So, you are going to be a journalist?' she asked, settling back in her cozy-looking chair, cup in hand.

‘Yes. It’s been my dream since I was a child. That and travelling,’ I answered, blowing on the steaming hot tea.

‘Is there any particular reason why that profession appealed to you?’

‘Actually, there is, but it is a sad story.’

'I'd like to hear it, if you wouldn't mind telling me. I have a few sad stories of my own and I suppose that is why you are here. Why don’t you let me ask you questions first?’

I smiled. ‘Okay. Let’s do that. Who knows, I might get some interviewing tips from you!’

Lise laughed at that and I had a very good feeling we were both sort of kindred spirits. I felt as though I had known her a very long time, instead of the short time I had been here so far today. Her smile and everything about her was somehow familiar to me.

‘Tell me about your sad story.’

I sighed deeply and wrapped my hands around the warm cup, gaining some comfort from its heat.

‘My parents were killed in a fire when I was a child.’

‘Oh, no you poor dear. That is a shocking revelation. What caused the fire?’

‘It was during the Troubles in Northern Ireland[29]. We lived in an area called The Triangle[30] – because there were three hotspots where the worst of the atrocities took place and we lived in the most dangerous of them. At that time the government decided to build these huge housing estates and blocks of flats for both Catholic and Protestant families. The theory was such a development would link together the populations of bigger towns in the North of Ireland, who were unable to remain in their homes due to the fighting and were separated in terms of social class and religion. It was hoped they would rub along nicely together in a peaceful way. That didn't happen. What happened was an all-out war between the two fractions on the estates.'

Lise pondered silently on this for a moment then asked. ‘What caused the fire in your home?’

'The investigation by the RUC and the fire officers concluded that my father, who was a mechanic, had

---

[29] *See Historical Notes*

[30] *Lurgan was mainly known as a terrorist stronghold, where Protestants and Catholics were kept apart by a wide main street. Along with the derided new town of Craigavon and neighbouring Portadown, Lurgan became known as the ‘murder triangle’ of Northern Ireland.*

spilled petrol or left clothes with petrol on them in the hallway – where the fire had broken out - and one of my parents must have knocked over an ashtray with a smoldering cigarette in it igniting the fire.'

‘But you don’t agree?’

‘Absolutely not. I know for a fact that it was not true as neither of my parents smoked. My mother had asthma so she had never smoked and my father gave up cigarettes when he began going out with her. They didn’t even have an ashtray in the house as nobody was allowed to smoke in our home because of Mum’s condition. Dad took his overalls off at work before he came home because even the fumes of petrol or diesel would give Mum an attack.’

‘So you think that it was done deliberately?’

'I know it was. There was an investigative journalist at the time who wrote about the murder, for that is what it was. Houses were set on fire all the time then, but not when people were inside. This was an intentional murder and the journalist, her name was Cathy Lynn, wouldn't let it go. She was threatened herself, with a petrol-soaked rag thrown into her letterbox and a lighted match on top of it. Thankfully her boyfriend was worried about retaliation for what she was writing, so she had been staying at his parents' house. But what was done to her, was exactly what she had written in the paper must have been done to my parents.'

'But do you know why?'

'Yes. I knew very well the reason at the time as did everybody else, only they wouldn't say it out loud. But Cathy Lynn was the person who brought it out into the open. It was her tenacity and bravery that made me want to become a crime journalist too. I admired her so much. She even interviewed me with my grandfather's permission and I told her exactly what I remembered.

My mother was in our sitting room with me early one morning. We were arguing because I wanted to go to a sleepover at my friend's house and Mum wouldn't let me cycle there. It was only about fifteen minutes away, but she said it was too dangerous with so many bombs going off and I had to wait for Dad to come home from work so he could drive me. I was cross because Saturday was Dad's busiest day and if he was home late, I'd miss watching the Saturday Show with my friend.

Suddenly there was a thump at our window. We had this huge floor-to-ceiling window overlooking the small, green area set in the middle of our estate. A soldier on foot patrol slumped against the window and to our horror blood began to run in rivulets down the glass. My mother immediately ran outside and screamed at me to go to the phone box at the end of the road and ring for an ambulance. Our neighbours on either side came out of their homes and as I ran to the phone, I heard them shout at my mother to get back indoors and leave the soldier be. I could not make the call as the phone box had been vandalized, but when I ran back my mother was being forced into our house by neighbours and the fallen soldier was surrounded by the army men, all holding guns and yelling loudly for everybody to go into their homes. There was pandemonium.'

'Am I right in presuming your mother made herself a target by coming to the aid of a British soldier?'

'Yes. That is why they murdered her and my father. I would have died too most likely, if I hadn't been staying at my friend's house as planned. Those pre-fabricated houses were made with the very cheapest of materials. My Dad used to joke and say he could put his hand through the ceiling and put the kettle on from his bedroom, the ceilings were so thin. Also, there was some kind of insulation that was toxic if on fire and breathed in. My parents were both found in bed, so it appeared they were not even aware of a fire, the fumes alone killed them as they slept. The houses on either side were separated by a brick shed so at least the fire didn't spread.'

'How horrific. How did you find out? You poor thing and were you an only child?'

'Yes, I am an only child. My grandfather came for me. He was my mother's father. As far as I know, the RUC contacted the Gardaí where Grandy lived over the border (that's what I called him) and he had his driver take him straight to the North.'

'His driver?'

'Yes. Grandy was a wealthy man. He had lived abroad since his twenties and built up a transport business that started with just taxis at first, then lorries and he ended up with haulage companies all over Europe. Eventually, he moved back to Ireland but to a different part from where he was born and married my grandmother. I think he knew her from where he used to live. I am not sure. He never spoke about his younger life. Dad had worked for one of his companies in Belfast as a mechanic.'

'So he told you about your parents? That must have been heartbreaking for him to have to do.'

'It was horrendous. But the thing is, I knew.'

‘You knew?’

‘Yes. I can always sort of tell when something terrible is going to happen. That evening when Dad left me at Linda’s house I got that feeling I still get – like a horrible sense of foreboding.’

‘Tell me about that,’ Lise coaxed.

And I did and when I reached home afterward I realized she knew more about me than I knew about her. What a great crime journalist I was going to make! I'd have to make sure next time it would be me doing the interviewing.

8

Maggie

Aghameen
1919

Maggie wracked her brains, trying to think of something she may have done to make her father have that look on his face – the one he always had when something serious happened or he heard some bad news.

'I need to have a talk with you in the house, Maggie love,' he requested.

Maggie put down the pail of feed she'd been carrying and wiped her hands on her apron, then followed her father inside. She felt a quickening in her heart when he closed the front door behind her. They rarely closed the door during the day.

'Sit down, Maggie,' he said, gesturing to the small table under the front window.

This is where the three of them usually sat for breakfast, or when having a cup of tea during the day. The window looked out onto the small, front lawn where now Mam's daffodils were in full bloom, lining the narrow pathway from the gate to the front door. The farm sheds, chicken and pig pens were located at the back of the house, so as not to be seen from the road. Mam liked to think to anybody passing, it looked like a nice townhouse instead of the farmhouse it was. Maggie took her seat with its back to the door. Her father always sat facing the door and Mam's seat was the one facing the window. It had been this way for as long as Maggie could remember.

'I am going to talk to you like the adult I know you are becoming, Maggie,' John-Joe said, placing his hands over hers, nervously resting on the small, wooden table.

'What is it, Daddy?' Maggie questioned, worriedly. 'Is something the matter with Mam? Is she sick?'

'Ah no, love,' he answered, his face softening. 'It's nothing like that. Listen, I know you will understand what I am going to tell you. I kept it from you until now as I believed the less you knew the better for you. That if you were ever questioned by the authorities, you could truthfully say you didn't know anything. However, it has come about now that I am going to have to share confidence with you. But, you need to keep this conversation between us and not let anything on to your mother. Do you understand?'

Maggie nodded. With eyes wide, she waited to hear what her father was about to divulge.

'You know the way your mother keeps going on about getting the roof slated?'

Maggie nodded again. 'Yes. She told me she's going to keep at you until she drives you mad and then you will give in. Like you always do, she said.'

John-Joe raised his eyes to heaven. 'You have to talk her out of it.'

Maggie wrinkled her brow. 'But why, Daddy, and how am I going to do that? She has her heart set on it. You know she has. Can we not afford it?'

'It's not anything to do with money, love.'

'Why do I have to worry about the authorities questioning me? What do they have to do with you slating the roof for Mam?'

'We can't slate the roof, Maggie, because the thatch is full of guns.'

Maggie drew in a breath. 'Guns?'

'Yes, love, and not only that, there are right now, two Volunteers hiding in the attic. If there is another raid on the house, they won't be able to get out through a slated roof. So, you can see why there is a need to keep the thatch!'

Maggie was stunned. Then a thought occurred to her and she asked 'You wouldn't happen to have somebody hiding close to the pig pen too, would you?'

This time it was her father's eyes that widened.

'Because I've heard them, you know,' Maggie continued. 'Well, I mean at least I wasn't sure. But now I am. They are underneath the ground, aren't they?'

'They aren't in a very secure place so,' John-Joe replied, shaking his head, disturbed by this revelation. 'Not if you could hear them.'

'It was only on two occasions, Daddy. It was that time I fell at the pig pen over a year ago. Remember? I knew I felt hands shove me, but you told me later on that it must have been one of the pigs that knocked me over. I knew it couldn't have been. And another time I could have sworn I heard a whistling sound from under the pigpen.'

John-Joe hissed. 'That bloody Tomás Óg. He was warned about that. He's gone now, thank God.'

'But how, I mean … how can they possibly live under there?'

'Come on,' John-Joe answered, standing up and putting his cap back on. 'I'll show you.'

Maggie stood also and followed her father out the front door and around the back of the house. Minutes later she stood transfixed as her father scraped away some of the pigs' droppings and straw with a long-handled shovel, then after knocking a sort of code onto the ground, he stood back while suddenly a piece of the ground moved and seconds later a head popped up.

'Oh, my word,' Maggie exclaimed, raising her hands to her mouth in disbelief. 'It's you, Conall. What are you doing down there? Sure you are not in hiding anymore. I don't believe it. Did you whistle at me one morning?'

Conall grinned. 'I knew you would recognise our little code. Myself and Tomás were on our way to the tunnel and I was trying to get your attention to let you know we were in the trees over beyond, but Tomás, in trying to protect me, just shoved you out of the way when I was trying to make a dash for cover. I am only here this morning for a quick meeting with the men.'

Another head popped out of the opening then. Not somebody that Maggie knew.

'This is Anthony Fox,' Conall said. 'And I had the misfortune to be stuck down there with him and my mate Bartle.'

Anthony threw a questioning look at John-Joe and the older man put his hand on his daughter's shoulder. 'She can be trusted,' he said.

And Maggie never felt as proud. Looking at her father, she felt she had grown an inch taller and asked 'Who else is down there? Can I go down? How big is it? Can I see?'

Anthony again looked at John-Joe for his reaction and when John-Joe nodded in acquiescence, he opened what appeared to be a hatch door even wider and Maggie walked towards ıt, peering down.

'Here,' Conall said, offering her his hand. 'I hope you haven't got your Sunday best on.'

Maggie shook her head and took his hand.

'Best thing to do first is sit down at the edge and hang your legs down. Then keep holding onto me and jump down. Just the way I showed you when we were children. Got it?'

Maggie nodded. Then without hesitation, she jumped and Conall caught her in his arms, as he had promised.

'This is amazing,' she exclaimed, her eyes beginning to adjust to the dark tunnel she found herself in. Just a metre or two further along, she could make out a dim light. 'But when did you do this?'

John-Joe was now behind her after jumping down himself.

'Wait,' Maggie continued, turning around to face her father. 'Was that why you sent Mam and me on that trip to Rosses Point?'

He nodded, sheepishly. 'Yes. Myself and the lads built this then. It was a tunnel that was here going back to Cromwellian times, for the monks to escape if there was an invasion. I brought it up at a meeting, the possibility that it could be turned into a safe place for hiding the men on the run. Once the decision was made we had to get yourself and your Mam out of the way so we could work on it, so that was why I came up with the idea to send you both on a little holiday.'

‘Come on,’ Conall suggested. ‘Meet the other lads. They’ll be real happy to have some visitors.’

Maggie eagerly followed where Conall walked slowly towards the dim light with her father behind her, and then almost laughed with surprise when she saw how roomy and well-furnished the living area was, even if it did smell awful. It was an odour of unwashed feet, male sweat and something else she didn't even want to think about.

‘Well, it’s like a little house,’ she said, appraisingly. ‘Where does the air come from?’

The man named Anthony Fox pointed to a sort of funnel in the roof and then pointed to where several more were along the ceiling.

‘That is what we use as air vents,’ he explained.

'It's incredible what you have done,' Maggie acknowledged, looking around.

There were many books and board games scattered about, including various pictures stuck to the makeshift walls. Some were pages torn out from newspapers with information about the Volunteers. There was a copy of the Proclamation and Maggie also noticed quite a few pictures of females, the sort that made her raise her eyebrows and cast a discerning look at the so-called gentlemen around her. Especially to Conall, who put his head down and looked embarrassed.

'Follow me,' John-Joe said, trying to distract her attention. 'I'll show you where the tunnel leads to.'

It took almost ten minutes to walk in the darkness and Maggie shuddered at what sounded like mice, or maybe even rats, scuttling past her feet. Conall reached behind and grabbed her hand, knowing she had always been claustrophobic. When her father came to a stop he lifted a long, steel hooked pole and did the same coded knock. After waiting for another minute with John-Joe's head cocked as though listening for noise, he pushed the crook of the pole under a hook in the roof and slowly pushed up. There were small standing stones carved into the tunnel walls that John-Joe used to lever himself up. Seconds later Conall guided Maggie up the same steps and her father pulled her into the light.

'I don't believe it,' Maggie gasped. 'It's St. Agnes Church!'

They had arrived into the priest's garment wardrobe, in the vestry room and Fr. Nangle himself was sitting at his desk, having a cigarette and cup of tea.

‘Ah, it’s yourself, Mr. McGuill,’ he said, unperturbed. ‘And young Maggie,’ he then added with surprise and threw John-Joe a questioning look.

'Maggie has been taken into the confidence of the men,' John-Joe explained. 'It was agreed on at the meeting.' He squinted his eyes at the priest, as though waiting for him to make some objection. It was a well-known fact that Fr. Nangle was quite the chauvinist and had very conservative opinions about the role of women.

‘Well,’ Fr. Nangle continued. ‘On your own head be it. I wasn’t at the meeting – or indeed informed of it, so my opinion obviously wasn’t consulted. Had it been, she wouldn’t be here. For her own safety, of course,’ he added, on seeing the look on Conall’s face.

'Many a woman is doing their part in the fight for a free country these days, Father,’ John-Joe said. ‘Indeed, we couldn’t do it without them. Maggie has already proved her worth and is trusted by the men.’

‘Hear, hear,’ Conall agreed. ‘My cousin Sheila fought in the Rebellion along with the rest of us and did her time in Kilmainham too and she is back out there training the women and men.’

‘I never knew the tunnel was here all this time,’ Maggie said, looking around the vestry in wonderment. 'To think how many times I have been in this church and had no idea what was going on underneath my feet.'

'The church was built over the ruins of the old abbey that was once here, going back to around the 13th Century. Cromwell and his men burned it in 1649, but thankfully everybody escaped.[31] The abbey gradually fell into ruin and this church was eventually built on the site in 1812.'

'But how come nobody ever knew it was here?' Maggie asked.

'Some of the clergy who used the vestry were aware of a tunnel, but they were the only ones. There has always been a fear I suppose of Penal Laws[32] being introduced again at some stage and Masses being forbidden. Or if there were any other kinds of invasion, the priests and whatever parishioners were inside at the time could get to safety.'

---

[31] *The Cromwellian Conquest of Ireland or Cromwellian War in Ireland was the re-conquest of Ireland by the forces of the English Parliament, led by Oliver Cromwell, during the Wars of the Three Kingdoms. Cromwell invaded Ireland with the New Model Army on behalf of England's Rump Parliament in August 1649.*

[32] *Under the Penal Laws imposed by England, the Catholics could not hold a commission in the army, enter a profession, or own a horse worth more than five pounds. Catholics could not possess weaponry and arms, could not study law or medicine, and could not speak or read Gaelic or play Irish music*

'And end up at our pig pen,' Maggie surmised. 'Did you always know the tunnel ended up on our land?'

John-Joe nodded his head. 'Yes, of course. My father told me and his father told him and so on. And now I am telling you as the next generation. The tunnel was chosen to end there because of the proximity to the lake. The monks had a boat hidden under the trees if they needed to get away and there is talk about another tunnel somewhere they had access to not far up the lake. As far as I know, there are stepping stones under the lake somewhere that lead to it. They were well prepared. And indeed, they all survived. We know because years after the Cromwellian invasion they wrote a book detailing the whole event. That book is now in the Royal Irish Academy. Before it ended up there, the book was kept in the Goodville library until they donated it.'

'Gosh. So much history and now it is being used again as a tunnel and an escape route. It is fascinating, yet sort of sad too,' Maggie said. 'So, the Forces – they know nothing about it? Are you sure?'

John-Joe shook his head. 'They don't know. If they did, they'd have been here already. Very few are aware of it and I know you won't say a word. I needed you to know about it, should anything happen to me or I needed you to get word to the men.'

Maggie was both humbled and honoured to be taken into her father's confidence like this and above all to be included in the trust of the men. It was all she ever wanted, to be respected by her father. This was way beyond anything she ever hoped for and she would never do anything to lose that respect, for it meant the world to her. Believing nothing else would surprise her today, there was another shock in store when Maggie saw the person who came into the vestry. It was none other than her friend and neighbour, Matthew Goodville. Immediately she stood in front of the wardrobe door that was already closed – a quick movement that did not go unnoticed by her father and he was pleased her first reaction was to protect their secret.

'Mr. Goodville,' she exclaimed. 'How are you? This is not your usual place of worship.'

Matthew and his family were Protestant and their church was the other side of town. By his face, he was as surprised to see Maggie as she was to see him.

'Miss McGuill,' he acknowledged. 'Good afternoon to you. And you also, Mr. McGuill.' He nodded to Fr. Nangle and Conall and consequently turned on his heel and left as quickly as he had come in.

‘Well,’ Maggie said, turning to her father. ‘Wasn’t that the strangest thing? What do you think he wanted in here? And why did he leave I wonder?’

‘There is no use in keeping you in the dark, Maggie,’ her father answered. ‘Matthew Goodville is one of us.’

Maggie’s mouth dropped open and for once she was lost for words. It was Fr. Nangle who spoke first.

‘I still don’t trust him.’

‘I don’t trust you either,’ John-Joe said, ushering Maggie outside the vestry door leading to the side of the small church.

‘We’ll walk back this way,’ her father said, lighting a cigarette. ‘So we can have a chat. But we’ll wait till we get out of earshot of anybody.’

The day looked normal enough, even though to Maggie it had become the strangest of days. For February it was quite warm and Maggie chewed over everything she had seen and heard in the last half hour or so as she walked in silence next to her father. There was plenty to think about. She was impatient to hear how Matthew had become involved in the Cause. He was English. He might live most of his time in the same town as her, but he was born in London. He went to school there and went to University there also. He was Protestant and although he said he considered himself to be Irish, he wasn't. He was English, as far as she and the rest of the town were concerned. Finally, her father spoke.

'I know I don't have to tell you to keep everything to yourself, love, and I know you were a bit taken aback to see Mr. Goodville turn up there. He sure looked shaken to see you. He wouldn't be aware yet of what went on at the meeting as he's only off the mail boat from England, so he wasn't expecting to see you there today.'

'He looked more than shaken. He looked like he was going to have a heart attack.'

'I'd say he had arrived to give the lads word about anything he may have heard over in London. He'll probably go back again to the church now that we have left. He couldn't go down into the tunnel with you there.'

'I can't believe what you said about Matthew,' Maggie exclaimed minutes later. 'Sure, he is a British Officer. Has he become a spy?'

'Sort of, he approached me several years ago actually and told me about his wish to leave the army and join us. But I told him he would be more useful if he remained in it. This is of the highest confidentiality, Maggie.'

She nodded her head, still stunned, thinking of all the times she and Matthew had talked over the years and he had kept all this information to himself. Though understandably, she acknowledged to herself. His life was at stake as traitors to the Crown are immediately executed.

'Who are the other two men in the tunnel? I didn't recognise them.'

'No, you wouldn't. They are from Sligo. Eamonn Sheldon is the blond-haired one and the other fellow is Jack Kelly. Good lads. They got caught up in an ambush and there is a warrant out for their arrest.'

'What about the men in the attic? Mam would have a fit if she knew they were up there.'

'She would. Not because she wouldn't want to help, but because she'd be scared stiff. She would never sleep at night knowing they were above her head. I hope it won't affect you.'

'Nothing affects my sleep, Daddy. You know that. I'd sleep standing up in the rain. But who are those men?'

'They are Volunteers. Just like yourself, Maggie. I think they are going today, so no need for an introduction.'

☘

'Can't I let Mrs. Daly know that her son Bartle is alright, Daddy?' Maggie asked as she handed her father his customary mug of tea after dinner. Mam always used the teacups and teapot after the meal, but when the table had been cleared, John-Joe loved to sit with a huge mug of tea and smoke his pipe with it in front of the fireplace, before going back outside to the farm.

'Shush,' he whispered, looking behind to ensure his wife wasn't in earshot. 'Be careful where you talk.'

'I know that,' Maggie whispered back. 'I waited till Mam had gone for her lie down.'

'And the answer is a resounding, no!' John-Joe replied, taking a sip of his tea. 'I know the family is worried about him and Mrs. Daly is a good decent woman, but if they are even told in private and warned not to let it out, people around will sense they are not as worried looking as they were up till now. Especially as their father owns the grocery shop and pub, we absolutely can't have a stray word getting out there.'

Maggie nodded, resolutely.

'I guessed as much myself. It is just awful to see her so upset and knowing I could ease that worry. I am happy to know Bartle is safe. I was concerned about him.'

'I know that, love. I know well too that he is one of Conall's best friends. All I can say is, just take heart, girl, that Bartle's family will be put out of their misery soon enough. At least he will be one of the local men going home in a day or two when this current group of Tans is gone.'

After mulling over a solution to the ruse her father asked Maggie to come up with all night, in the end, it was her mother who gave her the idea and thankfully it worked. She knew her mother very well and one thing that was important to Brigid McGuill was never under any circumstances to be seen as common.

Because the McGuill family had always been held in high esteem in the county, it gave Maggie's mother a better standing in the town than the one she had known and with that, she aspired to a lifestyle she felt accompanied her new station as Mrs. McGuill. She always had a hankering for the finer things in life and her husband, John Joe McGuill, always felt he disappointed her somewhat. That was why he liked to try to please her by planting the flower garden, buying her new hats or something nice for the house she could show off, like a rug or new curtains. Her idea of having the roof slated was the most recent plan she had hatched and now Maggie needed to convince her mother keeping the thatched roof was her idea.

'I met with Lady Goodville yesterday, Mam, when I was doing your errand in town.'

'Oh yes. How did she look?'

'She looked a bit older I think. We walked down Main Street together and she commented on how everybody was now getting the black slate roofs. She said in her opinion, the houses had lost their character because they all looked the same and they made the town look common.'

'Really?' Mam answered. 'It is alright for her to say so with her large house.'

And that was the end of her talk about having the roof slated. John-Joe was so pleased with Maggie being able to change her mother's mind so quickly he gave her money for both she and Alice to go to the Picture House and also money for refreshments afterwards in Daly's grocery shop.

‘Now, why didn’t I think of that?’ her father had said. ‘You are a clever girl, Maggie.’

‘You didn’t think of it, Daddy,’ she mocked, playfully. ‘Because you think like a man, whereas I think as a woman.

9

Leah
Lise Interview
Aghameen

Lise thought it was funny I wouldn't allow her to ask me any more questions until I got some more information about her. During my inquiries as to how she ended up where she was and who looked after her, she somehow avoided the answers by talking about another topic; one that also intrigued me.

'I don't know why it happened,' Lise said, quietly. 'It is very hard to explain to somebody who has never experienced it.'

'Try.'

Lise closed her eyes, her face scrunching up as though trying hard to recall something. Even her hands began to form fists and her whole body immediately looked taut, as though suddenly gripped in fear.

'It is like that feeling you would get if faced with something terrifying. Imagine you are walking along a path and suddenly a lion just appears in front of you. Your heart begins to race, you sweat, your legs tremble with fear; maybe your whole body shakes.'

I nodded my head, understanding the feeling well. 'Like a panic attack? I've had those several times and yes, they are awful.'

Without opening her eyes, Lise continued. 'I don't want to undermine your panic attacks, but I have had them too and this feeling is worse even than that. I think it is because when you are having a panic attack, although it is terrible at the time, you know what it is. With this, you don't know why your whole body completely seizes up if you try to go outside. I get all the rotten symptoms of a panic attack, but this terror can begin hours before you know you have to leave your home. The anticipation of it is horrendous. Almost like a slow boil.'

'What do you think will happen if you go outside? I mean, further from inside the walls?'

Lise opened her eyes and joined her fingers together as though in prayer, the knuckles white.

'It is not that I fear anything in particular, but my body does, if that makes sense? I often thought I would much prefer to face a lion head-on, than experience this unknown terror I have. The physical feeling is much worse than any other experiences I have gone through.'

'Do you think, perhaps, that you are suffering from PTSD? Do you know of that?'

Lise nodded her head. 'I think so. Is it one of those new medical terms for a mental illness?'

'It is short for Post Traumatic Stress Disorder. They say soldiers coming back from the war experienced it – but there was no name put on it then. They just said the men suffered from their nerves or were shell-shocked. I would say you are suffering from the same illness, Lise. You can get treatment for that you know.'

'And would I have to leave home to get it?' Lise asked, tentatively. 'What kind of treatment would it be? Not that electric shock torture they used to do on people? I am much too old for all that. What is the point at my age?'

'No,' I answered truthfully, shaking my head. 'You can have therapy and medication.'

Lise remained silent, pondering what I had just said.

‘Can I do that from here? I wouldn’t have to leave my home?’

I nodded. 'I am sure a therapist would come here. I could try and organize it, if you like?'

Lise stood and began shaking her hands up and down by her sides.

‘You see! Just thinking about leaving here is enough to make me terrified.’

She leaned over as though about to be sick and reached her hand out towards the table to steady herself.

'I don't think I can, Leah,' she said, apologetically. 'I appreciate you trying to help me, but the thing is, I don't want to go out there anymore. I have seen what it is out there and it has been quite enough for one lifetime. As far I am concerned, there isn't anything else I want to see, to be honest. And here I can choose who I want to see. Out there, there will be hundreds of people all around at the same time. I couldn't bear it.'

My heart broke for her. I wished she could see the changes in the world, meet new people and share her life's stories.

‘I am quite content in my life. I wake when I want to and I can get up immediately and have breakfast, or lie in bed and read. I might even go back to sleep. Every day is so different. I have people who call who don't expect or want anything from me. I can go outside and walk in the lovely wooded area opposite or sit by the stream. I have my dog. There isn't anything I yearn for or miss by not going further than where I feel safe. So why should I?'

'When did you first experience a panic attack when going outside?'

Lise closed her eyes as she often did when recalling an event in her life. When she used to do it at first it made me feel somewhat uncomfortable, watching somebody talk with their eyes closed seemed odd. After a while, I would also close my own eyes and found in that way, I could almost visualize the events she described, with Lise as the main character in a movie taking place in my mind's eye. Other times I would quickly jot down everything she said and during those occasions, I would forget her eyes were closed as I would be so focused on writing.

'It was the second day that I remember being fully awake. The first day, I had gone outside and drank water from the rain barrel and washed my face in it. But when I say the first day, I may have easily been here for weeks, I don't remember. The next day I went outside and walked along the wall to the right to see where it ended. It seemed to go around a corner and then I saw several outhouses and stables. I don't know what it was about them, but I felt as though I'd been kicked in the stomach and I had to double over to try and catch my breath. My heart started to beat fast and I could feel it pulsing in my throat. I was sure I was having a heart attack. It wasn't like I had any pain. It was more of a sense I was sort of slipping out of my body and feeling like I was losing control of my mind. My throat felt as though somebody had their hands around my neck, squeezing it. That sensation seemed to cause another rise of panic and I began to run back to where I was staying. When I got in I fell on the floor, almost faint. I didn't pass out, but I lay there for some time, glad of the cold floor and the safety of my little home. Apart from going just outside to the rain barrel, for what must have been a month, I didn't go any further than that.'

The whole situation of Lise living in this place, especially in the first days and weeks, not knowing the person who was feeding her or even where she was, was something I could not fathom. I longed to try and retrieve more information from her about those days and how she ended up here, but from what I knew of Lise, she would tell her story in her way and in her own time. She didn't reply to questions she did not want to answer. She ignored them completely and moved to a different topic. Other times she would sit in silence and eventually, it would be me who would change the topic.

'And when was the next time you went out?'

'The next time I walked to the left to see what was up that way. I trailed my hand along the wall as I walked slowly, as though touching something solid confirmed to me I would not fall. I know it sounds silly.'

I shook my head. 'No. Not to me.'

'The wall ran towards the forest and ended there. As I wandered into the greenness I did the same with both hands this time, trailing them along the trees on either side. I began to think of the story of Hansel and Gretel getting lost in the forest, so I walked back. That day I was fine. I didn't experience any feelings of fear. I left a note with my clean dishes asking for any kind of paint and two days later some pots leftover paints and a large size paintbrush were left with my food. I think they thought by the size of the brush I was intending to paint the room, but that was not the reason for it.

The next day I walked to the left of the wall again and when I reached the forested area I picked as many pebbles as I could find and carried them back. I painted them with the first tin of paint I picked up, a bright orange colour.'

'What were the stones for?'

'I used them as breadcrumbs.'

'As breadcrumbs?'

'Yes. Just as Hansel and Gretel used breadcrumbs to be able to follow their way back home, I used the coloured pebbles to guide mine. I still don't know how big the forest is completely, but I have travelled around it quite a bit over the years. It is very dense and there are little streams and some amazingly huge trees with hollows in them, big enough to sleep in which I used to do sometimes.'

'You slept in the trees?'

'Yes,' she laughed. 'I love trees. But I don't sleep there overnight anymore of course, only in the daytime, sometimes. I find there is something quite protective about trees, as though when I am lying inside their hollow they have their arms around me, keeping me safe.'

'So, you don't get panic attacks there?'

'No. But the next time I tried to venture past the wall to the right, the same thing happened again. I couldn't breathe, my heart started beating frighteningly fast and I was filled with the most awful terror.'

'So, it is something to do with the outhouses or stables?'

'I don't know. Or perhaps I was afraid to see people.'

'But you see people here?'

'Yes. But they are people I know. I don't know who I might meet if I turn around that corner.'

I shook my head again, this time with exasperation.

'Who exactly are these people who feed you and get you things?'

'The first time I saw Katherine she knocked on the door, then entered quietly into the room. I was in bed, but awake and watching her, my head half covered under the blanket. I sat up and gave her quite the fright.'

'Oh, Lord,' she'd said. 'You gave me quite the turn there.'

'Who are you?' I asked her. 'And where am I?'

‘You are in a safe place,’ she told me. ‘And I am Katherine. I live near here and I have been instructed to look after you.’

‘I don’t understand,’ I cried out. ‘I don’t seem to remember much about anything. I don’t know how I got here and I know this isn’t my home, but I don’t recall where I do live either.’

Katherine sat on the wooden chair next to my small bed and she smelled of something familiar but I couldn’t say what it was.

‘You had a bit of an accident to your head,’ she told me. ‘You were taken to this place to give you time to recover.’

I put my hand to my head and could feel a lump the size of an egg on the right-hand side and a bandage stuck to it, thinking it was strange I didn't notice the injury before now. Perhaps since I have such long, thick hair I didn't even realize it was there. It didn't hurt to touch at all. It felt quite numb, as though I had no feeling on that side of my head whatsoever. Katherine asked if she could check the bandage and I nodded and turned my head so she could administer to it. It was she who had initially seen to my injury. I enquired from her what had happened to me and if the bump on my head was the reason I couldn't remember anything. She said my memory loss was quite obviously due to my 'accident' and the reason for my tiredness. But, I healed and forgot all about it, if you pardon the joke!' Lise laughed. I had laughed with her, amazed at her childlike sense of humour she showed evidence of regularly.

Later at home that evening as I re-read everything I had transcribed from Lise's interview, I concluded she evaded a lot of the questions I had asked. I was determined to find out more about her life before ending up where she had, but I realized my attempts at coaxing Lise to receive assistance from a therapist or begin a course of mind-altering chemical drugs, was, in fact, more for my benefit than hers. Just because I could not comprehend the notion of never venturing further than a mere few metres from your home for so many decades did not mean it was wrong. It would be wrong for me. However, for Lise, it was preferable. She wanted to stay where she was, in the confinements she had determined for herself. In that case, who was I to try to modify her decision, just because I felt she should conform to the traditional mien of society?

It would be different if Lise wanted to travel further than the boundaries she had set for herself. But she didn't. I am uncomfortable with her situation because I think it is sad. However, I had to admit that Lise did not come across as a sad person who felt they were missing out on life. Despite her self-imposed restrictions, I had to acknowledge she undoubtedly appeared to be much happier and a lot less stressed than most people I knew. In truth, the majority of people I know would give their right arm to live such a simple life. Don't many spend a lot of money going on silent retreats, or going off on nomadic trails, just to get away from civilization and all its problems for a while? Was Lise wrong because she chose to live the way she does? No. I don't believe she was. And for that reason, I decided not to ever broach the subject of her agoraphobia again. Just putting a name on her way of life was unwarrantedly labelling her.

10

Maggie

Aghameen
1920

'You are not going to be able to do it,' Donal repeated, frankly. 'This firearm is designed with right-handed shooters in mind. The controls on the revolver are on the left side of the gun to allow for convenient thumb manipulation. But if you use your other hand instead, your thumb will be where the controls aren't located. To use a gun designed this way, you would have to drop your preferred stance and switch hands. I just don't think it … actually … I know it's just not going to work. Not for you I'm afraid.'

'Please, let me try again,' Maggie implored, reaching out her hand for the revolver Donal had retrieved from her seconds ago. 'I can learn to do most things with my right hand, like use scissors or even a fishing rod.'

‘No, you can’t,’ Josie scoffed. ‘You can only fish because your father made you a special rod with the reel on the other side.’

Maggie seethed, well aware that Josie was one of their best shooters and didn’t want anybody else to forget it.

'Listen, ladies,' Donal said, rolling his eyes at the petty female jealousies. 'I'm not going to stand here wasting time. Maggie, no firearm drills for you. There are plenty of other things you can help with that Josie here might not be as good at as you are.'

‘Oh? Like what?’ Josie questioned, hand on her hip.

Maggie thought she looked quite intimidating and wouldn't like to meet her on the wrong side in charge of a gun. With her red, curly hair cropped short like a man's and her strong jaw, Josie could easily pass for a male. Especially as she stood inches over most of the men and had no qualms about it either.

‘I can learn to use a gun,’ Maggie insisted. ‘Just the way I learned to do other important things with my left hand. I am sure there are many left-handed soldiers. I’ve never heard a man couldn’t be enlisted into the army simply because he was left-handed.’

Donal found himself momentarily speechless, trying to find an argument for an opposing point of view and failing, he picked up one of the .303 rifles, lifting it in front of Maggie, making his point.

'Look at this,' he said, aiming the gun as if about to fire. 'Watch my actions closely as I do this shot with my right hand and watch where the shell goes after it ejects. Now stand back, but keep your eyes on my hands and then the shell. Is that clear?'

Maggie nodded and stood back, then fixed her eyes where she was told. The noise of the shot made her flinch, but she watched closely. The shell ejected to the right, landing at Donal's right foot.

'Did you see that?' he asked Maggie.

She nodded. 'Yes.'

'If you are left-handed …' he continued, '… the empty shell will fly across your body instead of flying away from your body. Some will discharge across your body and you don't want a hot bullet smacking you in the face or dropping down your jacket. From changing the fire mode, removing the magazine, or releasing the bolt as I said earlier, a left-handed shooter must drop their shooting stance to do these things.'

‘But can’t I learn?’ Maggie asked, again. ‘Even with the smaller gun?’

Josie laughed. ‘It’s called a revolver, Mag. At least get the name right.’

‘I am called Margaret,’ Maggie replied, sarcastically. ‘Try and get *my* name right if you can.’

‘Right, that’s enough ladies,’ Donal groaned. ‘Josie, go back to drill.’ Donal pointed to where two male Volunteers were instructing firearms to a group of young women. 'Maggie, you may go back to the hall. Nurse Moran is giving lessons on bandaging wounds. Go on,' he insisted, on seeing her crestfallen face. 'A wounded man would be happier to see a nurse than somebody brandishing a weapon. Believe me.'

Trying to ignore Josie’s sneering look, Maggie turned on her heel and went to find Sheila Daly, her O.C.

‘I’ve been told I can’t do firearm drill as I am left-handed,’ she told the other woman, after eventually finding Sheila sitting on the steps of a derelict house nearby. She was reading a letter and having a cigarette.

‘Who said?’ Sheila demanded without looking up and taking a long pull from her cigarette, before handing it to Maggie.

Maggie surprised, took the cigarette as offered, but held it in her hand as she answered. ‘Donal Redmond said so.’

Sheila huffed. 'That's ridiculous. If you were a left-handed man he'd have you.'

‘That’s what I told him,’ Maggie agreed, eagerly.

‘Did you really?’ Sheila replied, impressed. ‘And what did he say to that?’

‘He told me to go to Nurse Moran’s lesson on bandaging. But you said we had to let you know if any of us were leaving as we’ve to sign out first.’

‘Why do you want to shoot somebody so much?’

Maggie balked. ‘I don’t,’ she stammered.

‘What do you want to do? What are you here for?’

Maggie looked around, as though expecting somebody to give her the answer. Then, she recalled the words of her mother ‘*Never let anybody or anything stand in the way of what you believe is the right thing for you.’*

‘In normal circumstances, I would hope I would never have any reason to learn how to use a gun or shoot anybody. Unfortunately, we are not living in normal circumstances. We are living under the rule of a Sovereign. Not even a Sovereign, but a Dictator. Those men who gave their life for a free Ireland would turn in their graves if they could see what has happened to us Irish people, since they were executed.’

Throwing the almost burnt-out cigarette on the ground and stamping on it with her foot, Maggie continued,

‘As Padraig Pearse said himself ‘*Ireland unfree shall never be at peace.*’ We have been treated appallingly by Britain for too long and if the only way I can help in gaining our freedom is by learning to fire a gun with my left hand, I will learn. So God help me. Even without Officer Redmond’s permission. After all, doesn’t it say in the Proclamation of the Irish Republic that both men and women should be treated as equals? Or has that gone by the wayside as well as our at least attempting to achieve a free Ireland?’

'Bravo,' Sheila answered, slowly clapping her hands and rising to her feet. 'Strong words from a strong and intelligent woman, but you need to realize this if you are to be a soldier for Ireland – you need to be able to follow orders. It is not all about doing what you want, but doing what is needed.' She looked Maggie in the eye, appraising her, and noticed the other woman also looked her straight in the eye in return.

'To offer your services to the Cause, you must offer the best of you. Whatever your strengths are or wherever your talents lie, that is what we need. Not what you think looks the most exciting or will gain you the most recognition. That means some women will nurse, some will provide safe houses, others will physically fight with firearms. Some are never seen as they stay home knitting warm clothes for the men on the run, cooking meals to be brought to those in hiding and every single task is as necessary as the next. None is more important than the other either. And no Volunteer is more important than the other.'

Maggie nodded her head, having heard this speech from Sheila several times.

‘I know that. I agree with that.’

‘So, what do you believe in your own opinion is your greatest strength to bring to the Cause?’

Maggie thought for a few seconds then replied ‘Loyalty.’

Sheila smiled. 'That may seem like a noble reply, but loyalty is expected and a prerequisite on joining up, as you should remember from your initiation.'

Maggie blushed, feeling as though she was being questioned for an exam she had not prepared for.

'Have you ever heard the saying '*The pen is mightier than the sword?*' Sheila questioned.

'Yes,' Maggie replied. 'But I don't know who the quote is by.'

'It was created by an English author named Edward Bulwer-Lytton in 1839. It indicates that the written word is more effective than violence as a means of social or political change. From your passionate oration earlier, I think you would be excellent in the role of propaganda.'

'Propaganda?' Maggie repeated. 'Why? Doing what?'

'We could do with somebody who has a good way with words for writing in our newspaper, 'Poblacht na hÉireann' - and also somebody who can write propaganda leaflets and that sort of thing.'

'How would I do that and where would I do it? At home? Would I post whatever I write somewhere?'

‘I’ll be in touch,’ Sheila replied, squeezing Maggie’s arm before leaving in the direction of where Donal Redmond was giving his firearm lesson.

‘Oh, and by the way you can leave. I will sign you out. I presume you can write with that left hand?’ she shouted back, without turning around.

‘Yes, of course,’ Maggie yelled back in return and smiled, feeling she had somebody on her side.

The walk back home through the fields was pleasant, but as for everybody else in these troubled times, no matter where a person was going, it was always with an uneasy trepidation of who they may meet. There were many roadblocks and until reaching one, it was impossible to guess by whom it was assembled. For this reason, many, like Maggie was doing today, preferred to walk across the fields and turf bogs than have to risk a search or confrontation at one of these roadblocks if it was constructed by the Black and Tans or British Army.

The Black and Tans were the absolutely feared new recruits to the RIC in 1920 and 1921. Their name derived from their initial makeshift uniform comprising a combination of military khaki, police black and dark green, though they were later kitted out in standard RIC uniforms. The overwhelming majority of these recruits were British veterans of the Great War. They were known for their brutality and the Black and Tans were indeed responsible for some of the gravest crimes of the Irish revolutionary period. But many of the atrocities popularly attributed to the Black and Tans were in fact carried out by the Auxiliary Division RIC (ADRIC).

In July 1920, a new specialist force, that of ex-military personnel, all ex-officers, was assigned by Prime Minister David Lloyd George on behalf of Winston Churchill, to fight the IRA. They were incorporated into the police, with the new recruits being called Temporary Cadets who were to be deployed into areas where the IRA was most active, with the mission of *find, fix and destroy*. And destroy they did as they pillaged, murdered and burned out communities across the country of Ireland, in their attempt to enforce the rule of the British Empire. Following just a few months of training, these Black and Tans started arriving in Ireland and were immediately assigned to RIC barracks in Dublin, Connaught and Munster. Their orders by Listowel Divisional Commander, Lieutenant Colonel Smyth, were; *'If a police barracks is burned, or if the barracks already occupied is not suitable, then the best house in the locality is to be commandeered, the occupants to be thrown into the gutter; the more, the better – let them die there. Should the order 'hands up' not be immediately obeyed, shoot and shoot with effect. If the persons approaching carry their hands in their pockets, or are in any way suspicious looking, shoot them down. You may make mistakes occasionally, and innocent persons may be shot, but that cannot be helped, and you are bound to get the right parties some time. The more you shoot, the better I will like you, and I assure you no policeman will get into trouble for shooting any man.'*

The first victim of the Black and Tans on their arrival close to Maggie's home was a local farmer, Patrick Gill.[33] In their desire to inflict terror on the locals, they shot dead the forty-four-year-old man as he was returning home from a relative's wake in the company of his sister, Lizzie, for no reason other than they could. Then news came to them of the death of Thomas McDonagh who was also shot by the Black and Tans.[34] They tied his bullet-riddled body to the back of a lorry and dragged it through the nearby town

---

[33] *In September a man named Patrick Gill was murdered by the military as he walked along a public road near Drumsna, County Leitrim. Accompanied by his sister and a woman named Netley, Gill was bayonetted after he had fallen to the ground. A coroner's jury subsequently found that Gill had been murdered without provocation.*

[34] *See Historical Notes*

of Ballaghdareen, only releasing it later after the pleading of his fiancée and mother.

Then a day came when Maggie had her first encounter with the feared Tans.

'Officer Daly,' Maggie exclaimed, surprised at seeing Sheila at her front door. 'Good morning to you. Do come in.'

'Mrs. McGuill,' Sheila nodded, as Maggie's mother came out of the scullery to see who had been knocking.

People usually just walked in, calling out who they were at the same time. But to Sheila this was an official call and her actions were that of a more formal nature. Indeed, she was donning the green Cumann na mBan uniform for this purpose, consisting of a coat and skirt of Volunteer tweed and a hat of the same material. The coat had four pockets in front, a skirt that was the customary seven inches off the ground and a brown leather belt. She was not wearing the usual haversack containing necessary first aid supplies.

'Good morning, Sheila,' Mrs. McGuill answered in greeting. 'Did you walk here?'

‘No. I have the bicycle with me,’ Sheila replied, pointing to where it was lying against the wall under the front window. ‘May I have a word in private with Margaret, please?’

'Of course, you can,' Bridget agreed. 'Shall I bring you, ladies, some tea?'

‘I am in a hurry, I am afraid,’ Sheila replied. ‘But thank you. I won’t take up much of Margaret’s time.’

Mrs. McGuill smiled in response and closed the scullery door after her. Needless to say, she stood with her ear pressed to it, hoping to make out what the girls were saying on the other side. Aware her daughter had joined Cumann na mBan, she wasn’t completely sure what they did. Her husband had simply informed her they did useful things like learn the basics of nursing and how to read maps. She thought it might be helpful for Maggie to learn some practical talents as in her opinion women should be capable of performing more interesting duties than mere housework. Waiting until her mother was safely ensconced in the scullery; Maggie turned to Sheila and enquired if there was something she needed from her.

‘You recall I mentioned I may have some propaganda type of work for you?’

Maggie nodded. 'Yes, of course. How can I help?' she asked, with interest.

'I need you to write up a report about the recent fundraising events for prisoners' families in Leitrim. Also could you write a report on what other things our local Cumann na mBan are doing at the moment? Mention the support we give to the men on the run and that sort of information. And this is the most important part; can you get it completed and delivered to the train station in Carrick today, by the 6 pm train? It needs to go to print for tomorrow's newspaper.'

'Yes. Certainly, I can do all that you require,' Maggie replied, emphatically. 'Who do I give the correspondence to?'

'A man will get off the train in a Volunteer uniform and will be looking for a woman in the same. Is yours available?'

'Yes. It is in my wardrobe,' Maggie replied. 'Do I need to conceal the article?'

'Definitely,' Sheila answered and confirmed this by retrieving an envelope from underneath the front of her uniform skirt. 'Put it in this envelope in the same place as I had it hidden and make sure it is flat next to your skin so it cannot be felt if you are weapon searched. Wear a coat over your uniform and take it off at the train station so you will be recognised.'

'And if I am stopped and questioned by the authorities?'

Sheila put her hand on Maggie's arm. 'Then you need to use your initiative,' she answered. 'Like we all do. Present yourself at the Leitrim Observer building at St. Georges Terrace in Carrick and ask for the owner, Patrick Dunne. He is a Volunteer with the South Leitrim Brigade also and he will set you up with a typewriter and anything else you need.'

Maggie nodded then walked Sheila to the door. On taking hold of her bicycle, Sheila asked if Maggie had one. Maggie said she did, then after waving Sheila off she went to the shed where it was kept. After checking the tyres and that she had a pump in her basket, Maggie went indoors to prepare for her trip to Carrick. She had a mission to accomplish. The journey to the newspaper office was thankfully without any obstacles. Maggie did not meet any blockades on the road. This was surprising, especially as the road to Carrick was a main one. It would have been unfortunate if she failed in her first assignment by being unable to get to town.

Mr. Dunne was waiting for Maggie when she arrived, cold and soaked through after cycling to Carrick on a blustery winter's day. Kindly getting one of the other workers to fetch Maggie a cup of tea and 'something fancy' as he said, Patrick showed her into his office where a black Corona typewriter sat on a green, leather-topped desk. Maggie was astounded at the mountains of paper piled on top of one another all over the office. Shelves almost groaned with the weight of folders stuffed onto their shelves and looked as though they might topple over at any moment. Several steel filing cabinets were lined against one wall like grey sentinels keeping watch on their editor and chief. The office also had various newspaper cut-outs pinned to a huge notice-board on another wall with maps of Ireland's roadways, lists of names and hand-written notes haphazardly stuck all over the corkboard.

'Are you familiar with this type of machine?' Mr. Dunne asked, brushing cigarette ash off the top of the typewriter.

'Yes. I did typing at secondary school,' Maggie replied, removing her damp coat, gloves and hat.

'Here, let me,' the young woman offered, who had just laid a tray complete with a scone and pot of tea on the desk. She took the wet clothing from Maggie and organized them over the back of a chair in front of the roaring fire at the far end of the room.

'Thank you very much,' Maggie said, immediately sitting down and picking up a sheet of paper and inserting it into the paper guide.

‘I will leave you to it,’ Mr. Dunne said, picking up a fat, brown ledger from the desk. ‘There are extra ribbons in the drawer and paper if you need them. Good luck.’

‘Thank you,’ Maggie repeated, not looking up. She had been summarising in her head what she should write on her journey to the newspaper office and was eager to get it down on the inviting blank page.

☘

At first, Maggie didn't take much notice of the commotion she could hear from downstairs, only looking up from the typewriter, with her fingers poised over the keys, at the sudden sound of women screaming. Immediately she pulled out the paper she was working on and put it with the others she had completed, folded them carefully, and placed them in an envelope she then concealed inside her skirt as instructed by Sheila. Maggie then quickly grabbed her coat from the chair at the fireplace and buttoned it up, put her hat and gloves on and made her way to the door. As she placed her hand on the brass door handle the door pushed open and two Tans with rifles almost knocked her over as they burst into the editor's room.[35]

'You! Out!' they ordered entering the room and as Maggie descended the staircase to the bottom floor, she could hear crashes as though they were ransacking Mr. Dunne's office.

Mr. Dunne was outside the front of the building with the rest of his staff where Maggie was pushed forward to join them by another of the Tans. Many of the female staff were crying in fear and the editor was attempting to get back inside. Patrick Dunne had his arm around a woman who Maggie thought was his wife or office worker, but when she was questioned she said her name was Eliza and Mr. Dunne's sister. One of the Tans who had barged into the editor's office beforehand came outside and was waving a newspaper clipping in his hand.

---

[35] *On November 10, 1920, what is now known as the Black and Tans raided the office and caused such damage that it kept the paper out of print for two years. Patrick Dunne and his sister Eliza were held at gunpoint and the printing office was set on fire. Dunne was arrested three weeks later and interned at Ballykinlar Camp in Down.*

'This you have brought on yourself, Dunne,' the Tan shouted into the editor's face. 'Listen here to these words of condemnation against the Crown Forces this rebel wrote in his traitorous propaganda.

'The Crown Forces can shoot down Irish civilians without provocation and then hold a court of inquiry themselves and pronounce themselves justified. No such terrible weapons have been used to break people's will since the Tsar of Russia was forced to abdicate.'

Therefore, due to this tirade against the King's men, the rest of you renegades can all blame Dunne for your loss of employment,' the Black and Tan roared, waving his gun around the crowd lined against the black, iron railings outside.

With that outburst over, several of the Tans pulled rags out of their pockets while others of them came out of the building with cans of what must have had petrol in them. They lit the rags and the staff ran out onto the road. Within seconds the cloths were lit and thrown into the newspaper building. Patrick Dunne and his sister Eliza tried in vain to stop the destruction but were held back at gunpoint.

As Maggie joined the rest of the group on the road she watched the despised British Forces as they jeered like a gang of marauding schoolboys while the edifice was slowly engulfed in flames. In an even greater display of guileless thuggery, they refused to allow the fire brigade use their pumps to put the fire out. Instead, they bodily forced the firemen at gunpoint back onto the wagon and when the fire chief tackled the pseudo soldiers he was struck over the head with the butt of a rifle. As he lay prostrate on the road another fireman who jumped off the fire lorry to attend to him was also struck down. In the melee, Maggie took her opportunity and quickly made a run for it. Ducking around the corner she made her way around the back of the nearby courthouse and from there crossed over by the canal, and ran as fast as she could over the bridge in the direction of the train station.

At 5.20 pm, as instructed, Maggie removed her long gabardine coat and placed it on the seat next to her. By now she was sitting in the train station waiting room and thanks to the station master giving her a pencil, she quickly wrote the day's happenings on the back of one of the typewritten pages. She covered everything that had occurred in minute detail and kept removing the article from its hiding place to re-read it for the hundredth time. It hadn’t taken her as long to write the most recent event as it had been to write about Cumann na mBan activities.

The next morning Maggie was startled by Conall wrapping his arms around her as she pulled the water pail up from the well.

‘Conall,’ she yelped, jumping back from a spray of cold water. ‘I’m soaked.’

'You are famous is what you are,' he answered, brandishing the Irish Times newspaper in his hand. 'You made the first page.'

'What?' Maggie exclaimed, putting the bucket down and snatching it from Conall. And there it was, her article on the front page, just like he said.

CENSORSHIP: THE VOICE OF LEITRIM BURNED BY CROWN FORCES IN 1920, BY MARGARET MCGUILL.

‘I can’t believe it,’ she laughed. ‘I just can’t believe it.’

‘I am so proud of you,’ Conall said, putting his arm proprietarily around her shoulders. ‘Come inside and we will show your parents.’

John-Joe McGuill was ecstatic and immediately put on his good clothes for going into town, a newspaper under his arm.

'Oh, I can't wait to show the men this,' he cried, proudly reading the words his very own daughter had written.

'I didn't write the headline,' Maggie explained. 'They did that.'

Her mother wasn't as jubilant.

'You do know what happened to Mr. Dunne and his newspaper business is because of what he wrote about the Crown Forces? Now you have done just the same as him and they might react in the same way towards you. I don't see the reason for getting so excited about what you wrote. I think all you have managed to do is bring trouble on yourself.'

'I was under orders to write an article, Mam,' Maggie replied, defensively.

'Yes, about fundraising and the like. Not about this,' Bridget McGuill replied, just as defensively. 'This will enrage them.'

'But this is exactly the information we need to be made public,' Conall told her. 'We need people like Maggie to let the rest of the country be aware of just what the Forces are doing. It is illegal. There is such a thing as free speech.'

Her mother shook her head. 'You know that in Ireland there isn't. All Maggie has done is bring attention to herself. They'll be here next. Just wait and see. And no doubt you men will want to avenge the burning of the newspaper. This war is going to last forever with the lot of you and your carrying on,' she cried, becoming tearful. 'In the meantime, people lose their livelihood and their lives, and for what? Now I won't get a night's sleep, for every time I hear any kind of noise in the night, I'll think it is somebody coming after my daughter.'

Maggie looked crestfallen after listening to her mother's lamentations. At seeing the expression on her face, Conall took her by the arm and led her outside to the front garden. Leaning down towards her, he lifted her chin with his hand until she was looking into his eyes.

'Don't worry. They'll not be looking for you. And if they do come out, they won't make it up the road with all the look-outs we have around the place.'

'I was so proud for such a short time,' Maggie answered, regretfully. 'I didn't even consider the possible repercussions, Conall. I just wanted to get the information of what had occurred at the paper to Dublin when I had the opportunity, seeing as Mr.

Dunne wouldn't be able to do so anymore now that his newspaper cannot be printed.'

'You did the right thing, Maggie,' Conall assured her. 'And your father believes the same.'

Sheila Daly concurred with Conall when she approached Maggie at the next meeting of Cumann na mBan. 'You fulfilled your obligation as one of our members and I commend you for your quick thinking,' she told Maggie. 'Now the paper is out of action for the foreseeable future, it is up to us to get intelligence reports from this area to the rest of the country. Consequently, I am requesting that you undertake this task, if you are willing?' Sheila asked.

'I would be happy to,' Maggie replied, resolving to do so without her mother's knowledge.

And so it happened that Matthew Goodville allowed Maggie to use the typewriter in his office at the Manor House to carry out her intelligence assignments, telling his family she needed to practice her secretarial skills. His mother, Lady Goodville, was very supportive of this, believing it was important for young women of the 'lower classes' to train in skills other than household ones. Indeed, she often opened her home to one of her charities which enabled and encouraged young ladies to avail of their extensive library. Some of the locals said this was not an act of charity, but instead a way of keeping the Manor House from being attacked by the rebels, as many other of the landed gentry's homes were being, if there were young women of their side staying in it.

11

Leah

Lise Interview
Aghameen

Sitting at my desk in the small bedroom, I picked up a green cardboard folder with 5th Interview written on the front. Inside the folder was a foolscap copy with my interview notes written in green pen. It reminded me of the period when I used different coloured pens for various projects. Taking the copy over to the desk, I opened my laptop and began once again to type what I had written into Lise's file.

I vividly recalled when I did this interview. It had been a beautiful, sunny July day and I was wearing a plain yellow, cotton dress with white lace edging I had added myself and was one of the finds in my grandmother's suitcase of vintage clothes. I'd washed it in a whitening lotion then stitched it onto the hem of the dress. I always liked to make a piece of clothing more original by adding something personal to it, like the lace or sometimes a piece of thick ribbon tied around the waist or unusual buttons on the bodice. Lise had commented on the pretty lace design and ran her fingers over it, complimenting the good needlework.

This was also the first time we both ventured into her forest together. I suggested we do the interview outside as the day was so warm and she agreed, telling me she had been to the lake in the forest that morning and had a dip. I laughed with her as she described how she stripped off her clothes at the lakeside and slowly waded in 'In my birthday suit' she said, and how she swam the length of the lake with only the birds watching. I remember admiring her for this, considering her advanced years and declining when she asked if I wanted to join her.

‘I can’t swim,’ I told her.

She looked amazed at that.

‘I can show you, if you like,’ she offered. ‘It is easy. The hardest thing is trusting yourself.’

‘Who taught you to swim?’ I’d asked.

‘A friend,’ she’d replied.

‘Tell me about your life as a child,’ I asked her. ‘Did you have a boyfriend?’

'I do believe that I had everything at one time. But I remember there was a special person.'

She closed her eyes, reclining her head against the deckchair I had taken in my car.

'There was a day I can remember like it was yesterday. I was sitting up high in the hollow of a huge tree in a field close to my home. I craned my neck, eyes watering against the glare of a lowly hung sun to see only long, white legs dangling between the branches. I recognized the boots, encased as usual in wet mud and bits of rushes from the swamp we had just waded through. They had roughly made patches covering where the soles had worn through.

'You'll never make it this far,' he'd shouted.

With my foot already planted on the lowest branch, I yelled back 'Watch me.'

He did and within seconds we hugged as I pushed for space in the dip of the huge oak that covered us both with its leaves, and I received my gift of a kiss on the lips. I went to sleep that night with the taste of him still sweet on my mouth. It was a precious romance when innocence outweighs any physical pressures and the longing for each other is only due to the fun enjoyed in each other's company in childhood games. Oh, we had already agreed most solemnly we would marry when we were old, but until then our friendship remained unblemished by any future unforeseen adult responsibilities.

The three of us, he and his youngest sister who was my best friend, and I played endlessly in the fields around my home. We were not confined only to our small group; we were part of a large collection of children from the area with whom we spent our free time. In those days, children were expected to help out at home doing chores such as churning butter or looking after smaller children for the girls. The boys were a much-needed extra hand on the farms, dairies, or whatever employment their fathers worked in. But there was ample time for play and we took every opportunity to be together, running through the fields and forest, fishing, or swimming in the lake. We were a tight band of playmates, loyal to each other and any petty disagreements were quickly forgiven and forgotten.

As we grew older, freedom was not as plentiful of course. Our assistance at home was more needed as our capabilities grew and other outside interests took our attention. The boys began playing for local GAA teams, with hurling and football being the most popular. A lot of my female friends began to work in service as housemaids and some worked in local shops as serving girls. I was fortunate I did not have to work outside the home, but I was expected to go further with my education than the rest of my peers. Education was very important to my parents, to my father especially. My mother, who had not received any schooling after the age of twelve, wanted me to be different and to achieve as much education as I could. They had talked about the possibility of my attending Carysfort Teaching College in Dublin, the idea of which both thrilled and terrified me.

When I finished at the Intermediate School I was the only one who continued in education, by entering the convent school also for boarders. Indeed, only I and one other girl, who didn't finish the first year, were the only non-boarders. I was a very studious young woman. My father had a large collection of books and along the walls of our parlour were book-shelves. Mam would have liked to have a proper library for them, but there always more pressing jobs to be done first. I was aware growing up that my mother was disappointed my father had not become the scholarly gentleman she had hoped he would. Despite his intelligence and love of learning, Daddy was quite content to continue farming instead of trying to gain more of a white-collar profession. Anyway, where we lived, only the Protestants were able to obtain that sort of employment. None of the clerks, solicitors, or bankers were Catholic. Instead, they held the positions of barmen, farmers, shop-keepers, etc - trade jobs – which my mother looked down her nose at, even though she had once been a housemaid and her mother before her. Her father had been a blacksmith, but unfortunately died young and she and her mother both went into service, while her two younger brothers were sent to live with an uncle who had a creamery business in another town. The Catholics were prevented from moving up into a different class. The British government was afraid of our becoming too clever, too rich, or too rebellious. I remember one day in particular when my friend came to my rescue, but at the time it was one of the most awful, mortifying things that ever happened to me.'

'Tell me about it,' I coaxed, leaning closer as one does when being taken into somebody's confidence.

'The usual group of us were in the fields playing among the cocks of hay and I was typically climbing trees. Then one of the girls began to snigger at me.'

'You've got the curse,' she laughed, pointing at the red stain at the back of my summer dress.

I swiveled my neck and could feel the crimson stain of embarrassment creep onto my face.

'She got stuck on a branch,' he yelled back at them. 'Sure look at her legs, they're covered in scratches too.'

They looked, then wandered off, disappointed at having no drama to report back home. I was well known for my scrapes but if our playmate had said it was from sliding down the tree that I got the blood on the back of my dress, then that's what happened. Of course, he and I knew differently, but we kept that to ourselves and it was never mentioned between the two of us; one of many secrets we would share over the years.

I didn't see my neighbours as often as my other friends of course, because they were always away at boarding school in England. The brother and sister who were both a little older than us occasionally came home for the holidays, especially Easter and Christmas. In the summer they usually went to Europe and it was exciting to receive postcards and letters from their trips, with pictures of the places they had been on the front. I used to draw and paint copies of these photographs of the Eiffel Tower, the Colosseum and other famous sites. I liked the postcard of the Acropolis and for a while, I read everything I could find about Greece. I went through various phases in my reading material, all dependent on those postcards.

I wanted to have as much knowledge about the places the neighbours had visited so we could talk about them on their return.

Even though we often played together as children there was very much a 'them and us' class distinction. We didn't share the same schools or even share the same church. Our church was the Catholic one in town. It was huge and freezing cold in both winter and summer. Intimidating, it sat on top of the hill looking down over the town as though watching the locals comings and goings. We had the same parish priest for almost thirty years and he was proud of the fact he knew everybody in the town by name. He christened them, married them, buried them and knew all the secrets, weaknesses and sins of each one. In many respects, he was the most powerful and most dangerous man in our midst.

The curate who had been sent to assist him three years before was a much younger man and the Monsignor at first resented having to share his parochial house with a third person. There was another elderly priest who lived there before the arrival of the Monsignor, but he rarely left the parochial house due to severe arthritis. However, he was very popular with the older parishioners who visited him both for confessions and his sound, fatherly advice. The priest's housekeeper ran the parochial house with utmost efficiency and was very strict with the two domestic girls who took care of laundry and more difficult household tasks. Well known for her love of gossip, she was always avoided by the parishioners and most would call to the parochial house only when she was on an errand. Notorious for her fierce loyalty to the priests whom she guarded like a lioness with her cubs, she also had the convenience of having the priests in her confidence, a situation of which she took full advantage.

The older neighbour boy was never anything but a friend to me and I was the same to him. I think from quite a young age we were both mindful of the class difference and that our lives would go on very different journeys. We were well aware he would be going to university in England and would be expected to follow in his father's political footsteps there. My parents' plans for me, as I told you before, involved finishing secondary education at the convent and then attending Carysfort College to become a National School Teacher (N.T.) I was quite happy to go along with that. I enjoyed my studies and had already helped in assisting the teachers at the National School in my town, a role I liked. I found it satisfying having a part to play in filling those little minds with information and I already knew I wanted to work with disadvantaged children - those who may already think they have no chance of going further with their education due to their position in life, poverty, large families or no parental support. I believed it would be a huge honour to somehow enable these children to fulfill their potential and gain scholarships so they could avail of all the privileges open to every other child in the country, regardless of their background; and also regardless of their religion or parents political persuasion, but as equals as stated in the Proclamation.'

After that day's interview, I recall being delighted I got so much information from Lise. It was almost as though she knew it would be one of our last interviews. That was also the day she showed me the only photograph she had of herself as a young woman. She had found it in an envelope under her door one morning, another of her snippets of information that intrigued me. I mean, how did she not go crazy wondering who had done that? The photo was grainy, as though it had gotten wet at some stage, but I could see it was her, Lise. The deep-set dark eyes, the high forehead and smile were the same. She handed it to me and when I looked at it, then looked across at the old woman opposite, I could see it was her.

'Apparently, I am told that was taken just two weeks before. Though of course, I have no memory of it.'

‘Before?’

‘Before I started to become who I am now.’

I had a million questions. My heart was thumping strongly in my chest because somehow the photograph looked so familiar to me. I felt compelled to pick up my bag containing my notebook and pen. It was just at my feet, yet I was afraid to move or do anything that might change this moment. A moment I already knew was going to change something, but what it was going to be, I wasn’t sure.

‘It’s okay,’ she said.

I looked up at her.

‘You can write it down. I want you to write it down.’

And I did, but I did not know then, what she knew, that she had only about a year to live. Because of this knowledge, she had no more fear; only the fear of her story never being told.

‘Sure, they’d never believe it,’ Lise sighed, at the end of her narration. ‘That it could happen in Catholic Ireland, the land of saints and scholars.’

‘I believe it,’ I replied, my eyes misting with the story I had just heard.

Now, reading through the notebooks my interest in her story was reignited and I vowed to give it the attention it should have been given long ago. I had been offered to do work experience with a leading newspaper in London and it all happened so quickly that I didn't even call to say goodbye to Lise. It was through somebody that Grandy knew from the town, whose son worked on the same paper. I did write to Lise from London explaining the situation and she replied that she completely understood and was delighted I had received such a wonderful opportunity. Slowly, over time as I moved from one apartment to another, one country to another and as young people often do, I forgot about a lot of the people I had left at home and Lise was one of them. Apart from the very occasional visit to her in the first year of my leaving home when I returned more often due to homesickness, I gradually forgot about her altogether; until I was back for Grandy’s birthday and had a sudden urge to visit her. I asked Grandy to come with me to Aghameen that very afternoon, so strong was the feeling to see Lise and he eagerly obliged. Grandy had become much frailer since I had last been home just a few months ago and for the first time, I realized just how old he was, when beforehand it seemed he never aged and was strong as an ox. Perhaps my being away from home had made this more noticeable.

On reaching the huge gates to the hotel Lise had been living next to, I knew I would not find her there and I was correct. Firstly I noticed the hotel had been changed to a guesthouse judging by the green and gold sign swinging from a pole outside the entrance. The little home she occupied was still there and although the front door was now a new one, it pushed open easily, just as the older one had done. Inside was almost unrecognizable, so much so I gasped in pleasant surprise. The door opened into a bright airy room and the living area was much larger than I had remembered. A comfortable cream carpet covered the floor and the walls were painted an off-white colour with, I couldn't believe it, Lise's artwork on the walls. I was delighted, but there was no sign of Lise and that wasn't good.

The guesthouse was open and after enquiring at reception I was told that Lise was seriously ill in the Ashling Nursing Home, not far away. This surprised me. Not that she was ill since she was very elderly, just like Grandy was by now, but because she had left her home. In all the time I had known her, she never had. It didn’t take me long to find the Home and to my surprise, Grandy was quite insistent on coming with me to see her. Usually on trips we took together when I was home, he would stay in the car if I was going into a shop or somewhere.

'Help this old codger up the steps,' he had said, while leaning heavily on my arm. His embarrassing flirting with the matron, whom he seemed to know, got us quickly into Lise's room and then I saw her. She was alone and looked so tiny in the bed. Her face was turned towards the door. There were pink, fluffy slippers on the floor.

‘Lise, can you hear me? Can you see me?’ I asked, taking her limp hand in mine.

A nurse entered the room. She did some things with a drip and carried out other types of routine checks on Lise, opened her eyelids and felt her pulse. With a sad face, she shook her head at me.

‘She doesn’t have long.’

Grandy sat on the side of her bed and unexpectedly, he took hold of Lise’s other hand. At one stage the nurse leaned over my old friend and pulled the blanket a little higher over Lise's shoulders as she checked her pulse. I realised that I had tears running down my face. I wiped them with the side of my hand and kept the other hand in my friend's one. I could hear her breathing which was raspy and short, and then long slow breaths.

'Lise,' I called. 'I am here. It's Leah. Can you hear me?'

The nice nurse was checking again and shook her head at me.

'Is she gone?' I asked.

She nodded.

Grandy let out a sudden sob and I put my hand covering his livered speckled one, which he held over Lise's own.

'Grandy,' I whispered. 'Do you feel alright?'

He nodded, a single tear falling down his cheek.

'It is sad,' he murmured. 'It is all so sad.'

I expected more. What did I expect? That she would rise from her sick bed and sit up and welcome me? Or that I would see a vision … angels coming from heaven and carrying Lise off in a cloud? No. None of those things happened, but she did not die alone. I was there and Grandy was there and even the nice nurse was there. But even then, I still did not write her story as she had wanted.

12

Maggie
Aghameen
1921

'It is just as well we can read the screen,' Maggie whispered to her friend Alice who was seated next to her. 'The noise in here is deafening.'

'Michael Collins[36] is quite a handsome man,' Alice replied, flicking ash on the floor and rubbing it with the top of her shoe. 'He has a wonderful smile. It is funny that he once went to so much trouble to hide himself away and now here he is in the picture screen for all the world to see. It's an awful pity we can't hear his voice. I am positive it sounds silky.'

'Silky!' Maggie giggled. 'Honestly, Alice. Who has a silky voice?'

---

[36] *Michael Collins was an Irish revolutionary, soldier, and politician who was a leading figure in the early-20th-century struggle for Irish independence. During the War of Independence, he was Director of Intelligence of the Irish Republican Army and a government minister of the self-declared Irish Republic.*

‘That’s the traitor now for you boys,’ somebody shouted from the back.

‘Will you wait, Foxy, till we see what’s coming up next,’ another voice shouted in reply to Anthony Fox’s expletives.

They didn’t have to wait long and there was initially a stunned silence as the crowd in the cinema read the words visible on screen. Even the piano player at the front of the stage slowly trailed off the tune he’d been playing in the background, while he too began to read the words.

British and Irish leaders sign a Peace Treaty.[37] *There will be a new Irish Free State which will have full control of customs, tariffs, and economic policies.*

These words caused immediate cheering and clapping from the overflowing cinema hall. People stamped their feet, men threw hats in the air and women hugged each other. Some even cried. But the jubilation was short-lived for some.

The New State will resume under the British Empire as a dominion and will swear an oath to the

---

[37] *The Irish delegates concluded that they had secured as much as was feasible at that time and, under an ultimatum from Lloyd George, signed the Treaty on December 6th. The Treaty sowed deep divisions within the Sinn Féin movement that ultimately, and tragically, led to civil war after the Treaty was narrowly approved by the Dáil in January 1922.*

King. Northern Ireland will remain part of the United Kingdom.

For a second there was silence as everybody read the writing on screen. Then, pandemonium ensued. Men and women jumped from their seats gesturing angrily towards the screen. Some men even stood in their seats shouting their outrage.

'I'll swear no oath to the King.'

'We were tricked. We were bloody hoodwinked.'

'We are too close to freedom to give up now boys.'

These were just some of the statements being shouted around the noisy hall.

'Oh Maggie, let's get out of here,' Alice exclaimed, grabbing hold of Maggie's arm in a tight grip. 'There's going to be trouble. I know it.'

'Don't you see, Alice,' Maggie hissed. 'They've not given us our freedom at all.'

'I don't care about that right now. I just want to get out of here. Come on,' Alice insisted, pulling her coat and hat on.

'Long live the Republic,' a voice shouted and began to sing;

'Sinne Fianna Fáil

A tá fé gheall ag Éirinn,

Buion dár slua

Thar toinn do ráinig chugainn,' [38]

The words of the ballad were then sung by many others present, including Maggie. Louder and louder they continued to sing until a scuffle at the back of the hall drew their attention. Some of the young men quickly ran towards the double doorway where some sort of altercation had broken out. Maggie attempted to push past the people who were blocking the aisle but as she had been sitting at the front of the cinema with Alice, she was at the end of the crowd trying to get away. From what she could make out, there was a physical brawl taking place and a lot of shouting. The owner, Mr. Heaney, was trying to push people out of the front doors but eventually gave up and escaped for his safety. Instead, for some reason, he locked everybody inside – and then it was a free for all.

'Get down,' a voice commanded Maggie, pushing her in between a row of seats. Another young woman

---

[38] *Soldiers are we, Whose lives are pledged to Ireland, Some have come from a land beyond the wave,*

came in beside her and the two women held on to one another.

‘They are going to kill each other,’ the other women exclaimed.

‘Can you see what is happening?’ asked Maggie nervously, peeking over the red tip-up seats.

'It's some of the local Volunteers fighting among themselves about the Treaty,' was the reply. 'It looked like it started to get violent. Somebody has blood pouring from his nose and another fellow got hit with what I think was a bottle. My fiancé is caught up there. I hope he will be safe,' she continued, worriedly.

‘What is his name? What is your name actually, may I ask?’ Maggie questioned.

‘My fiancé is called Bartle Daly and my name is Kathleen Duggan.’

Maggie shook Kathleen's hand. 'I know Bartle very well, since I was a child. I am pleased to meet you, Miss Duggan, despite the circumstances! I am Maggie McGuill.'

‘Likewise,’ Kathleen replied. ‘I know of you. Bartle has mentioned you several times. Aren’t you his cousin, Conall Daly’s *special* friend?’ she asked, emphasising the word special. ‘Call me Kathleen, please. I don't think this situation calls for formalities.'

Maggie blushed, pleased at how Kathleen had linked Conall's name with hers. She was about to answer when suddenly there was the sound of whistles blowing and when the women peered over the seats, they saw the Auxiliaries burst into the cinema hall.

'Oh, God help us,' Kathleen cried out. 'We'll all be arrested.'

'Keep down,' Maggie implored, trying to see where Alice had gone. 'They mightn't see us.'

Crouched on the dirty wooden floor they clutched each other, afraid even to breathe too loudly. Desperately wanting to look up at what was happening, the women could only listen. What they heard was shouting from the police ordering the crowd to line up against the wall. They heard thumping and knew it was the officers hitting men with their guns.

'I won't ask you again!' a loud voice shouted. 'Give me your name this minute or you'll be taken to the Barracks.'

Maggie could just about make out the man's voice answering his name in the Irish language.

'Oh, dear God,' Kathleen whispered, painfully clutching Maggie's arm. 'It's Bartle. It's my fiancé. What is he doing? He isn't involved in anything – why is he behaving like a Volunteer and antagonizing them, the foolish man!'

Maggie stayed silent, aware that Bartle was indeed a Volunteer; and it was just like him to insist on speaking in his native tongue, despite knowing it would only get him into more trouble. Voices were raised once again while the officer continued to demand that Bartle give his name and address in the English language.

When the shot rang out, followed swiftly by another one, Kathleen sprang to her feet and began screaming hysterically.

'Bartle … oh dear God, please not Bartle,' she cried, running towards where the disturbance was taking place.

Chasing after her, with her hat falling off in her haste, Maggie stopped still on seeing the sight before her eyes. Kathleen and some other men were endeavouring to lift Bartle to a standing position from where he lay slumped against the wall, blood running from his head.

‘They shot him. The bastards bloody shot him. An unarmed man,’ one of the bystanders was shouting.

By now everybody was yelling and waving their arms towards the wounded man. Auxies were rounding up men and women, dragging them out as they fought against the armed forces with their hands and fists. Women swiped aimlessly against the uniformed men with their bags and umbrellas, only to be brutally punched to the ground or manhandled into the back of lorries waiting outside.

'The man was armed,' an officer yelled back at the angry crowd. 'Any rebels with firearms in their possession are to be executed. They know the rules.'

‘Where is his gun then, you bastard?’ Anthony shouted. ‘We want to see it.’

Amidst her tears, Kathleen and another man searched in Bartle's trousers and coat pockets.

‘Look,’ she cried out loudly. ‘It’s a torch! Kathleen waved the torch in the face of the Auxies officer who was still brandishing his gun. ‘It’s his Hylite Flashlight his uncle took him back from America. He’s not armed. You murderers! You didn’t even search him.’

'He was resisting arrest,' the officer yelled back. 'Every one of you swine is under arrest for disturbing the peace.'

Maggie, while looking around for Alice, found herself being dragged outside by the arm at the behest of another burly officer.

'I haven't done anything,' she shouted in defense, then recalled the words about resisting arrest and decided to remain quiet. She didn't want to end up like poor Bartle.

'I can't believe this,' a young woman sobbed, also sitting like Maggie on the floor of the tarpaulin-covered lorry. 'It is my first time at the Picture House. My mother didn't want me to go because she said it is too dangerous to go out these days, but I begged her. Now look where I've ended up. What's going to happen to us?'

Maggie tried to console the weeping girl, herself unsure what was going to become of them.

'They'll say we initiated a riot,' another woman said worriedly. 'We can be thrown in jail for that.'

Maggie tried to signal to her to keep quiet, but it was too late. Several of the younger women in the lorry began crying and lamenting about what could happen to them.

'They can't lock us up for nothing,' Maggie said, trying to reassure everybody. 'They will search us for arms or any evidence of wrongdoing and they will let us go.'

'Are you serious?' a woman with long, dark hair reiterated. 'The jails all over the country are full of Irish men and women who have done nothing.'

Maggie knew this to be true but didn't want to further frighten the other occupiers of the lorry. She was frightened also, but logic told her they must have arrested over a hundred people. They were not going to keep them all. If anything, it would take too long to book everybody in and the barracks would be stormed with families looking for their sons and daughters. Practically all in the Picture House were young, single men and women who still lived at home with families who would be missing them by now. As Maggie put her arm around the young girl who was crying uncontrollably, they both painfully banged heads as the lorry came to an abrupt stop.

'What was that?' people started to ask. 'It sounded like gunfire?'

'No. I think the lorry backfired,' Maggie answered, hoping that's all it was.

However, within seconds she was proved wrong, for it was indeed gunfire and complete panic ensued among the captives on the lorry.

'They are going to shoot us all,' a voice cried out, in terror.

Some of the women began praying loudly and some cried, and screamed. Others tried to scramble down the back of the immobile lorry.

'Get back in,' Maggie cried out to the women who were trying to climb out. 'It is safer to stay in the lorry.'

She attempted to pull one woman back inside but instead, she was pushed backwards.

'I'm making a run for it,' the woman shouted, as she jumped. 'I'm not letting them shoot me.'

The soldiers driving the lorry were shouting at each other, arguing over whether to get out or stay inside. Then, the windows smashed as guns were fired and both men's bodies were flung to the side as they were shot, several times. The women all started to scream. Clutching onto each other, they began shouting,

‘Who is it? Who is firing?’

Maggie knew. Seconds later, a familiar face appeared at the back of the lorry with an arm outstretched.

‘You are safe now, ladies,’ Conall said, assisting the woman with the long, black hair down from the lorry.

Making eye contact with Maggie, he did not acknowledge her in words while he lowered the back end of the vehicle to enable the women to climb down.

‘Oh, thank God,’ the women sobbed, reaching out their hands towards other Volunteers who had gathered around the back of the lorry to help them out.

When Maggie reached the grass bank she saw absolute carnage in front of her. There were several bodies strewn across the road, blood flowed from heads and torsos onto the road now running in a stream of blood, intermingling with the gently falling rain. One lorry ahead was on fire, creating a spiral of dirty, black smoke to fill the air. All along the edge of the road were the women and men who had been previously forced onto the lorries by the Auxiliary Army. One of the Volunteers began collecting weapons from the dead men and handing them to another comrade who was standing by a pony and trap.

Maggie looked around and began to walk along the road looking for Alice. On feeling a tap on her shoulder, she spun around.

‘Conall, have you seen Alice?’ she asked, with concern.

He nodded his head.

'Yes, she is unharmed. She got out before the soldiers arrived. It was she who got word to us about Bartle. We rounded up a Flying Column and got to you all as soon as we could. Are you alright?' he asked, scanning her face and body for any signs of injury.

'Yes. I am fine,' she answered, nodding in the direction of the soldier who had killed Bartle, now lying on the road dead.

‘You got him then,’ she acknowledged. ‘Bartle wasn’t even armed, you know?’

Conall nodded, grimly. ‘I know. I knew before Alice even told me, because his lady-friend is terrified of guns and he wouldn’t carry one when he is … sorry *was*, with her.’

They both looked in silence at each other and their eyes filled with tears.

‘I didn’t know he had a girl,’ Maggie said, quietly. ‘I met her today. Kathleen. She seems very nice.’

‘She is,’ Conall answered. ‘I met her only once and I could tell my cousin was very fond of her. He kept mentioning her name every chance he could get. His parents are on their way over there now. God help them.’

'Poor Sheila will be devastated,' Maggie said, sadly. 'She idolized Bartholomew.'

'What happened, Maggie?' Conall asked. 'Alice just told us there was trouble at the Picture House and that Bartle had been shot by an Auxie. We came straight out, but nobody knows what took place. Can you tell me?'

‘A row broke out about the Treaty, Conall, with those against and those for it. The owner locked us in and called for the police and the Auxiliaries arrived. All I know is they searched Bartle and felt the torch and thought it was a gun. They shot him in front of us all. Then mayhem broke out and they started forcing us onto the lorries and telling us we were all being arrested.’

'Maggie, stay where you are, people are coming behind us with transport to take you all home. Your father will probably be among them. Tell him what you told me and let him know I am paying a visit to Heaney who owns the Picture House. He'll not be locking anyone in anymore after I have seen him.'

Maggie nodded. ‘Be careful. They are going to be baying for blood after this onslaught.’

Conall slung a gun over his shoulder and turned in the direction of town. ‘Then they shouldn’t have shot Bartle,’ he answered, as he stamped off on the blood-stained road.

13

Leah

Lise Interview
Aghameen

'It had been the loveliest of summers. School was over for two whole months and not even the dread of moving to Intermediate School in September could dampen the days we spent mostly in blissful freedom. Luckier than most with no young brothers or sisters to look after, once the daily chores were completed I was free as a bird for the day. If you could have seen how charming the countryside was then, Leah, where I played innocent games with my friends. Oh, there was work too when the hay needed sorting and hard work, but we made a game out of that as we did with everything else. It was a good time also for courting,' Lise smiled, eyes twinkling with memory. 'All the young men from miles around would make up a *meitheil* and of course we young women would follow them around, with our bottles of tea and food.'

In answer to my questioning look, she continued.

'A *meitheil* is when a group of men would get together from neighbouring farms and take turns doing the farm work - gathering in the hay for the winter that is – on each other's land. The work was done much quicker when there was a gang of them and they'd share out farming equipment or whatever was needed. It worked very well for all concerned.'

'Did you come from a big farm?' I asked.

'It was a big enough farm I suppose. We had cattle and pigs and sheep. We grew a variety of vegetables. But it was once much larger. Oh yes. My father spoke about it bitterly many a time. Up until the time of the famine our family had the largest holding in this part of Ireland and had owned it for generations. The famine was the ruination of them, but mainly because of my grandfather's landlord, Denis Mahon of Strokestown[39]. He increased the rents almost by one hundred percent to pay debts to the Crown his predecessor Maurice Mahon had accrued.'

'By almost one hundred percent?' I gasped. 'But that is preposterous.'

---

[39] *Major Denis Mahon was the Irish Landlord of Strokestown in County Roscommon who was shot and killed during the Great Famine of Ireland.*

'Exactly what the tenants thought. When the famine gripped the country, my grandfather could not keep up with the payments. The potato crop had failed three years in a row. My family tried their best to continue to pay the lease but it was becoming more and more difficult to do so. They sold any valuables they had such as jewellery, paintings, clothes, etc … at the time they would have been regarded as quite well-to-do, but by the end of the famine they were almost destitute. Most of the farm had to be given back to the landlord, Denis Mahon, to pay the rent and arrears, including their large house which his English friends then moved into.'

'The Manor House that you told me about – was once your own family home?' I asked, astounded by this revelation.

'Oh, yes. By the time I was born, their family was well established in our former house and my grandfather, whom I never met, had built the smaller home where I grew up. Daddy was left the house and farm when my grandfather died and he gave some of his share to his younger brother. The two brothers were named after my grandfather as was the family tradition for many decades. So, by the time I was born, the farm had decreased again in size. The people next to us were good neighbours. They were very aware of the sacrifice made by my family and I think were embarrassed about it. Or maybe it was more fear than embarrassment.'

'Why were they afraid?'

'Denis Mahon had been murdered. I think it was in 1847, not long after the end of the famine, but of course, the country was still in a terrible state. Millions had died and millions more emigrated. Denis Mahon had sent many of his tenants on ships to Canada on an assisted emigration scheme[40] – to get rid of them really – but sadly thousands of them died en route, on what they called the Famine Ships, or Coffin Ships. This caused an awful lot of anger towards him from those people's relatives who still lived in the area. Also, many died on his lands due to starvation and the mass evictions he orchestrated. He was a much-hated man. Even the local parish priest, Fr. Michael McDermott, accused Mahon of amusing himself by *'Burning houses and turning out people to starve.'*[41]

---

[40] *Between 1856 and 1906 the Irish Poor Law Boards of Guardians financed the emigration of about 25,000 paupers, primarily to the United States and Canada. In 1882-83 Parliament passed legislation that subsidized transportation for over 54,000 more.*

[41] *"At the end of August 1847, Mahon returned from England to Roscommon where he had left local Catholic priest Michael McDermott in his place filling in as the chairman of the Strokestown famine relief committee. McDermott accused Mahon of amusing himself by "burning houses and turning out people to starve."*

The Reverend was accused of inciting violence against Mahon, resulting in allegations initiated by the local aristocracy that Denis Mahon's murder was caused by some kind of a Catholic conspiracy against Protestant landlords. The accusation against McDermott was made in parliament by Lord Farnham of the Orange Order. Farnham claimed at the Sunday Mass before Mahon's murder, Fr. McDermott had said from the pulpit '*Major Mahon is worse than Cromwell and yet he lives.'* The priest denied it of course, but well, the timing does point to the evidence he was guilty of the accusation made against him.'

'Is it known who murdered him?' I asked, agog with interest while busy scribbling all this information down.

'Yes. There were four men arrested. I believe one of them made some sort of arrangement for freedom in exchange for giving information and one escaped. But the other two men were hanged.'

'So,' I continued. 'You think maybe the reason the family beside you were good neighbours, as you called them, is more to do with the concern they too could be murdered like Denis Mahon – if they were thought to be mistreating their tenants?'

'Perhaps. Who knows? A lot of the local people from the town worked for them and found them to be good employers. There were never any complaints about them. But of course, in the end … they were English and could turn their coats very quickly. As you know, I was very friendly with their son and despite us being brought up quite differently and having different backgrounds, we were quite close. They lived right next to us because of course, the farm had one time been all the one so our land ran alongside each others.'

And on that note, the last of my interviews with Lise ended.

14

Maggie
Aghameen
1922

Maggie thought at first it was a trick of light, or maybe a rabbit speeding past that caused the tall grass to rustle as it did. Holding her breath, she squinted her eyes, staring right ahead. Something was moving, just about five meters from where she was sitting with her legs stretched out in front of her and ankles crossed. In one hand she held her drawing book and the other a pencil, almost just a stub now. She had been lost in her reverie for God knows how long, penciling drawings of the wildflowers she sat amongst and aware she had flattened a good part of them where she was sitting.

The colours had caught her breath yesterday while out walking with her dog Marley, and ever since Maggie had been mixing paint shades in her mind, aching to get them down on paper. Now she was occupied with copying the intrinsic detail of each flower, its stems, its petals, the flower head itself. It was mesmerizing how each had its own perfect symmetry and some asymmetrical. Just like every single person's thumbprint was different, each flower was different too. Even every blade of the long grass growing amongst the wildflowers was unique. Maggie bent her head right up to the flower as she drew, wishing she had a microscope to better see each individually defined mark on the plant.

Where did the wildflowers come from, she wondered and how did they get here? Did somebody one time plant them or did they just grow wildly by themselves? It was almost as though they had been perfectly planted with the way the flowers were mixed in splendid juxtaposition, complimenting each other in an array of colourful harmony. *Cno léana* showed off its vibrant display of stunning star-shaped maroon-red flowers that emitted an almost radiant reddish hue, the *dréimire mhuire* stood tall, with its mass of powdery pink flowers, bog rosemary with its purple buds beautifully complimented the vibrancy of the *bainne bó bleachtáin* with their cluster of small, drooping yellow heads. Entwined among these was the faithful wild daisy, simple yet also beautiful in its simplicity. Maggie picked one, and plucking each petal in a sing-song voice said in turn 'He loves me. He loves me not.'

‘Who is *he*?’ a voice asked.

Startled, Maggie screamed first, then turned bright red and lastly, jumped to her feet.

‘Who are you to be going around scaring the living daylights out of people?’ she demanded, pulling down the back of her skirt that had hunched up in a very unladylike fashion around her knees.

The stranger laughed and bent down to pluck a daisy of his own. Standing straight, he held it out towards the indignant Maggie and recited;

‘In youth from rock to rock I went,

From hill to hill in discontent

Of pleasure high and turbulent,

Most pleased when most uneasy;

But now my own delights I make,--

My thirst at every rill can slake,

And gladly Nature's love partake,

Of Thee, sweet Daisy!’

'That's Wordsworth,' Maggie said, proudly. 'I know him.'

The man theatrically waved his hat above his head and laughed playfully.

'I am impressed. Now are you going to tell me who *he* is? I am sorry I interrupted your little game. Does that mean you will never know if he loves you or not?' the man asked, taking off his jacket and laying it on the grass beside Maggie, then sitting beside her.

Maggie was incensed from absolute embarrassment at being caught performing such a childish act. Whoever he was had completely ruined what had been a perfectly lovely afternoon. She felt robbed and belittled to boot. What did he mean by 'I am impressed?' Did he think she wouldn't know who Wordsworth was? Did he think she was some stupid, ignorant female who still played childhood games? Quickly Maggie gathered up her belongings and flung them haphazardly into the wicker basket - her drawing book, uneaten apple, the cream woollen shawl she had been sitting on and her pencil box.

'Can I see your drawings?' he asked, extending a hand towards the basket, as though to help himself to her sketchpad. Then to her horror, he put his hand heavily on her thigh.

'Certainly not,' she responded, snatching the basket from the ground and beginning to get up.

‘Oh, please don’t leave on my behalf,’ he said, with a grin. ‘Major Hawkins,’ he added, offering his hand which Maggie studiously ignored, rising to her feet.

‘And you are?’ he enquired.

When Maggie didn't reply and instead began to walk away he called after her 'I will have that information by the end of the day. Perhaps next time you will deign to talk to me, Miss Moody.'

Annoyingly, Maggie realised quickly her calves had pins and needles from sitting in the same position for so long. She sucked in her lips and walked on slower, trying not to make it obvious to him she was in such discomfort. Never in her life had a man touched her in such an offensive way and inward she seethed with fury. If Conall and her father found out, the man would be fodder for the pigs. But little did Maggie know one of them already knew and the other soon would.

15

Maggie
Aghameen
1922

‘How do you know that?’

'Look at the rod,' he answered. 'Nobody local has a rod like that. It must be eighteen feet long.' He picked up the handle and turned the reel slowly in his hands. 'It's solid brass and so are the joints of the rod. And the line is silk. Look.'

Maggie looked and nodded her head in agreement.

‘I like the fancy fishing basket.’

He smirked. ‘It’s only a gentleman that has fishing tackle in a picnic basket.’ He lifted the lid.

‘Look at this equipment. It must have cost a small fortune.’

Inside were two compartments. In one were extra reels and fishing lines, artificial flies and brightly coloured floats. The other side was lined with wax canvas, presumably for taking the fish home. Also in the basket was a small loaf of wheaten bread wrapped in a white linen cloth, together with a hip flask.

‘Silver,’ Conall said, lifting it out. ‘And look. The owner’s name is engraved on it. C. J. Hawkins.’

Her blood ran cold. ‘Put it back,’ she cried.

Ignoring her, he opened the flask and sniffed, then putting the flask to his lips he took a long swallow.

‘That would put hairs on your chest like barbed wire,’ he exclaimed, his eyes bright. He took another swallow and then gestured to the grass bank close to the edge of the lake.

‘Lots of footprints up and down there and well sunk in too. I’d say he was here a while.’

‘But where did he go?’ she asked, looking around. ‘Nobody would just leave this expensive fishing equipment behind.’

‘Perhaps he was carried away by the faeries,’ Conall winked. ‘He must be a guest of the Goodvilles. Haven’t you seen any strange men around here?’

'Only you,' Maggie joked. 'You are definitely the strangest-looking man I have ever seen around here.'

She screamed then as Conall made a grab to tickle her. Running in the direction of the farm she held up her skirt and climbed over the low stone wall, laughing, she waved to Conall as he tried to catch up with her. But in a second she stood still on seeing the horrific scene taking place in front of her eyes.

Grey and black smoke billowed into the air and there was a sickening smell of burning flesh and horrendous squeals of pain. Rooted to the spot, Maggie could only throw her hands to her mouth, unable even to make a sound out of complete shock, as a ghastly feeling of absolute panic enveloped her senses. But Conall acted on instinct. Speedily jumping the wall, he shouted at Maggie to stay where she was as he ran towards the horrific incident occurring at her home. Army men toting guns loudly yelled orders as they ran around the farm. There seemed to be about thirty of them. Maggie could hear Marley barking manically as he circled the soldiers rampaging about the farmyard. Then she saw her parents. Her father came out of the house first holding the hand of her mother who had her other hand to her mouth, much like Maggie had now. A soldier pushed them both roughly against the front wall of the house. Her parents turned their faces toward the meadow that

Conall was now running through and then their eyes caught their daughters. Both heads began to shake, warning Maggie to stay where she was.

'Who are you looking at?' a soldier shouted, then turned around when Conall landed beside him.

'What do you want?' the soldier roared at him. 'Who are you? Are you the son?'

'No. They have no children,' Conall shouted back. 'I'm just a passerby coming to see what's on fire?'

'You are in for a good show then,' the officer laughed raucously. 'Just in time to see what happens to Irish rebels and the ones they hide.' With that, he lifted his gun.

Maggie screamed into her fist as she watched her mother throw herself in front of father when the first shots rang out. Slumping to the ground, she held on to her husband's legs and trying in vain to lift her, he was hit himself. They lay tangled together, a pool of blood around them and it ran mixed with the rain into Bridget's flower bed in front of the house. Maggie also fell to the ground, then retched bile onto the grass as the rain began thundering from the heavens, almost as though God had unleashed his anger at the horrific atrocity of this day. As the soldiers lifted their bodies, Maggie saw her father's leg twitch and so they hit him several times over the back of his head with the butt of a gun. Parts of his scalp lay on the ground when they threw him and her mother onto the rear of a lorry. Maggie watched in abysmal horror as the blood of her parents dripped through the cracks of the wagon's slatted floor as it drove off. Conall came for her then, where she lay curled on the soaked ground. As he lifted her, Maggie let out a howl that haunted Conall's dreams for many nights afterwards, as she cursed the soldiers; as she cursed them all to hell. When the neighbours started to appear out of their homes after hearing the commotion, Maggie cursed them too, kicking and screaming as those she was reared beside tried to hold her and she scratched the faces of women who had bounced her on their knees as a baby. At that moment Maggie hated them all and hated everything there was to hate.

'Somebody told,' she repeated over and over as Conall tried his best to calm his sweetheart down, aghast at the words she used and how her very body seemed to writhe with the repugnance she displayed. 'I want them dead,' she screamed in her anguish. 'I want to die. Why didn't they kill me too?' Then in another angry breath, she lamented, tears streaming down her face. 'No. I hate them too much to die. I wouldn't give them the satisfaction. I'll live them all out. I hope to God I do. I'll live them all out and *then* I'll dance on their graves. Someday I will find out who caused this. You watch me. All of you watch me,' she cried, as Alice also in tears tried to comfort her friend. 'Conall, if you love me, promise me … promise me you will deal with whoever is responsible for my parents' deaths. Promise me!'

'I do. I do. I promise you, Maggie love. On my oath and the lives of your parents, I will get them all,' Conall swore. 'Every last one.'

'Oh God, oh God,' Maggie wailed over and over, now beginning to tear at her hair and clothes. 'Oh I can't … I can't bear it, oh Jesus help me …' falling to the ground then just where her parents had breathed their last, she fought against Conall as he tried to lift her into his arms.

'Leave me. Leave me. I don't want it to wash away … I don't want …' and she tried to catch the blood of her mother and father as the rain washed it into the wet grass.

'We need to get the doctor,' Alice whispered to her mother. 'I fear for her sanity.'

Her mother nodded and went over to where her husband and the local men-folk were putting ladders up to the roof, trying to save the thatch, for as a parting gift the ruthless soldiers had set the house alight. It was only thanks to the torrential rain and quick action of the neighbours it didn't have a chance of catching enough to make much damage. But the damage done to Maggie was forever irreparable.

16

Maggie
Aghameen
1922

On entering her home for the first time after the neighbours had done their best to clean it up, the immediate thing Maggie noticed was the remaining stains of smoke damage on the white-washed walls. Her parents were lying upstairs together on their bed. The local women had made them look as presentable as possible for the wake. Only Maggie and the undertakers knew the back of her father's head was missing. There were no visible marks on his face, or on her mother's. They had been cut down in their prime. Her father had been a tall muscular man and handsome. His hair had only recently begun to grow grey. Unlike her mother's golden locks, his hair was dark. Mourners remarked when they visited her parents' bedroom to pay their respects at what 'a great head of hair he had. God bless him.'

When the laying out was completed it took a while before she could go into her parents' bedroom. There was a smell emanating from the room that made her head feel light. It was an odour of the church during a funeral, candle wax and incense, too foreign a scent to be in their home. Their home? It wasn't *their* home any longer. Now this house was just *her* home. Slowly Maggie lifted her eyes and settled them on the brass bedstead.

The window was open and a breeze blew across the bed, ruffling the lace-edged sheet which lay across her parents' bodies. The curtains had gone, burned in the fire. A fat, white candle sat on the wide windowsill. There were candles on either side of the bed also, in tall, black wrought-iron candlesticks. The dressing table mirror was covered over in a dark cloth. Maggie could not look at her parents' faces because if she did, it would be all too real and she didn't want it to be real. Not yet. Instead, she shook her head when offered a seat by Mrs. Daly and leaned against the wall, her hands folded in front of her. The prayers that had ceased on her entering the room took up once again and Maggie also murmured her responses to the rosary. A hand then enveloped itself in her left one, causing her to look up. It was Conall. Seeing his red-rimmed eyes brought a slight whimper from her throat. Digging her nails into the palm of her other hand, Maggie swayed a little and Conall pulled her closer to him, where she laid her head against his shoulder.

The ring Mrs. Daly had removed from Bridget McGuill's finger was given to Maggie. It had an indent where her mother's arthritic little finger had bent a mark never noticeable when she wore it. But now that Maggie held it in her palm, she could see it, just very slightly, on one side. She could tell where the finger had pressed and left its mark. When did that begin, she wondered? Was it a subtle change over the years? Was her mother aware of it? She remembered the day she had looked closely at her mother's hand as it lay still, for once, on the armrest. When had the fingers become ever so slightly crooked, at what age? Was it a slow happening? Did her mother wonder at it or not even notice? Surely, she must have noticed?

She recalled a time when her mother had been asked to remove her wedding ring, but not the occasion. Her mother had shyly laughed then and said it had never been removed from her finger since the day her husband had put it there. But she had seen the photos of the slim girl. She had tried in vain to put on the gloves her mother had once worn. They were flimsy, lace, and tiny. Those now plumper and arthritic hands would never fit inside. Yet the ring had stayed on, until rubbed with much oil and wax and soap to remove it from her dead body. She never felt closer to her mother than today when she put the wedding ring on her finger. It was worn thin from all the clothes washing over the years, yet it shone brightly. Good, clean, pure gold … simple and thin and her mother's one piece of real jewellery; the only solid gold piece she had ever owned.

When Maggie first approached her parents' bodies, she immediately commented her mother's hair should be let loose, instead of tied up in the severe fashion they had arranged, with it clipped high on her head. She wanted her to look as beautiful as possible so people could see how young her mother had been. Maggie pulled the clips out gently and began fussing with her mother's hair, laying it over her shoulders. Her hair was soft and wonderfully thick. Beginning to twist the tendrils around her fingers, Maggie repeated over and over 'Mam, I miss you. I need you, Mam.'

It was her older cousin, Ernie McGuill, who calmly pulled Maggie away from the bed. By now she had become aware of her sobs becoming louder and she could hear murmuring around her that was not the rosary the mourners had been saying minutes ago. Instead, Maggie could hear neighbours suggesting to each other that somebody take the poor thing outside.

It was Ernie who stepped up, as Conall had gone outside for a word with the undertakers.

'The poor girl is out of her mind with grief,' Maggie could hear somebody say.

'Come on, Maggie,' he whispered, gently untwisting her fingers from her mother's hair. 'Let's get some air.'

Maggie allowed him to take her arm and guide her as she stumbled from the bedroom, down the stairway, and out the front door. Ernie manoeuvred Maggie around the side of the house, obviously forgetting this was where the atrocity had taken place. When his cousin stopped walking, he noticed that she tensed up.

'Oh, I'm sorry, Maggie,' he said. 'I didn't think. We'll go back inside.'

She didn't answer at first. Instead, Maggie just stared at where the pig-pen had once been and she wondered for the first time what had become of the bodies of the men who had been down there.

'The men, what …?'

'They've been removed,' Ernie stated. 'They've been returned to their families for burial.'

Maggie nodded, relieved for both the families and herself. She couldn't have borne living next to what would have been a burial ground. They walked to the lake and sat on one of the low wooden benches John-Joe had placed near the edge. Maggie and her father had often sat here in the evening, watching the swans and geese and their young using the lake as their own private reservoir. The lake was shared between their farm and the Goodvilles. In the middle was a crannog, a small artificial island that at one time would have had a dwelling place. It had a little fort on it now that both Matthew and Maggie had built as children. They had spent many a day there building it with bits and pieces of un-wanted wood from the farm. The timber roof was covered over with tarpaulin to keep the rain out while Matthew and Maggie would lie back on faded, old cushions reading to each other, or silently to themselves. Telling each other their plans for the future, they would conjure up the wildest scenarios, of camel riding over the dunes of the Sahara and taking the Orient Express through cities such as Prague, Venice and Paris. Matthew had been to both France and Italy and Maggie would lie back and listen with fascination as he told her about the incredible sights he had seen. The last time they had travelled to the little island together on her father's small rowing boat had been on her birthday. Matthew told Maggie he had a surprise for her and as usual left a note in the latch asking her to meet him at the lake. The lake was calm that morning and the air so still. On the island, it seemed like they were the only people in the world. His gift was a huge artist's sketchpad, bigger than any she'd had before and a set of oil paints in a beautiful wooden box with her name engraved on the front, Miss Margaret McGuill.

'Oh Matthew, it is truly lovely,' she had exclaimed. 'It is the nicest gift I have ever received in my life.'

She threw her arms around his neck and Matthew kissed her on the top of the head saying 'I hope you draw something for me?'

'I will. Right now,' she'd answered, already settling down and opening the first page of the lovely sketchpad. 'Now, go away and leave me in peace.'

He'd laughed at that. 'I can't go very far. Unless I leave you stranded here with no way back if I take the boat.'

'Do that then,' Maggie suggested. 'I will be fine here for a while if you can come back for me later. Just don't forget me!'

To Maggie, those times and all the times before now were as though they happened to another person completely. Just as Conall had been changed irrevocably by his experience in the GPO, this recent atrocity had also changed her forever.

As happens at every wake in Ireland the neighbours and friends flocked to the farm to offer their condolences to Maggie. While Alice handed around the customary food, drink and tobacco she heard snippets of conversation from each corner of the house.

'I don't even know why she had so much respect for the Goodvilles. The older Lady Goodville was a nice person, but her son Matthew Senior is an arrogant man and his wife, Lady Mabel, is quite the snob. Bridget told me that Lord Goodville would call her Girl, as though she was unworthy even of an acknowledgment of her name. 'Girl,' he would shout, and she would come running. If too far away in the house for her to hear, she said he would simply jangle the bell cord next to the fireplace and continue to ring it until she appeared panting, her face red and hair falling loose from under her cap and then he would chastise her for looking like a harridan.'

‘I do believe the elder Lady Goodville was very fond of Bridget and her mother. I know that she put on a great show for Mrs. O’Hare’s funeral with no expense spared. And I believe that was because Mrs. O'Hare took some very questionable secrets to the grave with her. Do you remember there was all that palaver about young Lady Madeleine suddenly going to London and the shocking rumour about why?'

‘Oh goodness, I had quite forgotten about that. Wasn’t there a huge scandal? It was quietened down quickly when Lord Goodville put that classified advertisement in the newspaper saying anybody heard making defamatory remarks about any member of his family would be charged with defamation of character.’

'Yes, but not only that, the most frightening thing was they would also lose their employment and home if they were tenants or workers of his. Nobody dared mention the Goodville name in any manner, after that stark warning.'

‘There was talk you know about Bridget’s mother …’ a voice trailed off as Alice came within earshot.

‘Yes. That she was the actual offspring of Madeleine Goodville.’

‘No!’ another voice interrupted. ‘I had heard something, but …’

‘Oh, yes. I heard that too, so that would make Maggie who? Or what?’

‘It would make her a Goodville for a start. And Mr. Matthew’s cousin? Oh, my dear, we are so sorry for your loss …'

Maggie’s face went as white as the sheet that covered her parents’ bodies upstairs.

17

Maggie

Aghameen
1922

'What do I want to confess? I don't know what to say. How can I even trust you, Father? How do I know you aren't one of them, or if you are really one of us?'

Silence.

'I request a different priest,' Maggie said.

But it wasn't silence this time. It was a hand through the heavy, red velvet curtain that yanked Maggie from her knees and painfully grabbed her by the hair. In seconds she found herself thrown onto the cold hard tiles of her local church.

'You're nothing but a harlot,' he roared and as he swished past, the hem of his long, black priestly frock struck her face like a whip.

Again, there was silence. Maggie picked herself up from where she had been thrown and looked around. All eyes in the church were focused in her direction. Mrs. Daly tut-tutted, put her rosary beads into her pocket and crossed the aisle to where Maggie was dusting down her skirt.

'You probably didn't say anything we aren't all thinking, but haven't the nerve to tell him ourselves.'

'I don't know what to think anymore,' Maggie sighed, taking the other woman's offered arm as they began to walk towards the church exit.

Mrs. Daly didn't speak until they were outside and even then she looked around carefully before uttering another word.

'I understand you completely, Maggie. When Fr. Nangle refused to give my Bartholomew a Catholic burial because of his beliefs, I swore I'd never set foot in his church again. Only for Fr. O'Flanagan doing the funeral service over at Strokestown, I don't know what we would have done. Not to even be allowed to bury my son in the same graveyard as all his relatives … that's a sin. Not the one Fr. Nangle says my child committed. Sure, doesn't God forgive all sins?'

'I know it was him,' Maggie whispered. 'I know he gave us up to the authorities, but what I'd like to know is how he could do it. How he could be on our side for so long and then just turn us in, knowing what would happen?'

'I agree. But he is telling people that it was your neighbour, Mr. Goodville, who ratted on the men. He said Mr. Goodville came into the vestry and overheard your father telling you about the tunnel and that it was you and your father's fault. He said he told your father he didn't agree with you being privy to important information, as a woman couldn't hold her tongue.'

'He ratted us out because he is pro-treaty. That's why,' Maggie stated. 'He wanted to gain admiration from the Bishop because his heart is set on taking over from him in due course. We all know the church is behind the Treaty because they want the social policies of the new state to be based on Catholic teaching and then the Church's catechetical and pastoral mission will be safeguarded. Even Pope Benedict sent telegrams of congratulations on the outcome of the Treaty to the Cardinal in Armagh, as well as to the Dáil and King George. So, the priests are going to go against all Republicans. And the Bishop said that anybody interfering with the Treaty by taking up arms against those who are endorsing it will be excommunicated.'

‘I know,’ Mrs. Daly replied, nodding her head. ‘And then we have the likes of Fr. O’Flanagan and many other good priests who will allow Republicans to avail of Catholic rites and also offer their support in any way they can. But will they too be excommunicated if the Bishop hears of it?’

'I don't know. Nobody seems to have the answer,' Maggie replied. 'Those Capuchin friars from Dublin, Dominic O'Connor and Albert Bibby, and the Maynooth professor Pádraig de Brún, openly support the anti-treaty side all over the country and nothing has happened to them.[42] But to me, Fr. Nangle refusing to bury my parents in our own parish graveyard because Daddy helped the Volunteers is something I cannot accept. The Bishop said Volunteers who take part in guerrilla warfare are barred from receiving the sacraments – but my parents were not involved in guerrilla warfare.’

‘And neither was my Bartholomew,’ Mrs. Daly added. ‘It’s a disgrace. What did you say to Fr. Nangle? If it is private now, you don’t have to tell me anything.’

---

[42] *Clerics also ministered to the IRA, and they continued to do so after the Civil War began on 28 June 1922. Among the priests with a strong public profile as Republicans were the Capuchin friars Dominic O'Connor and Albert Bibby and the Maynooth professor Pádraig de Brún.*

'I thought I was going to Fr. Moran for confessions because his name was on the rota. I didn't realise it was Fr. Nangle until he began to talk and I couldn't speak at first because I was so shocked. Then he asked what I wanted to confess and I said I didn't know if I could trust him and requested another priest, and that was when he flung me out onto the floor.'

'Absolutely shocking,' Mrs. Daly hissed. 'It shouldn't be allowed for a priest to treat a person like that.'

'You know he does what he wants. What I am worried about is that he has so much inside information he is a danger to the rest of us. If it was him and I have no doubt it was, who gave information to the authorities, then none of us are safe in our beds or anywhere else.'

'Be quiet now,' Mrs. Daly whispered. 'Look who is coming up the road.'

It was Mrs. Devine, the priest's housekeeper and she rushed towards them excitedly.

'There is shocking news,' she exclaimed, breathlessly.

Neither Mrs. Daly nor Maggie asked what it was. It was well known the least interested you seemed, the more information you would gain from Mrs. Devine. Seeming eager to hear the news gave her a power over you that she revelled in, of just giving a snippet or two of a story until you begged her for more. Then she would give a lengthy oration on how she wasn't one to gossip before eventually gleefully revealing all she knew and also all she had fabricated. Those more experienced in listening to her knew if you seemed as though you were not bothered about her cherished gossip, then she would relay it all in one breath and wait in anticipation for your reaction. No reaction would deem you as somebody with more air than graces. Too much reaction would mean you were chomping at the bit for news. The best comment would be 'Why, Mrs. Devine, you are so knowledgeable.'

Therefore, the ladies simply nodded their hello and made as though to keep walking, when the housekeeper called out 'They are going to shoot the two young Fox brothers from the hill.'

This was indeed shocking news, but again, the usual method still had to be put into action.

'That is terrible news. Good day to you, Mrs. Devine,' Mrs. Daly replied, turning around to continue her journey.

‘Oh, but you have to hear,’ Mrs. Daly continued, beginning to walk quickly after them both. ‘Mrs. Fox got the letters from Dublin just this morning; one from each of her two sons. You could hear her screams of despair from up the hill and all over the town. Mr. Fox is on his way to Dublin now with their Josie to try and reclaim the bodies.’

The ladies stopped walking and turned towards her.

‘They were found carrying arms and were sentenced to death, just for that. Can you imagine? If they came here for the day, sure half the town would be executed.’

Maggie linked her arm to Mrs. Daly's. She knew this news would remind her of her own son's recent death at the hands of the authorities.

'They were to be shot at 7 am this morning in Kilmainham, the letters said,' Mrs. Devine continued. 'I pity that poor family.'

‘And will Fr. Nangle make them bury their children in another parish too, I wonder?’ Mrs. Daly asked, giving a steely glare.

Mrs. Devine squinted her beady eyes. 'Fr. Nangle answers to the bishop and it is his priestly duty to follow his Grace's orders. If you don't like it, you are quite free to go elsewhere where there are priests who disobey the Pope's orders. Good day, Miss McGuill.' And with that, she turned on her heel and left.

'That old bag,' Mrs. Daly exclaimed. 'She'll go straight to Nangle now and tell him what I said. I'll be called from the pulpit again. He'd put you off going to Mass at all. I would go to the other church if I could get to it, but Prionsias can't always get away to take me.'

'I'll take you then,' Maggie declared. 'I don't want to go back to his church either. I think we should boycott it until the bishop listens to his people. I can fit about six people in the cart, so if you want to ask somebody else to go with us it would be no problem.'

'You know, Maggie, I think that is exactly what we need to do. I will spread the word. I do not doubt in my mind that if God himself were here in this town today in these awful times, he would have no problem with allowing his people to receive the sacraments. Those who make up these rules are doing it only on the say-so of a Sovereign that isn't even Catholic. As always, it is all to do with power and money at the end of the day. Mark my words.'

And so it came to be in the parish of Aghameen, that not one single person attended St. Agnes Church.

As a result, Fr. O'Flanagan in the nearby town found his church overflowing, so much so he had to leave the doors open to allow the crowds outside to be able to hear Mass.

☘

‘If I am being honest, you were lucky even to get the bodies back as quickly as you did,’ Fr. Nangle said matter-of-factly, before the solicitor arrived for reading the will in Maggie’s home that afternoon.

‘Isn’t that a given?’ Maggie muttered, aware she was being sarcastic.

'No. It's not,' the priest replied, eyeing her as though trying to gauge the young woman's mood. 'They usually leave the bodies as an example in a public place and the family has to wait to be told when they can retrieve the remains. They don't usually let you take them this quickly. I'd say they only let your uncle take the remains home as they were afraid of reprisals if they didn't, seeing as your family is well respected in the town.'

‘I wasn’t talking about that, *Father*,’ Maggie replied, with the emphasis being on his title. ‘I meant, isn’t it a given that you would ‘be honest’ as you said, with you being a priest, that is.’

He looked around the room and then leaned towards Maggie, his whisky-tainted breath in her face.

'Don't you use that tone with me, young woman,' he hissed. 'You might think you are cock of the walk now you are the lady of the house, but watch how you go. You don't want to end up like your parents. Do you girl?'

Maggie bored her dark, green eyes into his, realizing this was practically his admission of guilt until finally, he looked away. There was plenty she could have said and he knew it. But this was neither the time nor the place. That would come, but not yet.

☘

Uncle Pat-Joe, Maggie's father's only brother, was another man who had words with her that day. He did not hide his anger when the family solicitor had read out her parents' wills dictating that Maggie was sole heir to the house and farm, including all or any assets that went with it.

'Preposterous,' he'd vented, angrily. 'What would a slip of a girl know about the running of a farm? I'll fight it. That farm belonged to my father and should go back to me on my brother's death.'

‘That’s not the case as set down here,’ the solicitor replied. ‘These are the terms her father drew up in front of me. The house and farm would have gone to her mother first and consequently Miss Margaret, but … due to the unfortunate death of both her parents, Miss Margaret is now sole heir of the family farm and that is that.’

‘Unfortunate deaths!’ Maggie hissed. ‘They were murdered in cold blood.’

She was not shocked by the contents of the will, well aware of what her father’s will entailed. Maggie was shocked only by her uncle's outburst. It was well known he was already sore with his brother due to his inheriting the full farm on their father's death. It was only out of generosity that John-Joe McGuill gifted a reasonable part of the large farm to his younger brother Pat-Joe, on which to rear and provide for his own family. However Pat-Joe believed the farm should have been halved equally between them, and it was a bone of contention he held against his older brother since their father's demise twenty-three years ago. He was hell-bent on having it returned to him if it was the last thing he would do.

18

Maggie

Aghameen &
The Four Courts, Dublin
1922

It was good to be home, but Maggie felt lonely despite the loving care given to her by the Dalys and other neighbours. Maggie had never experienced loneliness until now. Obviously, when her parents had died she missed them dreadfully and the following first number of weeks had been horrendous. The first few days the house had been full of people and even all during the night, various relations and neighbours had kept a twenty-four vigil around her parents' bed. Following their funeral, Mrs. Daly, Alice's mother, accepted no argument and Maggie stayed at their home for over a week. During this time she had been grateful for the company and kindness that came with it.

Alice and Conall accompanied Maggie on the morning she decided she wanted to go home. Their mother had washed the bedding on her parents' beds and Conall and other neighbouring men had whitewashed anywhere there had been smoke damage. The lingering smell of paint made the house smell fresh and new, as though the atrocity had never taken place. But nothing could erase the images that flashed through Maggie's mind or the memory of the smells and sounds of that dreadful day. They were etched into the fabric of who she was forever and she would never be that carefree young woman again who had left her home on that fateful day, unknowing her life would never be the same again.

In the days that followed, Maggie had wandered around the rooms of the house, picking up objects and putting them down again, leafing through her father's books and trying to fill her days with the usual farm work. This was in between the spontaneous fits of crying that caught her unawares at any moment. Then, another visit from her O.C. Sheila Daly changed everything once again.

'Sheila, do come in,' Maggie had said, opening the door wide in welcome.

'This is a formal visit, Maggie,' Sheila said. The last time she had been here was for the funeral. 'I know you are in mourning, but I thought perhaps you may wish to at least have the right to decide for yourself.'

Maggie was intrigued. Instead of asking if Sheila wanted tea, she began the preparations for making it, wishing to lengthen her caller's stay. While doing so, she asked what Sheila had on her mind.

'An official matter,' meaning whatever would be revealed, was confidential. 'We require as many Cumann na mBan members as possible to assist the men in Dublin. Is that something you think you could manage?'

'Most definitely,' Maggie replied, already feeling both excited at what the mission could be and relieved at having something different to focus on apart from running the farm. 'May I ask what will be required of me?'

'This is highly confidential, but I know I don't have to tell you that. Cumann na mBan women are needed at the Four Courts[43] to assist the men who are trying to hold it. Because it has gone on much longer than originally anticipated, our comrades who have been there since April need to be relieved and others take

---

[43] *See Historical Notes*

their place. Do you think you could do this? It is not an order. It is just a request.’

Maggie didn't need any time to mull the question over. Immediately, she nodded her head. 'When do I go?' she asked.

Sheila shook her hand. ‘You are a true soldier of Ireland,’ she said. ‘There is a contingent travelling tomorrow from Carrick train station. It will leave at eight in the morning and you will all be collected from the station in Dublin and taken to where you are most needed. There are four parts of the building under our control and I don’t know which one you will be sent to but you will be under the command of a Margaret Skinnider.’[44]

‘Will I know anybody else going?’ Maggie asked.

‘Margaret Sweeney and Anne Ryan are both going. Josie Fox will get on at Longford and there will be an Officer O’Shea coming from Sligo with her own brigade.’

‘Is it known how long we will be on duty?’ Maggie enquired. ‘I ask only as I will need to make arrangements for the farm before I leave.’

---

[44] *See Historical Notes*

Sheila took a sip from her teacup and then replied 'until you are told to leave.'

As soon as Maggie saw Sheila's bike disappear over the hill she ran across to Alice's house and around to the dairy, where she knew her friend would be at that time of the day.

'I've to go to Dublin,' she cried out, breathlessly. 'To help the Volunteers at the Four Courts. Sheila has just been to visit. I know you won't say anything as you will be aware this is a confidential matter.'

Alice stopped her churning of the butter and stared at Maggie in disbelief.

'You can't go there. It will be suicide,' she exclaimed.

'I am going,' Maggie answered, resolutely. 'I only came over to ask if you will lend me your bike. I still haven't replaced the one lost at the Leitrim Observer fire. And would you keep an eye on the farm for me, please? The workmen will need to be fed, but you can let them have the use of the scullery and whatever food is in there to help themselves.'

'Does Conall know you are going?'

'No. I just found out myself. I am sure you will tell him if I don't get to see him.'

'He won't be happy. He didn't even want you to go home to your own house yet. That's why he didn't go to Dublin himself, you know. Because he wanted to be here to look after you with all that has happened.'

'Then all the more reason not to tell him before I leave.'

'Will you call before you go to say goodbye?'

'No. I have to be on the eight o'clock train in the morning. Let's say goodbye now.'

The two women hugged tightly.

'Will you collect your bike from the station at some stage, if you can?' Maggie asked. She felt Alice nod her head while she still clung to Maggie.

'For God's sake, be careful,' Alice sobbed, with her eyes full of tears. 'You are my best friend. I don't know what I would do if anything happened to you.'

☘

It was seven on the morning of 26th June 1922, when Maggie left her home after eating a hearty breakfast of soda bread, eggs and porridge. She had been awake since five and washed in the scullery before donning her uniform. Underneath it, she wore a cream shirt with an olive green tie and she had a green felt hat perched on her head. The uniform also sported a haversack into which Maggie put another shirt, underclothes, some personal items, and the first aid kit. She also placed as much food as she could carry inside, cheese, ham, soda bread, a flask, boiled eggs and scones. She did not carry a gun.

With the animals fed and the fire dampened down, Maggie retrieved Alice's bicycle from the shed and began her journey. The sun was slowly rising to warm the chill of the June morning and a soft breeze caressed Maggie's face as she cycled. This time of the morning was busy in the countryside in June, when farmers were out early to start their day and the fields were a hive of activity. Some of the locals waved at Maggie as she passed by and perhaps made a correct guess at where she was going. The journey was not a long one, but time had to be allowed for the possibility of being held up at one of the dreaded checkpoints. Thankfully, luck was on Maggie's side this morning and the train station soon came into view.

After lifting the bicycle up the steps, Maggie went into the ticket office. Paddy Kelly the station master and his son Micheál Kelly, the new young clerk, were inside.

'Good morning, Miss McGuill,' Paddy said, tipping his hat. Noticing her uniform he told her she need not pay for a ticket and said he'd keep an eye on her bicycle. 'Till you get back, God willing,' he added.

'Thank you, Mr. Kelly,' Maggie replied, smiling at him as she removed her haversack from the basket in front. 'Alice Daly will be collecting it at some stage.'

Looking around the platform, Maggie noticed Anne Ryan and walked to where the other woman was sitting on a bench, her head in a book.

'Hello, Anne,' Maggie said, sitting next to her. 'Isn't Margaret here yet?'

'Maggie, it is good to see you. There has been no sign of Margaret but I overheard some men discussing a checkpoint on the road from Rooskey, so she may have got held up there. Or she may be at Dromod station. Did you get stopped?'

'No, thank God,' Maggie answered, putting her heavy haversack under the seat. 'I can't imagine a time when we can travel freely without worrying about checkpoints and being searched …'

'Or being shot,' Anne interrupted. 'That's why we are going to Dublin today, Maggie, to get back our freedom. It's either that or we lie down like dogs and take the beating they are metaphorically giving us.'

Maggie was about to reply when a young boy came running onto the platform and slid to a standstill when he saw the two ladies.

'I've to give you a message,' he gasped, holding on to his sides. 'My sister's been arrested at the roadblock. Margaret Sweeney is her name. I was sent to tell you.'

‘Oh, dear God,’ Anne replied. ‘Is she alright?’

He shook his head. ‘We don’t know. My Dad’s gone to the barracks. He said his revolver was missing so she must have taken it with her. If they searched her, she’ll be done for.’

With the train whistle blowing as well as the station-master’s whistle, the ladies could not hear anything else the boy said as he ran off, but it sounded like 'Up the Republic'. As the platform filled with engine smoke, they lifted their bags and ascended the step into where a whole carriage of uniformed women and men were engaged in song. As the train pulled out of the station to the Irish version of ‘Dawning of the Day' Maggie put the green hat on her knee and sat back as fields of yellow gorse sped by, a silent prayer on her lips. It was her first ever time in Dublin and Maggie was not prepared for the noise of trams and horses’ hooves, and the busy traffic as more motorcars than she had ever seen passed by. There were National Army blockades on every street.

'There,' she said to Anne, pointing over at a woman waving from the front of an ambulance.

The woman was dressed in a long, green olive skirt and a cream blouse, with a hat like Maggie's on her curly, brown bobbed hair. The blouse was blood-spattered and the woman who had a wide welcoming smile, introduced herself as Bridie Clyne[45] and was as dusty and dirty as the ambulance she drove. On her sleeve was a roughly sewn armband of a red cross on a white piece of material that looked like it was cut out hastily from a bed sheet or tablecloth. Handing over a handful of more such armbands to one of the other ladies who were climbing in the back, Bridie told them to 'Put them on your sleeves and hold tight' as she banged the door shut and took up her place once more at the wheel, with Maggie and Anne sitting next to her.

'You came from Leitrim, yes?' she asked. 'I am from Rooskey.'

'Oh, really?' Maggie replied. 'I was involved in the election there with Plunkett. I met his daughter, she had got lost in the crowd. Actually, Margaret Sweeney

---

[45] *See Historical Notes*

from Rooskey was supposed to be with us but she was arrested at a checkpoint on the way and apparently, she had a gun on her.'

'I know Margaret,' Bridie answered, not taking her eyes off the busy road in front. 'Her brother Hughie is in the Four Courts with us. He almost took a bullet last night but it went straight through his hat. He calls it his lucky hat now!' she giggled. 'He's a bit of a ladies' man mind, so keep him in his place.'

'We'll remember that,' Maggie laughed, but the ladies' mirth was short-lived.

It seemed as though from out of nowhere rubble began to fall heavily on the ambulance roof as they neared the Four Courts and screams could be heard from the ladies in the back.

'It's the artillery at the Liffey,' Bridie told them. 'They have eighteen-pounder guns[46] over there and they've been firing at us all day.'

'Holy God,' Anne exclaimed. 'When did they start that? We got no word about it.'

---

46 *Two 18-pounder field guns were placed on Bridge St. and Winetavern St., across the River Liffey from the Four Courts complex. After an ultimatum was delivered to the anti-Treaty garrison on the night of 27 June / early hours of 28 June, the National Army commenced the bombardment of Four Courts.*

'Just recently,' Bridie replied, skilfully manoeuvring the ambulance past huge mounds of debris that littered the streets. 'Listen, ladies,' she continued minutes later. 'I had a hell of a job getting out of the Courts earlier to pick you up and I am quite sure it isn't going to be easy getting back in. So, hang on to your hats, alright?'

Both Maggie and Anne nodded, with Anne putting her hand to her head and covering her hat, much to Maggie's amusement.

Approaching the Four Courts both women gasped to see the damage to the building. Surrounded by soldiers with smoke rising out of its roof and windows, Maggie realised she was indeed entering a battlefield. As briefed by Bridie, any possible entrance was cordoned off by barricades that to Maggie's eye looked completely impenetrable.

'What are we going to do?' she cried to Bridie. 'How are we going to get in?'

'The same way I got out,' was the reply.

Advancing towards a blockade on the entrance opposite the River Liffey the ambulance picked up speed.

'Get down,' Bridie shouted.

The ladies didn't have to be told twice. Holding on tightly to one another, they impulsively called out in terror as the ambulance rammed at a high speed and they heard the crash as it burst through a barricade. Staying in their crouched position and keeping their hands over their head as shots rang out, both ladies were amazed to hear Bridie laughing out loud.

'We did it,' she cried. 'We're in.'

Taking up position once again beside her, Maggie looked at Bridie awestruck.

'*You* did it you mean,' she exclaimed. 'I can't believe it. You were like a white knight on his steed charging into battle.'

Bridie laughed once again as she pulled the ambulance to a screeching stop in a courtyard. Immediately the women in the back climbed out, declaring how scared they had been but how brave Bridie was.

'Now, your first mission ladies,' Bridie told them, as with the women's help she began pulling out the wooden boxes they had been sitting on. 'Get these inside.'

'Are they coffins?' one woman asked, looking shocked.

‘No. But come to think of it, they could be used as that,’ Bridie answered glibly, instructing Maggie and Anne to lift one end. ‘They are guns,’ she stated, calmly. ‘Let’s get them in.’

As the women began carrying their much-needed cargo indoors, Volunteers began coming outside to give their assistance. Maggie noticed the men all looked exhausted, some wore bandages on their heads or limbs, but they all showed relief at seeing both the arrival of Cumann na mBan and the weapons they carried.

‘You are a sight for sore eyes,’ one of the men shouted. ‘And literally, some of us have them. The dust in this place would blind you.’

Immediately, Maggie arrived into chaos, one collapsed wall to the right of her had steps swinging precariously over its gaping stairwell. Ash, powder and soot permeated the air, and the ground was awash with stones and bits of wreckage from the constant bombardment by the Forces of the new Provisional Government.

‘Here, quick, we need hands,’ a man called out from over the banisters on the left of the wide hallway.

Maggie, Anne, and one of the men who helped carry the guns, all raced upstairs, taking the steps two at a time.

'Go get a door,' the man shouted.

'A door?' Maggie repeated.

'Yes, a door to carry him on.'

'Who?'

'Just get a bloody door, will you,' he ordered.

Maggie ran along a corridor and seeing a door hanging from its hinges she pulled hard, trying to loosen it. Anne helped her pull it and both women nearly fell back when it almost came down on top of them. Turning it on its side they slid the door along the rubble-strewn corridor to where the Volunteer had run into another room. Maggie gasped. A young man was lying on his back after being hit with a bullet while firing his gun from his seating position on a window ledge. His upper arm was leaning into a shard of glass the size of an open palm on the side of the window frame and blood gushed from the wound onto the ground. His left hand was missing fingers and with all the blood it was impossible to see how many. He was screaming and trying to free his body as more shots were being fired in his direction.

‘No, don’t,’ Maggie yelled, as the man who had ordered the door tried to pull him onto the floor. ‘Let me see his arm first.’

Dragging the haversack off her back, Maggie pulled out the roll of bandages and first aid kit from the front pockets. She also pulled out the flask that held not tea, but her father's homemade poitín.[47]

‘Give him a swig of this,’ she asked the man whose name she discovered was Harry. ‘Anne, take these,’ she handed over a roll of bandages. ‘Hold his hand up and wrap the severed fingers. Make a sling for him so the arm is supported.’

Anne went around to the man’s left side and began doing as asked while Maggie took a pair of scissors out of the bag and began cutting the material from the sleeve where the shard of glass was inserted.

'Good. It is not going into any veins,' she stated. 'I need you to get a hammer or something similar and knock the end of the glass that is stuck into him out of

---

47 *Poitín is a traditional Irish distilled beverage (40–90% ABV). Former common names for Poitín were "Irish moonshine" and "mountain dew". It was traditionally distilled in a small pot still and the term is a diminutive of the Irish word pota, meaning "pot". The Irish word for a hangover is póit. It can only be made from cereals, grain, whey, sugar beet, molasses, and potatoes.*

the window frame, and slowly, please. What is your name?' she asked the injured man.

‘Donal,’ he answered. ‘Donal Daly.’

‘Daly?’ Maggie repeated, slowly pulling the shard of glass from his arm. ‘I need the Poitín,’ she asked.

‘I’ve just given him some,’ Harry replied.

‘I need it for putting over the wound,’ Maggie answered. ‘Where are you from Donal? I have friends who are Dalys in Leitrim. Are you related?’

In between his screams, Donal attempted to reply. ‘… Dad’s family … Leitrim,’ he murmured. Then his head rolled back.

‘Is he dead?’ Harry cried.

‘No,’ Maggie answered, quickly wrapping his arm with the bandage. ‘He has passed out. Slide him onto the door, gently now.’

‘How is his hand?’ she asked Anne.

'Just half of his ring finger and his little finger are gone,' she replied, holding up a blood-stained golden band. 'Who will I give this to?'

‘Here,’ Harry said, removing a silver chain and cross from around his neck. ‘Put it on this and put the chain on him. ‘No, wait,’ he continued, removing the cross. ‘I need this,’ and he put the cross into the front pocket of his uniform jacket. ‘It’s kept me safe so far.’

Both Maggie and Anne together with Harry and another man called Ernie carried Donal’s make-shift stretcher out of the room away from the gunfire still ricocheting through the windows of the front of the building.

'Where are we taking him?' Maggie asked, holding onto the door with both hands. It weighed a ton.

'We need to get him downstairs,' Harry shouted back in reply. 'There's a make-do first aid station in the courtroom and doctors there.'

It was no easy task to carry the patient down the stairway and it was lucky for him he was still unconscious as it was a bumpy journey. As soon as he was handed over to the care of the medical team, Maggie and Anne were approached by Margaret Skinnider, their O.C. who was holding a note in her hand.

‘Names?’ she asked.

‘I am Maggie McGuill and this is Anne Ryan from the Leitrim Brigade.’

‘I need you to get these guns over to Headquarters in the North Block. You go out the back way and cross the courtyard. Ask for Ernie O’Malley[48] and give these guns to him’.

‘Ernie?’ Maggie repeated. ‘We’ve just been with him.’

‘He’s gone back to the North Block,’ the O.C. told them. ‘They couldn’t carry all the boxes. Carry them over there and check on any wounded.’

But the women faced a problem immediately. The box of guns was too heavy to lift, even between both of them.

‘Can we kick it with our feet?’ Anne asked, trying it out, but that seemed useless. ‘What are you doing?’ she continued, watching as Maggie began opening the lid and pulling out rifles.

‘We can carry them this way instead. It’s the box that’s the heaviest,’ Maggie replied, putting the slings of several rifles around her body. ‘You do the same.’

‘There’s ten altogether and ammunition. That’s five guns each and the ammo,’ Anne said, also putting guns over her shoulder. ‘They are too heavy to carry all at once.’

---

[48] *See Historical Notes*

‘We have to,’ was Maggie’s reply. ‘It won’t be far.’

The Courthouse was a maze of corridors, doors and staircases but the women soon reached the courtyard. Here the shooting was less with most of it being aimed at the front and back of the buildings. The ladies gasped at seeing dead bodies strewn on the ground, one with limbs missing. One man moaned and Anne went to move towards him but Maggie shouted at her to come back.

‘We’ll see to him after we drop these off,’ she insisted. ‘We need to get these over first.’

Due to the smoke and dust, they were not sure if the building they entered was indeed the Headquarters, but as soon as they were inside they were immediately relieved of their load.

‘God bless you,’ Ernie exclaimed. ‘Can you do another run?’

‘Yes,’ Maggie replied. ‘But there is a wounded man outside we need to see to first.’

'You,' he said to Anne. 'You see to him. And you, Maggie, is it?' he asked, to which she nodded. 'You go get the guns, but we need ammunition. Get that first. But hang on, can you see to him?' He pointed to a young man who looked only about sixteen years old. 'He's got hit in the leg.'

Once again, Maggie took out her scissors and bandages. The young lad was whimpering, trying to be brave. Tearing the trousers open Maggie could see a large piece of flesh hanging off. If the bullet was still in there it needed to come out and he needed to be stitched up.

'I need help to get him to the medical station,' she shouted. Nobody came forward.

'Will I lose my leg?' the young lad asked, between gritted teeth. 'Will I still be able to play hurling?'

'Sure you will,' Maggie assured him. 'It doesn't like too serious at all. But I need you to put your arm around my neck. I'm going to try and get you across the yard.'

As they both slowly limped back in the direction she had come from, Maggie saw Anne leaning over the wounded man. Anne looked up and shook her head.

'Help me,' Maggie called. 'Take his other arm.'

'That man,' Anne sobbed. 'He asked if I was his mother.'

‘What did you say to him?’

‘I told him I was.’

‘Good. You gave him comfort at his end, Anne.’

On returning to the room where the guns were stashed, the women were astounded to see there were none left.

‘Ernie is relying on us to get him more,’ Maggie exclaimed.

‘That man, the one who was dead in the courtyard,’ Anne answered. ‘He had ammunition on him. I’ll get it and bring it over.’

Maggie nodded. ‘And I will go around the other bodies to see if they have any.’

For the rest of the day and night an exhausted Maggie ran from pillar to post completing whatever tasks were required of her, including ones that she came across that needed to be taken care of immediately such as wounded men, hungry men, and men for whom only a priest was needed. Being part of this battle was far from any of her expectations, where she had naively imagined she would be assisting in some simple nursing and perhaps handing out food to the men in action. Instead, she found herself ferrying weapons and artillery, carrying notes from one building to the next of which there were several. The huge complex included the Garrison's headquarters and barracks living quarters in the North Block, the Public Records Office, and Land Registry Office, and then there were the East and West Pavilions of the main Four Courts itself with its myriad of corridors, rooms, and several floors. Some of the blocks were used as munitions factories and explosives and incendiary material storage, and all areas of the huge complex were occupied by the Volunteers who were fighting hard to keep hold of them.

All the time Maggie was under constant gunfire and just getting from one area to another could take ages as she ducked under windows to prevent being hit by a stray bullet that could come from either side. Sometimes the amount of smoke made it impossible to see in front of her and it was easy to lose her bearings, not knowing what part of the building she was in. She had not seen Anne since the day before and the last time they spoke her comrade told her she'd been dispatched to the munitions block to make an inventory of what armoury was left.

A note was given to Maggie by a military courier at 3.30 am on 28th June 1922 that she carried to a

Thomas 'Skinner' O'Reilly.[49] It took her ten minutes to locate him due to not knowing which part of the building he occupied and her journey being precariously under constant bombardment. The document caused him to look horrified when he read it and Maggie almost felt as though it was she who had written the words that caused him such obvious upset. She knew what was in it. She had been told she needed to read every note that passed through her hands. If in the event of it being lost in transit at least she would be able to recite the message word for word.

Thomas swore once more when he re-read the document for the second time.

'Come with me,' he said to Maggie, and she followed him up to the Central Hall under the huge dome where he gave the note to Rory O'Connor[50] who read it out loud.

TO THE OFFICER IN CHARGE

FOUR COURTS

I, acting under the order of the government, hereby order you to evacuate the buildings of the Four Courts and to parade your men under arrest, without arms,

---

[49] *See Historical Notes*
[50] *See Historical Notes*

on that portion of the quays immediately in front of the Four Courts by 4 a.m.

Failing compliance with this order, the building will be taken by me with force, and you and all concerned with you will be held responsible for any life lost or any damage done.

By order

THOMAS ENNIS[51]

O/C 2nd Eastern Division

'It is already 3.40 am now. What date are they talking about? Do they mean in just twenty minutes? We need an immediate meeting,' Rory declared. 'Maggie you need to get hold of Ernie O'Malley and Liam Mellowes[52] and get them all to meet in the main hall.

It was no easy achievement to get word to all the men Rory listed. To do so meant that Maggie once again had to run from building to building under smoke and heavy fire. She found Ernie O'Malley and Liam Mellowes on the roof, with Liam lying on his

---

[51] *Commandant Tom Ennis was given the task of removing the anti-Treaty forces from the Four Courts.*
[52] *See Historical Notes*

stomach on a ledge, revolver in hand. Lying there on the roof edge he looked almost like a black cat stretched out, ready to pounce on his prey.

'Liam Mellowes,' Maggie shouted. 'Rory O'Connor needs you for an urgent meeting at Central Hall.'

'I'm a bit tied up right now,' he roared back, not even turning around.

'He said it's to do with an urgent document from Thomas Ennis,' she hollered, attempting to wave the plumes of smoke away with her hand.

Yelling at another man who turned out to be Andy Cooney[53], all the men jumped down and followed Maggie. Each man wanted to know why the urgency of the meeting and Maggie did not wish to divulge any information, only to say it was important they were present. The journey back to where Skinner was in the main hall was a treacherous one under a constant barrage of fire and bits of broken glass and masonry falling on their heads. As the men assembled one by one from their various posts, Maggie's heart went out in pity for them. They all looked bone weary. They had been here since April, almost three months ago,

---

[53] *See Historical Notes*

and the stress and strain showed on each face. Their once neatly pressed uniforms were now torn and filthy while unkempt beards and whiskers covered taut, grey faces. Liam Mellowes, Andy Cooney, Ernie O'Malley, Rory O'Connor, and Seán McBride[54] huddled into a corner to discuss the document Thomas read out to them.

'Absolutely not,' Liam Mellowes hollered. 'Skinner, tell them there is no reply.'

This is the message that Maggie then relayed to the dispatch driver to be carried back to Thomas Ennis.

'There is no reply,' she said, blissfully unaware of just what her simple message would unleash.

Reports came to the occupiers inside that an armoured Lancia tender was driven up to block the main gate of the Four Courts and then disabled and abandoned by its National Army soldiers. The garrison in the Four Courts gave no response as they were under strict orders not to fire the first shots.

'You know it is one of our own former comrades who is firing on us. Michael Collins, the new Commander-in-Chief of the National Army himself!' Ernie O'Malley exclaimed, as the bombardment

---

54 *See Historical Notes*

commenced at 4.10 am. 'I never thought I would see the day.'

Collins' plan was to cause such an assault on the Four Courts that those inside would have no choice but to surrender. On Friday the 30th of June, a huge explosion made holding on to the building impossible, and surrender was inevitable. At 4 pm on Friday, 30th June 1922, after holding out for three days since the demand for surrender, the anti-treaty army which consisted of 140 men, unconditionally surrendered to the Free State Army. This fight was over, but for the country, Civil War had just begun.

19

Maggie
Aghameen
1923

A feeling of heat overpowered her. Even her hair tingled on her scalp and she could feel sweat run down the side of her face. Maggie squeezed her fists. Her hands felt damp. Unable to lift her head for fear they would all see the horror in her eyes, she replied.

'I can't.'

Her shoes were navy and scuffed at the toes with thin straps over woollen stockings. These things she focused on: a flash of light, a cigarette thrown on the ground in annoyance. All she could see were the men's boots. Men, she wondered. They were boys really, who still had their mother washing their underclothes and none of them were probably able to make any kind of a meal without a woman around. In fact, some of them were even younger than Maggie and yet were asking she do this dreadful thing. She waited for

Conall to speak and say he disagreed. But he didn't. Instead, her uncle Pat-Joe spoke. She had mended the shirt Conall wore now. That's where her eyes were focused. There had been a tear just under the armpit. So well repaired only she could know it had been done. She recalled the faint smell of his sweat as she sewed and how fresh it was, pleasant.

His arm reached for the bread she had baked just that morning in anticipation of his arrival. She could not look at his face. Her hands clasped tight to her light dress, the perspiration leaving an imprint. Her legs shook and she crossed her ankles, tight, and lifted her teacup, the steam rising from the hot tea scalded her nose and she breathed in deeply. Put down the cup, for fear they could see how her hands shook and replaced them to her side. Kept the ankles crossed so her feet would not portray the fact her whole body was shaking. Focusing on the fireplace, she could hear the words being spoken above her head. I should get more turf, Maggie thought.

'We all know it's a lot to ask, lass. God knows none of us here would want our womenfolk doing it. But we are asking you.'

She heard murmurs of agreement. Dusty boots scuffed the floor and somebody had stormed out, slamming the front door after them. This caused her to lift her head and breathe with relief on seeing it was he who had left. At least he had done that.

‘You know and we all know it’s yourself he is interested in,’ her uncle said, following her eyes to the doorway. ‘He won’t let any harm come to you. Sure none of us will.’

‘They’ll shoot me. You know they’ll shoot me.’

'Shoot you for what? For saving our country from those bastards who are trying to ruin it? Nobody's going to go shooting you. Sure, won't they know you are only following our orders?'

‘Is it crazy you are?’

‘It’s the only way.’

‘And what will happen to me afterwards? Can you tell me that?’

Nobody answered.

‘You’ll see. You all know what will happen to me. It’ll be the jailhouse or the madhouse or worse.’

What could be worse she thought? Death would be better and maybe even the madhouse would be better than prison. They had completely taken away any pleasure she had felt on receiving the invitation to the Easter dance at the Goodville home. It was a huge event when guests from all over the country would arrive in their droves and The Manor would hire extra staff from the town to prepare for the party and feed and cater to the guests. Due to their past history with the Goodvilles, the McGuill family was invited every year as a show of courtesy. John-Joe McGuill always had an excuse for not accepting, but his wife and daughter could not bear to miss it. The invitation was always a bittersweet one as the pressure of what to wear would cloud their excitement and John-Joe McGuill often had to sell some livestock to cover the expense of new dresses. These dresses were usually sold afterwards as the ladies would not have an occasion to wear them during the year and naturally they could not be worn again to the next party. However, this year was going to be different on two accounts. The first one was that her mother would not be accompanying her and the other was the men had asked her to attend for a grave reason of their own.

'I had planned to decline the invitation this year due to my parents' murders and I am quite surprised the Goodvilles even extended the invite.'

'Oh, the English have no regard for our traditions,' Pat-Joe answered, gruffly. 'We'll get you the money for a dress or whatever fancies it is you need for the party.'

‘I won’t do it,’ Maggie answered again, resolutely. ‘You can’t make me.’

‘Listen here, girleen,’ Pat-Joe said, taking the seat next to her and putting his arm around her. ‘Those people murdered your father and mother and those men your father died to protect. They killed Bartle and all our other comrades without even a fair trial.’

‘I heard you myself, Maggie,’ Mick O’Connor said, softly. ‘When they shot your parents, I heard you shout that you’d kill them all. Have you reneged on your word now?’

‘I was half mad with grief,’ Maggie snapped. ‘Are you going to make me do this thing because of that?’

The men looked around at one another and some shrugged their shoulders, as though to say ‘What can we do?’

Then Mr. Daly spoke. He was Prionsias Daly, father of both Bartholomew and Sheila and proprietor of Daly’s public house. He was also Conall’s uncle.

‘If my Sheila, God rest her soul, was alive, I know without a doubt she would do this thing if asked. But she can’t. She can’t do it because she is in her grave alongside her brother and my only son Bartholomew, after that recent skirmish when she got fatally shot.

My two children lie above there in the cemetery in the next town because that priest wouldn't have them in our own local parish church. And why is that I ask you? Because of the Treaty and because of those English tyrants who forced it on the people with threats of a war mightier than one ever seen, if they didn't agree to it. That man who will be wining and dining himself at the Goodville's big party is the very man who was given the job to enforce martial law on anybody who resists the armed forces. He is the man responsible for my children, your two friends and your parents being murdered in cold blood. And you have an opportunity to prevent him from doing that to any more men and women of Ireland.'

'Thcy will just send another in his place,' Maggie insisted, but her resolve was beginning to weaken.

'And by God, we will find him too, if we can,' Prionsias replied, looking Maggie in the eye. 'Till they run out of bastards who will take the position, for it will be known as a certain suicidal one.'

Maggie looked around at the men she had known all of her life, men who had come to her aid when her parents were murdered and had done the repairs to her home. These were the men who carried her parents' coffins and dug their graves in the next county and who she knew would do the same for her, if needed. How could she refuse them?

They instructed her two nights later exactly what the plan was. They'd called to her home, Micheál, Padraíg and Prionsias. While she had been reading by the fireplace, the knock came to the door and looking out the window first, she saw three dark shapes. Unconcerned that it was the authorities, for she knew they didn't knock but burst their way in, she answered. It was who she had been expecting. She didn't offer any niceties such as a cup of tea. This was not a social visit but instead a formal meeting. Micheál did most of the talking. The men took off their hats, holding them in their hands. Maggie did not even offer them a seat.

'Here is a picture likeness of the man,' Micheál said, holding a newspaper cutting out to her.

Maggie took the piece of paper and looked at it, then handed it back. She nodded her head.

'Do you want to hold on to it?' Micheál asked. 'In case you forget his face?'

'I know his face,' she answered.

‘Have you seen him before?’ Padraíg asked this time. ‘Where?’

‘In the meadow,’ she replied.

‘And did you talk to him?’ he asked, excitedly.

‘Yes. I did.’

‘Champion. This is great news,’ he said. ‘So you have made his acquaintance? And was it amicable?’

Again Maggie asserted that it was; for him at least.

‘We’ve already made great inroads so,’ Padraíg agreed. ‘He’ll recognise you at the event and he will more than likely ask you out for a dance. Sure, it’d be rude if he didn’t. And he’s not a married man. We know that much. This will make the whole thing a lot easier now.’

‘Absolutely,’ Micheál acknowledged. ‘It means you won’t have to go trying to catch his eye or initiate any kind of conversation with the man. You will just have to be within his vision and then he’ll do all the work himself. It couldn’t be better. It’ll look completely natural and nobody can say later you led him on.’

‘All you have to do is fake a headache or come over all faint and if he is any sort of a gentleman at all he will offer his assistance,’ Padraíg said.

‘Then you tell him you need to take some air,’ Micheál interjected. ‘Be sure now that you get as far away from the house as you can. Walk over towards the lake. They’ll not hear a thing inside with the noise of the band. Afterwards, go back inside and talk to as many people as you can. You have to be sure to be seen so you will have plenty of alibis if needed later on.’

‘Oh please, for God’s sake, don’t shoot him in front of me. I’ve seen enough of death to last me a lifetime,’ Maggie pleaded.

The men looked at each other in consternation.

‘There is no way around that unfortunately, Maggie,’ Micheál answered, shaking his head. ‘What possible reason could you give for leaving him standing by the lake on his own while you walk away?’

‘If I think of something, can I go?’

‘Look,’ Padraíg replied. ‘The main thing is that we get him. We can understand why you don’t want to be present when we take him out, but as soon as we do you have to quickly go back to the party and you can't appear to look the least bit distressed. Immediately when you return you must talk gaily with somebody and act completely natural.'

There is nothing natural about it, Maggie thought to herself. She looked over at Prionsias Daly. He hadn't spoken a word the whole time they were in the house. Was it because he felt ashamed they asked her to do this deed or was it because he was aware of something the men were not disclosing to her, she wondered?

'Is there anything else I need to know?' she asked. 'If there is, this is the time to tell me. I don't want any surprises on the night in question. I will be nervous enough without the possibility of that.'

Whirls of tobacco smoke swirled in the air from the men's smoking. She longed for the strong inhalation to quench the taste of fear in her mouth and the sweet release of exhaling. It felt like she had been holding her breath for much too long. Words spun on her tongue, words of anger swam in her head and she could feel them like a river whose banks were about to overflow; the words she could not say.

'Have ye a dress?' Micheál asked. 'Something fancy like, that you can catch his eye in?'

'No,' she answered, truthfully.

The men looked around at each other with their eyebrows raised.

'We'll get ye one so,' Micheál replied.

Maggie couldn't raise her eyes.

'So, you know what you've to do then?' a gruff voice asked.

It was Padraig who spoke this time. Calling to her home for years as her father's best friend since she was knee-high to a grasshopper – now expecting her to do this shameful thing. She'd never forgive him. Or forget. Maggie nodded. And as the men took their leave the only one she looked at was him, and his eyes wouldn't meet hers, for the shame.

20

Maggie

Aghameen
1923

‘Isn’t that Matthew Goodville,’ Alice asked, pointing to where a car was driving into the village with people in the back, Matthew and the driver in front.

‘Oh, yes,’ Maggie answered, happy to see Matthew was home. She waved as the car slowed to a stop and Matthew got out.

‘It’s good to see you home,’ she told him, placing her hand on his shoulder.

Feeling him tense a little, Maggie stood away as he turned back to the car.

‘May I introduce you to Lord and Lady Thompson and their daughter Miss Isabella Thompson.’

Maggie nodded her head.

'Pleased to meet you,' she answered and then continued. 'You are here for the party I presume?'

'Indeed,' Lady Thompson replied.

The ladies were dressed exquisitely. Lady Thompson hardly looked old enough to be a married woman, never mind a mother. And Miss Isabella looked the epitome of chic. Her dark hair was cut in the newest fashion of an *Ina Claire* bob, named after the famous American actress. She wore a very daring sleeveless dress with a long string of beads hanging down to the waist and was even holding a parasol. It was to keep the sun off her pale face, Maggie presumed, her cheeks reddening with embarrassment as she hugged the simple brown woollen cardigan around her body, aware she looked exactly like the country farm girl she was.

'I bid you good day,' Maggie said, in the classiest voice she could muster, then smiled and nodded at Matthew as he climbed back into the waiting car.

'That was a tad uncomfortable,' Alice whispered, as they drove away in the direction of the manor. 'Didn't she look like a film star?'

'Yes,' Maggie replied. 'I've never heard Matthew mention them before.'

She noticed him immediately. He was the tallest and most dignified-looking man in the room, head and shoulders above anybody else. Broad-shouldered, his military uniform only served to enhance his physique and as soon as Maggie walked into the room, he saw her.

Maggie felt extremely ill at ease. Used to having her mother's company, she hunted the room with her eyes for Matthew. Of course, he was in conference with Miss Isabella and her family. She could not intrude on that congregation unless invited. Accepting a glass of champagne served on a silver tray from a waiter, Maggie slowly made her way to where a group of elderly ladies were seated at a table. She missed her mother and she missed how they would have commented on what everybody was wearing and who was who. Bridget McGuill had revelled in this social highlight of the year and it would make for colourful conversation for weeks afterwards. More than anything, Maggie just wanted to go home.

She wore a dark blue dress, not wanting to appear too brightly dressed in honour of her parents. The colour suited her perfectly and with her blond hair artistically swept up in a magnificent chignon, courtesy of Alice and Mrs. Daly's handiwork, Maggie was the belle of the ball, a fact she was quite unaware of. Major Hawkins was still looking in her direction, yet when she caught his eye, he turned his head toward where the band was playing. Maggie knew it would be impossible to ask him to dance, even during ladies' choice, when women could ask the men to join them on the floor. He was an army Major, so no way would she be able to ask him to dance. During ladies' choice women still only asked their partners or male relatives to accompany them onto the dance floor. Maggie could never approach a man like him, not in a million years, even though they had already made each other's acquaintance. He would have to make the first move. It didn't take him long.

From the corner of her eye, Maggie saw him approach their table and she began talking in earnest with the quite deaf mother of Lady Goodville. She turned her back slightly so that the Major would have to make a point of singling her out. This was important and would be noticed by the gathering at her table, and the fact that it would be witnessed by Lady Goodville's mother was a great advantage.

'Good evening, ladies,' she heard him say. 'Mrs. DeVere, how are you enjoying the festivities?' This question he aimed towards Lady Goodville's mother, as it would be polite to acknowledge her first.

‘What did he say, dear?’ Mrs. DeVere asked Maggie.

This was Maggie’s prime opportunity.

‘The Major asked if you are enjoying the party?’ she said, nodding her head at the Major.

'Oh, not at all,' Mrs. DeVere replied, shaking her head vehemently. 'I do dislike these bawdy affairs, but one must support one's family on these occasions.'

‘Indeed,’ the Major replied, winking at Maggie. ‘I do believe we have had the pleasure of meeting previously,’ he smiled, offering his hand to Maggie which she took with her gloved one.

‘May I?’ he asked, gesturing to an empty chair next to Maggie.

‘Certainly, Major,’ she replied. ‘And are you enjoying the frivolities?’

He nodded. ‘The night just became much more fun,’ he answered. ‘And tell me, have you done any more painting or fishing?’

Maggie was about to answer when the band struck up a rather lively piece and the Major offered her his hand again.

'Perhaps you would do me the honour?' he suggested. 'And you can answer my inquiry on the dance floor?'

‘Is this music to your liking, Miss McGuill?’ asked the Major, as he slowly put his hand around Maggie’s waist, causing her to wince. ‘Or do you prefer the new faster sort of music that is becoming popular?’

Maggie had never heard of whatever music he was talking about but didn't want to let him know that.

‘I prefer this music,’ she simply replied.

To an outsider, Maggie would just appear like any young lady on the dance floor being whirled about by her partner without a care in the world. They would never imagine what was going through her head and would be completely aghast if they did. As she answered the Major’s questions about her art, Maggie’s mind was in turmoil. Now the night had arrived and the target of the operation was literally in her arms, she wished with all her might she was somebody else and anywhere else but here and part of this gruesome scheme.

‘Don’t you agree?’ he asked, and Maggie nodded her head in assent.

‘Oh, yes. Of course,’ she replied, not aware of what the Major had even asked.

‘You see, one has to take emotion out of the situation,’ he continued, slowly beginning to stroke Maggie’s back with his long fingers. ‘I mean … less than a year ago I was informed of a hide-out where those rebels were holed up. Not very far from here … you may have heard of it yourself? I had to make the unfortunate decision to …’ he trailed off. ‘I say, are you quite alright?’

Maggie felt as though cymbals were clashing in her ears. Her head began to swim and more than anything she had to get away from him.

‘I need to … I have to get some air,’ Maggie cried. ‘I do apologise,’ and blindly she half ran towards the open veranda doors.

Lifting each side of her dress in her hands, Maggie bolted across the garden area and kept running until reaching the beginning of the field, across from which her own home was situated. She could hear the Major hot on her heels.

‘Wait. Miss Margaret. Wait,’ she heard him call after her. ‘What is wrong?’

‘Get away from me,’ she screamed. ‘Get away from me. You killed …’

The shot rang out and Maggie watched him slump silently at her feet.

☘

‘Good morning,’ Maggie said, opening the door a little wider. ‘Can I help you?’

‘We need you to come with us, Miss McGuill,’ the Sergeant replied.

Maggie stood back. ‘What for?’ she asked.

‘Get a move on,’ he ordered, as the other policeman took her arm.

‘Wait. I need to close the door,’ Maggie said, turning around. ‘And may I take my shawl, please?’

The sergeant pulled the door behind him and pushed Maggie roughly towards the lorry outside. As she climbed into the back, Maggie was surprised to see many others were already inside. Some of the men were still in night-shirts. One woman had a baby wrapped underneath her shawl and both were crying.

'Maggie,' she heard and looked up to see her mother's friend, Maura Sullivan, sitting at the back.

'Why did they pick you up, pet?' Maura asked in a worried voice, making a space for Maggie to sit next to her.

‘I don’t know,’ Maggie replied, settling herself down on the floor. ‘I have no idea. Do you know anything?’

‘There was a shooting last night at Goodvilles,’ Maura answered. ‘A Major Hawkins got killed.’

‘Oh, my word,’ Maggie exclaimed. ‘It can’t be. I danced with him last night. That is shocking. How did it happen?’

‘You danced with him?’ Maura queried. ‘Then that is why they are bringing you in.’

‘But why are you and everybody else here?’ Maggie questioned, noticing almost all of those on the lorry were Goodville employees. Some of the men were Volunteers too and Maggie did not make eye contact with them. It had not been disclosed to her which of the men would perform the deed and it could easily have been any of them on the lorry.

‘Anybody who was working at the Goodvilles last night has been lifted for questioning. There have been several lorries doing the rounds since early morning. Lord Goodville is baying for blood.’

Maggie looked over at the young woman nursing her baby. 'And her?' she asked.

'She was serving the meal last night,' Maura told her.

Maggie lay back against the side of the lorry and pulled her knees up to her chest as there was no room in which to stretch them out. This was a situation she had not even contemplated happening; that innocent men and women would be rounded up like this to be taken to the barracks for questioning. Truth be told, Maggie had not even considered what would happen afterwards. All her thoughts had been about doing exactly what was requested and having to live with the ramifications afterwards. Hearing the Major speak so flippantly, almost proudly, of how he had initiated the murder of her parents and comrades had left her reeling. Maggie had no memory of running off, but she recalled the sound of the gunshot and the Major slumping to the ground. After that, she had walked in stupefied silence back to the ballroom as ordered and calmly sat next to Lady Goodville once more, also as directed. The events of the night thereafter had been a blur of banal, polite chatter and the occasional dance. Maggie did enquire of Matthew if he had seen Major Hawkins who had offered to fetch her a drink and not returned. But, by his knowing look, she could tell Matthew was quite aware of her task that night.

21

Maggie

Aghameen

1923

Maggie raised her head on hearing the cell door scrape open. It was still dark and the scant amount of light that came from the corridor made it just possible to see two men standing in the doorway. One was a policeman, but the other she did not recognise. She could make out that he had a beard and glasses and was wearing a dark-coloured suit, and fedora hat with a blank band around it.

'Get up, McGuill,' the policeman barked. 'You are being released.'

Maggie got to her feet and attempted to smooth down her crumpled skirt. Pushing her hair away from her face, she held on to the wall as she moved towards the men. Her head felt light and when she staggered, the gentleman put out his arms to grab her.

‘Hold on to me, Miss McGuill,’ he offered. ‘I have a friend of yours waiting in a buggy outside and we will get you home in no time at all.’

Clutching the man’s arm, Maggie inched along the dark corridor.

‘Just a minute there,’ a voice called out. ‘The prisoner must be formally dismissed. You can’t just …’

‘I believe I can and I am,’ the man replied, determinedly. ‘Now open the doors.’

Maggie did not look up until she reached the step onto the buggy.

‘Alice,’ she cried. ‘Did you get me out?’

'It was Conall who put the wheels in motion,' Alice replied, assisting her into the buggy. 'He contacted Count Plunkett and this gentleman, Mr. Lawlor, who is a solicitor, arrived at our home late last night. My parents insisted he stay with us instead of the hotel. I think Conall was afraid Mr. Lawlor might disappear if we let him out of our sight. You look dreadful.'

‘I feel it, but I am so grateful to be out of that place, Alice,’ Maggie said, leaning into her friend for comfort, while Mr. Lawlor took up the horse’s reins.

‘The Count will be relieved also,’ Mr. Lawlor added. ‘He told me how you had come to the aid of Miss Plunkett while he was here canvassing a few years ago and all the support you gave to his election campaign. He was stricken to hear of the fate of your parents. I am so very sorry for your horrific loss.’

'Thank you,' Maggie replied. 'And thank you also for coming to my aid today. Or should I say, last night? That was so unbelievably kind of the Count, to even think of assisting me in my plight.'

‘Conall was quite insistent,’ the solicitor acknowledged. ‘He came up to Dublin himself you know, to plead your case. But it didn’t take much convincing. Plunkett sent me here immediately and Mr. Goodville kindly lent his buggy for the journey to retrieve you.’

‘I wondered how you had got hold of it,’ Maggie answered, having recognised it immediately she sat inside.

‘Matthew had also been to the barracks to petition on your behalf,’ Alice interjected. ‘He told the police you could not have committed the murder but they had to wait for the Inspector to return from Athlone before setting you free. The Inspector arrived back last night and Mr. Lawlor approached him first thing this morning. Whatever they both said resulted in your release. Thank God.'

Alice took hold of Maggie's hand and squeezed it warmly.

'Do you want to come back to our house or go to your own home?' she asked. 'Conall is insisting you can't stay there on your own anymore.'

'I need to be home to look after the farm and animals. And it's my home, Alice. Why should I leave it?'

'Conall and the other men have been looking after it. But in the long-term, Maggie, a woman on her own in a house is not safe.'

'Rubbish,' Maggie retorted. 'If somebody wanted to harm me, they could do it in a hundred different ways, regardless if I had an army protecting me. Look what happened to my parents. They thought they were safe in their own home. And anyway, your family is right across the road. You can see my house from yours. I am sure you would notice if something was amiss.'

Alice shook her head. She had said as much to Conall herself. In her opinion she thought he should just marry Maggie quickly. He had made it clear that

Maggie was the woman for him, so why wait? Then he could move into the McGuills and Maggie would no longer be on her own. Alice vowed to have a word with him as soon as she got the chance. The last time she had suggested it, he had said it was not the right time and the last thing he wanted to do was leave Maggie with a family and no husband if he got caught up in something.'

‘At least come to our house first,’ Alice suggested. ‘Get something to eat and rest and then go home.’

‘No, but thank you,’ Maggie insisted. ‘I just want to get to my own bed. Please, leave me be today, but do come over tomorrow.’

Alice nodded. ‘Alright, if that is what you want. I will leave some provisions in the scullery later, but I won’t disturb you.’

On reaching the farm, Mr. Lawlor helped both women down from the buggy outside Maggie’s gate. ‘I will be returning to Dublin later today,’ he said. ‘I will inform the Count of your release.’

Maggie spontaneously threw her arms around him. ‘Thank you so much and please do thank the Count for me. I am very grateful to you both.’

There is nothing as comforting as your own bed, in your own home. These were Maggie's thoughts as she snuggled in between the blankets. She had stripped off every stitch of clothing and put them aside to be washed. She didn't want any reminders of that awful prison smell on her clothes or person. Not wanting to wait for the water to heat at the fireplace, she filled a basin and using a bar of scented soap she had once given her mother as a gift, Maggie scrubbed every inch of herself. Pouring the water over her head, she rinsed it again and again with clear water from a jug and rubbed it half-dry with a towel. Eventually, feeling rid of any reminders of her captivity, barefoot and with a clean nightgown on, she wearily climbed the stairs.

It was dark when she finally awoke. The moon cast shadows on her bedroom wall and Maggie sat up, wondering what time it could be. Padding to the door, she retrieved her warm dressing gown from its hook and wrapped it around herself. It was cooler now. The house was quiet and opening the door, she could hear only a ticking downstairs from the mantelpiece clock.

As promised, Alice had kindly left food on the table. Lifting the cloth, Maggie found a fresh batch of homemade bread, cheese, ham and butter, as well as an apple tart. Her stomach growled and wrapping the cloth around her hand, Maggie lifted the black kettle from its hook over the fire and prepared to make some tea. It always made her breath catch in her throat when she saw her parents' cups hanging on the dresser, her father's chipped mug and her mother's bone china cup that matched the dinnerware received from the Goodvilles on their marriage. Maggie still used the small pink teacup that was part of a set she had been given as a 16th birthday present from Alice and Conall. It came with a saucer and side plate and her two friends joked they would give her the rest on each birthday, though of course they never did. She used the set daily, even though the cup was quite small and she had to refill it several times from the teapot to get a decent amount of tea. Measuring out the tea leaves, Maggie noticed her hand shaking, most likely due to hunger as she had not eaten since the evening before she was freed. That pitiful meal consisted of a watery stew with indigestible fatty meat and unpeeled potatoes. She had eaten what she could but afterwards suffered from colicky cramps.

The taste of fresh food was glorious but Maggie found although very hungry, she could only manage one serving of the delicious bread and one slice of cheese. She dug a fork into the apple tart and revelled in its sweetness. It was obviously baked by Alice's hand as she was always very generous with the honey she used instead of sugar. Their father kept bees and donated some of his supply to several of the local homes. Opening the front door, Maggie emptied her hand of the leftover food she had gathered from the table, throwing them as breakfast for the birds. Her ears pricked at the sound of footsteps and wrapping her dressing gown around her, she felt her pulse quicken. The prison and recent developments had made her highly sensitive to any strange noises. It was Conall. Thank God, it wasn't the police. She had seen enough of them for a lifetime.

'How did you know I was awake?' she asked, watching as he walked the garden path towards her. 'Where have you been at this hour?'

Steering Maggie back inside the house, Conall gently coaxed her into one of the fireside chairs.

'We have to get married,' he said, his eyes bright.

She giggled. 'Is that a proposal?'

'It is.'

'You said not until Ireland was free.'

'Ah, Maggie, will you just marry me, for God's sake.'

'But, why the sudden rush?'

He looked at her with a fire in his eyes.

'Well, it might have something to do with you running off to Dublin trying to get yourself killed. Or ending up in jail, or …'

‘Wait a minute,’ Maggie answered, holding her hand up in front of him.

‘It was *you* and the rest of the men who were responsible for my ending up in prison.’

‘They’d never have asked you if you were a married woman.’

‘And that’s the reason you want to marry me now, is it?’

Conall sighed and took her hands in his, then knelt in front of her.

'Maggie McGuill, the most stubborn, beautiful, brave and loyal woman I know. Will you marry me because I love you and I want to protect you, and together we can watch as a free Ireland happens one day. What do you say?'

‘I say, yes,’ Maggie answered, quietly. ‘Now get up from the floor or you’ll wear a hole in your trousers and I’m not patching them for you yet!’

22

Leah
2016

I had to go to Aghameen. I found myself dreaming of Lise every night. I'd always had the most vivid of dreams, so detailed that sometimes I had a problem the next morning trying to fit back into the reality of my life. Perhaps it was part of my second sight, but in dreams I often found things that had been lost by me or other people, even dreaming I was at a person's funeral and then heard they had died. This time I kept dreaming I was in Aghameen, even walking along the village as it would have been almost a hundred years ago, with Lise chatting by my side. Flashes of her warm smile kept coming into my head and sometimes in my dreams she looked the same as in her photo as a young woman. I couldn't get the nagging feeling of guilt out of my system because I had not told her story as she had asked, nor indeed discovered what the rest was. In my dreams she kept saying *'I will rest when the truth is out and you clear my name because they took that too.'* If there was one thing I was making a priority, it was to do what she had asked so long ago, but how?

Then, a visit to Grandy's solicitor made it even more imperative that I go back to Aghameen.

'You took your time,' Seán grinned, as I let myself into his untidy office. 'Coffee?'

'Is it Italian?' I asked, raising my eyebrows as I grinned back.

'You know it isn't,' Seán replied, already standing up and taking his suit jacket from the back of the chair, he put it on. 'After you.'

I smiled and went back onto the tiny landing where Seán followed me down the crooked staircase and I blinked when the strong sunlight hit my eyes.

'Why don't you do the office up a bit?' I queried, as we walked along the busy footpath towards the nearby coffee shop. 'It's been the same way since I was a child. It is so dark.'

'I know. I know,' he replied, opening the glass-fronted door and allowing me to walk through first. 'I just haven't got around to it yet. Somehow it makes me feel that Dad is still here if I keep it the way it is.

And, by the way, when are you going to do up your own place?'

‘Okay. You got me,’ I laughed, putting my handbag down on the floor and picking up the menu. ‘I kind of feel like Grandy is still around if I keep everything the same way.’

‘How about I do up your place and you do up mine?’ he suggested, winking at me.

‘How about we make this a wine instead of a coffee?’ I winked back. ‘We keep saying we will do that every time we talk.’

‘Deal,’ he answered, then ordered two glasses of Merlot, knowing it was my favourite tipple.

‘Jill tells me you are ‘in the zone’ as she calls it.’

I nodded. ‘I have so much to tell you about a project I'm working on. I think we should get a bottle.’

The bottle ended up being another bottle in the little wine bar right next door to Seán's office. He was fascinated, or at least pretended to be, by my story about Lise and asked many 'solicitor-type questions' as I referred to them, just to annoy him.

'How do I know that?' I answered when he asked what had happened to Lise’s belongings after she died.

'I might look into it for you if you are interested,' he suggested. 'See what I can find out about her.'

‘Yes, that would be great if you could. I am thinking of doing a book on her life story. I sort of feel I owe it to her and it might get me over this bloody Marc Lewis business.’

I had told Seán the short version about my so-called boyfriend turning rogue and he had been indignant on my behalf, offering to look him up and see if we could get my money back.

'I'd rather you didn't,' I told him. 'I am just going to put it down to a hard lesson learned and busy myself with this new project to keep my mind off him.'

He wasn't happy with that, but accepted my wishes and by the time he left me in a taxi hours later after a pleasant few kisses, just like we had shared many of since teenagers, I had completely forgotten why I had called to him. Thankfully he hadn't and texted me later to see if I got home alright. He asked me to call in two days' time when he would clear his afternoon for me to go over Grandy's papers. I was grateful he didn't make the appointment for the following day, as that promised to be a hangover one!

23

Leah
2016

Tears sprang unbidden from my eyes as I held the childish copybook in my hand containing Lise's beautiful penmanship. If only I had opened this envelope years ago when I should have done, instead, I had let the grief of Grandy's death prevent me from going through his papers although I had been asked over and over again by his solicitor. But no, I stayed abroad, too wrapped up in my sorrow and instead allowed other people to concern themselves with his affairs. It was only after the firm insistence of Jill to 'not put it off a day longer,' as she had said, that I eventually visited his friend's office, now run by his son, Seán Keenan, who was only delighted to hand over Grandy's documents and leave me alone in his office to peruse them at my leisure.

'Some amount of stuff in this,' Seán said, giving me Grandy's brown, leather Italian briefcase I had given him years ago on Father's Day, that I had renamed 'Grandy's Day'. 'There is more but probably best not to overwhelm you all at once,' he told me, causing me to ask exactly how much more there was.

'Start with this,' he simply replied. 'I'll be on the mobile if you need me to come back.'

I nodded and opened the briefcase then wept as I pulled out my handmade birthday cards that he had kept, my school reports, letters I had written to him from various travels, old love letters from my grandmother and baby photographs of my mother, even her hospital band from the day of her birth was there. My hospital band had burned in the fire when my parents had died, along with other mementoes of my childhood. I grinned when I found a half packet of his cigarettes and placed them to the side with his pens and then took out the bulky brown envelope, taped tightly in the way he used to do with my birthday and Christmas gifts, wound round and round until he must have used up the whole roll.

What was inside shook me to my very core and I cried out loud in surprise. They were copy-books of Lise's. But how did he get them and when? Why did he never show them to me, or tell me about them? Then I got my answer. A brown manila envelope like Grandy used for his business letters was inside one of the copybooks. On the front was written *For Leah. After my death.* Filled with trepidation I sat on the worn, leather swivel chair where Seán's father had conducted his business for many years and opened the envelope.

My dear Leah,

If you are reading this, then I have gone to join my parents and for this, I have waited a long time. I believe that you will return someday to pick up the threads of my story and I fear by that time, I will no longer be here to tell you myself. I have begun to note down my memories, so that you may weave them together with the others I shared with you. At this age, most people find that they forget much of the account of their life, but for me, it is the opposite. I find that I am remembering it all as though watching on a large technicolour screen, and lest I forgot it all again, I have taken up the pen and have discovered that I had never really forgotten anything; but instead had chosen not to remember. At this stage of my letter, I would suggest that you read the first copy book, with Number 1 written on the front, then perhaps come back to this letter. You will notice that some of my story may not be in the order of the events as they happened. Also, please forgive me if I repeat myself.

This is due to my writing them as they came back to my memory.

Doing as bid, I tentatively opened the first page and began to read.

I recalled that during my training with Cumann na mBan I was not permitted to use a firearm, neither a revolver nor a rifle, due to my being left-handed. My O.C. agreed with me I could be taught, but the IRA officer wouldn't allow it. I wanted to prove them wrong. It wasn't anything about wanting to be able to kill somebody or be involved in an ambush. Women were not permitted to be involved in combat. We were trained in firearms only as a means of self-defence. My wishing to be trained in the use of a firearm was more about wanting to show that being left-handed wouldn't stop me from being able to do anything, as though it was some kind of handicap. It was stubbornness I suppose that had always made me want to prove I could do anything a man could do. Since I was a child, I always felt my parents wished my brother had survived, instead of me. I wanted to be as useful to them as a male heir would have been.

Matthew understood this and he offered to teach me to use a gun, privately. He knew how much it meant to me and so he would take me over the fields when there was nobody around and give me lessons in shooting. Conall had refused to teach me saying there was no need for me to be trained in firearms as I wouldn't be in combat. That morning I had been out feeding the animals as usual in Dad's old coat - the tan-coloured gabardine I'd begun wearing around the farm even though it was far too big for me. It still smelled of my father and I got some comfort from it. Matthew had left a note for me in our secret hiding place – one we had used since we were children. It was rolled up small inside the big iron latch on the feed shed. The inside of the latch was hollow and was where we stored our notes so they wouldn't get wet. Matthew would hop over the low stone wall where his field ended and ours began and leave it there for me. It became a habit when Matthew was home, I would check the latch just in case there was a note. On this particular morning, there was. It was written on the Goodville personal writing paper as always. It read,

Usual place. 3 pm. Shooting practice. Take the Web. M.

The Web referred to was my father's Webley revolver. It was the one I used when practising with Matthew twice before. It was smaller than a rifle and simpler for me to operate. Also, it was easier to hide on a person. I must admit, I did find it more difficult than I thought I would. The gun felt completely alien in my hands and trying to shoot with my right hand was a real challenge. Matthew was so patient. He tried over and over, getting me to stand this way and that, teaching me a rhyme to say in my head to remember all the movements. And don't forget, it had to be all done in seconds, no waiting around.

On the third occasion, we met again in the same field. We had our dogs with us. I had Marley and he had Salt and Pepper. His were ridiculous names for dogs! They were all sitting around my feet, tired out from running around in the warm sun. Matthew was in a giddy mood, saying he had something intriguing to tell me after our lesson. Of course, I pestered him to tell me immediately but he insisted it was not a story to tell in haste and there was somebody he wanted me to meet. I was teasing him about whether it was Miss Thompson who was still at the Goodville home since the party, while aiming the gun and saying the rhyme Matthew had taught me out loud. I pulled the trigger and nothing happened. Matthew ran towards me and the dogs suddenly darted – probably after spotting a rabbit. I tripped. The gun went off. Matthew slowly fell to his knees with a startled cry.

I screamed and fell to the ground where he lay collapsed. He had this terrible look of shock on his face and he whispered 'You shot me. You shot me.'

At first I thought he was joking. I couldn't see any blood and I even shook him and told him to stop larking about. But I think really I knew he was dying. I saw the blood. It began to seep through his fingers where his hands covered his chest. All I can remember is feeling suddenly terribly cold - as though somebody had poured freezing water all over me, from my head to my toes. This icy grip took hold of me and I began shaking and calling his name over and over.

'Matthew, don't die. I'm sorry. Wake up.'

I ran to the back of the Manor House and first I met his mother on the veranda. I was screaming for help as I ran towards her shouting 'I shot him. I shot him' and the first thing she said to me was 'What have you done to my son?'

I wasn't aware then that my skirt and blouse were covered in his blood. She ran in the direction I had just come from and then I met Lord Goodville. When he saw me crying hysterically and covered in blood, he shouted at somebody to ring the police and he also ran after Lady Goodville. All I remember is lots of people, the servants and guests from Dublin who were staying at the house. They all started running towards the field and two men who I'd never seen before grabbed me. They dragged me by my arms and locked me into one of the stables. I kept yelling and banging at the door for what seemed like ages. Then sometime later, the door opened and police charged into the smelly stable.

There were about seven or eight policemen, all shouting and yelling at me to stay still - as if I was going to attempt to make a run for it. There was no chance of that as I was rooted to the spot in fear. All I could see around me were flashes of uniform, shiny silver buttons, black polished boots, gold stripes on cuffs and truncheons. I could have walked out of the stable and into the waiting lorry had they asked me, but they didn't. Instead, six of the policemen lifted me by my arms and legs and manhandled me from the stable into the courtyard, where several of the servants stood gawping in horror. One of the younger housemaids shouted 'You murdering bitch. You will swing for this.'

Her words seemed to encourage the others as they all then began to shout 'Murderer, Fenian bitch,' and other such obscenities. I was carried in the air feet first, through the stable yard where Lord and Lady Goodville and their guests were waiting. Their silence was worse than the taunts of the staff members. To say I was thrown into the open lorry was an understatement. The police swung me first and then flung me in as though I was a sack of meal. I landed on my back on the wooden floor of the lorry, just exactly how my parents had been and it felt as though my spine snapped with their forceful throw.

'Get in there you dirty rebel … terrorist bitch … filthy pig …' these were just some of the names they called me. One even spat into the lorry and his spittle landed on my skirt. I remember it left a brown stain, as though he had chewed tobacco.

I attempted to scramble to my feet, but six policemen knelt on the lorry floor beside me and began to roughly tie my hands and feet. There was no need whatsoever to do this, as it was obvious there was no chance to escape, even if I had had the willpower to do so. My feet were bound together with rope and the same with my wrists. A cloth of some sort was placed around my mouth and tied at the back of my head, painfully catching my hair in the knot they tied. I felt strung up like one of the pigs I had often seen my father prepare for slaughter, helpless and unable to do anything to stop the terrible things happening to me. I tried to scream but muffled moans caught in my throat while tears ran silently down my face. The policemen were disgusting. They made crude comments about my vulnerability and talked loudly about things they could do to me in my defenceless state. They joked about the party they would throw while watching my hanging and how they would treat my body afterwards. The terror I felt was something I never imagined a person could experience.

The soldiers smoked over my head and continued to taunt me mercilessly as the lorry jostled over the road. Some even kicked me where I lay. I could visualize exactly where the vehicle was going. I had travelled this road many times myself and knew every turn on the road, and I also knew where I was going to end up. It was not a long journey yet I did not want it to be over despite my fear and discomfort, for I knew there was worse to come. All Volunteers heard the horror stories of what went on in the prison and how appallingly prisoners were treated. I was about to discover it first-hand and every cell in my body filled with dread. I was dragged from the lorry as unceremoniously as I had been put into it. I almost wished they had also covered my eyes, so I would not have to see the faces of the crowd who had gathered around the outside of the barracks. They did not yet know what had happened or who was being pulled out of the lorry. They were just bystanders, people who had been passing and stood to watch the spectacle. As I feared, somebody did recognise me. My long blond hair was easy to notice.

'It's Maggie McGuill,' I heard a voice shout out. I recognised the voice too. It was Mrs. Fox, whose daughter Josie was a friend of mine and also a fellow Cumann na Ban member. At least now word would get to them. However, despite my fear as I was carried by the soldiers into the barracks, all I could think about was Matthew and if he was dead or alive.

24

Prison
1923

He stank of sweat. Not the clean fresh kind, of a man who had been working hard in the field all day. He stank of many days of old sweat never washed away. His face was stubble-free, but tiny cuts from a blade pebble-dashed his chin. A tall man, he looked down at me with a menacing sneer. I noticed his hands shaking, fond of a drop perhaps. Or maybe he was nervous, nervous of what, of me? I doubted it was that. I dropped my head and faced the floor. His boots were so polished they gleamed. He must have a wife looking after him, I thought. Or perhaps he polished them himself. I doubted that too.

'Well,' he hissed. 'You've got yourself into a whole of trouble alright, Missy. You must know what is going to happen to you now?'

I shivered and not from the cold, although it did feel cold. My shivering was from sheer terror.

Remembering my orders not to talk if ever imprisoned, I simply nodded my head.

'Not so brave now, are you?' he snarled and the polished boots took a step closer towards me.

There were footsteps outside on the corridor and murmurs of conversation. Recognising the voice, I turned my head towards the door behind me. It was Father Nangle. I was saved.

The door burst open causing me to jump back.

'Father Nangle,' I cried, holding out my hands. 'Thank God …'

His punch knocked me to the floor and it seemed as though blackness came through a slow tunnel, then nothing.

☘

In my dream, I imagined I drank from the well, from the river, from a jug of cold milk. Yet every time I tried to put the liquid to my mouth, it was knocked out of my hand by black polished boots. I dreamt of licking the wet moisture of the giant, green leaves of the oak tree in our field, but when I put them to my lips, they flew away out of reach. My face felt frozen on one side and ached on the other. There was a taste of old pennies or copper in my mouth. My head seemed heavy. My eyes were still shut, but I had a feeling it was best to keep them that way. To stay in this strange dream would be better than opening my eyes. I knew I lay on a stone floor, but not sure where that was. It was so cold. My body was freezing and lying in the foetal position my knees felt stiff, as though I had lain this way for some time. Yet I was afraid to stretch my legs, afraid to open my eyes, afraid to see where I was and discover what my fate could be. Somehow I believed if I stayed very still within the darkness, I was safe.

I needed to use the lavatory. This most basic of needs would be the one to make me open my eyes. Stretching my legs out straight hurt a lot. My head pounded terribly, lifting it and trying to prop myself up on my shoulder hurt even more. Moving my head around the room caused bile to come to my throat and I retched, but nothing came out. I was in a small cell. There was a thin and grubby, straw-stuffed mattress on the ground and a dirty, brown blanket folded on the end of it. There was one window high up with bars but without any glass, an enamel bucket with a lid on the floor next to the bed and a white ceramic jug with blue edging. I reached out and pulled it closer to me. I drank greedily, first picking out the dead bluebottle that swam at the top. My bladder throbbed more.

There was nowhere in which to relieve myself. Probably that was the purpose of the bucket. Aware that the water in the blue jug might have to keep me for some time, I dared not empty it all at once.

I placed a hand on the edge of the bed and tried to stand up. My head swam and I felt once again I was going to be sick. My legs felt weak. I sat on the makeshift bed and looked around the room. There wasn't much to it. Just the mattress and blanket, the bucket and jug, graffiti-marked, whitewashed walls and a stone floor. I stood and holding my left hand against the wall, I reached the door. Of course, it was shut. I banged and called again and again. Lifting my dress and removing my undergarments I relieved myself in the bucket, then put the blanket over the filthy bed made of straw and lay down, but I didn't weep or call out again. Instead, I began to list facts in my head, the counties of Ireland, the rivers of Ireland, the … until blackness called me once more.

☘

The cold was shocking. I had never experienced cold like this, except for the time I fell into the lake while swinging over it on a rope Conall had hung from our tree. Calling it our tree sounded childish I know, but that was how we had once referred to it. It had been our meeting place.

'Meet you at the tree,' he would shout, or 'I'll be at our tree in the afternoon if you can get away.' Mostly I did get away to meet him and looking back now, I could scarcely remember what on earth we spent so much time doing and talking about.

The time I fallen into the lake and been stunned by the freezing water, at least then I had been quickly dragged out by Conall and warmed up in a few minutes. This was different. This cold was relentless and never ceased. Huddling in the corner of the cell where I had dragged the straw bed the furthest I could away from the window, I sat with my knees pulled up against my chest with my arms wrapped around them and my hands clasped together under my thighs. I still wore the long tan skirt and cream long-sleeved blouse I arrived in, grey woollen stockings and undergarments and my shoes. I wrapped the dirty blanket around my head and shoulders as best I could. It looked as though it had been roughly ripped in half and probably had been as the number of prisoners had grown daily. At night I rocked myself to sleep but woke many times with fleas biting at any piece of skin they could get at. Every part of me itched unbearably.

I could understand how the dampness got into the chests of those locked up around me. I could hear the fits of coughing of women who had been here longer than me which was not surprising, considering the wind that whistled through the stone, walled corridors and in through the barred open window. Even the soldiers wheezed and coughed like old men, not helped by their constant smoking. It was more or less similar to the workhouse conditions I had often heard talked about by older relations over the years. However, the workhouse inmates were not treated like criminals as we were.

Holding my head towards the sky, I took a long, deep breath. The rain on my face was welcome. Even more welcome was the gale-force wind that whipped around my legs and caused my hair to fly in every direction. I was one of the women still lucky enough to have that at least, for most of them sported shorn heads, some with cuts all over their scalp due to their barbarous hairstylists. The only misfortune in still having long hair was the scourge of head lice that plagued the inmates. Due to having my own cell, I had so far avoided this infestation. The telltale sign of one scratching their head was a warning to keep your distance.

In the daylight, I realised just how dishevelled I must look in my stained skirt and blouse. My fingernails were filthy and grown much too long. I dared not even remove my stockings to examine my feet. The pain of loneliness came in waves, I never thought it could hurt so physically and awfully that it made me gasp with its intensity. Yet in my pain, I felt somehow more alive than ever.

☘

The sound of the scraping of the latch across the door and the noise of keys jangling woke me. When the door opened it brought with it the sound of voices shouting at me. 'Wake up, you lazy Fenian bitch.' A rough hand pulled me from where I lay, forcing me to stand. Looking at their faces I saw the look of hate. To them, I was a rebel, a traitor and worse than dirt under their shoes.

'You are going for a little trip,' one of them sneered. Pressing his body close to mine, he put the hand not holding a gun around my neck and slowly squeezed. My eyes began to water and instinctively I put my arms up in an attempt to loosen his grip. It only served to make him squeeze tighter. Struggling to breathe, I began to fight for breath, hitting the soldier with my fists, willing him to let go. All the while the other soldier laughed raucously.

‘Not so brave now are you, Missy?’ he snarled. ‘Shall we have to do her for assaulting a soldier as well as murder then, Sarge?’

‘Oh, she is going to swing anyway,’ the one holding me by the neck replied. Leaning his red, sweaty face into mine he continued ‘I could just do the job now myself, but that would only save you the experience of walking to the noose and I would like to see that.’

Spitting into my face, he released his hand and I fell backwards onto the straw bed. Desperately trying to breathe, I bent over as my head swam, wiping at my cheek.

'Get up,' he yelled, once again dragging me to my feet. 'You are going on a little trip. Ain't that nice?' he sneered, while shoving me towards the cell door.

'And you won't be coming back either,' the other soldier mocked, pushing me along the stone-floored corridor with the butt of his rifle.

At the end of the passageway was an open door and I could hear raised voices, as though men were arguing with each other. They stopped when the soldiers came to the doorway and looked at me with contempt as I stood in front of them in my bedraggled state.

Yes, it was disgusting, but it worked. It kept them off us.

'Scratch yourself. Down there,' Helga said, pointing to her groin. 'Every time you see one of them, just scratch.'

I was appalled. But I did as they said and it worked. They never bothered me again. Other women, desperate women … the ones envied on the outside for their beauty but pitied on the inside, had to go to worse measures to keep the men away. They caught any insect they found and they were plentiful in the damp-ridden cells. On hearing the boots outside, these women shoved their prey inside their underclothes and delighted at the soldier's horror when they violently stripped the women to find insects crawling down their legs. They did what they had to, but some women welcomed the attention, gaining themselves some meagre favours such as extra rations, another blanket or cigarettes. These women were despised by the ones who resisted, warning the others what would happen when they got out for currying favour with the enemy.

‘We could be here forever,’ one of the women snapped. ‘I’ll do what I have to do to survive and I’ll do the same again if I get out.’

Cumann na mBan women were soldiers and acted as such. Because of their association with the Republican rebels they were held together at the top of Kilmainham Prison and treated with much more repugnance than the women in other prisons, who were held for petty crimes such as theft or prostitution. As far as the prison wardens and soldiers were concerned, these women were traitors and extremely dangerous.

I dreamt of the well and of how he had got behind me as I pulled the bucket, and how he had clasped his arms over the rope as I pulled the bucket in. I had felt he was too close, yet I liked the smell of him and his weight behind me. How his forearms had blond hairs, lots of them. He smelled of straw and the sun and sweat, and made me loosen my grip and how his arms tightened even more around mine as we lugged the bucket up together. And yet I had felt slighted and indignant.

‘I can do it myself,’ I’d retorted.

And so he loosened his grip and the water splashed with an angry authority onto my dress and he laughed. But I didn't laugh. Instead, I hauled the bucket up as I had done every morning for as long as I could remember. Only I had never remembered being splashed and my dress being wet and so I criticized him for his careless help in women's work. Now my tongue was dry and when I opened my eyes I realised I was in the depths of hell. I had been told the prison warders urinated into the bucket of water left in the cells. Thankful for the torrential rain all night that eventually lulled me to sleep and was still emptying its torrents through the small glassless window I caught the deluge of water still cascading through the bars into my palms.

How have I come to this? I asked myself. When I woke that morning the sky was grey and slowly from the edge of the tiny window, a dull sun began to creep its way from the left. I thought of the animals and wondered who would feed them. Who would make the breakfast of porridge and take the warm underclothes to my father? Then I remembered I no longer had a father or a mother. Who would look after Marley and feed the cats? Who would bring food to the farmhands and … the door clanged. A large hairy hand deposited a steel tray onto the floor. The door clanged shut. I inched towards the tray, a slice of brown bread, porridge and a tin cup of warm water. I didn't dare. I ate the bread and the porridge. Water poured in once more from the streams cascading from the barred window. I relieved myself in the bucket and climbing into the straw bed, I slept again. Day twelve was over.

There was another steel tray on the floor. Grey meat congealed in brown liquid and a quarter of potato. More thirsty than hungry, I warily spied the tin cup of water. The rain had stopped and I was thirsty. I drank it. The fatty meat took ages to chew and yet I swallowed it all. Remembering tales from the men about how hunger or thirst can kill you slower than a bullet, I ate all on the tray without thinking of the taste and afterwards refused my stomach to relieve me of its contents later. It was three days before they emptied my toilet bucket. And it was four more days before I was taken to the dark room.

25

My Death
1923

At the end of this exposé of Lise' were instructions to pick up the letter again, which I did.

There is a vacuum in my memory at this point, dear Leah. I recall only that there were a series of long, drawn-out interrogations by several men of the law where I had to recount repeatedly what had occurred on that fateful day. I was questioned over and again about the note I told them of, the one Matthew had left asking me to meet him for shooting practice, the absence of which I could not explain. My home was searched and nothing was found in my father's coat or anywhere else in the house, though I insisted the note was left in the pocket of the tan coat.

Sheila Daly was the only other person who knew that Matthew had been giving me lessons, but she was now deceased. I had kept knowledge of Matthew's teaching me from Conall, so he was honest when he said he knew nothing about it. Alice also was unaware of this. Therefore there was nobody on my side who could affirm what I had said at my trial.

The constant questioning went on for weeks during which time my health slowly deteriorated. I had begun to find it impossible to eat as there was a continuous churning in my stomach and I suffered with fainting spells. I also had terrifying nightmares where I relived my parents' deaths, Bartle's death, the death of the men in the tunnel and the Major's death, those others that I witnessed in the Four Courts ... I could see them all as though happening in slow motion in front of my very eyes. I began to have trouble remembering the record of events leading to Matthew's shooting and either through exhaustion or confusion, I began to refer to him as the Major, or the soldier who had shot Bartle, later killed by Conall. In doing so, I began unintentionally implicating myself in these murders too and the evidence against me was most damning. I was sentenced to death by hanging and when the words were said out loud I am told that I said 'Thank you'. I have no memory of it. What I have written in copy-book Number 2 is again a little jumbled and though I have tried my best to write as coherently as possible, I am afraid there might well be errors in what really occurred. Sadly, there is once again, nobody who can tell the true version of what happened. Only the writings of this old woman exist.

It was the sun that undid me. Remember, I had been in that cell for so long. When they took me out, that final day – or what was to be my final day here on earth, I had not seen sunshine for many weeks. It was dark when they put me into the cart that morning and I lay down on the bench at the back and pulled my shawl over my head. When they took me out … oh, the sun, Leah, it was so bright and it made me sway. They took me to a room. I knew I was at the place where they hanged people, but I didn't look. I kept looking only at the sun and I could feel it right on my face. Oh, the joy of it. Fr. Nangle came in and at first he said prayers over me and blessed my forehead with holy oil. Then he sat on the straw bed next to me and took my hands. He asked for forgiveness and he cried. He held my hands in his and sobbed while asking me to forgive him. He told me he was indeed the person who betrayed my parents and the Volunteer men and said he did it for selfish reasons. He apologised for striking me in the prison and explained there was a reason for that … he wanted to let the guards think he was angry with me for Matthew's murder. I didn't feel anger or hate towards him anymore. I felt only pity. He promised he would pray every day for the rest of his life for my soul and those of my parents and the men he had betrayed. He said he would pray for a miracle – but I had little faith in that. It was too late for me now, but I forgave him and asked him to care for my parents' grave in the next village. He said he would be with me at the end and everything would be alright. I could see the sunlight through the cracks of the door. They led me out again and that's when I realised.

I was going to die. They were going to hang me. And I felt the most primal instincts a human could have and I fought. Oh God, I fought, Leah. I kicked and I screamed and they put something over my mouth and I fought so hard to have it removed from my face. It was pressed right to my nose and I inhaled deeply, again and again.

It was his unique smell, the smell of him and home and safety. It was everything we both knew. It was fresh-cut grass and hay after the sun had scorched it. It was warm sweet, strong tea and buttermilk from a can. It was tobacco smoke and chimney smoke and sweat from a day's work in the fields. It was him. And then I saw his eyes … he was there, just before they put that black cloth over my head and I felt the rope tighten around my neck. The last thing I saw was his eyes and he then smiled and …

Conall
1923

Do you remember the tree house we made in that hollow of the tree where you used to hide? I can still even now envisage every branch that we took to get to that hollow. Do you remember it? Maggie? Do you remember? Seven, you used to say. Seven steps to heaven. You were sure those seven branches to the top were the seven steps to heaven. Seven branches to the hollow and it was as though it was carved out just for the two of us. You always sat on the right side. Remember Maggie? I always sat at the higher end, because I could jump down. Do you remember that?

Remember how I would show off and jump down and then play dead. You would scream my name and hurry down the seven branches and then hit me when I laughed? Do you remember when I would shout up and give you that smile, encouraging you to jump and you would be too scared to? And one day you did. Remember Maggie? One day you did jump, even though you were scared - because I gave you our special code. Our special code when each of us needed help. We smiled our special smile. Pretending we had cross-eyes like Master O'Malley. You jumped because I smiled our smile.

You jumped because of the bees. Remember Maggie I am terrified of bees and you aren't. And you saw me give you our special smile. You knew I didn't want to lose face in front of our friends, so you just jumped and pretended you had hurt your feet and I took you home. You saved me then Maggie, just like I am saving you now.

Maggie
1923

I felt it, Leah. I felt the tightness of the rope, then it got tighter again and I felt the floor give way. Oh my God, the fear. My feet and my legs lifted and I could feel the terrible pressure in my neck. And then I dropped. I dropped and there was no sun and there was only pain and I knew I was dead. It happened, oh, so quickly, my leaving this world and yet much less painfully than I had thought, but so terribly and horribly quickly; my life was no more. Then apparently Conall took me here and said to wait until he got back. That was a lifetime ago, but I still wait. You see, I jumped, when I saw him give me our special smile. I jumped.

How did I jump when I was hung by the neck? I just did. I jumped. Because he obviously had it planned all along. I jumped and somehow he had arranged it, he and Fr. Nangle, that when I fell below to where the dead people end up, I would not be one of the dead. Conall was dressed as the other priest you see, they somehow had engineered my escape, but I cannot tell you how, for only they know. But I was carried out as though I was dead. I was carried out covered in straw and put in the back of a cart. I remember being lifted by several arms and being covered in straw and placed into some kind of cart and it began to move. I thought I was dead and in a hearse wagon. Then I felt terror like nothing on earth, as I believed that I was being buried alive. Perhaps whoever they were, did not know I still breathed. I cannot tell you what went through my head. I felt straw get into my mouth, I tried to struggle and cry out. There was a foul smell and I remember pain in my head and my neck, then nothing after that until I awoke in this place, where I still am.

I woke here in this room. Both my head and my neck ached terribly. I opened my eyes and I felt comfort. I felt softness underneath me. I moved my sore neck and head to the left and there was water and I lifted myself slowly up from the bed and put my hand out and picked up the jug and drank from it. The water splashed onto my chest wetting my dress and it ran down my chin, and I continued to drink thirstily. Then I lay back down and slept again. The next time I awoke I sat up in bed and glanced around me. It did not feel like I was at home, yet it felt familiar to me. I did not feel afraid. I had a feeling of security, as though I was safe in this place. I moved my legs to the left and put my feet on the solid ground and I stood up. I was wearing a black dress to my ankles and my feet were bare. My hair hung heavy around my shoulders and I reached up to touch it. I knew it was my hair, and this was my body. But I did not know my name, only that I knew I should have had one.

I did not feel afraid. I felt, more like a calmness one feels after they have been through something that had scared them, but it turned out to be alright. However, I was very aware that something was amiss and I should not be here, in this room – and I should know who I was. I walked around the small room, touching everything. I touched the table, a chair. I touched dishes on a dresser and discovered I could also reach the ceiling with just an outstretched arm. I walked to the door. I opened it and looked outside. I could see it was early morning. I heard birds and saw there was a path outside the door. It was mucky and my door was the only one along a high white-washed wall nearly half a mile long. Opposite the mucky path were high trees amongst wildflowers and it looked like the beginning of a forest. Outside my door was a huge black rain barrel and I put my hands into it and drank and washed my face. Then I went back inside the place. And this has been my home ever since.

I can only describe those first days as a child being born, unknowing where they have arrived and how.

We have no idea what their thoughts are, or indeed what our own thoughts were at that time, just that we survived them and forget them later. It was like that for me. I barely remember much of it and just like when a person is unconscious, or in a coma, they do not have any memory, just flashing images and recollections they can't tell are dreams or reality. Perhaps it is God's way of protecting us. I like to think it is.

I slept a lot. Food appeared and I knew not where it came from. I would wake and it would be there, on the table where we both had sat together so many times over a pot of tea. Days passed and I could not tell you how I filled them. I felt as though I was waiting, for somebody or something. I cannot explain it, but there was very much this strong feeling of expectation and I often stood at the door and looked up and down the track, but I did not know who I was searching for. I had that feeling of leaving something very important behind, like the feeling you get when you have gone out and are unsure if you left a pot boiling. But I could never acknowledge what it was I had mislaid, or forgotten. I was no longer the girl I used to be, but a whole new person who had been through a terrible darkness, but mostly, I began to learn who I now was, and who I would never be again; because to me, Maggie McGuill had died. I had no memory of my life before I ended up here, none at all. I had headaches. Not terribly painful, but they made me want to sleep a lot.

☘

I had lived in this way for many years and I was content. The day of the torrential storm something sparked in my mind and everything came back to me. One of the people who arrived to do repairs to my little home, was somebody I remembered or recognised. It was a slow awareness. Not a 'light-bulb moment' as you used to say. The storm had battered the door all night. It had never closed properly and for this reason, I would put a chair against it before going to bed. Not because I was afraid of somebody breaking in, that would have been futile – but because the door often banged if there was a wind and woke me up. During the night in question, a loud crash woke me and when I put my feet on the ground to investigate, water reached over my ankles. I quickly put a coat over me and shone a torch around my home. I saw, to my distress, it was completely flooded and some of my meagre belongings were floating along in the water. I began to pick up bits and pieces, placing them up high, on top of the dresser, the bed and the wardrobe. There was little point in trying to prevent any more rainwater from getting in, so I simply sat on my bed with my feet up and waited. I eventually fell asleep and then woke to somebody shaking me.

'Lise,' a voice asked. 'Are you alright?'

It was a woman who lived nearby and called to see me sometimes. It was she and a few others in the area who kept me in food and other necessities.

'Yes,' I replied. 'I am absolutely fine.'

'But your home,' she answered. 'It is flooded. You can't stay here. Come with me and we will get you sorted out.'

'No!' I cried out, in terror. 'I will stay where I am. It will dry up and everything will be alright.'

I could see her and the other woman named Joyce looking at each other. Ana shrugged her shoulders. They knew I found it impossible to go further than the length of an acre from where I lived.

'Look,' Ana said. 'Patsy and Ernie will do what they can here but you need to be out of their way so they can fix the place up a bit and get it dried out.'

'I know,' Joyce said. 'Our caravan. Can't Lise stay in that until the men finish what they have to do here?'

‘Great idea,’ Ana answered. ‘Get Patsy to drive it over and park right outside. How does that sound to you, Lise? Would that be alright?’

I nodded my head and thanked them. The women left and very soon afterwards I could hear the old caravan pulling up. Patsy came into the room and silently began moving my things out. I had met him before. He had often called to do maintenance work in my home. He was a silent man who never spoke when around me, exactly what I wanted.

But the other man, Ernie, when he came into the room I felt a chill go right through my body. I began to physically shake and Ana started to fuss saying it was the cold and my damp clothes. She bundled me into the cosy caravan and I lay down on the bed listening to the sound of rain pouring on the roof. As I drifted to sleep, Ernie’s face came into my dreams and then the faces of others. And when I awoke, I remembered I hadn’t died at all.

It was not a sudden recalling of my memory, but a slow process. When I returned to my little home I began to go through my sketches and paintings … ones that had been brought to me bit by bit over the years, from where I do not know. I searched first for the one I was looking for, the one of Ernie and I found it quite quickly. He was with another young man and they were crouched down in a grassy meadow with daisies around them and Ernie had his arms around a dog. I looked at the back of the painting and in pencil was written, The Meadow – May 1914 and the initials MMcG. I began to pull out other paintings I had faced towards the wall – mostly because I had previously found they disturbed me in some way, yet I couldn't allow myself to get rid of them. I spent the next few days barely sleeping, just going through the paintings and drawings and bit by bit memories came back. Some paintings made me gasp out loud when I saw them and burst into tears. These were the ones I realised were of my parents, confirmed by names and dates on the back of each one. There were many of these, some with my parents together, some with them on their own. Looking into their faces caused a grief in me I felt would kill me with its intensity. It was almost like a dagger being pierced into my heart.

I could only look at the drawings every few days and in the meantime, I kept them facing the wall, as looking at them still upset me. It was during this time you came into my life and I began to tell my story in pieces as I remembered it. Sometimes you would ask me questions and I was aware I was being evasive, but some things I could still not recall and others I found too difficult to tell you. I was still trying to process everything. When you left, I resolved to ask questions of those I saw in my life. I think they were shocked at first but then they got excited and began to bombard me with so much information I had to tell them to give me time to digest it all. It was the most wonderful time in my life and I thank God he gave me that time to somehow be reborn again, because that is what I had been, Leah. When I came to this place and lost my mind, my memory, my existence as I had known it, I was reborn, with a new name and no past. I had an awareness of another time, another life, but it was like everything was behind a veil in my brain and I did not know how to pull it back. Seeing Ernie that day removed the veil ever so slowly, as though my soul knew if it happened too quickly, my mind simply wouldn't have withstood it.

The day I found the pencil sketch of who I now know as Conall Daly – that day I wept so much. I hugged the picture to my breast and sobbed. Ana found me this way later, curled on my bed with his picture wrapped in my arms and it was she who told me what she knew of Conall, and my ending up where I was. She had been through so much in her own life and when she told me about it afterwards, I cried for her heartaches, as she too cried for mine. She told me when she moved to Aghameen from England, her friend Joyce had given her an account of my story. Joyce was the daughter of Alice, who had been my best friend. Alice and two other women, named Charlotte and her mother, Katherine (or Kate as I called her sometimes) looked after me since I arrived here. Conall (who had been my intended) had to go into hiding abroad because the law was after him for organising my escape. He first went to America, then various parts of Europe, anywhere that wasn't under British control. He did come back when he could to visit me, and he hoped when I recovered I would join him. Unfortunately, I did not recognise him and I am said to have recoiled when he came into my home. I seemed to have a dislike of men! He was broken-hearted and it was he who also brought these paintings and sketches, and the photograph of me he had taken from my home … where Ana now lived. Her husband, Ernie McGuill, my cousin, had been left the farm after the death of his brother and father, Pat-Joe McGuill, in a farming accident.

Apparently I had suffered some sort of brain trauma – either due to being short of oxygen for a while, or a fall – it is unclear – but I did have a head injury when I arrived here first, which Katherine and Charlotte treated themselves. I could not be seen by a doctor or taken to a hospital as there had been a warrant out for my arrest for several decades. I had to be kept hidden. Ana told me the women always blamed themselves for not doing more for me and perhaps preventing my memory loss, but what could they have done in reality? I was so lucky they had kept me alive at all. I feel surrounded by love since the day I had the pictures hung in my home. All the faces and places from my past are looking down on me, and every morning is like a gift with a new memory coming back. I have begun writing my story as I remember it and have a very strong feeling you will get these copy-books some day and write the ending for me … which I feel will not be too long away. I am so happy to have had this wonderful gift of clarity before I join my loved ones, Mam, Dad, Alice, Matthew, Bartle, Sheila, those brave Volunteer men, Charlotte and Kate, even Marley …and who knows, maybe even Conall. The only wish I have before I join them all is that somehow my name would be cleared, that the only evidence of my existence will not be as a woman convicted of the murder of my dear friend, Matthew.

As I write this I am watching a butterfly hover around the table where I sit. I've always felt a kinship with butterflies, as they too undergo a complete metamorphosis in life where each stage is completely different and serves a different purpose. I think perhaps the butterfly is proof you can endure a great deal of darkness and it can still somehow be transformed into something beautiful. Thank you for the time we spent together, Leah, and if I would have one piece of wisdom to impart to you it is this – there are no heroes in a war. There is only death and heartache. I know you lost your parents through another terrible Civil War in our country, a death caused by those who I once fought with in hopes of winning a free country. My parents were killed too, as you know, by the other side – and their side also suffered horrific heartache and loss. Yet we still do not have that united Ireland we made more important than our own lives. Do not do this, Leah. If you have to live someplace else for peace in your soul, do that, as I have done all these years. If you find somebody to love, do not let them easily go, and only allow yourself to be loved by somebody who can give you their whole self, and not put you in second place. Above all, be yourself, Leah. We've always had some sort of affinity with each other and I look on you as the daughter I would have loved to have had, with Conall.

Till we meet again, someday, somewhere. Maggie McGuill (Lise)

Lise was Maggie McGuill! I typed her name into Google on my phone. I knew it was a dead end. She had no birth cert or marriage cert, or any kind of cert to go by that I could find. Then I typed in, Margaret McGuill, 1920s, Aghameen, Ireland and found this.

Margaret McGuill, Aghameen, Ireland. Tried and convicted of murder and treason against the United Kingdom. Sentenced to death by hanging.

My heart skipped a beat. There were reels and reels of information on the internet. I read on. An article from the 1920s showed a horrible photograph in black and white of Lise leaving a cell accompanied by two priests and a policeman. Then it showed an empty scaffold and the heading 'Justice for a heinous murder'.

Margaret McGuill. Born to John-Joe and Brigid McGuill. Aghameen, Province of Connaught, Ireland. Only child. Convicted of murder of an Officer of Her Majesty's Army, 1923. Sentenced to death by hanging.

Said, Margaret McGuill, was convicted of the murder of Matthew Goodville by her own hand. Matthew Goodville, of Goodville Manor, Aghameen and Officer of Her Majesty's Army, was cruelly and unlawfully murdered by Margaret (Maggie) McGuill.

Her Majesty's jury found Margaret McGuill guilty. Witnesses at the court said they saw Margaret McGuill waiting on the Goodville land with a revolver in hand for the officer who had taken his dogs for a walk. It is said she cast blame on him for the death of her parents. Later his remains were found by his distraught Mother, Lady Goodville. McGuills blood-stained clothing and admittance to the crime convinced a jury that she was to be found guilty and the accused was sentenced to death as befitting a murderer.

There was so much information from so long ago and so many witness statements.

'Yes, Sir, I did see Maggie McGuill entering the Goodville property with a revolver in her possession.'

'Yes, the accused shouted 'I shot him. I shot him,' as she ran toward the Goodville home.'

'I believe she was jealous of Mr. Goodwin's paramour, Miss Isabella Thompson. It was a crime of passion.'

'She would never have shot Matthew. He was her friend,' was the only reply from a distressed Miss Alice Daly, friend of the accused.

A male acquaintance of Margaret McGuill upheld her innocence.

There was no body and no funeral. Nobody knows of her burial place. Presumably, it was taken care of by the prison service.

'No. Nobody saw her remains after the hanging.'

'Her death certificate is probably with whoever took care of the papers after the deed was done.'

'Yes. It was true that Count Plunkett called her a true Irish woman and wrote a letter of commendation to her Officer in Command.

'Yes. The letter from Plunkett was unfortunately said to confirm her guilt.'

Whatever happened to Margaret McGuill?

Where are her death records?

Where was she buried?

Why is there no record of Margaret McGuill after her sentencing?

The last known record of Margaret McGuill is that she was taken from her cell at 5.40 am and hanged by the neck until she died.

Witnesses say they saw her being taken to the scaffold. The local priest also confirmed he gave her the last rites.

But what happened afterwards?

There were no witnesses to the deceased body and no witnesses to her burial.

26

Leah
2016

It took me days to read through everything in Grandy's briefcase. I found I had to keep taking long breaks in-between to go for walks and mull over everything. In my sleep, I dreamed of what I had read and during the day I spent time typing everything into my laptop, trying to do so in chronological order, beginning with Maggie's (or Lise's) story. What information I had went back to 1916 when Conall had been involved in the Easter Rising.

I began spending my nights watching any movies I could find from that time and my days reading books on the War of Independence and Civil War, researching interviews from Volunteers in the Military Archives and even visiting Kilmainham Jail where Maggie had been. I shuddered when the guide showed me what used to be the Hanging Room, knowing this was where Maggie had found herself. Seán thought I was becoming obsessed.

‘I know you wanted to throw yourself into this project,’ he said. ‘But there is an actual world going on here in 2016 you are missing out on.’

Rolling my eyes, I picked up another bundle of letters and documents of Grandy’s I was intending taking with me to Aghameen in a few days.

‘Are you jealous of the men I am involved with in the 1920s?’ I joked. ‘Matthew Goodville does seem quite a catch!’

Seán came behind me then where I was crouched over some papers at the opposite desk and put his arms around my shoulders, kissing the top of my head.

‘Do you want me to drive you over there?’ he asked, this time planting a kiss on the back of my neck causing a pleasant shiver to go right through me.

'No. I will need my own car when I am there,' I replied. 'But do come over on Friday evening. I will need your company by then,' I winked at him, reaching behind me and grabbing his tie. 'And I shall require your devoted attention.'

‘And you shall have it,’ he answered, twisting the chair around so I faced him and leaning in for a kiss. ‘I have no intention of letting you disappear out of my life again, as you've been doing since you left here as a trainee journalist, breaking my poor wounded heart.'

I silenced him with a kiss and this time I had no intention of leaving him. Something inside me had shifted, perhaps it was because of Marc, perhaps it was reading all the information from Maggie, but I was beginning to realise that where I wanted to be right now was here with Seán. I also wanted to focus on the promise I made a long time ago to Lise/Maggie.

☘

It was many years since I had returned to my grandmother's home village. There wasn't a huge choice of accommodation, only the guesthouse formerly the hotel I had previously known. It had obviously changed ownership and some renovations had taken place. I booked myself in, remembering the hotel as being a relic of olden times and hoping it still was. Jill was bemused at my 'tearing around the country when you're only home' but she sent me off with a kiss and hug, and made me promise to ring when I arrived. However, now that I was here I suddenly felt completely out of my depth, wondering what I had taken on. It had all seemed so easy in my head or at home while I typed out a list of research.

Here alone in a village where I didn't know anyone and with only notebooks of Lise's story, I realised I had absolutely no idea where to start.

What was I expecting? That people of Lise's past would reappear from nowhere and take me to the places she had told me about? Impossible, as they were all dead now. The guesthouse was the only one in the tiny village, no longer a town, which seemed to comprise one pub, two churches, a graveyard and a small school. Dotted around were surprisingly large houses with intimidating tall iron gates, not at all what I remembered. The entrance to the guesthouse was also guarded by gates that opened easily once I punched in the code given by the booking agent. A sign reminding visitors to 'Please close gates – horses are loose' was taped to a pillar. The long driveway was lined by tall trees, with fairy lights strung on them. As I inched my car along it seemed very grand judging by the lamp-posts guiding my way. A scene dating back to a time when landlords ruled the country was the first thing that came to mind. A huge, centuries-old grand house greeted me when my car eventually reached the visitor's car-park. A lake glittered in the distance and horses galloped freely in a nearby paddock, and when I reached the top step leading to a Georgian door, I found a note.

'Welcome Leah. We are up at the farm. Come and join us if you feel up to it. Your room is first floor, on the right. Left food in fridge. Help yourself. A & J.'

They already seemed my perfect kind of hosts. No weary tour of the house or offers of tea and questions about my trip that I didn't want. I could just get in, dump my bag unhindered, and grab a hot shower without any niceties. That was exactly what I wanted. The door pushed open and for safety, being a woman of the world and so on, I flicked the latch on the inside, checked it was locked and immediately felt I had gone back one hundred years in time. The photos on the website did not do the house justice. This place was amazing. It was definitely Olde Worlde with bells on. The bed was so soft and it felt like my whole body sank into a cloud. My last memory was putting my hand out to feel for a socket to charge my phone and then exhaustion overcame me.

☘

It was still not completely dark outside, so thankfully I hadn't slept the whole night away. Even though it seemed like I'd been asleep for an eternity, it must have been only an hour or so. It felt eerie being in the house alone. Remembering I had a jumbo-size bag of crisps and a can of Coke in my car, I quickly ran outside until realizing I'd forgotten to take down my keys. Then to make matters worse, as is typical of the calamities I sometimes have, I knew I couldn't get back into the house because I had put the latch down and the door had shut tight.

Now what? I was stranded outside in a thin dress, in weather that was starting to turn nasty with only light, black pumps on my feet. No phone, no money, no keys and no way into the house. After checking the back door and windows I was faced with two choices. Should I wait in one of the stables or sheds for the owners to come back, or should I walk to the farm where A & J had said they would be? I had no idea where the farm was or what was going on there. As I meandered down the tree-lined avenue I noticed the twinkling fairy lights had been switched off, which only served to make my walk more difficult. Thankfully there was a full moon lighting my path. The air was still with just the sound of cows lowing nearby and as I opened the gates with the code I hesitated, unsure of which way to turn. I recalled one of Grandy's silly sayings 'If you don't know which way to go, turn right.' Then I would ask why and he would explain with a wink 'Because it's the right way to go.' We shared many of these little jokes between us and some of them even made sense! So, naturally, I took the turn to the right and hoped it wouldn't let me get lost.

There was no footpath and I felt a bit uneasy walking on the road, so I kept close to the low stone wall on my right. Used to the busy city streets, I was unaccustomed to not having any traffic speeding past and was thankful for it. To my right was an old abbey surrounded by gravestones, causing me to shudder as every horror movie I'd ever watched flashed through my mind. I presumed it was the same abbey Lise had told me about and vowed to have a look around it at some stage. Definitely not in the dark though! The walk was pleasant and I was admiring the unspoilt view when I heard the sound of galloping hooves coming behind me.

☘

I noticed lights ahead and quickened my step. A & J had simply written they would be at the farm, but was this it? Smoke billowed from a chimney and a large crowd of people were gathered around a doorway, some smoking and others quietly talking. As I grew closer, they parted to let me through the open front door. Instead of going into what sounded like a full house, I approached one of the people outside. In the dark, it was almost impossible to see who exactly I was talking to. Everyone was in dark clothing.

'Excuse me,' I asked. 'I am looking for the Purcells. Are they here, please?'

A man turned in my direction. 'Purcells? I've never heard of any Purcells around here.'

'They are from the Big House, beside the abbey. Andrew and Janet,' I replied, hoping I was at the right place.

'I don't know who they might be, but there were some staff from the Manor here earlier and they just left.'

'Oh? I didn't pass them on the road.'

'Ah, they probably took the path through the field,' the man answered. 'It is quicker and safer that way. You never know who you'd meet on the roads these days. They'd be home by now, I am sure.'

Perplexed, I looked about me and indeed noticed some people taking a route through a gate dividing the garden from an adjoining field. Suddenly the heavens opened and a deluge of rain caused the crowd to either run down the pathway I had just walked up, presumably on their way home, or shelter inside the house.

'Get in Miss!' somebody shouted from a shed at the side of the house, where they were standing out of the rain. 'You'll be soaked through.'

I shook my head at the man holding the door open. ‘No, thank you. I think I’d better get back.’

‘Here,’ he said, retrieving an old coat from a hook inside the shed door, and threw it out to me. ‘You can return it another time. You’ll catch your death in that dress.’

The coat smelled old as though worn by many bodies. Not unclean as such, but it had an odour like my grandmother's dressing-up box, of clothes that held many stories, been many places and seen many things. There was a faint smell of the tobacco Grandy once smoked. It was difficult to tell in the darkness if the coat belonged to a man or woman and I discovered trying to put it on, that it was inside out.

'Wait there, Miss,' the man shouted, as I began to walk towards the path where the others had gone. 'I'm going that way if you want to walk with me and the wife?'

‘Oh, yes. Thank you,’ I replied, grateful I didn’t need to venture into the dark forest alone.

‘Did you know them well?’ the man asked, as his wife walked behind, sounding as though she was quietly crying.

‘Them?’ I asked, picking my feet carefully through the damp grass.

‘The deceased,’ he added, with his head down as he walked in front of me, also watching where he was stepping in the darkness.

‘Wait,’ I said, stopping in my tracks and looking around. ‘This is not the right place.’

Both the man and woman stopped walking and looked in my direction. I could not see them properly, just two old white faces, one under a black hat and the other under a black scarf.

‘Where is it you want to go to?’ he asked patiently, even though the rain was pouring down on the three of us and his wife was shivering with the cold.

‘The guesthouse.’

‘The what?’ He stared like I spoke another language.

‘The Big House at the lake,’ I told him, beginning to feel a creeping sensation that all was not right.

‘Ah, yes. I know where you are going. Sure, it’s only another few steps.’

He stopped walking again and looked once more in my direction.

‘Are you lost?’

I nodded. ‘Yes. I seem to be.’

‘You must’a stood on the stray sod,’[55] he said.

‘I did what?’ I asked.

‘The stray sod,’ he said. ‘You must’a stood on it. You’ve lost your bearings like.’

‘Will you just tell me where I am? Please,’ I asked. ‘Nothing looks familiar to me.’

'Well, right now, you're on McGuill land. Belonging to the couple that was killed?'

This time it was I who stood still in my tracks. ‘Which couple?’ I asked.

'The McGuill couple who were shot by the Tans. Miss Margaret was saved thankfully, but people say she lost her mind with grief. It's hard to know if they were brave or foolish hiding those men as they did. There's the house,' he said, pointing where the guesthouse sat surrounded by trees and the lake shimmered in the moonlight.

---

[55] *In ancient Celtic mythology, specifically Irish folklore, a stray sod is a clump of grass enchanted by faeries. If a person steps on one, they will become disorientated and lost, even in familiar surroundings. Wearing an item of clothing inside-out breaks the enchantment, allowing the person to find their way again.*

‘We’ll say goodnight to you now, Miss,’ he said, tipping his hat and walking into the darkness, before I had a chance to ask him more about the story he had told me. I’d say he was glad to be rid of me.

Tiptoeing my way to the edge of the lake, I felt the uneven stony ground under my feet and was grateful I hadn’t worn stiletto heels. It was so quiet. A full moon and thousands of stars were reflected on the still water almost next to my feet. How cold it was. Finding pockets, I pushed my hands inside. They were empty, except for a hole in the left one. Feeling something rustle against my leg, I lifted the bottom of the coat and with my right hand patted the lining on the inside. A tissue I supposed. My fist curled around whatever it was. It felt more like paper. Reaching inside the left pocket, I worried my fingers further into the tear until eventually I got my whole hand inside. Digging deep, I pulled out a page and held it under the light of a full moon.

‘Matthew Goodville’ was the heading in golden type. There was a family seal and address centred under his name; Goodville Manor, Aghameen, County of Leitrim, Ireland. The page was embossed and good quality. The top left of the page was slightly torn and had an oily thumbprint on it. Further down the page a message was handwritten in ink, in neat scriptwriting.

Field. 3 pm. Shooting practice. Bring the web.

M

Frowning, I turned the page over. Nothing on the back. 'The web' I read out loud. What on earth did that mean? Folding the page I put it back into my pocket and stood at the lake's edge, admiring the starry sky, something seldom visible in the busy city I was accustomed to. This is what is really meant by pitch black, I thought. The only small bit of light came from the stars that looked so close, almost within an arm's reach. It looked as though I could simply put my hand into the dark abyss and pluck a star from that inky blackness with my fingers. Would they burn, I wondered? Are stars hot to touch? Raising my arm, I smiled. Amazing to think I was here in this place where Maggie, one time stood. How extraordinary to think of all the events those very same stars had witnessed, the wars of the past and the many different lives, all under an Irish sky.

Thankfully the front door was open this time and I was happy to note there were dimly lit lights on. From the outside I could see shadows moving behind net curtains.

'There you are,' the plump, matronly-looking woman exclaimed, shaking my hand when I walked through the door. 'I thought you'd got lost.'

I smiled, relieved at finally meeting one of my hosts.

'Not yet,' I replied, too tired and bewildered to say a word.

I wearily entered the bedroom without turning on a light and crept into bed, pulled the blankets over my head and dreamt I was back in civilisation.

27

Leah
Aghameen

It was the birds that woke me and I welcomed the sound rarely heard in the town I left the day before. I sat up in the high bed, rubbed my eyes and fumbled for a light switch. I stretched my arms over my head and looked around the room I had checked into the last night. My wheelie suitcase was open on the floor with clothes discarded around it. I felt like I had slept for years and put my hand out for my mobile phone, always near to me. Turning on my phone I saw that it had gone into reset mode. It was impossible to know what time it was with no clock around. I needed an upgrade, but when I got used to an appliance I was reluctant to change it for a newer version unless mine was broken beyond repair.

Unable to find either a socket or light switch, I went into the adjoining bathroom, admiring the free-standing bath and the olden style décor. However, I was not so happy to see there was no shower. I turned on the bath-tap and luckily hot water ran through it, but there was an awful roar, making a sound like thunder. After just a few minutes and another roaring sound, the hot water trickled to a stop, but enough for me to have a hip bath in at least. Later, when changed into a simple black dress and tights, I took the stairs to where I had remembered the kitchen was the night before, expecting to find A or J! On descending the stairs, I reached the hallway of black and white tiles and the front door was open. I could see horses in the paddock and hear dogs barking in the distance, but nobody was around.

I entered the kitchen. A freshly baked loaf of bread was on the long oak table beside a teapot. I felt it. It was warm. I picked up a teacup laid out with a plate, a knife and a boiled egg in an egg cup. Hungrily, I quickly picked the cold, hard egg from its cup, peeled and smashed it with my fork, as I liked it. I spread egg over a slice of the bread, added some salt and welcomed the freshness of both. The tea was strong and to my surprise, it had been made with tea leaves, but thankfully my invisible host had left a fancy, silver tea strainer for my use. The kitchen was exactly the type I would have chosen if I ever decided to upgrade Grandy's house. All the pots and pans were on show and dishes were displayed on a dresser. The teacup was vintage and the jam I planned on having after my delicious egg, looked homemade. It was in a glass bowl, covered in a gingham cloth and I could smell the freshness of the fruit.

There were footsteps and I sat up straighter, wiped my chin in case of any egg stains and waited to see who would arrive. I heard somebody kick boots on the outside wall before entering the kitchen. It was the man who had accompanied me back to the guesthouse last night. He sat ungraciously on the seat opposite and looked expectedly at the teapot on the table. The man was younger than I had thought, perhaps in his forties, but he looked weather-beaten and his clothes more those of a tramp. His working gear I presumed.

'Would you like a cup of tea?' I asked.

He nodded. 'I'd like nothing more.'

I stood and removed a cup and saucer from the nearby dresser and began to pour tea through a strainer from the pot. I placed it in front of him. He waited.

'Milk?' I asked.

He nodded and as I poured, I felt him watch me.

'Did ye sleep well?' he asked, taking a sip from the cup.

I nodded my head. ‘I did. Thank you.’

He waited for more information and as I was unwilling to offer any, he drank his tea silently for a few minutes as I continued with my breakfast, feeling uncomfortable as one does, eating while somebody watches.

‘I’m going into the village if you are wanting to go?’ he asked, putting his cup down on the saucer with a heavy hand.

I did and nodded my head to acknowledge the fact.

'The name is Mick O'Connor,' he said, with a look that requested I tell him my name.

‘Leah Kennedy,’ I answered.

‘Are you here for the writing and reading?’ he asked, his eyebrows raised.

‘I am. I’ll just get my bag,’ I added, getting off the chair and going in the direction of the stairway.

'I'll wait outside so,' he answered and also stood up.

It was something as simple as the smell of the air that made me realise with sounding clarity, what I had subconsciously refused to acknowledge. I still refused to acknowledge it as I climbed up onto the horse and cart Mick had waiting outside in the courtyard, because to acknowledge it was something I could not do. Not yet. As we travelled the tree-lined avenue and exited onto a dirt track road, I felt a shiver go through my whole body as I realised I was no longer in the world I was accustomed to. I should have felt terrified, but I wasn't. Perhaps I was in some kind of trance. But I felt strangely calm, too calm maybe as I took in the scene around me. I didn't even know who the man was. Was he a workman for the house? He said he was driving a pony and trap, not a horse and cart. I knew this because to break the silence of the journey to the village, I had asked the name of his horse. He'd laughed.

'She's got no name,' he said. 'And she's not a horse. She's a pony.'

I commented then on how comfortable his cart was and he said it was a fine trap, and had taken him on many a trip. It felt as though I had wandered into a film set of bygone days. Maybe I had. Maybe was something I kept saying to myself over and over. Maybe I am dreaming. Maybe I am in a strange kind of hallucinatory experience. But it didn't feel so, because I could smell what the pony had just dropped. I could hear the chatter of the people in the village and

I could feel the man's hand in mine as he helped me off the trap, and it was warm, calloused and kind.

'I have a few errands to run,' he said. 'But I'll be back in …' he looked around. 'Ah, I'll leave word if you're waiting on me, I'll be told.'

He walked off then and within seconds was lost among the crowd gathered around the tall clock in the middle of the town square. I didn't know which way to turn or what to do or what to feel. So, I walked to the only place a woman will go when she doesn't feel safe on her own and that was towards another group of women. Then I knew for sure I was on the stray sod, as Mick had said. As I neared the chattering group gathered around a fish stall, I began to walk slower to better observe the clothes they were wearing. As a lover of all things vintage, I was mesmerized by the cloche hats and leather ankle boots; the poorer-dressed women wore shawls and long dark skirts with high-necked blouses. Two women walking slowly past me were dressed in long skirts that were higher over the ankle and more colourful, with one of the women wearing a long, velvet dark blue coat that I couldn't take my eyes off. It was beautifully embroidered with bright flowers on the lapels and as she walked by me I noticed her blue hat was also velvet and embroidered with flowers to match her coat. Despite my fears of what was happening to me and around me, I vowed no matter what, I was going shopping, somehow! Well aware I had no money that would be acceptable, I hoped whatever fate had in store for me would include an opportunity to buy some vintage clothes!

The first time he touched me was when I felt his hand on my cheek. It was warm and it revived me. He had a hat on and in the bright sunlight I could not make out his face, but immediately felt I could trust him. He held me because I cried, aware I spoke incoherently. I was tired and said I wanted to go home, but even saying it made me cry more because I believed I had no home to go to and I didn't understand anymore what was happening to me.

'Are you quite alright, Miss,' I heard a concerned voice ask. 'May I be of assistance to you?'

I felt strong arms lifting me from where I had fallen on the dirty, dusty road. A group of women gathered around me as I was manoeuvred into a seating position on a low wall surrounding the town clock, while the strange man kept a hand on my arm.

'I am fine. Thank you,' I answered, looking at my grazed palms and wondering what had happened to me.

‘You got knocked over by that billy-goat,’ a woman told me, pointing to my assailant, now being tied to the back of a cart.

It would have to happen to me, wouldn’t it? It wasn’t enough I somehow seemed to be back one hundred years in time, but then of course, I had to be almost killed by a goat! Who would ever believe it? Spontaneously and surprisingly even to myself, I began to laugh and when I started, I couldn’t stop. Tears ran down my face as I clutched my sides, but the tears of mirth quickly changed to real tears and before I knew it, I was sobbing my heart out.

‘Can I get you something?’ he asked. ‘Or someone? Can I find a family member for you?’

‘I don’t have … have any …’ I cried out, with both tears and nose running at this stage. ‘I am stuck in the wrong time. I want to get out. I want to go home. I don’t know what is …’ I was not making sense either to myself or the bystanders by now.

‘Oh, my dear,’ an elderly lady exclaimed, putting her arm gently around me, while the man rubbed my back as though I was a child being winded.

‘She’s in shock,’ another woman whispered. ‘She needs a sup of something strong.’

‘Or should I fetch a doctor?’ the man asked, looking about as though expecting to see one nearby.

‘No!’ I cried out. ‘No doctor!’

'Can I offer to take you home then at least?' the man enquired. 'Where do you live?'

‘I am staying at the Manor House beside the abbey. Do you know it?’ I asked him, trying to wipe my face with my sleeve.

‘Oh, yes. I know it well,’ he replied, smiling at the other ladies standing around, who were watching the spectacle I was obviously making. ‘I will retrieve my car and return to you in a few moments. Ladies, would one of you please remain here until I return?’

On securing a companion for me, the man left and returned minutes later in a wonderful car. I had only ever seen one like it in a period drama movie and couldn't wait to get inside. The man helped me climb into the back of the car and then took up a position at the front. I actually would have preferred to sit in front also, to better see the workings of the vehicle, but I presumed this was the norm for the lady to sit in the back if she was not known to the driver. The seats were of shiny leather and I could smell polish from the interior. The upholstery was spotlessly clean and I imagined this was a car well looked after. Everything seemed to gleam.

'Is this a new car?' I asked, breaking the silence, as he had not uttered a word since we began the journey.

'It is relatively new,' the man replied. 'I bought it almost a year ago from Dan Leavy's in Dundalk. He is the closest Ford Dealer. It's the new Model T Ford with an electric starter and lights. Do you like her?'

'Her?' I questioned.

'Yes. All modes of transport are called her. Cars and boats too, of course.'

'Oh, I had forgotten that. And aeroplanes.'

'Aeroplanes? I suppose they would be also. Tell me, have you flown in many aeroplanes?'

'Too many I am ashamed to say,' I laughed. 'But they are so bad for the environment.' Then I realised my mistake.

He also laughed. Assuming, I imagined, that I was joking.

'Oh, I doubt a handful of aeroplanes will make that much difference to our environment.'

I smiled to myself. Oh, I love your naivety, I thought. I sat back and lapsed into silence, revelling in my unusual transportation and as I had done on the journey this morning, I enjoyed watching the unspoiled countryside as I passed by. Used to seeing the ruins of old stone cottages which pepper our Irish landscape, it was a treat to see them in their prime. Some were thatched and proudly showed off white-washed walls with lace curtains at the windows and looked exactly like the idyllic tourist cottages I had seen in the village of Cong in Mayo, where the Quiet Man movie was set. Some buildings were made of brick with black slated roofs. Others appeared to have a public house on one side with a shop on the other. Smoke swirled out of chimneys and there was a distinct smell of turf. I was surprised at the amount of people walking about or on bicycles. He dropped me at the entrance of the Manor and I couldn't remember if he offered to walk me to the door because I was too tired and my legs just made it to the room where I had wakened that morning. And I slept.

28

Leah
Aghameen
2016

I woke to the sound of my mobile phone ringing. Sitting on the edge of my bed watching the light shining from it, I saw Seán's name glaring from the screen. I answered and told him all that had been happening to me, and he said 'I believe you, Leah. I believe you.'

When I woke again, my phone was gone and I waited, because I had no idea what else to do or what was going to happen next. To accept what my conscious mind was telling me, would only affirm something I could not comprehend. It would contradict any of my personal conventional beliefs and above all, would be much too distressing to acknowledge. It sickeningly made me think of a chicken with its head cut off, yet still running around, unaware of its death and disbelieving its plight. How could it ever possibly be real? Used to working with facts and evidence of proof as I was – this new reality was way out of my comfort zone. It was incomprehensible. For this reason, up until now, I had stubbornly refused to countenance the incredible fact I was no longer inhabiting 2016 but somewhere in the 1920s. However, it had become impossible to ignore.

Now that I had finally yielded to the extraordinary circumstances I had found myself in, my customary reaction was to think firstly as a crime journalist. That meant I had to conduct and gather research, make a hypothesis and test it through various means such as statistics and data, formulating conclusions based on evidence gathered. However, my body had finally caught up with my brain and I realized I was beginning to shiver uncontrollably. A feeling of fear I'd never experienced rushed like molten lava through my veins, causing a rise in both my temperature and blood pressure. As my heart began to pound and a ringing noise sounded in my ears, I experienced the instinct of whether to fight or flight and so I ran - down the wide-stepped staircase, out through the opened front door and across the cobbled courtyard until I reached the edge of the lake, suddenly coming to a halt. Wrapping my arms tightly around my upper body to stop the shivering, I attempted to recall the advice given when having a panic attack; 5,4,3,2,1 – 5 things you could see, 4 you could say, 3 you could touch, 2 you could smell, 1 you could taste. Or was it something you could hear? Yes, it was something you could hear, not say.

Okay, I thought, still holding my arms around myself; I can see the lake, the sky, clouds, birds and my feet; then realised when I looked down I had run out without any shoes. Touch; I can touch my hair. I dipped one bare foot gingerly into the lake. It was freezing. Then I leaned down and touched the grass at the lake's edge. I could smell smoke from a chimney and rain. I know people laugh when I say I can smell rain. I really could, but don't ask me to explain it. I could also smell if somebody was pregnant, that was easier to explain. It is kind of a milky, warm smell and I could likewise smell if somebody was seriously ill. That odour is musky and a bit woody. Mum and Dad had grown used to my idiosyncrasies, saying it was like having their own little fortune teller in the house. It was particularly useful for predicting the weather when Dad had wanted to go fishing as I could also smell if a storm was imminent! Friends often made fun of my eccentricities, calling me The Sorceress. They'd even bought me a little silver brooch of a witch on a broomstick as a birthday gift one year. It was quite a conversation piece!

By now my breathing had become almost normal and I began to slowly walk back towards the large house. And as for what I could taste – it was metal. That was the taste of fear. The scientific explanation is anxiety causes your mouth to become dry. Combined with the chemicals released in your brain when you get an adrenalin rush, it creates that metallic taste. At least that phenomenon could be rationalized.

During my walk the first evening I arrived at the Manor House things began to get odd. When I put the old tan gabardine coat on at the McGuill house and followed the older couple back to the Manor, I knew something was strange. Even the very air smelt different, but I didn't let myself dwell on it as it was much too bizarre to be real.

☘

What happened next? He was in the house - the man who had left me home. Not the man with the pony and trap, but the man who had put me in a big shiny car the day before and taken me here. He was standing in the hallway when I came downstairs wearing the black dress and tights I had worn the day before and slept in. Unable to say a word I simply sat on the third last step, staring at him. Oh God, he was handsome. He was straight out of one of those black-and-white movies. Clark Gable eat your heart out, was the first thought I had. To me, he looked just like those photos I had seen of Michael Collins. He wore a dark suit, starched collar, tie, and a fedora hat. The whole works. But he was even more handsome than Michael Collins, and he was alive and standing there in front of me with a concerned look on his face. The first thing he said was 'Good morning, Miss. May I ask your name?'

'Leah,' I replied, then added a cursory 'Good morning.'

'Do you have a surname, Miss Leah?'

I smiled.

'Yes. Leah Kennedy.'

He lifted his hat and tipped it, just like in the old movies.

'Matthew Goodville,' he replied.

☘

How can one possibly tell another person you are from the future, from a world one hundred years later than now? In those times people got locked away for the rest of their lives for showing any kind of mental illness, especially women. There was no way I wanted that to happen to me. I mean, imagine being locked up in a mental asylum, one hundred years back in time. It would be just my luck, I thought. I had debated whether to show Matthew my mobile phone and laptop, but what if they didn't turn on? He would be perplexed by the design of them, but that could be explained. Other things I had in my luggage that could prove my story would be the novel I was currently reading, with the date printed on the inside, but even though the cover was modern, it could still be explained. There were other things like my contact lenses, modern makeup, clothes etc, but I needed more proof if I was to try and make him believe my story.

The fear of being classed as mentally ill and being incarcerated in one of those awful asylums made me too afraid to divulge anything. Thankfully, being a woman who had a love of vintage, a lot of my clothes were from bygone days. I might be able to pass for a woman of the era, though if they saw my underwear, particularly my Mickey Mouse nightdress, it might cause an eyebrow to be raised. Was the famous mouse even around then? I doubted it. For now, I decided to keep events to myself. I felt almost as though I was in a novel and was waiting to find out where the author was taking me next. It was terrifying, yet strangely exciting at the same time. Mostly, I felt anxious. That butterflies in the tummy feeling was now a butterflies all over my body feeling and not in a pleasant way. I was tempted to take Xanax which as a sufferer of panic attacks, I always had on my person, but I was afraid it could enhance the strange occurrences taking place in some way and I had enough to deal with right now.

This morning I knew I was back once again in the 1920s, or thereabouts. I was aware this was the town-land where Maggie had lived and so far, the only person I had met who she previously mentioned to me was Matthew Goodville. I began to believe the Manor House I was staying in was the Goodville home, but under what guise I wasn't sure. I hadn't seen anybody else in the house and when Matthew discovered where I was staying, he did not seem the least bit perturbed, as though he was used to strange women being here.

'Are you staying here too?' I asked him.

'I live here,' he replied.

'But how?' I asked, completely confused. 'It is for guests.'

'Well, yes and no. Mother often has lady guests here, as you probably know, for painting and writing and so on. But I can assure you that I *do* live here,' he answered, with a twinkle in his eye and his mouth turned up in a smile.

‘Do you know what date it is?’ I asked.

Looking surprised, he first checked the newspaper under his arm and then replied with ‘it is 7th of September, 1920.’

'Thank you,' I answered, running back up the stairs, very aware of his eyes watching me.

29

Leah
Aghameen
1920s

I went into journalist mode and opened my notebook. I wrote everything that had happened since I arrived in Aghameen. I mentioned every little thing, from the weather and the temperature, to what I had to eat, and then I began to make other notes under various headings - the people I had met so far through this experience or dream or whatever it was, and what they wore. I described the buildings, even the animals I had seen. Again, I made a note of everything I could think of no matter how mundane. This was how my brain worked best – when I could see things written in front of me. I tried to gauge how much time I had spent in the 1920s and how much time in the present, and what times of day I had spent in each. I wish I had the internet so I could Google anything to do with going back to the past, but realistically I know it is only something made up by imaginative authors and movie script writers. It was not possible to go back in time, unless in a dream. Yet, here I was, having what seemed a very real experience.

I wondered if this was just a heightened version of the second sight I have experienced since as far back as I can remember. The first time it happened was when I was only about three or four years of age. I knew my neighbour's baby was dying. While my mother and her friend were sitting chatting in the kitchen I got that cold, shivery feeling I get when around death, or someone/something dying. I wasn't even aware there was a baby, or anybody else, in the house. I remember sitting on my mother's knee, watching the plumes of cigarette smoke swirling in the air when I got a sudden, peculiar chill all over my body. A pull, almost magnetic-like, made me jump from my mother's knee and run into the sitting room, where a baby lay in one of those old-fashioned cribs. I knew instinctively the baby was dying. The awareness was so strong I didn't even have to look into the crib to check. I simply ran back to the kitchen and said 'Baby is dying.' My mother and her horrified friend ran to the baby and I recall there was pandemonium. I was sent to fetch my father and the husband of my mother's friend, both tinkering with a car in the driveway. I still have the vivid memory of the young mother screaming hysterically and bundling the baby into their car and speeding off. For years my mother often recounted the story, telling people how I had saved the baby's life. The baby had almost been the victim of a cot death, and could have died except for my weird premonition. The strange thing was although I knew she was dying, I also knew she wasn’t going to.

These occurrences happened regularly but I thought everybody else experienced the same thing. It was only when I began to get older I realized not everybody experienced these things and actually, it was something viewed as odd or unnatural. So, I learned to keep these incidents to myself, until the day I discovered I had an ally. My grandmother, on my mother’s side, came to visit. These visits were rare since we lived during the terrible time of the ‘Troubles’ and people who lived over the border were very reluctant to travel to the North of Ireland, except my grandfather who had businesses there. However, my grandmother was very nervous about travelling north, so we would usually make the journey to see her instead. On this occasion, she was making the trip for my First Holy Communion. Nothing, not even the fear of bombs falling, would make her miss that.

On the way to the church, in one of my grandfather's fancy new cars, I began to kick up a fuss that I didn't want him to drive a particular route. My parents, who sat either side of me in the back seat, tried to placate me and asked why I didn't want to go the usual way, apologising to my grandfather and trying to explain I was just nervous and never usually behaved this way. My grandmother asked Grandy to pull over as she wanted to talk to me. She lifted me out of the back seat and we walked to a bus stop where there were seats. I remember she put a handkerchief down on the grimy bench so my white dress wouldn't get dirty.

'What is going to happen if we go the way you don't want us to go, Leah?' she asked me.

'Lots of smoke and fire and I will get all bleeding,' is what I remember informing her.

We took another route. Back at our house where we were going to have a party, our neighbour, who had stayed behind to make the tea and sandwiches, informed everybody the court-house had been blown up at 11.45 am, exactly the time we would have been passing on the way to church. She had been worried sick we had gotten caught up in it. Even at the tender age of seven, I understood the significance of this. I remember staring at my grandmother and she had a strange look on her face. Grandy also was ashen, as were my parents. Afterwards, I was on the swing in our small back garden being pushed by my Dad, my grandmother came out and told him she would take over. Before she did, she knelt in front of me taking my hands in hers.

'You are like me, Leah,' she said. 'You have second sight; that means you are a very special little girl because you have a magic gift inside you that comes from God and the angels. It makes you know things and see things other people can't.' I remember nodding my head in agreement and was aware this was a solemn conversation and a private one.

'You can talk to me about this magic, love. But sometimes people might think you are telling lies or making up stories. But I know you aren't. When you get bigger you will know what to tell people and what to keep inside your head like a special secret. Do you understand?'

Again I nodded my head. Throwing my arms around my grandmother's neck I snuggled into her as she kissed the top of my head. My little heart was sore because I already knew I had a special magic secret I couldn't share with her, that she was going to join the angels soon. I was left without my ally but with some little information about second sight. Years later I looked it up in the dictionary and found this. Second sight - *an unusual ability that some people are thought to have that allows them to know without being told what will happen in the future or what is happening in a different place.* However, I took my grandmother's advice and kept my special gift, as she had called it, to myself. Occasionally, I would share some things with my parents. My mother had some knowledge of it because of my grandmother, but the gift had not been passed to her. They say it becomes evident in every second generation and usually the eldest daughter receives it. Mum and Dad joked about it, but there were times when I dumbfounded them and although they may have discussed it out of my hearing, they neither criticised nor acknowledged my so-called gift in front of me.

Over the years, I began to look at it more as intuition or a gut feeling. After getting in trouble more than once at school as a child, for telling what were deemed lies, I also learned more and more to keep my second sight private. And more and more I began to ignore my gut feeling and always regretted it later, especially in matters of the heart. Grandy was used to my grandmother's ways with her second sight and he took my own experience of it with a pinch of salt. After my parents' murders when I went to live with him in the south, I was filled with guilt because I hadn't warned my parents that I had a bad feeling about them being at home that night. I knew if I had warned them they wouldn't have taken me seriously. They definitely would not have gone elsewhere and explained to friends their daughter had a premonition they should vacate their home for the night! But because I didn't tell them, I was saved while they died in the fire.

I didn't speak a word on the journey to Grandy's house and when he gently walked me indoors with his arm around me, I simply sat dumbly on his brown, velvet sofa staring into space. He had no idea what to do with me. My grandmother would have known what to do, but Grandy was totally out of his depth. It was only when I remembered he too was dealing with the grief of losing his daughter, that in my sympathy for him, I jumped from the sofa and ran into the dining-room. He was sitting on a kitchen chair, his head in his hands and tears silently running down his ruddy cheeks. Emphatically, I put my arms around his heaving shoulders and rocked him as though he was the child and I the adult. He kept repeating the same words over and over.

'My little girl. My poor little girl.'

And I knew he was not talking about me. Grandy and I supported each other through our shared grief.

At the funeral we held hands while allowing tears to flow unrestrained. It became our custom to speak openly about our loved ones, often bringing their names into conversation and in this way we slowly learned to live without them and build a new way of living, together. Over time I grew used to missing them and Grandy did the same. We rubbed along very well together. I had made a conscious decision not to be difficult and instead, I felt, mostly later on, I had somehow skipped an important part of my life, those of the rebellious teenage years. Feeling bad about the fact my last conversation with mum had been an argument, for this reason, I avoided any kind of confrontation from then on.

My new school was the same one my mother had attended and for this reason, as many of the teachers were those who had taught my mother, I received a lot of kindness due to her sad death. I breezed through my school years there. I quickly made friends and was envied as I got a dispensation from having to do Irish classes, due to never having been taught Irish in my Northern Irish school. Grandy spoiled me. Birthdays meant being allowed to bring as many friends as I liked to the local hotel for a birthday meal and in those days this was a huge deal. Grandy was quite happy to ferry a gang of us girls around in his car and didn't mind seats getting covered in sand or later on, false tan staining his lovely upholstery.

It was Grandy who taught me to drive or tried to. Always on car journeys, I would put my hand on the gear stick and he would cover my hand with his larger one, showing me how to change the gears when necessary. I loved car trips with him when he would put on one of his tapes of old music, as I called it, usually Frank Patterson or John McCormack. Together we would sing our heads off as we travelled the roads while he visited his many businesses. The song I loved the most was 'Jerusalem' and we would try to outdo each other by seeing who could sing the chorus of Hosanna the loudest. Always it was him. As a chocolate lover, Grandy always had a stash of sweets with him in the glove compartment. He was a stickler for habits and would only ever buy Cadbury chocolate and HB ice-cream. However, he relaxed his rule when I became addicted to Yorkie bars made by Nestle, despite his belief they tasted plastic, although he'd never tasted one himself.

I never thought about how it must have been for my grandfather once again being a parent of a teenager, but I do think he enjoyed it. I know my mother marrying so young and moving to the north broke his heart and I had a feeling although he never said so, I think he blamed my father for her death by moving her to what he called a 'war zone.' He often said I kept him young and I believed it. He struck quite a handsome figure. About six foot three, he dressed impeccably, wearing a suit every day and his shoes polished to a high sheen. A tie always matched his handkerchief and on colder days he wore an old-fashioned fedora hat and great coat. I never saw him in casual clothes in my life and also never saw him in pyjamas. The only concession was his wardrobe for a trip to Rome. For the occasion he had two linen suits made by his tailors with short-sleeved linen shirts – a huge change for him, complete with his Panama hat. He was the epitome of a perfect gentleman – and I vowed to settle for nothing less. A promise I wish I had kept.

30

Leah
Aghameen
1920s

The idea came to me as I lay in bed that night. I had been thinking of my grandmother and our only conversation about our shared gift of second sight, and then I began to think about the fact she would have been alive in these times. Doing the maths in my head I realised she would be now somewhere in her twenties. I knew where she had been brought up as a child because I had visited her home when my grand-uncle, who was her brother, Gerard, had died. It was not very far from here. Sitting up in bed, my pulse racing, it dawned on me if I could only find her, she might be able to help me. By this age, she was well used to her gift and might already be aware somebody would be looking for her, or going to call. That awareness, if it was the same as mine, would give her the feeling of anticipation, a knowing that something important was going to happen. She would be on high alert, waiting for a sign of what it could be. I had this feeling several times already, like the time I had received an offer of a job in Germany. I knew I would soon be getting news that would change my life in some way, but I didn't know what it could be.

Grandy always knew when something was brewing as he referred to it because he said I paced like a cat that could smell a mouse, and my grandmother had done the same thing. That described it perfectly. It took me ages to fall asleep that night, when up to now, despite all that was going on, I was out like a light as soon as I hit the pillow. I found myself trying to think what would be the best way to approach my grandmother if I was able to track her down, until eventually I remembered what she had said to me when I was a little girl.

'If you need me to help you, but you think I won't understand, just say you need to talk about our name.'

It was Shailagh, pronounced Shaylah. It is the Irish name for *from the fairy place*. Both our middle names were Shailagh and my mother's also, down through the generations. With this memory, I was finally able to close my eyes and wait to see what year I would wake up in. Somehow, believing I could have my ally by my side once again made everything thankfully, seem less daunting.

Wakening next morning, I knew before opening my eyes I was back in 2016, as I could hear somebody outside on a ride-on lawnmower. I am quite sure they didn't have those in the 1920s. Immediately, I jumped up and plugged my phone into the socket magically back beside my bed. I got out of bed and plugged my laptop into a socket on the other side and next, I sprinted into the bathroom to avail of the shower which had also magically re-appeared in 2016. After a shower, I was grateful to be able to use both my hairdryer and styling wand and began to feel more like me. The free-standing bath looked lovely, but you couldn't beat the pleasure of a strong, hot shower. Washed, dressed and face and hair done, I sat on the bed and put the laptop on my knee. I was ravenous but thought it best to take full advantage of the wonders of the internet in case I was swept again into a different century.

What I wanted to find out first was the exact address of my grandmother. Logging into the 1911 census I was able to find her quite quickly, including the home address where she had been born. Grabbing my notebook from the bedside locker, I jotted down the information. My next port of call was to look up Time Travel on Google. After reading Stephen Hawking's theory on it, I became more confused than ever. According to him *time travel is possible, and not just in the way we might think. Backward time travel is not supported by Hawking's theories, because new matter (a new you) would need to be created – one existing in the past and one in the present, travelling back in time. This doesn't hold up, because matter cannot be created.*[56]

This made my mind dive into a hundred different scenarios. So, what if I was time travelling to 2016 when I was really living in the 1920s? Although it was only eleven in the morning, I felt that I could do with a strong alcoholic drink. Or a hot toddy at the very least! Venturing downstairs in my stocking feet, I could smell the aroma of fresh bread and my stomach gurgled. Then, I had a sense of *déjà vu*. That was the same smell I had encountered when I came down for breakfast in the 1920s. Oh no, I thought. Not again! Tentatively, I pushed open the kitchen door and yes, my suspicions were correct. The fridge was gone and on the table the same breakfast, a boiled egg, fresh bread and tea, this time on a silver tray. There was the addition of a housekeeper, or cook, in the kitchen.

---

[56] *https://www.pbslearningmedia.org/resource/can-we-time-travel-lesson-plan/can-we-time-travel-lesson-plan/*

Whoever she was, was smiling at me and wiping her floured hands on a long starched, white apron with lace edging.

'Good morning, Miss,' the woman said, lifting a tray from the table. 'I will serve you in the morning room.'

'Oh, this is fine,' I replied, beginning to pull a chair out.

The woman looked horrified and realizing that perhaps I was intruding in her domain, I nodded and said 'Thank you. That would be lovely.'

Following her as she walked down the hall to a front room, I noticed little things I had missed beforehand. First of all, I noticed the wonderful paraffin lamp and gas wall brackets in the entrance hall with their arms forming a loop, gracefully curving down around the glass lampshade with the lamp cradled below. The glass shades were coloured and were extremely ornate, with cut glass decoration that cast wonderful kaleidoscope-like shapes across the white, painted ceiling. I have to say, although the house was still magnificent in 2016, I liked it more in this era. The blinds were gone from the front window and instead long, white broderie anglaise curtains hung down from brass curtain poles with white, wooden shutters pulled back to allow the daylight in.

I once again seemed to be the only guest and was thankful. It would have been extremely difficult to keep up a charade with another human being. The housekeeper did not hang around long enough for chatter, but I noticed she gawped with disbelief at my stocking feet. Thankfully, I was not wearing jeans! They were not a favourite of mine as I preferred long flowing dresses and skirts, though I did wear more conservative trouser suits and skirts when doing interviews for the paper. She probably also disapproved of my makeup. Though not too liberally applied, I remember reading only 'working ladies' painted their faces in these times. I was in the process of lifting a very delicate, china cup to my lips when that familiar feeling of uneasiness came over me, like butterflies were flapping their decorative wings and dancing the Mamba in all my major organs, except, of course, the Mamba wasn't developed until the 1940s in Cuba. However, butterflies were very definitely alive inside me now in the 1920s. I put the cup down and pushed my breakfast dishes away from me. There is no way I could continue to eat when all my nerve endings were in flight or fight mode once again.

As if guided by an unforeseen force, I walked up the winding, ornamental staircase to my bedroom. Of course, the laptop and phone were gone. Stepping into my flat, black pumps, I pushed the page with my grandmother's address into one of the deep pockets of my long dress. Then I made once more for the stairs. Unsure yet of where I was going, I opened the front door, lifted one of the black umbrellas from a hall stand and walked outside.

It was raining softly this morning. Are the Irish the only people who use that expression about rain? Or describe a day as soft also, I wondered? Reaching the gate, I wished I had the use of my phone to open Google Maps. I found out on my internet search this morning my grandmother's home was just nine miles from here, but nine miles is a good stretch of the legs and I didn't think there would be a bus or taxi passing by anytime soon. I knew to walk in the direction of the town and that meant once again taking the right turn past the abbey. The old map I had looked at earlier showed I should then continue across a bridge and keep following the road until coming to the village of Seanchros (Old Cross). In 2016 this village was no longer there, as what was left of it had been demolished to build a motorway. I remembered my grandmother's home was just a little outside the village and down a boreen. I hoped I would be able to find it easily. Grateful for the umbrella, I put it up as the raindrops grew heavier. It didn't take me long to realize that due to a lack of footpaths, my lightly soled pumps had begun to squelch as the dust and dirt of the road mixed with what had become a downpour. This soon developed into a river of muck that I was trying to carefully tip-toe through.

Although the umbrella was strong and very large compared to the small, fold-up handbag-sized ones I was used to, it wasn't long before I was soaked. My long, sopping dress clung to my body and my woollen tights were splashed with mud. It wasn't cold as such, but I did feel extremely sodden and uncomfortable. Trying to keep one eye on the road ahead and one on my feet, I kept walking and it wasn't long until I reached the bridge. At least I knew I was on the right track. As far as I remembered, from the bridge it was approximately four miles to Seanchros village, which meant, thankfully, I was over halfway there. A shout from behind made me turn my head and notice two young people approaching on a pony and trap. They both looked as drenched as me, but they kindly stopped and offered me a lift. The girl looked around twelve and the boy was perhaps eighteen years old.

‘Where are you headed?’ the boy asked.

‘Seanchros,’ I replied. ‘To the McKeown house.’

‘Jump in the back,’ the young lad replied. ‘We are going there ourselves.’

The young girl had remarkably huge, dark eyes with long, thick eyelashes. She didn’t speak a word when I ungracefully climbed into the back of the cart and sat down on a damp blanket covering whatever goods they carried. Thankfully it didn’t seem to be anything alive! Whatever it was felt more like a seat or a long box of some sort. I could only see the back of the teenagers' heads. I must remember not to call them that, I thought to myself. I think that term only came about in the 1950s. The girl had a black shawl wrapped over her head and shoulders. Not even a wisp of hair showed. The boy wore a cloth cap and a dark, tweed jacket with leather patches on the elbows. It reminded me of when Grandy had that done to his suit jackets; the ones he had demoted to wearing if doing work outside, which I had to admit, wasn't very often. He'd always had a man in to do any house or garden maintenance.

As if being in the 1920s wasn't terrifying enough, what happened next was probably one of the most petrifying events of my life. As one could imagine, the pony and cart weren't going at any type of speed. We plodded along slowly on the mucky road while I still held the umbrella above my head with one hand, the other hand holding on to the side of the cart, in a vain attempt at keeping myself steady. As we turned around a bend I heard the young man exclaim, then curse, while the girl sounded as though she had begun fervently praying. All I could hear were the words 'Holy Mary, pray for … something, something … at this hour.'

Turning my neck to see what was going on, I gasped aloud on seeing soldiers standing at a blockade, guns raised and pointing in our direction. For the first time it dawned on me this time was during the War of Independence, one of the most devastating wars in Irish history. My heart began to bang in my chest as judging by their uniform, these were none other than the dreaded Black and Tans.

'Turn round! Turn round!' the girl pleaded.

'I can't,' the fellow replied, pulling on the pony's rein and beginning to slow down. 'They'll shoot us.'

'Oh, Jesus Christ, save us,' the girl cried, beginning to sob in terror.

'Don't worry, love,' the lad said. 'Don't say anything. Try to stay calm.'

I could see the girl's head nod up and down quickly as she clutched the front of her shawl in both fists.

'Halt there,' one of the men shouted, walking towards the cart with two others. They had guns toting at us, as did the others who remained at the blockade.

By now the cart had stopped moving altogether while the driver kept hold of the reins.

'Name, boy?' the man demanded.

'Gerard McKeown.'

I gasped out loud. It was my grand-uncle. It was my grand-uncle Gerard, my grandmother's youngest brother. I couldn't believe it.

'Where are you going, Gerard McKeown?'

'Home,' he answered, his voice unwavering, bravely hiding the obvious fear he must be feeling.

'And where is home?'

'Just a mile or so up the road, down the laneway, beside the schoolhouse.'

'Up the road and down the lane … sounds like some sort of stupid Irish nursery rhyme. Doesn't it boys?'

The others laughed, while one of them began to slowly walk around the back of the cart.

'And who have we got here then?' the man questioned, raising his eyebrows and giving me a lascivious look.

I was completely struck dumb with fear.

'Picked her up on the road,' the young lad answered.

'What's your name then?' he asked me, standing at the rear of the cart.

'My name is Leah Kennedy,' I answered, trying to portray confidence I didn't feel.

'From?' he barked.

'The Manor House in Aghameen,' I answered, hoping they would accept that and not question me further.

'Purpose of your journey?' he enquired further.

'To visit my …' I almost said grandmother. 'To visit my relatives,' I replied.

'And your relatives are?'

'The McKeown family in Seanchros.'

I could see Gerard looking at me quizzically. The soldier standing in front of the cart pointed towards the back of it with his gun.

'What are you carrying?' he asked Gerard. 'Show me.'

'It's a coffin.'

I jumped in shock when I heard that.

'Open it,' the soldier ordered.

'I can't do that,' Gerard replied. 'It's nailed down. Best not to open it on account of how he died.'

'Open it now,' the soldier shouted, beginning to pull Gerard down from the front seat.

The young man jumped down and walked around to the back of the cart, keeping his eyes on the girl in front.

'Who's your friend?' the soldier asked.

'My sister, Mary.'

I gasped at hearing that. Before Gerard climbed into the back of the cart, he reached out his hand to help me climb down. It was shaking. Mary was also beginning to get down from the front seat and then moved towards the side of the road. She had a stricken look on her face. With the point of his gun, the soldier pulled off the blanket covering the coffin. It was made of rough pieces of timber in different shades and must have had a hundred nails hammered into the top.

'Open it,' the soldier shouted, again.

'I've no tools to open it with,' Gerard replied, calmly.

'For Pete's sake,' was the reply. 'Hey, is there anything to prize this open with, in the lorry?' the soldier shouted to the men standing beside it.

'Just a hammer,' they shouted back, after looking inside for a moment.

'Bring it 'ere.'

Handing the hammer to Gerard, the soldier ordered him to break the coffin open, causing Mary to scream out in despair.

'You can't do that. Oh, sweet Jesus, you can't do that,' she cried.

Gerard looked beseechingly at the soldier who roared at him again to open it.

'Break it open,' he yelled. 'Do it.'

'I can't do that,' Gerard stammered. 'I can't.'

To my horror, the soldier raised his arms and aimed his gun at the coffin, pulled the trigger, again and again, peppering the coffin lid with a myriad of holes. What happened then was a furore of ghastly confusion. Some of the things I witnessed seemed to happen in slow motion. Other things came back to my memory later on. How the sight of Mary's almost bald and scabbed head was revealed when the soldier pulled off her shawl as she tried to run away on hearing the gunshots. The bits of wood and pieces of dead body that shot in the air as the soldiers fired bullets into the coffin lid. The stench. The roars of Gerard as he called out for his sister. The slump of her slim body onto the rain-soaked and muddy road as the soldier's bullets tore into her back and her slender, white neck. How quickly Gerard pulled a rifle from under the dead body in the coffin and in less than a minute, two soldiers lay dead just inches from my feet. How speedily the remaining soldiers departed. And then the silence.

I will never forget the wailing, of who I later realized was my great-grandmother, on seeing the lifeless body of her youngest daughter being carried into their home in the arms of her son. Lingering at the gate, I didn't dare go any further. With Gerard, I had rushed to Mary's side, both of us pointlessly trying to stem the flow of blood gushing from her back and neck. We knew she was gone, but instinct made us want to do something for her. I watched helplessly as Gerard gently lifted his sister and I wept as he kissed her tenderly on the forehead. From the front, she looked like she was simply sleeping in his arms, while blood dripped from her body as he slowly walked towards their home.

Numbly I followed, still holding the umbrella in my hand. The pony followed me, dragging the cart behind him. We made a pitiful procession as we passed the neighbouring houses, while people traipsed out of their homes to accompany the sad cortege. And that was when I met my grandmother; as she ran quickly past me towards the front door, her hair flying loose and wearing a light blue, high-necked lace blouse and long dark skirt. She was screaming her sister's name, a sound that reached an even louder crescendo when she arrived indoors where Mary had been carried.

'What happened, in the name of God?' a woman asked, who joined me at the gate.

'It's Mary,' I quietly answered. 'She's been shot.'

‘Jesus, Mary and Joseph,’ the woman replied. ‘Is she dead?’

I nodded my head.

'Oh, that poor child. After all, she's been through.'

I guessed that she referred to Mary’s shorn head, but dared not ask.

‘This will kill poor Kate, after what happened to her husband.’

‘Her husband?’

The woman looked at me derisively. ‘You know, after he was killed at that ambush.’

I nodded my head, not wanting to acknowledge my ignorance of the family history, about which I sincerely realised I was entirely uninformed. All I knew was my great-grandfather had died suddenly and I presumed it had been from an illness. I had no idea he died in an ambush. Also, I was aware there was a younger sister who had died, but again, I wrongly assumed she died from one of those common childhood diseases, as sadly, many young children did in those days. I wish I had asked more questions about my grandmother's family history. However, I knew most people of that generation never disclosed anything about the war. It must have been just too awful to discuss. Like the famine, it was something seen as a stain on our Irish history and repressed, as a way of protecting the new generation.

How awful both my great-grandfather and great-aunt had died in this war and so horribly. Then the thought struck me my grandmother most likely was alert to the fact death was approaching her loved ones and would have been vigilantly watching them, as I would have also done in the same circumstance. Is that why she was out of her home this afternoon? Was she looking for Mary? Trying to protect her little sister from danger? I was about to turn around and begin the long walk back to Aghameen as this did not seem to be the ideal time to meet my grandmother when Gerard came to the front door and began allowing people enter the house. If I walked away now, would it look rude, I wondered. They were expecting neighbours to come in to do whatever it is neighbours do in these situations. But, I wasn't a neighbour. A decision was made for me when the lady I had been talking with took my arm and began steering me towards the McKeown home.

'They'll be needing help with the preparations,' she said. 'And Gerard will have to go for the priest and the doctor. We can't leave them on their own.'

The house was almost as I remembered it when I'd visited as a child. There was a long wide hallway with a low, oak staircase in the middle and two doors on each side of the wall. I noticed the doorway behind the staircase was not there. That was where the bathroom had been, obviously not added yet. All the women entered the room on the right-hand side that I remembered as one large open kitchen and dining/living area when I visited. Now it was two smaller rooms. This room had a huge fireplace that seemed to serve as a stove with all the utensils hanging on a black iron crook over the fire, with various black pots and pans and a well-used, scorched copper kettle. In this room there was also a table with six chairs, a dresser displaying all types of crockery and a sort of wooden bench near the fireplace. Everybody except me seemed to know what to do. Some women went through a door to another room and from what I could make out, it looked like a pantry or kitchen area. Others rolled up their sleeves and pulled chairs out from the table, lining them along a wall and then placed the table in the middle of the room.

‘Is Gerard fetching Mrs. Ward too?’ a voice enquired.

‘Yes, on his way to the priest,’ somebody answered.

‘Is the girl upstairs?’

‘No. She’s in the parlour with Mrs. McKeown and Charlotte.’

‘And she’s definitely …’

‘Yes, dead, poor thing. Sure they riddled her with bullets. The swine.’

I pulled the curtains as ordered by a neighbouring woman and made my way to the fireplace where I’d also been instructed to fetch hot water.

‘And where was Gerard when they shot her?’ somebody asked.

‘He was on the cart,’ I replied. Then I yelped as I burned my hand on the kettle.

‘Quick,’ a woman cried, ushering me to the kitchen area and plunging my hand into a bucket of water on the table. ‘That’ll take the sting out of it while I make up a poultice. You forgot to cover the handle with a cloth … must be the shock of it all,’ she added.

Thankfully, I knew what a poultice was as my grandmother had treated us with them if we had any skin ailments. It was usually a piece of muslin soaked in warm milk or water, with a mixture made up of flour, bread and/or herbs and placed on a burn or rash. Everybody had their own method of making it and my grandmother's consisted of a cloth soaked in a bowl of nettles in warm water; then the cloth was wrung out and used to wrap some kind of concoction my grandmother would prepare. This was then placed securely around the sore and left for a few hours or overnight. It had always worked, without fail.

'You said Gerard was on the cart when Mary got shot?' she asked, bustling about to prepare my treatment, while I sat at a well-scrubbed kitchen table.

I opened my mouth to reply when I heard a voice behind me.

'Who are you?'

It was my grandmother and my mouth went dry. How on earth was I going to answer that question?

'My name is Leah Kennedy,' I replied, quietly. 'Leah *Shailagh* Kennedy.' I emphasized our shared middle name.

My grandmother's cheeks flushed, and then she asked the other lady whose name I now discovered was Mrs. Lambert, what she was doing.

‘I’m going to boil milk for the lady’s hand,’ she answered. ‘She’s just burned it lifting the kettle without a cloth. It was from the shock I told her.’

‘You don’t usc milk for that. I have nettle water that I keep for a poultice. I’ll see to it.’

‘Are you sure, Charlotte? You’ve enough to worry about right now.’

‘I will see to it Mrs. Lambert. Thank you for your help.’ And the other lady left, disappointed I think, on not getting to hear the story my grandmother was no doubt going to hear from me.

After I had relayed the events leading to her sister’s death that Charlotte did indeed ask for ‘without sparing the details' as she said, she turned from the window where she had remained standing looking out, while I told her. Her eyes were red and her face streaked with tears. Wiping them with a handkerchief taken from a hidden pocket in her skirt, she sat down on the chair facing me.

‘Who are you to me?’ she asked.

'I am your granddaughter.'

She didn't flinch but silently stared into my face for what seemed the longest time. I noticed that she too had long, dark eyelashes and dark eyes. Like my own, they seemed at first glance to be brown, but they are actually the darkest green with flecks of dark brown. Exactly like both mine and my mother's.

'So, the *An Dá Shealladh* still surpasses a generation?'

At my questioning look, she added '*An Dá Shealladh* – the Gaelic for second sight. That's where our name Shailagh comes from.'

'Oh, I didn't know that. Then yes, my mother did not have it.'

She smiled. 'I will have a daughter.'

I was about to reply when she put her hand up 'Don't tell me anything about my life. It is not good to interfere with our fate. It is enough to know you will be in my future. That already tells me a lot.'

I nodded. I had guessed she would say something to that effect if ever I met her.

'You will say you are a distant relative, on your way to … let's say Belfast … and decided to call in passing, and had the misfortune to be caught up in the death of my sister.'

Again I nodded. I was finding it very difficult to put into words things I needed to ask her and explain.

‘We will need to get time alone to talk, but it will be difficult today as you can understand. Very soon this house will be swamped with family and neighbours. You are welcome to stay here, or would you prefer I find somebody nearby to take you in. Have you just … arrived?’

‘I am staying at the Manor House in Aghameen. I arrived there a few days ago.’

‘From when?’

‘From when?’ I repeated, confused.

‘What year?’

‘2016’, I replied, finally understanding. She sounded as though this was an event that had happened before, that is, somebody from the future approaching her.

She shook her head, her eyes scanning me from my head to my toes. ‘Incredible. My mind is bursting, but my heart is bursting too and I must return to my mother. She is in an agony of grief.’

‘Of course. I will go back to the Manor.’ Then a thought occurred to me.

‘But, I might, you know … go back to 2016.’

'I think you must stay here. I will say that you have been sent by Cumann na mBan to help the family.'

'Cumann na mBan? Won't I need a uniform?'

'Yes. You can use mine. Come upstairs with me.'

I was astonished. My grandmother had been in Cumann na mBan! It was extraordinary. I had absolutely no idea. Following Charlotte up the stairs I once again had that feeling of *déjà vu*, remembering visiting here when I was a child and following her, just like this, up to what had been her bedroom. That was where I had stayed when I was here as a child. It was the same room and almost completely unchanged. The low roof with white timber beams, the window that you could only see out of if you lay in bed; the same two single beds with brass bedsteads and even the dressing table with a deep dip in the middle and drawers higher up on either side. When I was there it was painted white instead of the dark, brown wood it now was and the colourful eiderdowns currently lying across the beds had been changed to flowery duvet covers. The dark wardrobe Charlotte now opened was not there in my time, instead, there was a built-in wardrobe with pine-slatted doors. My grandmother pulled out a green uniform, complete with brown leather belts of some sort looped around the hook. Looking down at my shoes she pulled a face, then rummaged at the bottom of the wardrobe and took out brown laced-up ankle boots, telling me to try them on.

Sitting on the bed I took off my still wet pumps and loosened the laces on thc boots. They were leather and looked as though they'd been recently polished. If I'd seen them for sale in 2016 I'd definitely buy them, but being 100% leather they would be expensive. About to put my foot inside, Charlotte said

'Take off those wet stockings. You'll get the insoles soaked. They are sopping wet.'

Inwardly I smiled. She already sounded just like my grandmother. Reaching under my dress I began to peel down the black tights, while Charlotte handed me a pair of beige woollen stockings complete with a garter-type thing for holding them up.

'Put them on,' she ordered. Which I did and she took my wet shoes and tights and left the room.

Pulling the damp dress over my head, I let it fall to the ground and removed the uniform from the wooden hanger. I was surprised at how heavy the uniform felt and the material was quite coarse. There was a label at the back of the jacket saying *Made in Dublin by Co-op Workers.* On the jacket lapel was a badge made of silver with the words Cumann na mBan and a motif of a rifle neatly intertwined in the initials. It was an intricate design and although I had seen one of the badges in a photo, I had never seen one in reality and wondered what had become of this one of my grandmother's. There didn't appear to be a shirt or blouse to go with the uniform and when I tried it on, I found the jacket buttoned right up to my neck. It fitted well but did feel quite cumbersome and I had difficulty figuring out exactly how the belt fitted across the jacket. It had a little pouch hanging off it and there was a thicker brown leather belt for the waist. I did like the saddle bag which came with it. Made of pure leather, it was also dark brown in colour with two pouches inside. Again, I wondered what my grandmother had done with it. Sitting on the bed, I pushed my feet into the boots, wincing at the throbbing in my right hand. I guess they didn't have any anti-inflammatory medication in the house. Finding it difficult to do up the laces, I was grateful to see Charlotte (it seemed strange to call her that) arriving back into the room.

'Let me,' she said, kneeling on the floor in front of me and tying up my laces, and to my delight she did them up with 'bunny ears' in the exact same way she would do for me as a child!

'They are back,' I said, pointing out the window. 'It's Gerard with the priest and another man.'

Charlotte turned around to see out the window. ‘It’s the doctor and the old woman getting off the cart, that’s Mrs. Ward.’ I heard a catch in her throat and put my hand sympathetically on her shoulder before she stood up and left the room, telling me as she did to come downstairs when I was ready. Going onto the landing I was met with Gerard once again carrying the body of his sister, this time up the stairs. The priest was behind him, then the doctor. Mrs. Ward was holding on to Mrs. McKeown who was crying loudly.

‘They had it in for her,’ she was sobbing. ‘They had it in for her all this time. My poor girl. My poor daughter. Only thirteen years old. Thirteen years old,’ she repeated.

Standing back to allow them pass, I couldn't help but stare at Mary's shorn head and determined to find out what had made somebody do that to her. I had heard in Lise’s interviews how women who had done something considered traitorous to the Cause had the humiliation of having their hair cut off as a form of punishment. Surely Mary was too young to have been guilty of that? And what did my great-grandmother mean by 'They had it in for her' I wondered. It did not seem to me the soldiers knew either her or Gerard, but perhaps they recognised her name? I had so many questions and just hoped I would be able to find out what had happened. After all, this was my own blood family.

Mrs. McKeown did not even seem to see me when she passed me by, lost instead in her depth of grief as she followed the others into her own bedroom. As the door closed, I made my way to the front room once again and later Gerard came in behind me.

'You said you were a relative?' he enquired. 'I've never heard of a Leah Kennedy.'

'She's father's cousin,' Charlotte answered for me, thankfully, as I had no idea how to respond.

'And you just happened to be passing?' he questioned further.

'No. She's a comrade also, Gerard,' Charlotte replied, again. 'You should know better than to ask too many questions.'

Gerard shrugged his shoulders and went out to the scullery and I heard him opening the back door and going outside.

'You had better remain close to me,' Charlotte suggested. 'With all the people around, you could be asked anything. In these times we are very suspicious of strangers.'

I nodded, gratefully. By now, I had a terrible headache with all the stress of the day. I really wanted to lie down somewhere, take a tablet and sleep it off, but that was not going to be happening any time soon. The whole time since I'd been in Aghameen I seemed to have this strange, aching feeling in my head and neck along with flashes of lights.

'May I have some water?' I asked Charlotte.

She looked at me intently. 'Have you eaten?'

'Not yet today. No,' I replied, realizing that could be the reason for my headache as I tended to suffer from hypoglycaemia if I skipped a meal. I would get a headache and then feel ill and shaky. Normally by the time my legs began to feel weak, it was really time to eat something or I could easily pass out.

'Go into the scullery,' she said. 'There is food on the table there. Help yourself to something and there will be tea too I am sure. There is always tea.'

'Thank you,' I replied and ventured into the scullery where there was already an assortment of food laid out on the table covered with a white linen tablecloth. I noticed how everything in this era was so beautifully made, curtains, bed sheets, and even simple objects like napkins were all exquisitely handmade. They were far superior in quality to the ready-made duvet covers, bed clothes and curtains I was used to.

'You'll have tea?' a lady asked me and already pouring a cup before I even replied.

‘Yes, thank you,’ I answered, helping myself to a huge doorstep sandwich with a thick slice of ham and wedge of cheese inside and a generous helping of butter. Thank God I did not time-travel back to the famine was a thought that guiltily crept into my head.

‘You’re the one who was there when they shot Mary, aren’t you?’ the lady asked and immediately all faces in the small room looked in my direction.

I could only nod as my mouth was full of food.

‘Tell us what happened,’ she coaxed.

I swallowed as quickly as I could and took a long drink of the scalding hot tea. Boy, they sure made it both hot and strong.

‘I wouldn’t like to add to the family’s distress,’ I replied.

The faces looked disappointed, but their owners nodded in understanding.

'Officer Kennedy, my cousin, is here on official business,' Charlotte said, once again coming to my rescue. 'She'll be making a full enquiry and will not be in a position to discuss that.'

I simply nodded my head, trying to look as formal as I could, back straight and making eye contact, but I was an absolute bundle of nerves. In truth, I just wanted to go home and I didn't mean back to the Manor. I meant back to my own world and I was beginning to feel really afraid that I might never do.

31

Leah

Aghameen
1920s

Charlotte hadn't exaggerated when she said the house would soon be swamped with people. I had been to funerals before, but this was in a whole different league. It was a different era of course and the death was a particularly violent and horrendously sad one which caused, despite the many brutal deaths during this terrible War, a monumental outpouring of grief and anger in the locality. After the funeral, I heard about the awful event that had caused my great-aunt to lose her hair.

The story as it was told around the huge open fire-place in my grandmother's parlour made me react so violently, I had to run outside and relieve myself of any food in my body. The words churned my stomach like a Catherine wheel and spewed out of me like putrid poison in a rage like I had never before experienced. I could understand now more than ever the desire to rid our country of those who had delivered this barbarous and inhumane deed on my own blood family members. I also could understand with lucidity why my grandparents had been so against my mother moving to a place where yet another war raged in our country, resulting in their greatest fear – her death. I now knew the reason why my great-grandfather had died in an ambush when beforehand he had no affiliation with the war in any aspect. He was a peaceful, devout man who quietly worked his business and farm, reared his children and believed the God he prayed to would protect him and his own. Until the awful night of horror came to his door, the account I had just heard with my own ears and wished to God I hadn't.

The McKeown home and public house was the largest establishment in the area, located just between the North and South of Ireland, indeed it was hard to tell to which county it belonged. In this prestigious position, it was the ideal place for a barracks and when Mr. James McKeown was approached to release his home to the Crown Forces, he refused the request and was relieved when this was accepted. Or so he thought. It began with small acts of intimidation, the first one being the mysterious poisoning of the family's much-loved sheepdog, Molly. The chicken coop wire was cut and all their poultry was destroyed. A barn was set on fire. Farm equipment was stolen and windows smashed in the bar adjoining their home while they were at church. James McKeown and his son, Gerard, took to sleeping in the cattle shed, guns by their side, taking turns to keep watch. Then there was the night when Gerard woke his father to say there was trouble up at the house. Grabbing guns, the two men stumbled in the dark across the muddy farmyard in the direction of where they could hear the gut-clenching screams of their womenfolk.

'You could hear them from our house,' Mrs. Lambert whispered. 'I thought at first it was the banshee, but then the children came running into our room shouting that something was happening up at the McKeown place. They heard it more because they slept at the front, you see,' she added. 'I'll never forget it as long as I live,' as she blessed herself. 'It took years from my life, that sight. Isn't that right, Harry?'

Her husband nodded, taking a long drink from the porter bottle. Wiping his mouth with his sleeve, he carried the rest of the story.

‘They'd Kate up in the room there,’ he recounted, pointing to the ceiling. ‘Three of them assaulted her and she was in the family way. Another two had Charlotte above in her room and young Mary was lying across just there,' he pointed again at the door leading into the bar. 'Several of them were at her and one of them cutting her lovely hair with a bloodied knife.'

'Then James came in the back door,' his wife continued. 'Sure, I had begun tearing at them with my own hands to get them off her and they belted me.'

'The roars of James I'll never forget,' Harry told them. 'And then Gerard ... he ... well, he was like a man possessed by the devil.'

She nodded. 'It was him more than any of the rest of us that took them all out. I think he'd lost his mind and he probably had. Who wouldn't?'

'He started shooting and of course, the neighbours by then had all started appearing and by God, there wasn't a man left, between them and Gerard, and the father. The soldiers, if you could give them that name, were too out of their minds with lust and drink to have a second to grab their guns. Sure they had raided the place of alcohol and their bellies were full of it.'

Murmurs of assent were heard around the room as neighbours recalled their memories of the horror.

'And poor Mary, God rest her little soul,' another woman said. 'She never said a word the whole time we washed her. Just like a little lamb she was, shivering with the shock and the blood pooled around her in the tub while we tried to salvage what we could of her hair.'

'And Charlotte, all she cared for was her mother,' she recalled. *'We are still alive, Mam. We are still alive. All of us.'* Do you remember?'

'Ay. And Kate lost the baby that night too. The doctor said he'd never seen women more defiled.'

'And now this has happened. I don't think she will ever get over it.'

It was at this point I left the room, my ears ringing with the sound of blood, *our* blood, *their* blood in my body, now pulsing loudly with outrageous indignation throughout my veins. It was Charlotte who came outside to check on me.

'I am sorry you had to hear that,' she said, gently smoothing my hair back from my face. I was sweating as you do after having been sick and felt wretched, never mind completely shocked by what I had just listened to.

‘I can’t imagine what you all must have been through,’ I sobbed. ‘I am so sorry. I never knew. Nobody ever spoke about it. *You* never spoke about it. I didn't even realize this house used to be a public house also. I thought the burned-out building at the side was an old shed or barn.'

Charlotte shook her head. ‘Why would I talk about it?’ she replied, quietly. ‘What good would there be in bringing it all up for anybody? Father and Gerard burnt the bar down afterwards and put the bodies inside. They said the soldiers had broken in and were asleep when the place went up in flames.'

‘But, did you get … I suppose there had no such thing as counselling or anything?’

She smiled. ‘The priest called, but sure, what can a priest say to a woman in a time like that? He couldn’t look me in the face. Mother was too distraught about losing the baby and Mary turned in on herself like a snail going into its shell for comfort. She never spoke a word until Gerard said she did when the ambush happened and she was killed. I know this may seem incredible for you to hear me say of my own sister, but somehow I think it was a kindness in itself. It would have been very quick and no pain, because she lived in silent agony since that night. She had tried to drown herself in the lake on two occasions.’

Putting my hand to my mouth, I let out a cry. ‘Oh, the poor girl. But you seem so … normal now. How do you survive it?’

‘How? I have no choice but to. I have to look after my mother and Gerard and the farm as it's our only income now. I only blame myself for ignoring the feeling that night I had to go away … my legs had … you probably know what I mean … that restless feeling like …'

‘Like shocks going through them and you know you are in the wrong place and have to get away.’

‘Yes, exactly. But how could I tell my family we had to get out of the house? I should have set fire to it … anything to prevent what happened.’

‘It’s just like what happened to my …’ I trailed off and then stopped myself. The last thing Charlotte needed to know was what would become of her daughter.

'Happened to your who?' she asked, with the same questioning look she would give me many times in years yet to come.

‘Happened to me one time when I was young and you helped me.’

She smiled and held me close. 'I am happy that I will do that,' she murmured. 'But please, do try not to reveal too much of the future to me. It is not wise.'

I nodded, enjoying being hugged once again by her and closed my eyes treasuring the moment.

It was Lise. I knew it was, even though she had her back to me, just by the turn of her head and the way she stood with her hands clasped behind her back. Seeing her, stunned me in a way that I had not at all expected. I wanted to cry out and run to her and hug her and touch her face. I wanted to look into those blue eyes and see them as they once were, young, without the lines of age around them and without them having yet seen the things I knew she soon would. Our worlds had collided. What should I do? Should I run over to her and tell her who I was, or would be to her? How could I do that? What could I say that would make her believe me and not think I was some crazy woman? The Lise I knew would believe me, but this Lise, she had not yet lived that life. I heard her voice then. It had the same lilting words. All I heard her say was 'It is surely' but the way she said it was the way she would still say it many decades later.

On her feet were boots, dark in colour and the soles were muddy. Everybody's shoes and boots were mucky today as the rain had come down heavily earlier, but now as Ireland would still do years later, the sun shone as though it had forgotten the recent deluge and already the people who had arrived for young Mary McKeown's funeral were feeling the heat, opening coats and removing wet shawls. Lise had a bicycle with her, painted black with a basket on the front. Inside was some kind of parcel. I inched nearer. She was engaged in chat with two women, one older and one around her own age. I could clearly hear their conversation about a raid on another local pub by the Black and Tans the night before.

'Minnie was inside with the children,' the older woman said, shaking her head. 'It is just shocking. They were told to get out and she had to get the two boys from their beds, not even giving them time to get dressed. She carried young Joseph outside and then went back for James. I don't know how she managed to get them down those winding stairs on her own in the dark.'

'Seamus will be beside himself when he gets the news,' Lise added. 'And the brutes love nothing more than to transfer bad news to a prisoner, knowing they can do nothing about it.'

‘Why did they do it?’ the other woman asked. ‘Seamus is in jail, so he wasn’t their target.’

‘It’s to break him,’ the older woman replied. ‘If they can’t get to you inside to break your spirit or get information, they target your family and home. I just thank God they didn’t burn the pub down with the family indoors. They’ve done that before.’

I looked over at the smouldering ruin of what had once been The Bridge Inn situated on the same side of the road as the graveyard, burned to the ground last night by the Black and Tans. They didn’t give a reason. They didn’t have to and yes, it was surprising they allowed the family to get out first.

‘What about Maureen?’ Lise asked. ‘Wasn’t she there?’

‘No,’ the older woman replied. ‘She went away somewhere on the train yesterday. Dundalk, I think, to visit Seamus. That’s where he is being held. She would have stayed with his family there.’

I noticed Lise and the other young lady give each other a knowing look, that the other woman picked up on.

‘What’s going on?’ she asked.

‘Oh, I remembered something,’ Lise replied. ‘We have a meeting tonight.’ However, Lise and her friend were aware there was a prison break-out planned for Dundalk and the real reason Maureen was on her way there.

‘You are great young women. If I was a young one I’d been in Cumann na mBan too. The men would be lost without you all.’

As the crowds turned to follow Mary's coffin being carried by Gerard and other local men, I too walked behind. Apparently, women didn't usually go to funerals in these times but they were making an exception today given the distressing events. Lise had never mentioned being in Cumann na mBan. I decided if I came across Lise alone I would make an introduction. But perhaps I should check with my grandmother first. She would know if it was the right thing to do. But right now, I stood next to Charlotte and Kate as the priest read words of comfort over their loved one and as the sun shone its rays of brightness on the heads of the mourners I looked over at Lise in her uniform, to find she was staring straight back at me.

It was later at the house when Lise first approached me and I stammered foolishly when she asked from which Cumann na mBan group I was from as she did not recognise me.

‘I am a family relative,’ I stammered. ‘From Dundalk. I am here to give my assistance if needed.’

Lise nodded, but her eyes scanned me. ‘And will you be staying for long?’ she enquired further. ‘I ask only because perhaps we could have a little talk about what is going on in Dundalk amongst Cumann na mBan there as I write about our events for the Republican newspaper.’

I nodded my head, still flabbergasted by having Lise stand in front of me as a young woman and a very beautiful young woman at that. 'Yes, that would be nice,' I replied, my heart hammering in my chest at this unbelievable development.

‘What is your name?’ she asked.

‘Leah. Leah Kennedy,’ I answered and held out my hand.

'Maggie McGuill,' she replied, smiling as she shook my hand firmly. 'Please, do call to the house. It is in

Aghameen, next to the Manor House. It is not difficult to find. Come when you can. I know you will have much to do here at the moment. It is a very sad affair and I am so very sorry for your family. I didn't know Mary well, but her death was a cruel thing.'

32

Leah
Aghameen
1920s

'Do you know a Maggie McGuill?' I asked Charlotte, as we stripped the clothes off her mother's double bed where Mary had been laid out this morning before the funeral.

'Maggie? Yes. A lovely girl. We went to the same school together.'

'I met her before. But she was called Lise.'

'Oh, it must have been somebody else.'

'No. It definitely is her. I saw her photograph and it is Maggie. No doubt about it.'

Charlotte sat down on the kitchen chair then and I sat on the other one opposite. 'You need to explain to me, Leah,' she stated. 'Start from the beginning.'

So I did and it took some time.

Gerard left me to the door of the Manor House the next morning. He was fairly quiet on the journey, no doubt thinking of the last one we had been on together, as was I. With both of us lost in our thoughts I almost jumped with surprise when he announced we had arrived.

'I am sure I will see you soon,' I said, as he helped me down from the cart. Though in honesty I didn't know if I would see him again until many years later, when he was a much older man and I was a much younger version of myself.

'Thank you,' he replied. 'Your presence was a comfort to us all, especially to Charlotte. Do come and visit when you can.'

I promised I would and knew it would be a promise I would keep, but not exactly when. The Manor House was the same as I had left. No sudden surprises of it being back to the guesthouse I had booked into just a week beforehand. Had it really only been a week? I felt as though I had lived a whole other lifetime since then and in some respects I had. The front door was open when I arrived and I wondered if Matthew Goodville was around. We had not spoken to or seen each other since the day I had met him in the hallway.

On reaching my bedroom, I kicked off the black pumps I was now wearing once again, having returned the uncomfortable uniform to Charlotte, along with the boots. The dress smelled of the soap I had used to help her wash the bed sheets and I had to admit it was a much fresher and longer-lasting smell than the fabric conditioner I was used to, that seemed to vanish after an hour of wearing. Perhaps it was the hand-washing and drying in the open air that made a difference. It also took out stains better than any bleach I had tried. I definitely had learned some good tricks on this strange adventure I found myself in.

It was comforting to have my things around me again, like my toothbrush and paste, cosmetics and creams; my own Mickey Mouse nightdress even seemed to welcome me back to some kind of normality. I eyed the tan coat still hanging in the open wardrobe with suspicion, then dug into the pocket again and retrieved the note, re-reading it once more.

Field. 3 pm. Shooting practice. Bring the web.

M

Exhausted from the last few days at Charlotte's home, I lay on the bed, my mind whirring with all the occurrences of the last week. Then, jumping up, I opened the front zip of my wheelie case and pulled out the bag that had been there since my flight from Germany … gosh that seemed like a million years ago and I realized I had not thought about Marc Lewis this whole week. Well, that was a good thing. But there are easier ways to get over an ex, I thought, than time-travelling! Yes! They were there - a bottle of wine, screw-top thankfully, cigarettes and lighter. If ever I needed both it was now!

Putting my dressing gown on and shoving the bottle of wine into one pocket, I put the cigarettes into the other one and made my way downstairs. Once more walking towards the bench at the lakeside, I sat down and pulled the wine bottle out of the pocket, unscrewed the lid and drank straight from the top like a thirsty sailor. Putting the wine down in between my feet on the stone gravelled ground I took out a cigarette, lit it and then inhaled deeply. Boy, I needed both like a fish needs water. In about ten minutes my head felt lighter and that was just the relief I wanted, that feeling of release for just a little to make things feel less crazy. Taking another long sip from the bottle I turned my head on hearing footsteps behind. Oh no, I realized, it's Matthew. Crushing the cigarette under my foot, I tried to conceal the bottle under my dress but it was too late. He had seen both me and it.

‘Miss Kennedy,’ he said, with his broad smile. ‘It is nice to see you again. I believe you have been away, as I have?’

'Yes,' I nodded, moving towards the end of the bench when he took a seat next to me.

‘You were at a funeral I heard?’

I nodded again, sheepishly aware he could see the bottle protruding from under the long dress between my feet. He gestured towards it.

‘We have glasses in the house if you would like me to fetch one?’ he queried, raising his eyebrows.

‘I …’ my face blushed and I didn’t how to respond. He put his hand out as though requesting the bottle and I bent down and picked it up, then handed it to him like a child caught with a stolen toy.

‘Where did you get this?’ he asked, turning the bottle around in his hands. ‘Merlot 2014.’

He sniffed the open bottle and took a sip. ‘Unusual. Where did you get it?' he asked again, reading the label at the back. 'I've never seen anything like this. What are all these symbols and warnings for?' and he began to read them out loud.

I was completely dumbstruck, unable to think of anything in reply.

He ran his right hand over the label and I noticed he had a birthmark like the wings of a butterfly on his hand, just between his thumb and forefinger when he joined them together. Seeing me looking at it, he said 'Yes, uncanny that. It seems to run in the family, but only with some of us. Strange.'

I nodded dumbly again and he handed back the bottle.

'Who are you, Leah Kennedy?' he queried. 'And again I ask where you got this bottle?'

So I told him. What else could I do? I showed him the cigarette box and the lighter with *Stuttgart Millennium Hotel 2015* written in black on the side. Did he believe me? He didn't say. He simply listened and took the things I showed him in his hands and turned them over and back, investigating them like they were ancient artefacts.

'Show me the coat,' he asked, already standing up and offered me his hand. I took it and he followed me up the stairs where I opened the wardrobe. The coat was gone and as I turned slowly around to the doorway where he had been standing, I knew he too would be gone. Immediately my first thought was my phone and laptop and like lightning, I raced to both and turned them on.

He was there when I awoke after I had slept only two hours or so, my night spent in tears of desperation and fear. He was not *in* the room, but as near as he could get to it. Right outside my bedroom door, tap tapping.

'Miss Kennedy,' he called. 'Are you awake?'

I ignored him. Instead, I pulled the covers over my head and once again began to cry. I simply could not cope with another day of this incomprehensible situation.

'I say,' Matthew called out again. 'I shall have to come in to check that you are quite alright, so I am giving you fair warning.'

I refused to come out from underneath the blankets, so instead he first gave me a gentle shove and seeing I was indeed breathing, he sat on the edge of the bed and began to talk.

'I do believe you, you know, about what you divulged yesterday. Do you know that when you walked into this room last night, you simply vanished into thin air? I followed you right to the door. You opened it and walked in first and I waited to be invited. When no invitation was forthcoming, I ventured in behind you to find the room empty. There was no other exit for you to have left from. The window was much too high and hadn't been opened. You certainly didn't fly up the chimney … the room was empty of any of your belongings, even the coat you spoke of. Look here,' he continued, shaking my hiding body once again. 'You need to come out from under there and talk to me. I quite insist.'

Doing as he asked, I sat up and he immediately could tell I had been crying. I was not one of those women who looked sweet and vulnerable when I was upset. Instead, I looked like I'd been struck down with the flu, sporting a snotty nose, blotchy face and red-rimmed eyes. As if that wasn't bad enough, I found it hard to stop once I had started. So, I did not look one bit attractive to Mr. Goodville, together with my having several years on him (and then some if you add on almost a century) I must have looked quite the sight.

But it wasn’t my face that Matthew Goodville found hilarious – it was my night attire.

‘What on earth are you wearing?’ he laughed, tugging at the three-quarter length sleeve of my Mickey Mouse nightdress that had illustrations of Mickey Mouse running up it after a mouse.

‘It’s Mickey Mouse,’ I gulped, then just as I had the first time we met, my tears turned into laughter as I pulled the embroidered sheet down and pointed at the red glittery bow that bedecked the character flaunted on the front.

'Is that what women wear as their nightwear in 2016?' he chuckled, pulling at the large sparkly bow around the famous mouse's neck. 'If so, I think I will stay in the 1920s, thank you very much.'

Despite my distress, I found myself in fits of laughter with Matthew.

‘I suppose it is not very ladylike, is it?’ I joked, taking an unladylike pose by pulling my knees up and stretching the nightdress over them.

'This is the most bizarre situation,' he said then, his face suddenly becoming more solemn. 'Strangely, in my heart, I am somehow accepting everything you are telling me, yet my head is screaming that it is simply much too extraordinary to be real.'

I nodded. 'How do you think I feel?' I asked. 'I don't know if I am dreaming or hallucinating or both. Maybe I am reacting to some kind of drug, but I've never taken drugs. Perhaps I was spiked?'

'Spiked?' he questioned. 'What … no, don't explain just now. Yet, here we both are. I can touch you,' he said, touching my face gently. 'And you can touch me.' He took my hand and placed it on his face. 'See. I am as real as real can be.'

Immediately I felt a shiver go through my body, like that feeling when I know something important is about to happen. He noticed and asked if I was cold.

'No,' I answered, truthfully. 'But I feel strange. There are so many things I need to tell you, about the note I found and other things I discovered just last night.'

Taking my face in his hands he looked into my eyes.

'I can see my reflection,' he murmured. 'How can this be happening? But right now I don't want to talk. Not about the past, or the future or about anything. I just want to …'

When he kissed me, there were no years between us. There was only a magnetic pull and a passion that surprised us both with its force and could absolutely not be ignored or refused. Days, months, years and decades were swept away, as together we broke all tangible realities and joined together in an illogical union. We didn't speak when afterwards limbs entwined, we trailed our fingers over each other's arms and faces, as though trying to ensure the other was not going to disappear again. I traced my fingers around the edges of his butterfly birthmark and leaning across him, I kissed it, wishing I too could carry some mark that would prove this time with him had been real.

'What is going to happen to you?' he asked quietly, turning his head towards me and the look of concern on his face etched my own fear.

'I have honestly no idea,' I replied.

'I was to have an appointment at this time,' he said, looking at the mantelpiece clock. However, I can simply remain here. I'd much rather stay with you.'

'No,' I answered, shaking my head. I needed to sleep. Last night I barely had any and I was beginning to feel exhausted. 'You go. I need to rest.'

As he dressed, he asked what I had wanted to show him in the coat pocket the night before.

'I'll show you later,' I told him, selfishly anxious to be alone, to wash and then sleep while thinking over all that had occurred between us. I had always been that way – needing time alone 'afterwards' to reclaim ownership of my body once more to myself.

As he pulled the heavy coverlet over my naked body, Matthew leaned down and gently kissed the top of my head. 'Till we meet again,' he whispered.

As his footsteps retreated I had all intention of rising from the bed and making an attempt to fill the bath, but sleep instead had other ideas and as I drifted off, images of butterflies peppered my dreams.

'At last, you are back to the land of the living,' Seán whispered, stroking the top of my head. 'How do you feel?'

His words sounded as though he was saying them through a megaphone, so loud in my ears that I winced.

'Are you feeling alright?' he asked with a concerned look on his face.

I opened my mouth to answer him. It was so dry. Seán lifted a bottle of water with a straw and placed the straw between my lips. I drank thirstily. Examining his face, I expected to see somebody else but couldn't remember who that could be.

'You are in hospital,' he told me, placing the bottle back onto the locker. Then he took both my hands in his and I noticed there was an IV running from the back of my hand to a drip next to the bed.

‘Do you remember anything at all?’

My brow furrowed and I shook my head.

‘You have been in a coma on and off for several weeks,’ he told me gently.

Startled, I whispered ‘Why? How?’

He grinned at this. 'It is so good to hear your voice. Well, at least making sense,' he continued. 'You've been telling the wildest stories, so real I almost believed them myself. It was almost like you were describing scenes of a movie going on inside your head and getting things mixed up with stories you had told me about Maggie. Obviously it’s due to all this research you've been doing.'

I tried to sit up but my shoulders and neck ached.

‘Careful,’ he coaxed. ‘You broke your collar bone and still have a brace on it.’ He guided my hand to my neck and I could feel a brace around it.

'What happened to me?' I asked again, almost afraid to hear the answer. I immediately put my hands on my legs and thankfully I could feel them.

'The horses got out after you forgot to close the gate,' he told me. 'You were knocked by one or maybe more than one. A neighbour found you on the road and got an ambulance. You received a bad blow to your head and had a blood clot on your brain. But miraculously it seems to have dispersed.'

I must have looked frightened because he smiled and called a nurse over.

'Will you inform Dr. Bryant that Leah has woken,' he said. 'He can give her a better explanation than I.'

The nurse smiled. 'It is good to see you awake, Leah,' she said. 'This man has been by your side for weeks, reading to you all the old stories from your notebooks and letters.'

'I expect a full recovery,' Dr. Bryant said, putting the instrument he had just shone into my eyes inside his pocket. 'You had us quite worried for a while, but there are things even our medical profession can't explain and the blood clot on your brain is no longer visible on the scan. It is remarkable, but not unusual. The body has an amazing ability to heal itself.'

'When can I go home?' was the first thing I asked. The other medical questions could wait for later.

‘Not just yet,’ he answered. ‘There is another matter that you seem unaware of.’

At my questioning look, he continued. ‘Your pregnancy. You are only in the early stages, but so far everything seems to be as it should and thankfully your baby has not been affected by the accident.'

I could not speak. Hairs stood on my arms and my pulse raced. I felt as though I had just taken a sip of something really strong to drink. My head swam and my stomach was queasy. I looked at Seán and he looked worried, as though this information would upset me.

‘I’ll leave you both alone now,’ Dr. Bryant said, patting Seán’s arm. ‘Come and see me before you leave,’ he asked.

I waited until the doctor had closed the door of my private room and then I turned to Seán.

‘I don’t understand?’

He smiled. ‘Well, as he said, you are having a baby. I know it is another big shock but hey, a good shock, right?’

‘But who … I don’t know …’

Sitting beside me once more on the bed, Seán kissed me on the forehead.

'Does it matter? After what you've been through and the hell of thinking I could lose you, I vowed that *who* doesn't matter one jot. Unless of course, you want to, you know, get in touch with … just in case you think …'

I shook my head, tears of joy or shock or fear beginning to well in my eyes. I didn't know which.

'But right now,' he said. 'Do you want to hear about the crazy stories you told me in your lucid times? Why, I could write your book myself. You really have a vivid imagination.'

Epilogue

Leah
Dundalk
2017

'I still find it hard to believe Grandy was Conall,' I declared, straightening the painting of him hanging pride of place in the gallery.

Simply named, *Margaret McGuill – Pictures of a Remarkable Life* – was now a section of a new wing donated in memory of the deceased Conrad Delaney, in the National Gallery of Ireland. The walls proudly showed off Maggie's paintings and sketches with a detailed history of each picture. Glass cases also displayed Maggie's original memoirs, as well as my early interviews. A signed copy of my book 'Margaret McGuill – A Remarkable Tale' – was also on show here. A special frame held the infamous note, later found by myself in the place I had dreamt while in my coma. It was inside the lining of an old tan coat, hanging under many others in a dilapidated shed next to the ruins of an old cottage. This torn scrap of paper, yellowed with age, was instrumental in Margaret McGuill being posthumously cleared of any charges against her in the murder of Matthew Goodville, almost a hundred years ago.

'I knew when you mentioned the name to me I had heard it before,' Seán acknowledged. 'But I couldn't think where.'

'So Grandy changed his name to Conrad Delaney while in America then?'

Seán shrugged his shoulders. 'It appears so. You must remember there was a warrant out for his arrest for many years, but he kept the same initials – just like you did,' he grinned. 'Mrs Keenan.'

I grinned back. 'Well, Leah Keenan and Leah Kennedy sound quite similar, and at least I don't have to go changing initials on my things, like my luggage and my purse.'

'As we have both his original birth certificate and the false one he had made up in the States, do you think we should add his real name to his headstone? But then, we'd have to change your grandmother's also, to Charlotte Daly, instead of Charlotte Delaney.'

'No,' I said, resolutely. 'My mum was known as Kate Delaney until she got married to Dad and became Kate Kennedy. It would be too confusing to begin changing things now. Let's leave things as they are. My book will explain everything anyway. But this little lady knows who she is, isn't that right?' I murmured, tickling our beautiful, curly-haired daughter under the chin. She gurgled back, as I traced my finger over the little butterfly birthmark on her tiny hand.

'Maggie Keenan will always know who she is,' I said, 'and exactly where she comes from.'

THE END

Historical Notes

James Stephens was an Irish Republican and the founding member of an originally unnamed revolutionary organisation in Dublin. This organisation, founded on 17 March 1858, was later to become known as the Irish Republican Brotherhood. *Wikipedia*

The Great Famine also known within Ireland as the Great Hunger or simply the Famine was a period of starvation and disease in Ireland from 1845 to 1852 that constituted a historical social crisis which subsequently had a major impact on Irish society and history as a whole, with the most severely affected areas in the west and south of Ireland, where the Irish language was dominant. The worst year of the period was 1847, which became known as Black '47. During the Great Hunger, roughly one million people died and between 1845 and 1855, at least 2.1 million people left Ireland, one of the greatest exodus from a single island in history. *Wikipedia*

The Cromwellian War in Ireland (1649–53) was the conquest of Ireland by the forces of the English Parliament, led by Oliver Cromwell. Cromwell imposed an extremely harsh settlement on the Irish Catholic population. The practice of Catholicism was banned and bounties were offered for the capture of priests, who were executed when found. The Cromwellian conquest completed the British colonisation of Ireland, which was merged into the Commonwealth of England, Scotland and Ireland in 1653–59. It destroyed the native Irish Catholic land-owning classes and replaced them with colonists with a British identity. The bitterness caused by the Cromwellian settlement was a powerful source of Irish nationalism from the 17th century onwards. Oliver Cromwell left behind him death, exile, persecution, indentured slavery, and a form of 17th-century ethnic cleansing. His name is forever associated by the Irish people with a burning hatred and his slogan 'To Hell or to Connaught with them' i.e. the Irish people, is long linked to his name.

https://www.lurganancestry.com/cromwellsconquest.htm

The 1917 North Roscommon by-election was held on 3 February 1917. The election took place nine months after the 1916 Rising and was contested by Thomas Devine, and Jasper Tully, a lo cal newspaper owner who was running as an independent. An outsider candidate was proposed as an Independent candidate: Count George Noble Plunkett, the father of Joseph Plunkett, who had been executed for his role in the Easter Rising. Count Plunkett was proposed by John J. O'Kelly (Sceilg), P. T. Keohane and

Fr. Michael O'Flanagan. Though often credited as Sinn Féin's first victory in a Parliamentary election, Plunkett was not a member of Sinn Féin. *Wikipedia*

The Proclamation document was a formal assertion of the Irish Republic as a sovereign, independent state, and also a declaration of rights. The seven signatories, Thomas J. Clarke, Seán Mac Diarmada, Patrick H. Pearse, James Connolly, Thomas MacDonagh, Éamonn Ceannt and Joseph Plunkett, would all be among those court-martialled and executed after the failure of the Rising. *The National Museum of Ireland*

The Rising began on Easter Monday, 24 April 1916 and lasted for just six days: the official surrender occurred on Friday 28 and all fighting ceased on Saturday 29 April. The rebels numbered around 2500; by the end of the fighting, there were around 20,000 British troops in Dublin. The Easter Rising was an armed rebellion against British rule in Ireland, staged by several militant republican groups working together, including the Irish Volunteers, the Irish Citizen Army and Cumann na mBan. These men and women took up strategic positions in buildings around central Dublin and then repelled British attempts to remove them. They publicly read a proclamation of Irish independence from Britain (which was also printed and posted in the streets), though the rebellion itself had very little support in the community. The headquarters of the rebellion was Dublin's General Post Office, on O'Connell St. *State Library Victoria*

Cumann na mBan was officially founded on the 5th of April 1914 at a meeting held in Wynn's Hotel, Dublin led by Kathleen Lane-O`Kelley and attended by Bridie O'Rahilly (nee Clyne). Translated as the *Women's League*, Cumann na mBan was originally formed as an auxiliary formation to complement the Irish Volunteers. The constitution of Cumann na mBan contained explicit references to the use of force by arms against Crown Forces in Ireland. Under its constitution, the primary aim of the organisation was to 'advance the cause of Irish liberty' and 'teach its members first aid, drill, signalling and rifle practice in order to aid the men of Ireland'. *The Irish War*

The Black and Tans and the Auxiliaries were part of the British Crown Forces in Ireland (which also included the Royal Irish Constabulary (RIC), the Dublin Metropolitan Police (DMP) and the Ulster Special Constabulary) and both groups were recruited during the War of Independence to supplement the regular police division. *The Irish Story*

During the Easter Rising of 1916, **the GPO** served as the headquarters of the uprising's leaders. It was from outside this building on the 24th of April 1916, that Patrick Pearse read out the Proclamation of the Irish Republic. *Leaders* of the *1916 Rising* · Eamonn Ceannt · James Connolly · Joseph Mary Plunkett · Patrick Pearse · Séan Mac Dermott · Thomas Clarke · Thomas MacDonagh. All were executed.

The Troubles, also called the **Northern Ireland conflict**, from 1968 to 1998 in Northern Ireland between the overwhelmingly Protestant unionists (loyalists), who desired the province to remain part of the United Kingdom, and the overwhelmingly Roman Catholic nationalists (republicans), who wanted Northern Ireland to become part of the Republic of Ireland. The other major players in the conflict were the British army, Royal Ulster Constabulary (RUC), and Ulster Defence Regiment (UDR; from 1992 called the Royal Irish Regiment), and their avowed purpose was to play a peacekeeping role, most prominently between the nationalist Irish Republican Army (IRA), which viewed the conflict as a guerrilla war for national independence, and the unionist paramilitary forces, which characterized the IRA's aggression as terrorism. Marked by street fighting, sensational bombings, sniper attacks, roadblocks, and internment without trial, the confrontation had the characteristics of a civil war. Some 3,600 people were killed and more than 30,000 more were wounded before a peaceful solution, which involved the governments of both the United Kingdom and Ireland, was effectively reached in 1998, leading to a power-sharing arrangement in the Northern Ireland Assembly at Stormont. *Wikipedia*

Thomas McDonagh, (who was born in the U.S. but then a resident of Cloonloo, County Sligo) became the first casualty suffered by the IRA in Roscommon during the War of Independence. It was discovered later that McDonagh's revolver had faulty ammunition and had misfired, resulting in him being unable to defend himself from the opposing fire. The ambush proceeds included rifles, revolvers and ammunition, equipment much needed by the volunteers. In the aftermath of the attack, the Black and Tans descended on the scene and seized the body of Thomas McDonagh. They placed it on a lorry and brought it into Ballaghaderreen. They then tied the body to the rear of the lorry and had it dragged through the streets of the town. Thomas McDonagh's remains were eventually released after his relatives and his fiancée pleaded with the authorities for possession. *Roscommon People Newspaper*

At the **Four Courts**, the women of Cumann na mBan helped to organise the evacuation of buildings at the time of surrender and to destroy incriminating papers. More typical was the General Post Office (GPO), where Pearse insisted that most of them (excluding Carney, who refused to leave the injured James Connolly) leave at noon on Friday, 28 April. The building was then coming under shell- and machine-gun fire and many casualties were anticipated. The following day the leaders at the GPO decided to negotiate a surrender. Pearse asked Cumann na mBan member Elizabeth O'Farrell (a midwife at the National Maternity Hospital) to act as a go-between. Under British military supervision, she brought Pearse's surrender order to the rebel units still fighting in Dublin. Over 70 women, including many of the leading figures in Cumann na mBan, were arrested after the insurrection and many of the women who had been captured fighting were imprisoned in Kilmainham; all but twelve had been released by 8 May 1916. *Wikipedia*

After the Rising **Margaret Skinnider** was active in promoting the Republican Cause and was imprisoned during the War of Independence. Skinnider became Paymaster General of the anti-treaty IRA in the Civil War. She was elected a member of the Executive

Cumann na mBan in 1921 as part of the Fairview Branch and was appointed as Director of Training, a position she held until 1923. She was in charge of Cumann na mBan operations in Dublin during the attack on the Four Courts. Skinnider worked in charge of the Accounts Branch in the Quartermaster General's Office in December 1922. She was arrested in December 1922 and released from prison in November 1923· She applied for a pension in 1925 based on her activities and service but was refused payment as she was a woman. *Central Statistics Office*

Born in 1898, **Bridie Clyne** grew up on a small Shannonside farm. She emigrated to Edinburgh as a teenager where she worked in a cafe, but still kept strong links with her native country joining Cumann na mBan. The incredible story of Rooskey native, Bridie Clyne, has been immortalised in a new panel recently unveiled at Dromod Railway Station. Serving on the Anti-Treaty side in the Irish Civil War, Bridie rammed the barricades around the Four Courts in 1922 driving an ambulance filled with guns, despite coming under ferocious fire from an 18-pounder gun across the Liffey. Part of the Dromod panel includes an artist's depiction of the ambulance she drove that day. The panel also details how Bridie was by Éamon de

Valera's side when the future Irish leader narrowly avoided assassination in Ennis - she later risked her own life driving him to a safe house. Bridie worked for the Republican underground through the Civil War, delivering weapons, clothing, and medical supplies. She even spent three months in jail under the assumed name of Anny Hardwicke after a raid on a 'secret' house in Merrion. Bridie also went on hunger strike for a month and during her stay in Kilmainham suffered lifelong injuries to her leg after a warden pushed her down the stairs. *Leitrim Observer*

Ernie O'Malley, who assumed operational command of the Four Courts occupation after garrison commander Paddy O'Brien was injured by shrapnel was ordered by his senior IRA commanders – over his objections – to surrender to the Free State Army on the afternoon of 30 June. That evening he escaped from temporary captivity in the Jameson Distillery along with Seán Lemass and two others. The next day he travelled via the Wicklow Mountains to Blessington, then to County Wexford and finally to County Carlow. This escape probably saved O'Malley's life, as four of the other senior Four Courts leaders were later executed. *Wikipedia*

This document (**order for surrender from Thomas Ennis**) was received by **Thomas 'Skinner' O'Reilly** who later said *'I went up to the Central Hall under the dome and gave the note to Rory O'Connor. He went into a huddle with Liam Mellows and some of the others and then told me to go back to the gate and tell the dispatch rider there was no reply.'* Skinner followed his orders. *The Clock is Still Going.*

Roderick (Rory) O'Connor (28 November 1883 – 8 December 1922) was an Irish republican revolutionary. He was Director of Engineering for the IRA in the Irish War of Independence. O'Connor opposed the Anglo-Irish Treaty of 1921 and was chairman of the Republican military council that became the Anti-Treaty IRA in March 1922. He was the main spokesman for the Republican side in the lead-up to the outbreak of the Irish Civil War in June of that year. On 30 June, O'Connor was taken prisoner after the attack by Free State forces on the Four Courts in Dublin. On 8 December 1922, he was executed along with four other senior members of the IRA Four Courts garrison. *Wikipedia*

William (Liam) Mellows was an Irish Republican and Sinn Féin politician. He was active with the Irish Republican Brotherhood and Irish Volunteers and participated in the Easter Rising in County Galway and the War of Independence. Elected as a TD to the First Dáil, he rejected the Anglo-Irish Treaty. During the Irish Civil War Mellows was captured by Pro-Treaty forces after the surrender of the Four Courts in June 1922. On 8 December 1922, he was one of four senior IRA men executed by the Provisional Government. *Wikipedia*

Cooney, Andrew ('Andy') (1897–1968), a Republican and medical doctor, was born on 22 April 1897 in Ballyphillip, Nenagh, Co. Tipperary. Joining the IRB at the end of 1918, he assisted in the December 1918 election by protecting candidates and acted as a guard at the sittings of the first Dáil. In 1920 he played a major role in the attack on Borrisokane RIC barracks (26 June), took part in the Bloody Sunday operations (21 November) at 28 Upper Pembroke St. where several British agents were killed, and attended Croke Park afterwards. He was captured at the Four Courts there at the surrender (30 June 1922). After sojourns in Newbridge and Arbour Hill, he was moved with the other leaders to Kilmainham, where he spent forty-one days on hunger strike. Removed (1 January 1924) to Harepark Camp, the

Curragh, he was among the last to be released (29 May 1924). *Dictionary of Irish Biography*

Seán MacBride was the son of the Irish actress and patriot Maud Gonne and her husband, Major John MacBride was executed in 1916 for his part in the Easter Rising of that year against the British. Seán joined the Irish Republican Army (IRA) during the Anglo-Irish War (Irish War of Independence,1919–21). He denied the legitimacy of the Irish Free State established in 1922, and he remained a member of the IRA during and after the civil war of 1922–23 and became its chief of staff in 1936–37, severing his formal ties because he believed the 1937 constitution met republican objectives. MacBride then became a barrister and specialized in defending his former IRA associates. He was awarded the Nobel Peace Prize in 1974 and the Lenin Peace Prize in 1977; also in that year he was appointed president of the International Commission for the Study of Communication Problems, established by UNESCO. *Wikipedia*

About the Author

International Best Selling Author, Nicola Kearns, has published three novels - Under a Maltese Sky (2015), The Azure Window (2017) and All the Seas Between (2018). Nicola also has many stories and articles published in women's magazines, including a selection of anthologies. She is a regular contributor to radio and selected podcasts for her book reviews and writing experience. Nicola is also a Writing Coach/Editor and Italian Teacher and lives in the North West of Ireland.

By the same author:

Under a Maltese Sky

Being caught up in war is not what Ana Mellor expects when she lands in Malta to join her Wing-Commander father. Amid horror and destruction, the courage and resilience of the Maltese people are revealed as they struggle to survive.

Ana falls in love but treachery intervenes with catastrophic consequences.

Meanwhile, disillusioned with Ireland's fight for political independence, Ernie McGuill leaves home to join the British Army. Due to the outbreak of war, he trains as a fighter pilot and is posted to Malta.

It is against this background that the characters of Ana, Ernie and many others are interwoven in a story of betrayal and intrigue. This is not unravelled until generations later when two women make a journey to Malta - a journey that is to have astonishing consequences.

PROLOGUE

Malta 2001

Ana was very happy. Today she had met Pope John Paul II and as she told her granddaughter, if she died now, she would do so contentedly. As the rest of the group was busy chatting and drinking wine, Ana gazed out the window. From her seat, she could see down into Grand Harbour. Although it was dark, Fort St. Elmo was lit up as was the whole harbour below. She wondered what had happened to all the people she had loved on this island. Where was the man who had never been far from her thoughts for over fifty years? Where were the girls she had been to school with, the nurses she trained beside and lived with through those terrible war years? She remembered vividly the horror of the war. It was almost impossible to visualize battleships moored where there was now a pretty marina, or to imagine the frightening sound of an air raid siren, breaking the silence of the night to warn them of yet another air raid.

Sadly Ana knew the fate of some of the friends she had loved in her time here during the war. Looking over at her granddaughter she smiled to herself as she realised that when she was Jessy's age, she had been here in this country of sunshine and sadness, of laughter and loss and love. Thanks to her granddaughter she was now back in Malta. Although she had been shocked and excited when she realised she was to return to the island, Ana was happy now that she had come. The place she had tried to forget for years was still familiar and just as beautiful.

By the same author:

The Azure Window

Spanning over sixty years, from an island torn apart in the Second World War, to what is now a tourist's paradise, the story intertwines three separate love stories. The focus is on three generations of women, who like The Azure Window, are beautiful, fragile and enigmatic.

Primarily set in Malta in present times, Jessy McGuill becomes drawn into the past and the life of her mother, Maria, whom she never knew. The truth she learns of her grandmother Ana's endurance as she struggled to survive severe loss and heartache during the Siege of Malta, forms the backdrop to Jessy's own story.

Like Ana, Jessy also finds love in Malta, until her grandfather arrives on the island, with a relative in tow. This young man Neil brings with him his own secrets and the friendship between him and Jessy soon causes a ripple of unease for several reasons. A plot unravels that provides a particular and unbelievable twist which will captivate the reader.

PROLOGUE

Malta, July 1943.

The wind whipped wildly around her head. Ana put an arm up, grabbed a handful of blonde strands and pulled. Opening her fist, she watched as the hairs blew away like ribbons in the air. Her scalp tingled and she felt her heartbeat accelerate rapidly, as though it was going to burst out of her chest.

The sea was rough. Angry waves danced into the air, green and blue and brown. Ferocious. Would it be quick she wondered? Will I die before hitting the sea, or will my heart stop on the way down, like what happened to people who jumped off high-rise buildings? Her mouth had a funny taste, as though even panic had a flavour. This must be what it would be like to face a firing squad or an axe murderer when you know you are going to die soon and crazy thoughts go through your head. It was as though the whole world had stood still and it was just she, Ana McGuill, poised in terror on the top of The Azure Window in the middle of the Mediterranean Sea, trying to find the courage to end her life.

Franco had brought her to this place of natural wonder. They had held hands as they walked across the arch in the sea, he gripping hers tightly to keep her safe. He had always kept her safe and she believed that he always would. But he was gone.

They had stood looking out over the blue water. It had been warm and sunny then. Not like today. Today the sky was much darker, like her heart. The pain in her heart was unbearable. It lay like a heavy stone in her body, gnawing at her like a beast. Unable to sleep or eat, she went through her days on autopilot. Until today. Today she had said, enough. That word had brought her here, almost seven hours later. This place where she and Franco had stood and planned their life together. How did so much change in so short a time?

She turned at the sound. There was nobody. A bird perhaps, or some animal.

~~~~

In a crib just a few miles away, an infant whimpered fretfully. A kindly face looked down and clutched a tiny finger. 'Ssssh little one, all will be well.'

She heard it again. The sound of a baby's cry. Turning around quickly once more, her foot slipped and she tumbled. An immense feeling of terror
~~~~

gripped her. Opening her mouth to scream she found that no sound came and it seemed as though her whole body was suddenly engulfed in an intense heat. On her knees, she saw a hand outstretched. She grabbed it, pulling herself to her feet. Looking up, Ana turned her head left and right. Nobody. 'Hello,' she called. Where could they have gone? There was no place to hide.

Ana tentatively stepped across the stony ground until she was off the arch.

The baby closed her eyes.

All was well.

By the same author:

All the Seas Between

Italy. June 1940. Benito Mussolini declares his country is at war. Serenella Inglima, a young noblewoman, suddenly finds herself estranged from both the man she loves and her Sicilian home. A shocking personal incident, involving one of the twentieth century's most formidable Dictators, has consequences affecting Serenella and the Inglima family for decades.

Malta. October 2003. A young Irish woman, Jessica McGuill, has been living on the small Mediterranean island for almost two years. Engaged to be married, her world is suddenly thrown into turmoil, when two men in her life, from very different backgrounds, make unexpected declarations.

These women's lives are intertwined through familial ties and two different types of war. One is forced on a country, the other is a battle of wills - a conflict between right and wrong and the grey area in between. Because life is never simple really, is it? Especially in matters of the heart.

PROLOGUE

Forli, Italy. March 1944.

'Marius,' Signora Inglima called with vexation. Where had the child got to? These tireless games of hide and seek every time they needed to leave the house were maddening. Usually indulgent with her youngest child, this time she had no patience for his frolics. Serenella had always been the one to eventually find her brother in some cupboard or under a bed, giggling mischievously to himself. The study door was open which was unusual, but the weeping she heard from inside was not her son's. Tentatively pushing the door open, she saw the sorrowful sight of Rachele, leaning with her hands across the ornately carved desk.

'Rachele,' she whispered, concerned. 'What is it?'

Her friend shook her head and turned to face Maria-Angela. 'This,' she replied, holding a piece of jewellery on the ends of her fingers. 'He's had yet another *puttana* in here.'

Maria-Angela took the necklace out of Rachele's trembling hand.

'Can I get you anything?' she enquired gently.

To try and sympathise was futile. This was a common occurrence and platitudes only added salt to the wound. Rachele shook her head and together they left the room silently. As Signora Mussolini walked towards the kitchen, Maria-Angela stalled in the hallway and examined the piece of jewellery in her hand. It was a long gold chain with the links roughly snapped, as though pulled violently from somebody's neck. Cheap gold she believed, typical of a working-class woman. Opening the clasp she gasped out loud, recognising the face which looked back at her from inside the locket. But how? Then realisation dawned. Her daughter had owned this chain and had been in this room. When? It was a recognised fact that Il Duce took his many women visitors in here for one reason only. 'Oh my God,' she cried, suddenly comprehending. 'My poor, beautiful daughter. What have I done?'

All novels by Nicola Kearns are available to buy on Amazon.co.uk

Nicola Kearns contact:

leitrimwritingcottage.com

nicolakearns3@hotmail.com

Printed in Great Britain
by Amazon

26045552R00273